SO I'M A HEEL

It's just a lucky break the way blotter that tips him off on the arrest-and-release of his rich neighbor, Otto Weylin, for molesting a minor. Nobody ever gave Hawkins a break, and he doesn't intend to give Weylin one, either. He figures that Weylin is good for ten grand to keep this little bit of information out of the papers, and maybe he's right. But why all of a sudden is his 10-year-old son becoming so friendly with Weylin? What is the secret that Weylin's sex-starved wife keeps hinting at? The blackmail scheme is rapidly backfiring and Hawkins can't trust anyone, even his own wife—and now his own boy has gone missing!

FLINT

Flint took a bullet in the lung during that last job, a hole that just won't seem to plug itself. But hired killers don't get to retire, and Flint is called out to Colorado for one more job. A rancher named Mr. Good wants his competition removed, and he's got a pretty plan on how to get away with it. So Flint rides out and meets the local sheriff, a man so fat he spends all his time in his office—should be easy to work around. He meets his victim, Thomason, a poor but honest man, who naively hires him on the spot. And then he meets Thomason's wife, Cora, who seems….very friendly—but is she all that she seems? And can Mr. Good really be trusted? This is supposed to be Flint's last job, but it's funny how a simple plan can soon get so complicated.

THE BIG OUT

Brick Palmer, catcher for the Blues, gets a call after the game. His kid brother Johnny is in trouble again. Johnny is the brilliant one, the one who's going to be a doctor, but he's forged Brick's name on a $10,000 Syndicate debt. So Brick does what he has to do, he pays off the Syndicate punk, then busts his nose. Randy York of the *Herald* sees the payoff and reveals the meeting in his column the next day. Unable to rat out his brother, Brick is thrown out of the league. All he can do is play for one of the outlaw leagues. So he and wife Cathy move to Montreal and try to start over. But they're all out to get him—the fans and players for selling out, the umps for dirtying the game. They're all out for blood. But for the Syndicate punk it's personal—he plans to make it murder.

ARNOLD HANO BIBLIOGRAPHY

Fiction

Western Roundup (editor; 1948)
Western Triggers (editor; 1948)
The Big Out (1951)
The Executive (1964)
Marriage Italian Style (movie tie-in; 1965)
Bandolero (movie tie-in; 1967)
Running Wild (movie tie-in; 1973)

Sports

A Day in the Bleachers (1955;
reprinted in new editions in 1982, 2004)
Sandy Koufax: Strikeout King (1964)
Willie Mays: The Say-Hey Kid (1966)
The Greatest Giants of Them All (1967)
Roberto Clemente: Batting King (1968)
Willie Mays: Mr. Baseball Himself (1970)
Kareem! Basketball Great (1975)
Muhammad Ali, the Champion (1977)

As Gil Dodge

Flint (1957)

As Matthew Gant

Valley of Angry Men (1953)
The Manhunter (1957)
The Last Notch (1958)
The Raven and the Sword (1960)
Queen Street (1963)

As Ad Gordon

The Flesh Painter (1955)
Slade (1956)

As Mike Heller

So I'm a Heel (1957)

For Nancy & Cal. *(handwritten)*

SO I'M A HEEL

FLINT

THE BIG OUT

BY ARNOLD HANO

with love (handwritten)

Arnold Hano   11/11/12 (handwritten)

1/28/14 (handwritten)

STARK HOUSE

Stark House Press • Eureka California

3 STEPS TO HELL: SO I'M A HEEL/FLINT/THE BIG OUT

Published by Stark House Press
1315 H Street
Eureka, CA 95501, USA
griffinskye3@sbcglobal.net
www.starkhousepress.com

SO I'M A HEEL
Originally published by Gold Medal Books as by "Mike Heller" and copyright © 1957
by Fawcett Publications, Inc. Reprinted by permission of the Author.

FLINT
Originally published by Signet Books as by "Gil Dodge" and copyright © 1957
by Gil Dodge. Copyright renewed 1985. Reprinted by permission of the Author.

THE BIG OUT
Originally published by A. S. Barnes and Company and copyright © 1951
by Arnold Hano. Copyright renewed 1979. Reprinted by permission of the Author.

"The Author's Preface" copyright © 2012 by Arnold Hano

"Welcome to 3 Steps to Hell and the Work of Arnold Hano" copyright © 2012
by Gary Phillips.

"A Conversation with Arnold Hano" copyright © 2012 by Dan Duling

ISBN: 1-933586-50-8
ISBN-13: 978-1-933586-50-2

Cover design and layout by Mark Shepard, www.SHEPGRAPHICS.COM
Proofreading by Rick Ollerman

The publisher wishes to thank Gary Phillips and Dan Duling for all their work on this project.

PUBLISHER'S NOTE

First Stark House Press Edition: October 2012
First Edition

Welcome to 3 Steps to Hell and the work of Arnold Hano

• •

With the flickering ghost of Jim Thompson at my shoulder, I was going to write a bunch of lies and half-truths in this intro to *3 Steps to Hell*, this most audacious effort from Stark House collecting for the first time three of Arnold Hano's novels that cover a range of undertakings by his troubled protagonists. *Flint* is a western take on Thompson's *Savage Night* which Arnold edited, *The Big Out* is Arnold's first novel set in the sport he played and loves, baseball, and *So I'm a Heel* is a nervous crime story taking place incongruously where there are no looming buildings and men in fedoras hugging dense shadows but sunshine, sand and surf. For Thompson simply reinvented various parts of his life in his supposed memoirs *Bad Boy* and *Roughneck*. While I'm also mindful Arnold has mentioned to me and Dan Duling, our mutual friend, a writer lies for a living. So why not weave in recountings of how we initially met that could have taken place? Nobody would know except the three of us – and we're all writers.

I might have used the time I was delivering dog cages for an upcoming charity dog show given by the Daughters of the Indistinct. Wheeling my load in, I inadvertently spy this wiry built older gent in a pin-striped suit down on a knee behind some cubicle panels injecting a clear substance into the hindquarters of an off-colored Lhasa Apso. Or when I was in the far end of the bar in the Clown Room dive in a Hollywood no one remembers now having a jolt of Jack, and this solemn-eyed guy took a seat on the stool next to me. We make small talk and then he mentioned there was this guy across the street in the gray office building who owed him his cut from a chemin de fer grift they'd been running with a couple of gap-toothed nuns. That maybe seeing as how I'm broke down now, but look like I used to play football in school I could help him out for no more than say ten minutes of my time and a couple of C notes.

While the reality of our first encounter, facilitated by Dan, was more mundane, on a sunny, blustery day in Laguna Beach (are there any other such days down there behind the Orange Curtain?) the thinly disguised Laredo Rock in *So I'm a Heel*, it was nonetheless a memorable day for me. By then I'd heard of Arnold from mystery booksellers and bibliophiles. So when Dan told me he'd known him for years, well that sealed it. Way back I'd initially read about Arnold in the pages of the factual Jim Thompson biography, the fully-realized *Savage Art* by Robert Polito, which won the Edgar from the Mystery Writers of America.

As Polito observed, it was under Arnold's incisive editorial hand at Lion Books that in a brief spate, '52-'54, Thompson wrote feverishly, producing 14 novels, more than half of all his books.

"This is hard for me to talk about." Arnold recalled in *Savage Art*, "but I think I became a kind of surrogate father for him, a big brother, or uncle, God knows what. He was a few years older, but that didn't seem to matter. Jim was always needy in terms of other people. He had to have other people, because he really didn't take care of himself."

The need can be tracked to the three different main characters, tarnished, hardened yet vulnerable men you'll find in these stories. William "Brick" Palmer is no kid, but he's still giving it his all as a major league catcher for the Blues. Until. Not to give anything away but Brick gets banned for life from the majors, from the game that defines him. Then an offer to play the goat, the villain in ball in the outlaw leagues of Canada and he accepts because he has no choice.

The need gnaws at him.

Unlike pro quarterback Michael Vick, who truly needed redemption – after all Brick was only accused of taking a bribe, not backing dogfights – the irony was the world perceived Brick had fallen and would be damned if they gave him a hand up.

The gunslinger Flint would like nothing more than to put the blood and bullets behind him. "My name is Flint. I'm wanted in ten states and territories. I haven't touched a gun in six years." Of course a man like him, doing what he'd done, there's no escaping for him. But in this Old West noir, better pay close attention to what Flint, the narrator, is telling us. Everything just might not be on the up and up. For when was the last time you read a western about a cold-eyed killer who admitted he fainted once after cutting down a trio of men? There's a distance between Flint's fast hand and the sweating brain under his weathered hat.

Then there's Ed Hawkins, the anti-hero of *So I'm a Heel*. He's a decorated World War II vet with a slapped together jaw of bone and plastic he's frightfully aware of as his souvenir from the sniper's bullet. Yeah, he's looking out for number one, so what? Screw you, buddy. He's a working stiff equally alienated and attracted to his wife and son. Like any guy just getting by, he could use a little more. Then his chance to get ahead falls into his lap and damned if he's not going for it – setting in motion a series of events Hawkins will have a hell of a time not being sucked under let alone working his grab. Then he really gets socked in the gut.

Not only is it significant this collection includes Arnold's first novel taking place on and off the diamond, his place in history is made given he wrote the classic book about baseball from a fan's perspective, A Day in the Bleachers. The book is constructed around the first game of the 1954 World Series, the New York Giants versus the Cleveland Indians. That was the game where Willie Mays, the Say-Hey Kid, made the Catch deep in center field off a hit by Vic Wertz. Not only does Mays get the out; the ball dropping over his shoulder, his back to it as he runs toward the wall, he turns in the same motion and throws a rocket to second base, keeping the runner there while corkscrewing his body to the ground.

Palmer, literally and Flint and Hawkins, figuratively, are also running for the ball. They can see it, that most desirous of objects and it's shimmering right out there on the horizon. Beyond their grasp but not so much so they aren't willing to stretch, to claw and tear, and reach, and maybe get burned...or maybe pull down the prize. Nothing big really...but enough...just enough as you'll discover in 3 Steps to Hell.

Gary Phillips
Los Angeles, Summer 2012

The Author's Preface

● ●

Some years ago at a party thrown by a major magazine for writers, editors, agents and wannabes in a fancy-schmanzy Hollywood eatery, a writer came up to me and asked rather briskly, "How do you do it?"

Bewildered, I said, "Do what?"

"Write. Write your stuff. You're the best."

Flattery replaced bewilderment. So I launched a professorial lecture on thematic and character development and very soon my writer-student fled. I had failed to answer his question. It was not until the next morning that it came to me.

I solve mysteries.

Or try to.

Be it a novel, a short story, a magazine article, a play—whatever—problems lie within and must be addressed.

Why did Sam Houston abruptly abandon his governorship of Tennessee and his beautiful bride to join the Cherokee Nation?

How does an aging baseball player, banned for life for a crime he did not commit, respond?

Why does a hired killer kill?

I go about answering those questions.

I dig. I pry. Sometimes I steal.

I have a disabled veteran as my protagonist in *So I'm a Heel*, a man whose jaw had been shattered by a Japanese sniper's bullet during our invasion of a tiny island in the Pacific. I borrowed the injury from that suffered by a Chicago newspaper war correspondent, Keith Wheeler, who accompanied us onshore and was promptly felled by a Japanese sniper's bullet that shattered his jaw. Wheeler spent months having his face put back together. So had my protagonist. I guess I got it right; Anthony Boucher of the *New York Times Book Review* liked my opening pages though he was not happy with my ending. Judge for yourself. If I do a lot of borrowing in solving my mysteries. When Jim Thompson turned in his manuscript, *Savage Night*, to Lion Books where I was Jim's editor, I immediately saw the possibility of writing a Western along the same lines. I asked Jim if he'd mind if I tried my hand at it, and he said, Go ahead.

Which is how *Flint* came about and why in this edition it is dedicated to Jim's memory.

The baseball crime novel, *The Big Out*, deals with the relationship between two brothers, not unlike my relationship with my big brother, my only sibling, my hero.

There is a scene on a lake with a loon; I had lived exactly that scene once on a lake in Lee, Massachusetts. No, I never knew a loon.

So that's how I write. I hope you like the results. I wrote these three novels back in the 1950s. I am now 90 years old. I can take it.

Arnold Hano
Laguna Beach, California
May 2012

So I'm a Heel

By Arnold Hano
writing as Mike Heller

CHAPTER ONE

I shouldn't have been looking at the dame, I guess—she came jiggling her way across Wood Street, her hips rolling and jouncing and her ankles flash-ing, but even so it wasn't my fault. I had the tow truck halfway up the ramp and headed for the open garage door when I took my eyes off the dame—she was one of those dames who don't wear underclothes, you could see—and I saw this jerk coming down the sidewalk, lost in a dream. I honked and braked, but he took the next step anyway, and I bumped him.

Hell, I wasn't going three miles an hour, but he was an old geezer with dangling eyeglasses and he must have been scared stiff. He walked into the left front fender and bounced about two feet out of the line of the truck and then landed on his right hip. He got up right away—sort of like a fighter who gets spilled and has to get up right away, hoping he'll make you forget he was ever down—and suddenly there was a crowd all around.

Now, as I said, it wasn't my fault. He should have stopped. I had honked and honked. But if it hadn't been for the dame, I wouldn't have hit him. And I'm a married man, with a ten-year-old kid. The boy's a peculiar boy, in a way, and there are lots of times when I don't like him. Know what I mean? He's sort of dreamy, too, with floppy soft brown hair that spills over his face and a lower lip that hangs down like a little pink pillow, a kid who'd rather read books—he's a helluva reader, for a ten-year-old—than play football or go out and steal a smoke behind the house.

But that's another thing, and I'll get to it. It all fits in, I guess. As I said, looking a dame over isn't so important—every guy does it, of course—but when there's an accident on the Coast Highway and we're the only AAA tow truck available, the driver better make damn sure he gets his butt mov-ing and out. They come down the highway lickety-split, sailor boys mostly on their way back to San Diego or marines to Camp Pendleton, and maybe they have a bottle in the front seat making the rounds, and they don't see the truck pulled off to the side of the road, the driver grabbing a snooze before barreling the rest of the way down. And they get off on the shoulder and plow into the truck, and before you know it, the alarm is ringing like blazes in the garage and we're expected to get out and scrape up the boys.

So when the tow truck itself gets stalled right at the garage door, it makes the company look pretty sick. It's like a firewagon, say, that gets to a fire and finds it forgot the hose, or a cop who forgets his gun.

Carlstrom came out of the little office to the side of the garage proper, and he saw me at the wheel, glaring down at the old geezer who was looking for his eyeglasses on the pavement. Carlstrom owns the garage. He sort of sighed and waved me out of the cab.

"Hawkins," he said, "you're on the job two weeks and you're in an accident already."

I said, "It wasn't my fault, boss. Ask anybody."

Carlstrom said, "It's never the driver's fault. I know. It's always the pedestrian's fault." He went inside and yelled, "Anderson, on the double."

Anderson came out, a bit peeved, I guess, but moving pretty fast toward the truck. He was the other driver on duty, and he had been playing a running game of gin with two of the grease monkeys in the back when the accident was reported. So he and I had tossed a coin and I lost and went out. Now he was going to have to go anyway. He hopped up and gave me a sour look.

I said, "Look, it wasn't my fault, Andy."

Carlstrom said, "Get going, Anderson. They say it's a mess down there," and Anderson gunned the truck and turned left onto Wood Street and headed for the Coast Highway.

A cop shoved himself forward and he said, "You the driver?"

I said. "Yeah. What about it?"

"You're Hawkins, aren't you?"

I said, "Yeah."

In a little town like Laredo Rock—pop. 8,000, situated halfway between L.A. and San Diego right near the Orange County-San Diego County line—everybody knows everybody. With me, it's easy. I'm a big guy, six-two, two hundred and five, plain ordinary looking except for my jaw. A piece of steel sliced off my lower jaw in the Marshalls back in February of '44. I put in a law suit against the ammunition manufacturer that made the shell—it blew up in one of our guns, killing a dozen men, and catching me with a flying chunk right at the lower gumline—and the ammo maker (you know who I mean) paid off finally because of the lousy publicity they were getting with pictures of me in every paper, my new jaw wired on, not quite fitting right and captions yapping, "GI War Hero Sues for New Jaw."

They probably wouldn't have had to pay. It really turned out that the guy who loaded the gun—a 155 howitzer—had grabbed up the wrong fuse and screwed it on and shoved it in, and somebody else had slammed the breech shut, and the gunner yelled, "Set," when she went off. I was a hundred yards away, digging a nice little hole back at Div Arty when I got rapped.

The dough went into the bank—five gees, it was finally settled for—and I got a half-disabled pension on top of it. Now I look sort of like a man sucking eggs or like a little boy drawing in his lower lip before he starts to cry. Or maybe like Andy Gump.

It's not funny.

The cop said, "All right, Hawkins, come on down to headquarters. You'll have to file an accident report." He had his little book out, making notes and talking to people, and I started rubbing my jaw as if it ached. People are suckers. They all know about my jaw and the trouble I had trying to get it settled (nobody likes ammunition manufacturers, that's a cinch) so it's always been easy working up sympathy. Though somehow it never lasts long. I don't know why. Well, anyway, I rubbed my jaw and the people the cop was talking to looked over at me and sort of smiled: It was like a salute, like they were saying, "Don't worry, buddy. You won't get the wrong end of the stick. We'll take care of you."

Then the old geezer—who wasn't hurt, you understand, not the slightest, not even his hip where he landed—and I piled into the patrol car and went to headquarters. In a town the size of Laredo Rock, that's a three-minute ride. You can go any place in that town in three minutes. I ought to know. I've had a dozen different jobs in the ten years I've been out here: wrapper and runner for the ceramic shack, where they finally canned me after I dropped a couple of expensive bowls; I couldn't stand the place, always jammed with guys talking about glazes and kilns (they pronounced it kills) and making sissy motions with their hands and wrists. I was a dairy driver working the canyon route at the east edge of the town until I started coming in late too often mornings—getting up at five in the morning is for the birds; pin boy and general clean-up man in the bowling alley on the highway, over the pizza place, was easy work until things got slack in the winter, when the tourists are back East and they had to let somebody go and they picked me, though I wasn't the last guy hired. The last guy hired was a boy out of high school, all get-up-and-go, who used to pride himself that he could set pins in three alleys at once—can you imagine such a talent? Then I was delivery boy in three or four places, liquor stores, dry cleaners, a florist and so on. I know Laredo Rock like you know your own face—and, by the way, take a look at your face. How does your jaw look? Imagine the lower half off and a piece of dry flexible pink plastic wired on, complete with plastic gumline and false teeth. Try smiling into the mirror with that thing, the top half of your face all lit up and the bottom a sort of half-sneer, half-grimace. How would you feel? That's how I feel. I tell you, it's not funny.

I told the sergeant behind the wooden rail at headquarters what had happened, and the patrol cop said that was the way it had happened all right, and he had in his little book the word of two witnesses who saw it and said that was the way it had happened. So nothing came of it, and the old guy and I signed the accident report, and then the old guy went out. He was a nice guy, only a little scared and a bit seedy looking. He was holding his broken eyeglasses when he went out and I guess he figured ten or fifteen bucks shot to hell.

Well, that's the way it goes.

Then the cruiser cop went to his car, and the sergeant—Sakimoto, a big, good-looking Japanese—and I were the only ones in the outside room at headquarters. He looked across the rail at me and said, in a slow way, "You're pretty lucky, Hawkins."

I started to say, "What the hell does that mean?" pushing myself up against the rail, my face over the top so he had to take a good look at my face, at the thin line where my lower jaw had been sliced away, and so he'd know I wasn't lucky at all, when the teletype machine behind him began to clatter.

Now, I'm not usually a nosy guy—looking at that dame wasn't the same as being nosy; that was just normal, even for a married man with a ten-year-old boy—but here I was, leaning over the rail, steamed up at the desk sergeant, and him looking at a piece of paper in the teletype machine, words starting to appear over the top. It was natural, I guess, letting my eyes drift from the cop's shoulder to the paper, and I read the little bit that I could see, which wasn't much.

There was some code stuff first, in numbers and letters which didn't mean a thing to me, and then it said, plain as can be, "*Otto Weylin picked up last night drunk susp molesting minor 15 years old.*" Then the cop's shoulder got in the way and I couldn't see the kid's name. When the machine jumped, I read, "*Doubt family press chg. Shall release your juris?*" After that there was some more code.

I didn't have to figure out the part I missed or the code. I had it all figured. Otto Weylin—he's a big-shot lawyer here in town, one of the biggest lawyers in the county, I guess, and a wheel in county politics with the party in power; his wife's on the school board and in all the big snooty clubs where you have to be rich and a big shot to get in—and white and Protestant, too, I'll tell the cockeyed world, they don't want ordinary jaw-shotoff ex GI's who drive tow trucks—Otto Weylin had been picked up someplace, in another city or county, messing around with a high school girl.

I remembered reading in the local paper that Weylin's wife had been sick or something and was away on vacation for a month. So the old boy was having himself a ball. Well, I thought, it wasn't any skin off my lip (I like to kid myself like that; it's sort of funny when you realize there is no skin on my lip, at least on my bottom lip)—it wasn't any of my business.

I swear, that's what I thought when the sergeant—Sakimoto—waved me out of the headquarters a couple of minutes later. He had turned around, snatched the paper from the machine, and he seemed surprised to see me still there—I had moved a few steps from the rail so he'd figure I was a polite cuss who didn't read other people's mail—and then he said, "All right, Hawkins, beat it," sort of absent-mindedly. Then he went into one of the inside rooms with the sheet of paper, and I walked out.

And I wasn't thinking a thing about the message. I don't care what happened later; that was all an accident, too, I guess. When I walked out, the message was behind me and I wasn't paying it the slightest mind.

Let Weylin worry about himself, I thought. It's not my business. I've got worries of my own. It isn't true that I started to link his situation and my worries. I didn't see, then, how I could make one work with and for the other.

In fact, I laughed as I walked back to the garage—past the fire station, the city hall, the big Presbyterian Church, the Playhouse, and onto Wood Street and three blocks back to Carlstrom's. Weylin was beyond me. It was tough enough, apparently, on the city where he had been picked up. I could imagine the cop's surprise when it turned out the guy he had was Weylin. No wonder they wanted to release him to Laredo Rock. Then I figured why the family wasn't pressing charges. The cops had probably told the family it wasn't smart to mess around with a man like Weylin; he'd drag them through court proceedings, with slick legal moves designed to sap a family that didn't have as much dough as Weylin could command until they'd be sick of the whole smelly business.

So much for the family, I thought, and so much for the city that picked him up. Weylin was in with all the local moguls of the party, and I'd heard it said there wasn't a cop or a fireman or even a schoolteacher in the county who didn't owe his job in some degree to Weylin. So I knew what would happen when Weylin, very much sober, arrived back in Laredo Rock. They'd maybe talk gently to him—but straight enough—so he'd know it wouldn't do him any good if it ever leaked out he was in such a jam. The other political party would love to know about it—the cops would tell Weylin—and if he just made sure he behaved himself, there'd be no report, no nothing.

That's the way it shaped, with Weylin slipping some of the boys on top a twenty, and the rest on down ten spots. And making sure they all climbed on his Christmas list. Nobody would be the wiser. The cops would know, of course, and Weylin, and the family of the girl, but they would have signed some paper saying nothing really had happened. Weylin's wife would never know about it. Nobody would.

Except me.

...But as I said, it had just about slipped my mind altogether once I left the police building and went back to the garage.

Carlstrom walked over to me when I sauntered in. He looked like white paste. He said, "Get that grin off your face, you stupid jerk. It's no laughing matter."

I said, "What's up, doc? Expect me to weep because some old geezer gets out in front of me?"

A little color struggled back to his face. His mouth started to twist and I swear for a minute it looked as if he was going to poke me. Ain't that a laugh! He's a good fifty pounds lighter and four or five inches shorter, and, of course, twenty years older. But he had turned himself a bit, his right arm drawn back, his fist crawling up to his hip. He said, "Listen, Hawkins. There were four sailor boys in that car. The car was on fire when Anderson got there. He got there right along with the fire truck. They say if he or anybody got there sooner, the boys might have been saved. It was a slow fire. The boy who was driving had his hand on the ignition. He had turned it off. So it burned slow, no explosion. But the doors had jammed tight shut. Andy got out and put a hook on the door and got it open and they tumbled out, on fire. A minute or two sooner, and they might have been saved."

I heard him.

And I couldn't see how it meant anything to me. It still added up to the old geezer getting in front of the truck. Or if Anderson was such a rah-rah college boy, up and at 'em in a big fat hurry, why did he agree to toss a coin with me to see who'd go? Why didn't he just pile into the tow truck and beat it?

I said to Carlstrom, "Throw another nickel on the drum. Your story touches me but it doesn't draw blood."

It looked then as though I'd hit *him*. He bounced back a little, his eyes squinting close together. Then he said, "Hawkins, if you ever come within six inches of hitting anybody with one of my trucks, you're through. Hear me?"

I said, "Yeah, I hear you." I had to bend a little to let him have the best view. I said, "I hear you, you dried-up rabbit. I'm through, now. The hell with your tow truck." And pushed his face in.

Not hard, mind you. I'm a big guy and Carlstrom's not. So I just shoved lightly and he staggered back and his heels hit some slick grease and down he went. I started to laugh and I was still laughing when I got to the bar on the ocean side of the highway, about a block and a half from the garage. I had three quick beers—just enough to take the edge off—and then I went back to the garage.

Carlstrom's face was whiter than before, white with a sick tinge of green underneath. He saw me and he said, "L-look here, Hawkins. Why don't you just go on home? I'm not going to cause you any trouble. I just slipped, that's all." He was afraid I'd come back all heated up from the saloon, ready to really tangle with him.

I said, "Why, Carlo boy, what kind of halfwit do you think I am? I came back for my pay and for my car." We parked our heaps in the garage, of course.

His lips thinned. He said, "This is Monday morning. You got paid for all of last week. This week's just begun. You haven't done a lick of work. I won't stand for any—"

Then he stopped. I guess he saw my face. He didn't know how much he was working me up, but he was starting to get the idea. It had been a bad day for me. There was the boy at home trying to make out he was sick and didn't want to go to school, and Mary—that's my wife, did I tell you about her? Well, that'll come, too—Mary sticking up for the boy, and me and her yapping at each other, and then my coming down, and even though it was my turn to take the tow truck out—Anderson had made the last call last week; that's how we worked it, by turns, but I wasn't going to do it so early in the day unless we flipped first, and I lost the flip and hit the old guy and had to

go to police headquarters—and then Carlstrom trying to con me into thinking it was somehow my fault four stupid drunken joy-riding sailor boys had
got creamed on the highway—well, I tell you. I could feel my temple start to
throb and my hands claw at my sides and I began to tremble inside just the
way a tea kettle does before the steam comes out. Only I ain't got a way to
make the steam come out. The beers helped a little to soften the edge, but that
was all. It was still there, inside me, bubbling away, climbing my throat like
hot blood, until—

With me, it sort of explodes. There was that guy in the ceramic shack,
once. He backed into me when I was holding a bowl. Or maybe my elbow
jabbed him and the bowl went down with a crash, and he turned around and
started to say, "Well. Of all the clumsy—" when I grabbed him. Oh, I
stopped him, all right, whatever it was he was going to say. I held him up real
close—you should have smelled the cologne on the guy—and I tapped him
right where the words were. He went limp as a rag in my hand, but I could-
n't stop and they had to pull me away.

...That's how I was getting with Carlstrom. He was riding me on top of
all those other things, and I was getting ready to let him have one. Not just
a little shove on his prat, either.

So he stopped talking and said, "Well, all right, Hawkins," and he went
into the office and I could see him rattling around the cash box, and he came
out with some money. "A week?" he said. "A week's pay? You'll just take
it, and go?"

I said, "Sure, Carlo," the feeling leaving me, and I took the sixty-five dollars, went up the ramp for my car, and rode out.

And I was thinking: it's not going to be a bad day at all. Not by a long
shot.

CHAPTER TWO

At first I thought I'd take the money and skedaddle home and put in a few hours in the sack. It's not often a man gets the chance to knock off work at ten in the morning on a Monday—and not have to go back the rest of the week. I had my pay and I had put in one hour. Sixty-five bucks an hour. Not bad, eh?

But not good, either, I thought. I drove to the end of Wood Street, where it runs into the Coast Highway. I rolled past the Hotel Laredo, where a man has to wear a tie to get a meal, and then past the dozens of realty joints, all advertising beach-front acreage at six or seven grand a lot or houses at thirty grand and up. This is a rich man's town, where old people come to die wrapped in cotton-white sand and sunshine. It rises up from the winding crescent beach like those postcards you see of southern France or the Italian Riviera, and climbs into the broadfaced canyons that hover over the village itself, hills that tingle with spiny cactus and iceplant and eucalyptus trees.

But if you go far enough into the canyons, into the hundreds of shaded hollows up there, you can find cruddy redwood homes that are falling apart, sagging beaver-board homes where a man can punch a hole clear through to the inside, bird-spattered, leaf-littered, skunk-smelling homes that are so many carbuncles against the sides of the hills. That's where the other people live, the people of Laredo Rock who don't come here to die, but die anyway, just about every day they live. They live and die in the dry-cleaning establishments, in the kitchens of the hotel's restaurants, in the motels, running errands and carrying baggage.

That's where I live, up in the canyon, me and Mary and the boy.

And that's why—with sixty-five bucks in my pocket five whole days before I expected to have sixty-five bucks in my pocket—I didn't want to go home. Not just yet.

I pulled up my '49 Chevy—with nearly 90,000 miles on it—in front of a saloon. I walked in but I didn't go to the bar—nobody was there. I took a table instead, near a window, where I could look out on the highway and watch the cars beat it down to La Jolla or Tijuana or up to Laguna or Santa Monica or further up to Santa Barbara or Carmel, the spokes of their big sports cars spinning like silver dollars. And when the dame came to my table to ask me what I wanted to eat or drink, it was all I could do to answer her as I watched those silver-dollar spokes go humming to places where other silver-dollar spokes were waiting.

I said, "Bourbon, on the rocks," and she said, "Ay, ay, sir," and wheeled away. I watched her from behind; she was tending toward flabbiness but the lines were still good. It's a strange thing, but Southern California has more good-looking women per square inch than any place I ever saw, and that includes Atlanta, Georgia. Well-stacked blondes, mostly. I'm from the East where you don't see so many blondes, so maybe it's still a novelty to me. But whatever it is, I find myself watching them more and more out here.

She brought me the bourbon with a smile, and I could see she wanted to talk. It was Monday morning, and nobody was in but me and nobody would be in for an hour or two, until the lunch crowd hit. And the lunch crowd would be two or three truck drivers.

I said, "How's business?" and she sort of brightened and said, "So-so." Then she waited and I could see it was going to be one of those question-and-answer games which I'd had enough of already this morning. So I decided to throw her a curve. I said, "What's your name?" and she said, "Susie," and I said, "Susie, what would you do if somebody handed you ten thousand dollars?"

Her eyes widened a bit and then she realized I wasn't anywhere near the guy who was going to hand her ten gees, so she said, "Keep right on dreaming, that's what I'd do."

I said, "No, seriously."

She said, "Buy me a big-screen TV set and a Thunderbird and a mink coat and—" I stopped listening.

I was getting mad at myself. I finished the bourbon and waved the empty glass at her and she went behind the bar and slopped another bourbon into the tumbler.

When she came back, I said, "Susie, are you a good girl?"

Her mouth snapped shut and she said, "Mister, watch yourself."

I said, "Susie, if somebody tossed ten gees on the table in front of you, would you care where they came from? Whether they were from a pimp or from a priest?"

She said, "Listen, mister, I don't get you. Go play your games someplace else."

You see? Here I was, face to face with the average palooka, and she wouldn't say whether it mattered if the money she had was clean or dirty. Maybe you don't think it proves anything. Maybe a sample of one doesn't count. I say it does, when the one is Susie. She didn't say she'd take that ten grand that came from the priest and bless it and spend it, wisely and well. She didn't say she'd take the ten grand from the pimp or whatever—and dump it back in the guy's face. It was all the same to her, and that's why she didn't answer.

It was all the same to me, too.

I had four more bourbons and the morning disappeared and then I had me a grilled steak sandwich and French fries, with a bottle of beer, and then I switched to gin on the rocks and the picture didn't change. It just got clearer. Don't ask me when it happened. I tell you, it didn't happen in the police station when I saw the message about Otto Weylin molesting a fifteen-year-old. I think it happened when Carlstrom told me about the four sailor boys on fire. I think that's when I started to turn and twist the whole thing in my head. Maybe you wonder how I take four dead sailor boys and Otto Weylin in a jam, and tote them up to blackmail. You can't, actually. There's more to tote than that. There's Laredo Rock and its six-thousand-dollar lots on the beach and sagging beaverboard homes—on the wrong side of the canyon. It's people who own hotels and people who wash dishes in the basement of hotels.

And it's a guy who sneers when he wants to smile. And it's not my fault.

But still, you say, how come blackmail? How come a guy like me—who maybe was a punk and a heel who'd just as soon hit you as spit on you, but who never robbed a bank or rolled a drunk or even snitched pennies from newsstands—how come now I was ready and willing to shake Otto Weylin down? Maybe everything I said about the wrong side of the tracks, and everything I said about my face being whacked out of shape—about Carlstrom egging me, and the four sailor boys creamed on the highway—maybe all that was enough to make me mad, make me want to take Weylin and slap him silly, just to teach him to keep his filthy mitts to himself and not all over the first teen-age dish that struts by.

But hitting a guy in the teeth is one thing, and blackmailing him is another, and I don't need you to tell me.

So how come?

So how come *you*, Mac, how come *you* lie on your income tax returns? How come you cheat the government—don't con me, Mac, I'm not that thick—how come you chisel Uncle Sam out of a hundred bucks every year, you and everybody else? How come you drive your car at seventy when the speed limit's fifty-five? How come you jaywalk, how come bartenders serve drinks to drunks and to under-age heroes? How come doctors double-bill you and lawyers tell you to go to court and lie, lie, lie—just to win a buck from the insurance house? How come guys shoot deer out of season and forget to toss back the five-inch fish in a seven-inch zone?

How come?

I'll tell you how come. Because we're a nation of crooks and cruds, of pimps, prostitutes and punks, of gamblers, grifters and grafters.

But most important of all, we're none of these when the heat's on. We're any of these when we can get away with it.

We're a nation of cowards and opportunists. We're quick on the uptake when the cop's walked around the corner and has promised us he won't be back on his beat for ten minutes. We're firm believers in the Eleventh Commandment. Don't get caught. It's okay if you don't get caught.

And that's how come. I was ready right now to shake Otto Weylin down, because I could get away with it.

Don't tell me you're different. Look at your income tax. Look at your speedometer. I know you, Mac.

And so, eight or nine or eleven drinks into the afternoon, all spread out so I wasn't the slightest bit drunk, not even wobbly, I said to Susie, "Here. Here's a five-dollar bill. I didn't steal it, but it's dirty." I laid one of Carlstrom's bills on the table and she fidgeted around, but she didn't walk away. She figured maybe it was her tip. And maybe it was. That was up to her.

"So?" she said, her eyes narrow and hard, and I wondered where I figured she was a good-looking dame four or five hours back.

"So this," I said. "So it's dirty. Let's say I did steal it, but it can't be traced. Would you take it?"

She said indifferently, "It's money, ain't it?" It wasn't a question.

It was my answer.

I took the five and I stood up and pulled her uniform out until it gaped at the chest, and I dropped it in. Then I dropped a ten spot on the table and said, "Keep what's left," and walked out.

CHAPTER THREE

I wound up the canyon and onto the dead-end turn-off where we live—and I pulled alongside the house. Mary hadn't come out to see who it was, which meant she hadn't heard me coming, which meant she was in the garage working the washing machine. It's a 1951 model which we bought at a church bazaar for twenty-five bucks, and it makes a helluva racket. So I was able to sneak up behind her and put my hands over her eyes. She sort of jumped and then she giggled, but she didn't try to turn around or take my hands away. I knew then that she had gotten over the yapping we'd had this morning before I left for work, about the boy staying home with his excuse of a cold.

I said, my hands still over her eyes, "Madame, I have a gadget that will add countless hours of pleasure to your day, to say nothing of your nights." She kept right on giggling, standing there, waiting for me to get to my punch line or whatever. I said, "It is certain, in the long run, to replace TV, reading, and even hanging the wash."

She started to bounce a bit from her giggling, and I turned her around and said, "Good afternoon, madame. May I demonstrate my gadget?"

She said, "Fresh," and then I was holding her and kissing her—and it was good, I'll tell you. I said before I had no way of letting off the steam, but that's not so. Mary, she was my way. Even while I was riding up the gravel road, just fifty yards from the house, I felt sweat on my palms, and my ankles ached from the way I was using the gas pedal and the clutch and brake. Not that I was going fast, mind you. Just that my foot was stiff all the way up my leg. I was tense and wound up. And now, with Mary's hair just resting under my jaw, the feeling was easing right out of my shoes and into the floor. Finally she pushed away and said, "Ed, you smell like a brewery. You've been cheating on Carlstrom's time, haven't you? You had a job up here someplace and you stopped off for a beer and now you've just sneaked over for a minute, is that it?"

"No," I said gravely, my face straight, "not for a minute. Like I explained, I have a gadget—" But the joke had gone its limit and I couldn't push it any further. "I quit," I said.

"Oh," she said, quickly, her mouth open and round, breath coming out with a tiny rush. "Oh, Ed, you should have seen what happened to the washing machine. A bolt came flying off and—and I had to crawl around looking for it, and—see, my knee?—I actually cut myself on a piece of gravel. But I found the bolt and put in on all by myself. Isn't that wonderful! Aren't I the one? Tell me, Ed, did you ever see such a wonder?" She was smiling brightly, her eyes crinkled and as blue as—

Let me tell you about Mary. You see what she did then, don't you? She thought she was fooling me, but she's done it so often that I'm on to it now. No matter, you still have to admire it. When I told her I had quit, the oh came out like I had hit her in the belly. That was what it was like, the open mouth, her lips rounded and the breath whooshing out. Like I had hooked my left to the beltline. But she didn't want me to know how she felt, so she just took that oh and tacked it onto something she wanted to tell me, something that was more important than my losing any silly old job. That's what she meant, and you have to admire it.

You—not me. I hated it. I knew what it meant, all right. I know more than you. It meant she was hurt, all right, but it meant she had to coddle me, baby me, make it look as if there were nothing wrong with me for leaving a job, that it was the most natural thing in the world, that no matter what had happened, I was right and they were wrong, and she was behind me.

Admirable? Not a goddam bit. For in order that she think and act that way, she had to think all the opposite things first. If it were necessary to tell me it didn't matter that I quit, she must have thought it mattered a great deal. Otherwise why the big act? Why not just say, "Again? Well, that's too bad. But we'll manage. You'll find something else."

That's what I wanted her to say; that would have meant something. It would have meant she felt it mattered, but not too much. This other way, the way she hid from me how hurt she was, told me what a heel she really thought I was, what a no-good bum without a thought in his head for his family.

I said, "Mary," holding her off at arms' length, "Mary, you're not to do that. You understand? You didn't cut yourself looking for a bolt, and you know it."

She said, "But, honey, I did. I showed you my knee. I was down on my hands and knees—"

I said, "Mary, please. No more. That's enough." I kept her off like that, looking at her, and the smile faded from her face and the hurt, sullen look started to crawl over and then she twisted away and began to pull the clothes out of the machine and pile them into the hemp basket.

I said, "Want a hand with that?"

She said, "No, thanks," in a kind of smothered voice and she ran out of the garage and up the back stairs to the porch outside the kitchen where the clotheslines were.

That's Mary.

Oh, I never did tell you what she looks like. She's blonde, and very small, small-boned that is, yet with enough flesh over those bones; and she has a cute sort of face, fresh, with a turned-up nose and crinkled blue eyes and some freckles on her face. And nice legs, trim and curvy, a nice figure, not too big but not too small, nice and solid.

No, that's not quite it, either. I haven't got it across to you what's wrong with Mary....

I met her twelve years ago, when I got my medical discharge, and I was on the streamliner headed up for Frisco to lay in a good old-fashioned drunk. I had to get myself drunk, you see, for they had just wired my new jaw on and it ached like the furies and it looked worse. Do you remember the movie Frankenstein? The scene where Karloff comes across the little girl tossing flowers into the stream? And how he sits down next to her and tosses flowers into the stream, too? Until he runs out of flowers and he's got nothing else to rip up and toss into the stream? And he looks at the little girl?

I tell you, I'll never forget that look. Like some thought was working in all that machinery and wiring that passed for his brain. There was a flash of tenderness and then a flash of cruelty, and then that marvelous combination of both that only Karloff can show you. But more than that, there was a look about his lower jaw, as if he was going to kiss the little girl or else tear her flesh apart with his teeth—both looks, actually.

That's how I looked then, right after they sewed a new lower jaw onto my face.

So I rode on up on the streamliner and the seat next to me remained empty half the way up, though the sun was in everybody's eyes on the other side. Mine was the only empty. Then a dame came into my car. She came in the front of the car, facing us, so it wasn't that she didn't see me. She came down the aisle slowly, carrying a bag and sort of swaying, a grin on her face like she was enjoying herself, and looking over the prospects of the car for small talk until she hit wherever she was going. Frisco, it turned out.

Because she got halfway down when she saw me. She had that grin on her face and I stared right into those blue eyes, waiting to see her change expression. There were two ways a dame's expression changed. Either they felt sorry or they felt disgusted, one or the other. Nothing in between. They'd either flinch and pull away, as if I was a freak, or else they'd get soft-eyed and grave and very very sympathetic as if I was a cripple or a blue baby or something.

She kept on coming, from about fifteen feet away when she first spotted me, until she drew up next to me, and my eyes had her pinned the whole time. I have good eyes and I was pretty expert at spotting the slightest little flicker that was the first giveaway.

But she never changed expression. The smile stayed put, not frozen there, either, but alive and flashing, and her eyes were smiling, too, warm and friendly, and she said, "Hi, soldier, is this seat taken?"

I must have mumbled something or else I shook my head, because she just turned around, dropped her bag in the aisle next to the seat and plopped down. She said, facing me, her eyes ten inches from my face, "On leave?"

Now you have to admit there's something wrong with such a dame. She saw my jaw and she knew it wasn't just a little pin scratch. She saw my ruptured duck in my lapel—my discharge button—so she knew I was out or on my way out of service. She had to know it. How dumb could she be? I could-n't figure it out. I still haven't....

I walked out of the garage and was half tempted to go on up the back stairs and help her pin up some of the clothes, but then I figured the hell with it. I had offered to help her, and she had turned me down. I went up the front steps and into the living room, and there was the boy sitting on the couch, his head in a book.

"Well," I said, clearing my throat, putting in that extra bit of heartiness to try and warm up the kid, "How's it going, Matt? How's the cold?"

He looked up with a start, as if he hadn't heard me—which would have been pretty strange, considering I had driven up and Mary and I had talked downstairs, right under the house, and then I had closed the door pretty hard. I had forgotten about the kid's being home.

He said, smiling a little, as though he were afraid to let go and really split his face wide open, "Hello, Dad. I think it's much better." Then he started to look down at his book, and his head jerked up quickly. He said, sort of fast and breathless, "Thank you."

He's a strange kid. He had forgotten to thank me for asking about his cold, and he had started to read when he remembered. He was actually scared be-cause he had forgotten. That was why the words were blurted out that way.

Or maybe he just blurted them out because he begrudged saying them. I had laced him this morning about his not going to school just because his nose was running. And when Mary had finally said, "Well, hon, it's not a good idea, really. Even if it's only a little cold and won't get any worse, he might spread it. The other kids might come down."

I had stared at her. "I don't see the other kids worrying about Matt very much. I don't see anybody coming on over here with a football or a bike and calling on him to go on out and play. If that's how they want to be, I would-n't care if they all caught rabies."

Mary had looked at me sort of hard and then she'd begun to giggle and she'd said, "Silly. You're so tough, aren't you? You're always ready for a scrap. My big tough hombre."

Matt had been smiling, looking at us both, liking us then for the way Mary was kidding me. And all I had to say was, "Yeah. Boy, I'm a real tiger," and then give her a little peck on the cheek or pat her behind, and rumple the boy's hair and go on out, saying, "Okay. Play hooky. Wait till the truant officer hears about this." Then I'd have been off for work, and it would have been a good day all around, and when the alarm rang in Carlstrom's I'd have hopped up and buzzed down the highway.

All the time that I said what I did say, I was wanting to say and do this other. But the words that came out were half a snarl, half a sneer. I said, "Or maybe it's his fault they don't come around and play. Maybe there's some-thing wrong with him. Is that it?"

And Mary and the boy just gasped together. That's when she laced into me and I yapped back....

I stood near the couch, looking down at the boy, his head back in the book. It was one of his school texts; he was trying to keep up with his class so the day home wouldn't matter. I said, "Matt, how'd you like to have a catch? The sun's out and it's real warm. We could go down the other side of the canyon to the empty lot and have a real good sweat. I think it would be good for your cold."

Well, you should have seen that boy. He was inside with his book and back out again with the ball and two gloves, his fielder's glove and my catcher's mitt, and his jacket over his shoulder, all in about twenty seconds. That's how eager he was to get out.

And Mary yelled when she saw us going down the side of the canyon wall, "Do you have a handkerchief, Matt?" and I yelled back, "Don't worry, he can use mine." I turned then and she waved. Not to us. To me. That's how it looked.

We went down the side of the canyon—it's a tricky walk down because it's pretty steep and when it rains, as it had a few days ago, it stays slicker on our side than across the way. So we stepped along pretty carefully and I finally said, halfway down, "Hey, boy, we'd better swap. Let me get in front of you, so in case you slide you can grab hold of me." Well, the boy beamed as if I had handed him a fifty-dollar bill and told him to blow it on books and ice cream sodas.

Well, we got to the big lot just below and behind the great big white house that sprawled on the canyon top—the biggest house in that part of town and probably with the best view, though I'd never been inside or around the front where the picture window is, looking out on the ocean, I guess—and I took my mitt and walked off about forty feet.

"Okay, boy," I said, "let 'er rip. The old fast ball and then the jughandle curve."

He grinned and tried to serve them up the way I signaled—one finger for the the fast ball, two fingers for the curve—but he just wasn't the type of kid who'd ever make much of a ball player. I'd played ball in high school and for a while with a semipro team back on Long Island—I caught and they had me batting fourth most of the time—and ever since Matt was born I was waiting for the time the kid would be big enough to slip his fingers into a glove. Mary used to say I was rushing the kid, but hell, didn't Bobby Brown's old man decide the boy was going to be a major-league ball player when the kid was born, and didn't Brown develop into just about the coldest, most deadly clutch hitter you ever saw?

Of course, Brown quit when he was still young and became a doctor, but the old man had turned him into what he set out to do, a boy who really could play ball.

So Matt grunted and threw and I would come out of my squat and dig the throw out of the dirt, and I'd toss it back. We kept it up for quite a while, and then I noticed the boy's face was getting strained and white, and I realized our game had become quite silent. He was throwing and I was catching, and that was all. No, there was more. I was starting to get irritated by his broken-wristed, elbow-snapping way of throwing and his inability to reach me without bouncing the ball.

So finally I caught one and said, "Okay, boy, let's take ten." He trotted over and we sat down on the grass, and I picked up a blade of grass and set it between my teeth. The boy eyed me and picked up a blade of grass and set it between his teeth. He said, "Dad, show me how to whistle on a blade of grass," so, of course, I showed him, though he couldn't seem to get it too well, and then he said, "Dad, show me how you hold the ball when you throw a curve."

I was staring at the big white house in front of us, sitting on the edge of the hill and looking out at the ocean, sixty thousand dollars' worth of house and a million-dollar view, and I said, "You hold the ball with two fingers and you twist your wrist and let it roll off your index finger when you release it."

"Which way, Dad?" he said, holding the ball in his right hand, two fingers gripping it as well as he could.

I said, "So the palm is facing to the left and slightly up. Unless you want to throw a screwball. Then you twist it the other way. But don't try it. You couldn't do it." I had my eyes set on that big house and I could feel the boy's eyes on my face, the puzzlement in them.

He said in a slow, almost pleading voice, "C-could you show me, Dad?" He had the ball held out in front of me, shoving it around so I'd have to see it. I grabbed the ball and I said, "This way for a curve, this way for a screwball," twisting my wrist first one way and then the other. And then I handed the ball back to him.

He should have dropped it then and there. He's a shrewd kid and he could see I wasn't interested any more in playing ball with him—hell, I'd done it for twenty minutes or maybe even half an hour—and now I was taking a breather, looking at that white heap of dollars in front of me. But Matt had an idea I wanted him to be a ball player above all else, and he figured he had me out where I could teach him; it was like a last chance for him, sort of. So he said, "Dad, could—would you take the glove and give me the mitt, and you toss me some curves, and tell me each time what you're doing? Maybe then I'll catch on. Would you, Dad?"

I got to my feet and we swapped gloves and he walked over and tried to squat the way I did, the glove up and practically hiding his whole head.

So I said, "All right, Matt, the curve ball," and I threw it at him, hard.

The instant it was out of my hand, I yelled, "Watch out!" but it wouldn't have mattered. He just froze there with the big glove out in front of his face, and the ball whipped in at him and then hooked like a jagged knife, down and to his right. It didn't hit him, but it didn't miss him by much, and it bounced behind him and skipped all the way to the rear grass lawn of the big house.

The boy lowered his glove and he looked at me. His face was white and there were tears in his eyes.

He started to say something, and then he turned around and ran after the ball.

But he didn't have to run far. The guy who owned the house had come through a door that led to the rear patio. He walked onto the lawn and picked up the ball. He had a friendly look on his face, and he turned the ball over a couple of times as if he was studying the stitching and the signature of Will Harridge, and then he tossed the ball the short distance to Matt. Matt caught it in the mitt and I heard him say, "Thanks."

I came on up and the man said, "That's a hell of a curve ball you threw, sir," smiling at me. "Where'd you pitch?"

Matt said, "He didn't pitch; he caught for the Cedarhurst team. And he batted cleanup."

I said, "I hope you're not sore about us playing ball on your property?"

The man shrugged. "What for?" He was a youngish middle-aged guy, about forty-five, medium height, stockily built, with dark hair parted in the middle. There was an old-fashioned look about him, as if you'd see him in knickerbockers, playing golf. He looked like Bobby Jones or Sarazen or that gang.

Matt said to him, "Do you want to play catch?" and the man burst out laughing. He said, "No, thanks, son—" and he paused, looking at Matt. "What's your name, boy?"

"Matthew Hawkins, sir," the kid said, standing there straight as an arrow, and for an instant I was proud of the boy. He was proud of me, too, you could see, and of being the son of Ed Hawkins, who batted fourth for Cedarhurst back in Long Island before the war.

"Matt," the man said, "how'd you and your dad like to have a Coke? I mean, after the workout, you're probably thirsty."

Matt said, "Oh, boy!"

I said, very slowly, "That's very nice of you. You sure you don't mind? The way we're dressed, and all?" I was still in my white T-shirt and cotton khakis, the gear I wear when I drive the tow truck.

The man frowned. He was in an open-necked beige sport shirt and dark brown trousers and brown-and-white shoes. His arms and face and neck were tanned. He looked like the kind of guy who goes to the private gyms and works the dumbbells for half an hour a day and then lies under the sun lamp. More likely, of course, he went down to a private beach every weekend.

He said, "You look fine to me, Hawkins."

He had seen my jaw, of course, but with men it's often different. They don't seem to react the way dames do. He had taken a good solid look at it when he came up to me, but when he didn't stiffen any or try to look sorry, I figured him pretty square.

We went in, and Matt and he jabbered away at each other about sports and books and movies and whether Cokes were really bad for your teeth which would have been too bad, because they really hit the spot when a guy was hot and thirsty, and Matt agreed very soberly, drinking his out of the bottle, the way we were. And I kept looking the place over, the shelves at the far end of the room where the fireplace was, a tall brick affair running right up to the ceiling, and the rug that squashed under your feet, the big over-stuffed chairs and couch, and the curved ceramic lamps and ashtrays. It was a nice room, warm and comfortable, and worth ten thousand bucks, not count-ing the price of the books, and there must have been six hundred of them.

I got up after we had been there about half an hour, and I said, "Okay, Matt, we'll have to run. Say thank you for the Coke."

Matt scrambled to his feet and said, "Thank you," and he extended his right hand. It was the first time I'd ever seen him shake hands with an adult without being told, and you could see it was a perfectly normal gesture. The man shook his hand and said, "You must come over and visit me again."

Matt said, "Gee, I sure will. Thanks again Mr. Weylin." We started out, the guy behind us, toward the door. All right, you figure it. Everybody has motives, all the time. You figure you're going out for a ride in the country, just for relaxation you think, but all the time—and maybe you don't even know it—you're aiming to spot the broads in the open sports cars. Or you go into town to window-shop, but you end up at a bar. So all the time you really know what you're aiming at.

Still, you come back from the ride all relaxed; it worked out the way you planned. Or you have a couple of shots at the bar, but on the way down and on the way back you have looked at the shop windows and you can tell the old lady whether the clearance sales are still on, or who's pushing what and at what price. It works out exactly as you planned, no matter what else you grab off on the way.

The kid needed some air; he needed some reassurance. He wanted his old man to play buddy with him. And I did. You've got to admit that. Maybe I steamed up a little, but still you should have seen the boy's face all the way back home. Like an Indian's, I tell you. Flashing, his eyes lit up like daggers and his teeth shining. He was loose, too, walking fast and easy, and I had to stretch out to catch up with him.

So the real reason I played catch was I wanted to see Weylin face to face if I got the chance, to size him up, to see the inside of his house. I had to case him. That was the idea in my head. It wasn't much more than an idea. I had no idea how to pull it off, but at least I saw it could be done.

I knew Otto Weylin had been pinched six or seven hours back, early this morning or more likely, the night before. Here he was back home again, wandering around, free and easy, steeped in money and comfort. They had dropped him because he was too hot to handle. And nobody was going to be any the wiser.

Here he was back home, and here I was out of a job.

The idea was so simple that anybody else probably would have thought of it on the spot, right in the police headquarters, but it took me a few hours and a dozen drinks. I was going to shake down Otto Weylin for all he was worth.

We got back to the house, and Mary had two glasses of milk on the table and a couple of brownies she had just baked. When Matt saw the milk, he waved his hand and said, "I don't want any, thanks."

There was an air about the boy, an assurance that had never been there before. It was as though our little trip through the canyon had matured the boy five years.

I said, "Matt, come here." The boy was on his way back to his room, to put away the gloves and jacket.

He came, smiling. "Yes, Dad?" he said.

I said quietly, "Drink your milk."

That's all I said. You wouldn't think that was so much. His mother had made the brownies and had poured the milk, but that wasn't the point. He had to learn that every day wasn't Saturday and everything wasn't Cokes and ball-playing. Some of it was milk when you didn't want any milk.

He frowned at me and then his face changed. The straight-as-an-arrow look sort of dissolved. And I swear, his nose started to run. Just like that.

He drank the milk.

Chapter Four

I heard Mary making little aimless noises outside the bedroom door the next morning, little shuffling-in-her-slipper noises. She wanted me to wake, but she was afraid to wake me herself. At first I started to roll over, thinking I had the whole day ahead of me to lie in the sack, but when the noises kept up I knew I wouldn't be able to sleep anyway.

Or maybe I figured there was money in the bank just begging to be picked up, without a cent of it ever coming out of my account.

So I sat up and looked out at the back of the canyon where the sun comes up except for eight months out of the year when all you get until ten o'clock is white fog, and Mary came in, bright-faced and looking surprised. She said, "Oh, you're up. I was going to let you sleep—"

"But?" I said. "You were, but you didn't."

She said, "Well, I was thinking you could drive Matt to the bus stop, unless you think it would be better for him to walk."

Up in the canyon, we're really out of the city. We're in the county, so if we ever had a fire, for instance, and the Laredo Rock fire engine came charging up to see what was happening, it'd first have to get clearance from county fire headquarters before the boys could let loose one drop of water. The school bus comes up the canyon, because we are in the same unified school district as the rich punk kids in the town proper, but it doesn't come all the way up. Some day this part of the town will probably vote to incorporate into Laredo Rock, because of such things as that. Still, it won't happen tomorrow. Laredo Rock pays whopping taxes; the county pays piddling taxes.

"Hell," I said, "let him walk. He's got two legs. It's not that far."

Mary frowned a little, thinking, and then she said, "Well, his cold's *better*, I guess—"

I said, "All right, I'll take him." Then I got out of bed and turned my back. I was sore, and I don't like starting the day sore. She wasn't nagging me the way another dame might, but she was letting me know I'd forgotten the boy had been sick and out of school yesterday, and his nose *had* still been running last night. So I dressed in a flash and went into the kitchen. The boy was drinking a glass of milk and when he looked up at me, our eyes meeting over that glass of milk, we both sort of flushed. Then he very deliberately drank it all down, not fast, not gulping it the way a hungry kid might, but putting it away because it had to be done. He didn't know it—or maybe he did—but he was slapping me in the face with that glass of milk.

I said, in a forced way, "Okay, Matt, pile in," and he wiped his mouth, grabbed his books and his lunch box and was out the front door. We didn't talk much on the way to the school bus stop. It's really too short a trip for much talk, and anyway I was just up, I hadn't brushed my teeth or washed or had a cup of coffee or even gone to the john.

And I was thinking of Otto Weylin.

So I braked to a jerky stop, and flung the door open and said, "End of the line, son. Keep your nose clean," and he said, "Right, Dad. Thanks. See you," and was gone to stand near, but not with, the three or four other kids jabbering away while waiting for the bus.

I drove back up the winding hill, the last part of it dirt, and went inside and cleaned up.

At breakfast, Mary was being so carefully quiet I finally said, "What's up? Out with it, girl."

She smiled and shook her head, the blonde hair dancing. "Nothing," she said. "I was just hoping you'd stick around today or maybe we could go to the beach or something."

I grunted. There it was again. Make a holiday out of what ordinarily would be considered a predicament. "Stick around?" I said. "What for?"

"Oh, you know. There're lots of things you always want to fix up, but you don't have the time. A paint retouch job, or that loose wiring in the basement near the washing machine. I'd like you to tighten the clotheslines. And I could get rid of all the cobwebs downstairs while you're working down there, or else wash down the back porch and sweep off the leaves and prune those bushes that always choke everything in the summer."

"Cozy," I said. And it was. We always worked side by side, or at least near by. Sometimes we'd chat while we worked, which had the effect of making it conversation, with work on the side, instead of the other way around, or sometimes we wouldn't, just working away quiet-like, me on the weeds, let's say, and Mary cleaning the steps, carefully picking up the snails and tossing them on the other side of the road because neither one of us liked to kill them and if we didn't get rid of them we'd find ourselves crunching them underfoot. And even working quiet that way, it wasn't really work.

Or the other. Going down to the beach. There's the glory of this place, that makes even the sagging beaverboard sores take on a richness I never knew when I lived back East. You can shut up the beaverboard and get down to the beach in three minutes, and in early spring the beach is a lonely golden strip, like some faraway South Sea island, or even better, a helluva lot better. Brother, I've seen some of those South Sea islands. They're no bargain.

I let my eyes stray out the kitchen window across the canyon to the other side where the empty lot gave extra dimension to Weylin's place. Not that it needed it. Half an acre at least, riding that soft peak like a white yacht on a still, green sea.

"No, thanks," I said softly. I wasn't going to let a day go by. No, not while Otto Weylin could play king of his hill, and didn't have to go down to the beach to get away from it all, from paint that needed retouching and the faulty wiring and the snails that left their slimy Morse-code prints wherever they moved. No, Otto Weylin could stay at home and have it rich, a lawn like a polo field, an outdoor patio fireplace as big as Matt's bedroom, and all those goddam books.

"No, thanks," I said again. "I'm going out this morning. They don't let the grass grow under Ed Hawkins's feet," and I could see that even though Mary would have liked my sticking around, she seemed relieved. She thought I was going out looking for a job, and that pleased her, because in the past I'd curl up for a day or two or else I'd tie one on downtown or get into a scrap, too much time and nothing to do gnawing away at me.

So I wet my hands and ran them over my hair and studied myself in the mirror—the jaw first because out of habit I always looked at it first, nodding at it, thinking it looked all right, and then dismissing it, and running down the rest of me. The rest wasn't much, big and rangy, a clean white T-shirt and clean faded khakis and clean unpolished heavy shoes. Maybe not the way you'd look for a job, but the only kind of job I'd look for if I were looking for one would need a guy who looked like me and dressed this way. Driving a truck, or wrapping liquor bottles, or throwing groceries into a box or into a couple of heavy paper sacks at one of the supermarts and toting the whole shebang to some dame's car. The kind of work that paid maybe as low as forty-five bucks a week and should have had a high-school boy handling it; or else as much as seventy-five or eighty, with prospects or not, depending on the geezer behind the steering wheel. Me.

Mary came up behind me and put her hands on her hips and cocked her head. "Not bad," she said. "Not Van Johnson, but not bad. I'll take it."

"For how much?" I said, trying to keep it light, and because I was trying, it slipped away.

"Oh," she said, and she was forcing it, too, hamming it up, making believe she was really weighing it, "three hundred a week. No, three hundred and fifty. *After* taxes."

I swung around and kissed her, and that should have been light, too, but it wasn't, and somehow we ended up wound around each other, digging in like crazy, a guy and his girl kissing each other as if it was the first time they'd ever gone that far or maybe the last time they'd ever get that far again.

Then we broke off and stared at each other, and I could see the fright in her face that she probably saw in mine. She said, breathless and husky, "Stay home, Ed. I want you to stay home."

I held her away, and took one deep breath and then another, and that changed the mood. I touched her lightly on the chin and said, "Sorry, hon, the bread's got to be won," and I went through a little feinting act I do with Mary, bobbing my head and making believe I'm going to belt her with my left hand. She bobbed with me, grinning her usual grin, and we crossed our rights together, little love taps on the side of the jaw. I used to think Mary liked that act because it gave her a chance to touch my jaw in a natural way, letting me know it didn't mean a thing to her and that it wasn't the kind of a jaw a man ought to have. But now, I think she does it because she likes to. Can you imagine a crazy dame like that?

The job I had in mind wasn't going to pay forty-five or seventy-five or eighty, nor was it going to pay three hundred and fifty, before, during or after taxes. It had a price tag of ten thousand dollars on it. But before I collected, I had a little groundwork to do.

I don't know much about local politics, but I know a little, because there's no way of not knowing at least a little around Laredo Rock. Laredo has two weekly newspapers, which is unique in this day and age, especially for a town of under ten thousand, and what is more unique is that one of the papers represents the Opposition political point of view. In a town like New York, with maybe eight million people and most of them Democrats, you get one paper out of seven or eight that's Democratic. So why should a town like Laredo, full of rich old people, full of high-ranking Marine and Air Corps officers at the two bases nearby, with a political registration that runs five and six to one in favor of the party of Otto Weylin and his crowd, why should a town like that have a rival paper?

It doesn't have to; the rich crums in this town could wipe it out in a minute if they wanted to. All they'd have to do is put a little pressure on the two or three supermarts who advertise in the rival paper, the three or four big local shops and a couple of others, and the paper would close down.

But they don't—don't ask me why—and the paper keeps open, and frankly it's a pretty good paper. It's all for public improvement bonds and school construction bonds and fluoridated water. And if you read it often enough, you get to know the poor slobs who try to do something about the beaches and the schools and the water even with that five-to-one registration against them.

I aimed the Chevy along Bel-Eyre Street and into the shopping area, confined mainly to three streets that come one right after the other, Wood, Sand, and Main. I turned onto Sand Street and went away from the ocean three blocks and parked the Chevy. The meter read *Violation* so I shoved a penny in for my twelve minutes, and I stood outside a double shop, half of which was marked "Kimball's Paints" with a man-wanted sign in the window, and the other half leased to the political party that's never won an election in Laredo Rock. There was nobody in the political headquarters, but that didn't matter, because Vince ("Win with Vin") Kimball *was* the political headquarters of that party.

I walked in and a woman with gray hair and eyes the same color and lipstick on her lower lip but not on her upper, walked along the wall behind the counter and said, "Hi, what can I do for you?"

I grinned and said, "Nothing, Mom. Is Vin around?"

She looked at me with a vague curiosity, because, I guess, people didn't ordinarily call her Mom unless they knew her. She obviously didn't know me. But then the little clouded look went away and I could see her filing my face, figuring she must have met me at a rally or something when she was too tired to notice the jaw, and she said, "He's in the back, Mr.—Mr.—"

"Hawkins," I said. "Ed Hawkins."

The little cloud came back again, and I knew she knew she didn't know me at all. But by then I was past her.

I *did* know Vinny Kimball. Not that I ever buy in his shop. I get my paint from Sears because it's cheaper. But I'd seen him around here and there, having rolls and coffee in the snack shop on the highway because maybe he was tired of breathing paint when he ate or maybe he was tired of looking at his wife's tired gray eyes. I'd be there myself between chores, having just delivered a load of asphalt or run a couple of cases of whisky to a shoe salesman entertaining in the Hotel Laredo. And people who grab afternoon bites are usually a gabby lot. Vinny Kimball and I had talked maybe three or four times.

I stood in the rear of the shop where it opened on a dim storage area lit up by a naked sixty-watt bulb hanging from a string straight down the center. Kimball was leaning over a couple of saw horses, working on a big placard.

I said, "Kind of early to get the campaign posters up, Vinny," and he grunted without looking up and said, "Little League." I came closer and rubbernecked over his shoulder. The placard read: "Let's Go, Rotary!"

I said, "You do all the Little League teams?"

He nodded, still working. "All eight teams. Both leagues. Have to have 'em ready for opening day."

I said dubiously, "Does that pay?"

He stiffened a little, and then he said in a different voice, "Pay? What the devil are you talking about?"

I looked over at the side of the wall. There were three other placards leaning against the wall, drying out. They read: "Come On, Kiwanis!" "Roar, Lions, Roar!" and one said simply, "VFW," and was decorated with gaudy stars. These were some of the sponsors of Little League here in Laredo; I knew the others—the Laredo Savings Bank, one of the sporting goods stores, the Optimists, and the American Legion.

When Matt was eight, I made him go out for the Little League tryouts. It was a laugh, of course, but I wanted him to see what he'd be missing. Last year, when he was nine (Little Leaguers have to be from eight to twelve) he came down with a bronchial cough that stuck practically all spring, so he missed the tryouts (and I've often wondered whether he wasn't coughing just so he *would* miss the tryouts). This year—well, I don't know. The tryouts would start in a couple of weeks.

I said to Kimball, "Don't tell me you do this for kicks?"

He stopped working finally and turned around. He frowned for a minute in the dim light, and then he recognized me. "Hawkins, you're pulling my leg. You know damn well that's why I do it."

I shook my head. Maybe he thought I was kidding, but I wasn't. Take a look at that roster again: Rotary, Kiwanis, VFW, American Legion, and on down the line. There wasn't a Kimball vote in the carload. Then I forced out a laugh. "Figuring on bolting your party, Vin?"

He walked away from me to the far wall and took a rag and wiped his hands very carefully, staring at his fingers. Then he said, "Come on up front, Hawkins. We can take care of whatever it is up there."

I followed him to the counter and his wife disappeared to the back, and I realized she was going to continue working on the Little League placards. For the life of me, I still couldn't see the angle, putting in ten or twelve hours at what looked like pretty damned skilled labor—for free.

Up front, Kimball looked less like a small-town paint store owner and more like a small-town politician. He looked crisper, sort of, and he made his five-nine imposing enough. He had a good jaw (I always see a man's jaw first; so would you) and a long thin nose that barely missed looking miserly and sharp blue eyes, crinkled at the edges like a farmer's or a smiling politician's. Fact is, he used to be a farmer, running a fruit ranch someplace around Rancho Santa Fe in the citrus and avocado country down there. But either you spend your life and everything you have nursing your fruit, or else you get out of the fruit business. Still, Kimball had a pile of money—family money, I understand—and nothing to do, so now he ran a little paint shop and supported the county political machine and kept running for the state senate or congress, and losing every time. The party biggies tolerated him and his dull speeches, I guess, because of his donations.

He said, "Now, Hawkins, what'll it be?"

I said, "Vin, I've got something I'd like to give to the *Laredo Sun*, because they'd sure as hell love to run it. But it seems to me there ought to be better ways of doing it than that." I paused, letting him wait until he saw I was going to outwait him.

He said, "Better ways of doing what?"

"Of handling this matter. Let me put it this way, Vin. I've got something of a political nature here, and it's all mine, nobody else's, and I think you'd like to have it."

"You trying to sell me something blind?" The crinkles had deepened until they were just plain lines, and the long thin nose had sharpened. But even if the face had been bland as a baby's, the words were still there, hanging over his dusty paint counter. *Trying to sell me something blind?*

If he'd left off the last word, you'd know he was an honest man, indignant as hell, getting ready to boot me out of his place. But the last word hung
him. It was a way of saying, "Sure I buy information or dirt or whatever you
want to call it. But I'm not a damn fool; I don't buy a pig in a poke."

It's too bad, when you think of it like that. Here's a man who runs a
penny-dimes paint shop, and who gives his time to a sagging political party
in the wrong part of the state. Up in L.A., for instance, or in Frisco or San
Diego, he'd do fine, but not down here. Though he doesn't have the time he
still finds some to knock off posters for Little League and God knows what
else just because he feels it's his duty or privilege or something. And yet, with
all that he has a price hung on his long nose.

I said, "Now, Vin, you know I wouldn't sell you anything blind. It's just
that I'm not ready to release it, or even to sell it. I wouldn't sell it, in fact,
even if you *would* want it blind."

Kimball was getting nervous. It was as if I was turning that sign on his
nose around where he could read it, and where he could keep knocking the
price down. He was more than plain cheap; he was fire-sale; going-out-of-busi-
ness, lower-than-cost, cut-rate cheap. He said, "Mom, come on out, will
you? Hawkins and I have to talk business back there."

Mom Kimball came out and shot her husband a smile, frightened, and pity-
ing, I guess, and a little scared. Kimball and I walked back and he sat on one
saw horse and I sat on the other. He said, "Hurry up, Hawkins, I haven't got
all day."

I said, "You've got me wrong, Vin. Honest, I'm not trying to sell you anything. It's just I need your advice. I've got this information—" He looked at
my pants pockets as though I were carrying a legal envelope, sealed, registered,
and notarized. I slapped my pockets and said, "Honest, Vin. Nothing on me.
I'm clean as a babe. All I want to do is find out the best way to do this. I've
got something on a big shot here in Laredo, one of the big shots, you might
say, and strictly on the square I want to make it worth my while. Not you.
You don't have to pay a cent for this; he'll take care of me, I think. But I want
to know how I can hold this thing over his head. That's all."

Kimball said, "What's it to me?" He seemed sore and a bit let down. If I
didn't want to sell the information to him, he couldn't see how he could use
it.

"Maybe nothing. Maybe plenty," I said. "Let me try an example. Suppose
I knew—I don't, but suppose I did—that the county leader of the party—
not your party, of course—had embezzled funds from a bank he worked for
ten years ago, maybe a hundred thousand dollars' worth. Would that be
worthwhile to know?"

Kimball nodded his head, his lips thin and his face thoughtful. He was siz-
ing me up, and he could see I was solid.

"What would you do with that info?"

Kimball kept nodding for a minute, still thinking. Then he said quietly, "I don't really know. It's the kind of dream you get sometimes of the big break. Here I am with a party that runs one in seven in bad times and one in four in good. They talk about a two-party system and all that malarkey, but it's absolutely mathematically impossible for us to win a local election. Did you know that, Hawkins?"

"Tough," I said. "You sure got it tough."

He nodded. "So the only thing I can do is dream that something comes along—like your embezzler, for instance—something really drastic to change our chances. An earthquake, that's what we need."

I said, "Embezzling be an earthquake?"

"I'll say. If he's high enough up."

"How about—say—a married man who's also a big party wheel, and who makes a pass at some teen-age girl?"

He made a face. "Get off it," he said. "*All* politicians have done that at one time or another."

"And got arrested for it?"

His breath came out slowly and it kept coming out until I thought for a minute he was whistling through his teeth. He sat on the wooden horse, side-saddle, looking out to the front of the shop, seeing how half his place was turned over to a political headquarters that was never open, his face a thin white glow, like a honed blade. He said finally, still looking away, "That's your dope, isn't it?"

"Yes," I said softly. "That's it."

"Golly," he said. "We use it in September, after Labor Day. No, not this year—we'll wait with it. Your boy had just better stick around—"

"He will."

"We spring it when the senatorial election comes up next year and half the assembly and state senate seats are up for grabs—*then* we spring it, right after Labor Day, a week before registration, but after all the conventions have met and all the nominations are in. Oh, golly, golly."

He was like a kid with Christmas candy, rocking back and forth on his horse.

"An earthquake?"

He nodded, swinging around to me. His face looked tired. He said, "You son of a gun, you better not be dangling me."

"Why would I do that, Vin? What's in it for me?"

"I wouldn't know," he said, "but you just better not."

"I wouldn't," I said very solemnly, because he seemed to think solemnity was called for, this honest joe who probably had never known what he really was and was just finding out and not even giving a rap. It was like my waitress Susie, not looking at the color of the money, but weighing it first, or the dame who'll put out for a million bucks but gets insulted for two bits. A country of whores, that's what I was finding. The woods were full of them, every one with his price.

I said, finally, "So how do I go about it? Do I write it out and put it in a safe somewhere and give you the combination, except you can't use it until I give you the word? Or what? How do I do it?"

He squinted at me. "I don't know," he said, a rueful grin on his face. "I never—did anything like this. Just tell the guy you've spread the word to a couple of people who have promised to keep it quiet, unless—"

I nodded. "Yeah, that's the way. I thought it would be like that, but it's so goddam simple I thought maybe I wasn't going about it right." I got up. "Thanks a lot, Vin," I said. "You've straightened me out." I started out and he grabbed my arm. "Don't spill it yet," he said. "You understand? Not yet."

"Don't worry. I'm not spilling anything. I'm still looking out for Number One."

He held my arm until I reached the door, and then he said, "I suppose if your man pays you off to keep quiet, you won't have anything to turn over to us?"

I looked down at Kimball. "Sorry, Vin, but that's the way I'd have to play it."

He chewed his lip, looking up and down Sand Street, the fire department at one end, the public boardwalk down at the other and a red-and-white caution flag up over the empty life-guard's deck down at the beach. "In a way," he said, "that would be better, wouldn't it?" He was speaking softly, remembering how once, ten minutes ago, he was an honest man.

"I wouldn't know," I said. "All I know is if my man pays me off, I'd have to forget it."

And the memory of his honesty vanished. All he saw, instead, were the five-to-one registration figures. "Would you?" he said, not looking at me. "Suppose he pays you off? Couldn't you let me know where to go for the same dope? I mean, if it's on a police blotter some place, I ought to be able to pay off a couple of cops to find out. So it really wouldn't be as if you told me, would it?"

I straightened up with a jolt. The cheap bastard. I hadn't thought of that. Christ, the police blotter, where Weylin got picked up, was practically public property. His name was down there some place. All anybody had to do was find out where Weylin was the night before last; a private dick would find out for fifty bucks.

Of course, Kimball didn't know it was Weylin. But it had to be Weylin or one of three or four other guys. Nobody else was that big. Kimball knew it was somebody big, the way I had put it. I was fouling myself up. Well, I thought, now the problem was to throw a chill into Kimball so he didn't get too busy playing Perry Mason.

I said, "Look here, Vin. This is a case of not being able to eat the cake and have it too. You got to respect my position. If my pigeon pays off, that's it. We can't keep cutting him up."

"No-o-o," he said, and I swear his nose got thinner. "*You* can't. But I don't see how that affects me."

I said, "Kimball," and when I called him by his last name, there was a little pained look on his face; you don't call local politicians by their last names; it's like insulting them somehow. "Kimball, we can't." I leaned into him a bit, swaying on the balls of my feet like a catcher coming out of the rocking-chair stance ready to peg one down to second, my right arm moving back a little. "We. You, me, anybody. I think I made a mistake, Kimball, telling you, but if I did, it won't matter, because you won't let it matter. You're the only person who knows what I know, the only person alive. So if it ever goes any further than this, it'll be because you spilled. And I won't like you to spill, Kimball. Understand?" I kept swaying and then I stopped, my feet spread just a trifle, the right hand where I wanted it, fingers balling a little. He looked the way Carlstrom had looked, pasty and scared.

Then I grinned, open and friendly. But when I grin, it comes out all twisted. "Hell's bells, Vin," I said, "let's not scrap over this. For all I know he won't kick in the way I want him to, and I'll hand him over to you on a silver platter and you can carve up on him. How's that sound?"

"Fine," he said mechanically, his face still pasty. "Just fine." He wanted me to get the hell away from him so he could mop his brow, but I knew that as soon as I was gone he'd start stacking the two pictures: the earthquake he could throw into the political picture here in the county and maybe all over the state, and the other earthquake I'd throw at him if he didn't do as I said. And I knew, too, that maybe he'd be scared I'd beat the hell out of him, but wouldn't it be worth it? So I had to tip the scale the way I wanted it.

"Vin," I said casually, "you'll have to believe me. I won't stand for it any other way. There would be people who'd be interested in hearing that you were involved in something messy like this. You know, do-gooders and bleeding hearts. A newspaper or two, for instance, or a national magazine. Get me?" Then I spun away and moved to the Chevy.

Let him stew on that one. Let him wonder how in hell a blackmailer could accuse anybody else. It was the kind of thing he would worry to death over. It was arithmetic, all legal as can be. Weylin wasn't going to blow the whistle on me, that was sure. He stood to lose too much. But I could blow the whistle on Kimball; one of those good-rep magazines could run a small piece about this smelly situation and Kimball would be finished in politics. Just enough people would be properly ashamed of Vin. Enough to wash him up.

There were no jobs to be had on Sand Street; there would have been openings in the summer when the tourists double the population, and every third business place in town has a sign in its window: Girls Wanted or Barber Wanted or Sales Clerk Wanted, No Experience.

In April there was nothing. Still, I drove slowly, looking. Then I turned over to Main Street, the third of Laredo's three main shopping streets, not counting the Coast Highway itself, and I wheeled along Main, looking. Nothing. I could have looked in the local paper at the classified to verify that there was nothing for me, but I knew there wasn't a chance.

And that was that. I'd looked, and the morning was shot, so I drove the Chevy into the town parking lot where the fee is a jit for two hours, and I had a slow lunch at the snack shop. Time passed, the fog burned out of the spring sky and the avenues were warm and friendly and uncrowded. Beyond the beach across the street the waves were feathering in; nobody was in the water, but a couple of dozen people were sopping up the sun.

It was a funny thing, that noon hour in Laredo—this noon hour. I never knew what high noon meant before. This one was high, all right. It floated like a balloon, a soft yellow light washing the streets and making everything look like cream. It was high noon, all right, everything up on a cloud or a space platform.

Maybe you figure I'm just handing you a song and dance now, trying to tell you I'm a patsy, a soft jerk with a heart as big as that yellow sun up there. You know better, you figure. You know about me and Vin Kimball. I'm not sure about this, and I wouldn't bet big money on it, but I think you're wrong. I think I went into Kimball's because I knew the man was honest, and I found out different. I figured I'd hit Kimball and he'd boot me into left field so hard I'd be sore for a month. Then he'd call me every name in the book and a few more he'd invent on the spot to fit me, and I'd go out and forget I ever heard of Otto Weylin, and I'd look for a job.

Hell, I did look for a job anyway, so that proves it. I had found out that Kimball was like Susie, and that they all had a price. Everybody. Damn them all, they all had a price. But I looked for a job, you can't take that away from me.

And now, softened up with the avenue outside and the sun on top of my head and the beach glinting and the ocean feathering the way the kids like it for surfboard riding—why, I couldn't run down a scorpion, much less a crumby guy like Otto Weylin.

Don't ask me what I was going to do. There wasn't a job to be had, that was sure. But this is Laredo, and five miles south is San Loma, and seven miles up is Dwight Point, and fifteen miles inland is Santa Maria, a city of forty-five thousand. Oh, there's a job—and decent enough for a punk like me—someplace around. The Chevy was resting up in the parking lot and I had practically a full tank of gas.

I said to the waitress, "That's it, sugar. Check me," and she toted up the damages and handed me the check, and I pivoted off the chair, looking at the check, giving it a quick add, and got halfway to the cashier's cage, ready to pay my eighty-five cents and get a dime for the girl behind the counter. Then I looked up and saw Otto Weylin walking in.

And there I was, adding up a lousy eighty-five cent lunch tab, hoping they'd made a mistake in my favor, and there was Otto Weylin.

I stopped where I was, so he'd have to run into me, and then I said, "Hello, Mr. Weylin."

He looked surprised for a second, and then he smiled and said, "Oh, Hawkins. How are you?" He nodded slightly as though that ended it, and I said, "Mr. Weylin, I'd like to see you some time this afternoon."

He frowned and his head tipped a bit and then he erased the frown and said, "Of course, Hawkins, I'll be back at the office in half an hour. I think I can squeeze— I think I'll have free time then."

Squeeze. Yesterday he didn't have to spend a goddam minute in his office because the cops had put him through the wringer and now he was going to do me the favor of squeezing me in.

I said, "That's swell, Mr. Weylin," and I paid my check and walked out, and I got into the Chevy and drove along the ocean before I realized I had forgotten to give the girl her dime. Well, I thought, most people around here don't tip counter help, so the hell with it.

CHAPTER FIVE

The girl had blue-rimmed glasses and black hair hanging to the shoulders, and a starched white blouse that she filled very nicely, and her hands looked cool on Otto Weylin's reception desk. She was not a California-looking chick, but a New York chick, the kind you see in the subways every day, wondering how in hell there are so many good-looking, neat, dark-haired girls with cool hands and nice busts and how in hell they keep their clothes so crisp in the subway.

She eyed my jaw and played it the I'm-so-sorry-for-you-but-I'll-be-brave-and-not-let-you-see way. Then she said, "Mr. Weylin says go right in; he's expecting you," and I knew she had come from the East with that unconscious superiority all Easterners have when they get out here, nothing phony or forced, mind you, just the natural knowledge that they're better than the rubes out here. That's the only rivalry you find in southern California, East and West.

I said, "Thanks, chicken," and I walked through the cane door and past the small open bullpen of a couple of desks and four or five files, and to the door at the end of the open area marked *Otto Weylin*. I started to knock, but he must have seen my shadow because he said pleasantly, "Come in, Hawkins," and I walked through.

His desk was big and neat, and next to it was a glass-framed bookcase with the usual fat volumes every lawyer puts in there and never cracks. There was a framed photograph on his desk, facing in to his seat, but as I sat down across from Weylin, I leaned forward and could see it was a dame, probably his wife, dark-haired, with a long thin face and not much else. No wonder he fingers cute little high school kids, I thought.

I said, "Thanks, Mr. Weylin," and I went through the motions of searching for a butt in my pants pockets. He immediately pushed his pack of Pall Malls across toward me, but I made a wry face, grinning a little and trying to look put out and embarrassed as all hell. "I'm sorry," I said. "I guess I'll go without. I'm one of those geezers who sticks to one brand. I smoke Camels, can't get used to anything else. Oh, well, it does a man good to go without." I sighed, and he said, "I'll send the girl across the street for a pack," and I brightened pretty fast so he'd know I really cared for a Camel and nothing else would make me happy.

He went outside, which let me know he didn't have a buzzer system on his desk, which was the first thing I wanted to know. The second thing I wanted was to find out how much sound filtered through Weylin's door. All I could hear while Weylin was outside telling the girl what I wanted was a low buzz, impossible to break into various sounds. Just to make sure, I wanted her out of the office for a couple of minutes.

Of course, I didn't know he didn't have the office bugged, but you don't figure people in Laredo go around wiring their offices for sound. It was a chance I had to take, but I didn't think it was much of a chance. Weylin hadn't been expecting me; I had parked across the street until he showed up and then I let him get inside maybe ninety seconds before I popped in the front door, so he'd had no time to monkey around with a Dictograph.

He came back in, smiling politely, feeling good that he'd done me a favor, and maybe wondering what the hell it was all about, because he could be remembering that I'd spent half an hour in his house yesterday and I never smoked the first puff of a butt. I don't smoke.

He swung around behind his desk and said, "Well, what can I do for you, Hawkins?"

I said, "You got arrested yesterday morning or the night before, Mr. Weylin, for fooling with a high-school kid. I know about it, and I think other people ought to know about it. Ten thousand bucks would keep me quiet."

It was like there was a soda straw stuck in his skin, and somebody took a good hard drag. The blood just sucked out of the man, then deep brown private-gymnasium, private-beach color drained so fast I thought for a minute he was going to faint. Then he said, "Ow," a little round noise of pain, and I guess he was hurt, all right. They must have given him a hard time, wherever it was, him probably still looped and the girl screeching away, a long red-painted finger pointing in his face, and a couple of beefy cops shoving him around and maybe belting him a couple of shots under the wishbone, maybe even a dirty scabby-blanketed cell for the night before they let him go. But at least it had ended, and they had let him go. He had thought it was over, finished.

Now he knew it wasn't over, and for all he knew, it never would be. So he'd give me ten grand, but where was the guarantee I wouldn't pop back for more?

He said quietly, still pale, but under control, "Blackmail is a crime, Hawkins."

I laughed then, not loud because I wanted this whole thing kept nice and quiet, and I wanted it over fast. I said, "So's fingering an underage kid."

"That was a mistake."

"Sure," I said, leaning back a little, enjoying this part. "Sure it was. You wouldn't do it again. I know that. But it happened."

"No," he said, shaking his head, hands gripping the edge of his desk, his body tilted forward from the waist, "no, it didn't. That's what I'm trying to say. It didn't happen. It was all a mistake."

For a minute I was scared, scared I was in too deep and couldn't get out. Maybe he was telling the truth. It was one thing being a blackmailer when the other guy's a child molester; but what if Weylin wasn't? Then I was out in the open. I shivered inside, for a naked second, under the hot glare of some imaginary cop's search beam. Me, criminal, on the run. Then the thought went as quickly as it had come. I said, "Is that what you told the judge?" I was still grinning at him, and, oh, how that grin must have looked.

He kept shaking his head from side to side, and he said, "You don't understand. It wasn't the way you think."

I stopped grinning. "Look, Weylin," I said. "I don't care whether it happened or not. I can't afford being out of work. You can't afford to have me talk. It's just a little deal we're making. That's all."

"You don't understand," he said, and then he started to say something else, but he stopped it short and he said, "You're a filthy bastard, Hawkins."

I nodded. "I guess so," I said. "At least, that's what I figured you'd say. It certainly is a dirty trick I'm playing on you. But look at it from my side. I'm going along minding my business when somebody comes up, figuratively speaking, and says, 'Look, Otto Weylin's been arrested for molesting a fifteen-year-old kid, what do you know about that, big shot like that, puts his dough in Community Chest and all the hospitals going up and all that jazz, and everybody says what a great guy Otto Weylin is, salt of the earth. And you, Ed Hawkins, you're a crumb. You don't put a penny into anything except your kid's piggy bank and you figured long ago how to shake it back out. Nobody gives you the time of day, and if they ran a popularity poll tomorrow you'd win the booby prize. On top of it, you can't even brush your own teeth on the bottom because your teeth are in the Marshalls someplace, floating around the lagoon with pieces of your skin.'"

I don't know how I got talking about myself, except that maybe that was the whole thing, like I said. There he was, and here I was, and you could drive a house trailer between us, that's how far apart we were, even sitting across the same desk.

He said, "Hawkins, you got a tough break. Don't take it out on me." He said it crisply, almost as though he were about to kick me out of the office in another minute.

"I'm not," I said very seriously. "I'm thinking of all those other little kids. I'm just protecting them, Mr. Weylin. And you—why, whenever you see me or think about me, you'll remember the mistake you made and you'll regret it." I grinned. "You sure as hell ought to. Unless ten gees comes that easy. Does it, Mr. Weylin?"

He grunted. "I couldn't give you ten thousand dollars if you took me before God Almighty and tried to shake me down. I just don't have it."

I made believe I was thinking that one over, frowning, looking down. Then I said, at length, still very serious, "Mr. Weylin, you don't understand, I guess. That must be it. Think of it this way. Make it seem as though I'm doing you a favor. Why, suppose instead of giving me ten grand, I went to a few people—just a few—like your wife, and one of your Elk or Lion or Rotary comrades, and a political boss or two, your party and the other party, that is, and told them what you'd done and how the newspapers really would love to know. Suppose, just suppose I did a thing like that. That would be a very dirty thing to do."

He laughed bitterly. "My wife is just returning from a long trip," he said. "She's preparing to go to Reno to establish residence for our divorce."

I didn't let him see that that made any difference. It did, a little, but not much. It sort of gave the guy some reason for kicking over the traces, for getting drunk anyway. But it wasn't going to change anything basically.

"So much the better," I said. "Maybe when she tells the judge why things are so tough on her, she can add the juicy little bit about your getting arrested for molesting." I nodded my head, thinking I had something there. In the local papers, anyway. They'd pick it up, sure as hell; it would sell papers like mad—local yokel accused of infidelity, and with a child, at that.

He was thinking it over, too, biting his lip, when there was a light rap on Weylin's door, and the girl said, "Your Camels, Mr. Hawkins." I got up quickly and opened the door and said, "Thanks, chicken," taking the cigarettes and closing the door gently, but firmly. When I turned back to Weylin, he had his check book out and I started to laugh.

"No," I said, shaking my head. "I don't want a check. Though I am surprised at you. You said a minute before you couldn't do it. Now you're ready to write out a check."

"I'm prepared to write you a check for a thousand dollars. Take it or leave it, Hawkins."

"I'll leave it," I said quickly. "Very defiinitely. I'll just leave it." It was a game now, the last couple of innings anyway, and he was taking his last few licks, trying to get back in. But it wasn't a close game at all, though he probably believed with some of the others in this country that the game isn't over until the last man is out.

"That's my final word," he said, closing the check book.

I frowned, trying to look surprised and disappointed. "Mr. Weylin," I said, "yesterday when I saw you at your place, I already knew the score. Why, I could have done this up brown yesterday, but I didn't. I didn't even do it first thing this morning, when I really should have. Do you know why?" I didn't wait for him to shake his head, though he was listening very hard. "Because I really don't want to do this. Think that over. I could have done it yesterday, just like that. I didn't. Appreciate that, Mr. Weylin; it's worth something."

By this time he had all his color back, or most of it. His face was taking on a new look, changing slowly, until I read it: he was amazed by what I had said.

"Hawkins," he said, "do you really think that makes a difference? That you didn't shake me down yesterday, but waited a whole twenty-four hours?"

"Why, yes," I said," I think it makes a very big difference."

He looked down and then he said quietly. "You're crazy. You know that, Hawkins? Why, you stupid bastard, what difference does it really make? A man thinks of robbing a bank when he's twenty-one, but he waits until he's twenty-five. What the hell do you think he is by thirty? A bank thief! What the hell do you think you are? A blackmailer! A bloodsucking son-of-a-bitch blackmailer!"

He was starting to make too much noise, and I didn't like that, and I didn't want it, so I knew I had to stop him. I said, "Please, Mr. Weylin, you're going to wake the neighbors. Pay me or don't pay me, but shut up." That's all I said, but the throbbing was at my temples, and I guess he could see it because he paled a little, and then he said, "Tell me, Hawkins, what do you really want? I'm just not going to give you ten grand in cash; I don't have it and I think you know I don't. Christ, nobody has that kind of cash."

I shrugged. I didn't care. Maybe this other way was better. It would be like a salary, sort of. I said, "That's all right, Mr. Weylin. Just give me a hundred a week—in cash, of course—for a hundred weeks. That is correct, isn't it? A c-note a week for a hundred weeks? Not quite two years?"

He went back to biting his lip, and then he said, "You're pretty good at this. You've done this before, haven't you?"

I cocked my head, chin up, and I said, "You know I have." I picked a stainless-steel letter opener from his desk and I tapped my chin. It made a dead sound. "Five gees for that."

He said, "You got away with murder that time, too. You know that, don't you?"

I shrugged. "Who cares?"

"The ammunition manufacturer wasn't responsible."

"My," I said. "Busy little lawyer, aren't you?"

"I can read."

"Believe all you read?"

He fidgeted slightly. "How is it that nobody else sued the ammunition maker? How is it you were the only one?"

I laughed. It was a hollow laugh, more a barking noise, I guess, but still in a way it was funny. "It's pretty tough suing when you're dead."

He frowned. "You were—the only one who was in that explosion that didn't get killed?"

"That's right."

He made his little grunting noise, tenting his fingers at the edge of his desk. "That was pretty lucky, wasn't it?"

"Was it?"

He looked up. "Oh," he said. "You mean your jaw. You're pretty sensitive about that, aren't you?"

"So-so. How'd you like to have it?"

"I don't know," he said. "I'm not sure it would bother me as much as it bothers you."

"But you'll never know, will you?"

He thought another minute and then he said, "Those people who were killed—their next-of-kin could have sued, but they didn't."

"They each got ten grand insurance for nothing. Just because somebody else got creamed, they each got ten gees. I was the only person involved who was still alive. The rest didn't matter."

"Still," he said, as if it was a legal problem they threw at law classes, something to take his mind off his own problem, "the fault was clearly established, wasn't it? Somebody made a mistake, put in the wrong fuse or something? Wasn't that it?"

"Something like that," I agreed.

"Yet you sued the ammunition maker."

Now I leaned forward. "So who else should I have sued? The government? Uncle Sam? Is that the way you figure it? Who in the hell was toting the load of that goddam war, paying your way so you could sit home and rake in the gravy? Who carried you on its back, you and the rest of the indispensables?"

He looked startled. "You've got me wrong; I was in the Navy myself, but even if I hadn't been, I don't understand you. The men who did the fighting carried the rest on their backs. That's who."

"And who the hell is the government?" I asked. "Everybody. The guys back home, taking it easy, and the guys in the holes, getting the crap beat out of them. You want me to sue the government? You want me to sue guys on the line, wading off the bullets?" It galls me, this sort of talk. It makes me mad. It frosts me to see guys like Weylin, up to their elbows in whipping cream and butter, telling me to go ahead and sue the government instead of some billionaire bastard who made a thousand mistakes and every time he made one, some poor jerk got an arm blown off or something worse, but this time didn't make a mistake, and expected me to put the blocks to the government instead. "Who the hell is the government?" I said. "Who?"

He mumbled something and then he said, red-faced, "You're right. You're right. Skip it. Christ, you're a funny guy."

"I'm the government," I said. "Me and guys like me. You, too, though I wouldn't have minded taking it off your hide. Hand me my hundred bucks. Right now, you cheap bastard. Right now."

I had him on the run, and I was loving how suddenly he was ashamed of himself. It was about time. Otto Weylin, right side of the tracks, right clubs, right wife—only right wives can afford to go to Reno; the rest of the poor suckers live with 'em because who can pay that sort of tab, and then the alimony—the right friends, the right notes in the right society pages. Rich and respected. They always said it that way—one word, sort of. Richenrespected.

If the guy is poor, he's poor but honest, as if it was unusual for a poor guy to be decent. It makes me sick. It frosts me.

He reached into his wallet and pulled out some bills and then he smoothed them out and stared at them. "Don't memorize the numbers, jerk," I said.

"You're a suspicious cuss, aren't you?"

"Around you, I am."

He shoved the money at me and I counted it fast and pocketed it. "Put the bills in the mail from now on," I said. "I don't want to have to look at you. I don't want to be around you." I took a quarter out of my pocket and shoved it across the desk top. "Here. For the Camels." I got up and walked to the door and then I turned and said, "Next time you'll think twice before you play around with some punk young dame," and I spun around and reached for the knob and threw the door open.

Behind me, it sounded as if he was gagging or crying, or something. He said, all thick in his throat, "Oh, my God."

I walked through the bullpen, and I patted the receptionist on top of her head because she was sitting down and I couldn't have found her fanny without digging. "So long, chicken," I said, and she said brightly, with that phony, intimate smile receptionists and manicurists develop, and with that faint unconscious superiority, "So long, Mr. Hawkins. See you."

I got into the Chevy and I started working my way inland from the beach on the canyon turnoff, and going up hill.

I stopped just before the road ran into dirt, and parked the Chevy for a minute. I had to tell a story to Mary. I had to tell how I had looked for a job— and that was the truth, I sure as hell had, up and down Wood, Sand, and Main, and along the highway, too. It was the rest that was going to be tough. I hated to lie. How come, she'd wonder, I'd be getting this dough every week? And mailed right to the house? What a dumb trick that was; I'd have to change that. I'd rent a post-office box. Even that was tricky. Somebody would see me in there one day, messing around with the box, and Mary would hear from some loose-tongued biddy how it certainly was smart, using a post-office box instead of relying on those outdoor rickety affairs two hundred yards from the house.

I nodded, grinning there in the Chevy. Oh, it was all so easy. It was always easier, more comfortable, telling the truth. I just hated to lie. I hate liars. I gunned the car and looked around. Nobody was nearby, and I had to figure nobody was looking. Our mailbox stands off the side of the road, where the asphalt ends and the dirt starts. The mailmen don't like driving their heavy trucks up that dirt road and then either backing down or else turning around in a pretty tight area. It isn't dangerous, but it takes time, and that's the thing a mailman can't afford.

I turned the steering wheel and stepped on the accelerator. The Chevy leaped, and I braked. I wasn't fast enough; I couldn't have been. The front right bumper and fender hit the mailbox and the post snapped off. I let the car roll back down and then I pulled up the emergency and let her squat. I got out and made believe I was sore as a boil at myself and at the post and I examined it (it was half rotten, so I had only to tap it) and then I slammed it down and shook my head and got back in. Now we needed either a new post or else a box in the post office. That was that....

I breezed in the front door, whistling. I had had a helluva nerve telling Kimball you couldn't have your cake and eat it. Look at me. It wasn't two o'clock and I was through. I still had time to mosey around the house. Mary was in the kitchen, ironing. I'd have me a glass of buttermilk, and then I'd go to work, the kind of work Mary and I liked.

I took off my shoes and socks, still whistling, and I washed my hands, and went into the kitchen, and poured the buttermilk.

Then I stopped whistling. Mary hadn't said a goddam word. How do you figure a dame like that?

I looked at her, and I could see she was full of words. I said, "If I tapped you in the belly, kiddo, you'd spit up a paragraph. Say it."

"Vince Kimball called, honey," she said, in a small explosion, her eyes all lit up.

I said dully, "Kimball?"

"It's about a job," she said breathlessly.

And there it was. She was so worried before that when the first sign of a job came up, she was just about off her rocker with relief.

"Job?" I said.

She nodded. "He's going to Sacramento to some convention or other for a week—didn't he tell you?—and then he and his wife are taking a vacation, for two more weeks. He wants somebody to run his shop."

I remembered the sign in the window. I had seen it first thing this morning: Man Wanted. A few minutes later I had heard him say he had only a month to finish his Little League posters—he had no more than four to go— and I should have known by that that he was going to be out of the shop for a few weeks. I remembered the way he and his wife kept running back and forth, just to finish up those posters, as if they had to be done in thirty minutes instead of thirty days. And how, if he was just going to be gone for a couple of days, he'd have shut up the shop as he'd done in the past, no need for a fill-in man. I had known it, all right.

There are times you kid yourself what a great guy you are, and everybody sort of nods their head and agrees, and it seems true. Then there are other times. You're thinking you're running holes in the wind like Nashua and hitting like Marciano, and you must look like Mr. America, but somebody shoves a mirror under your mug, and you get the real picture.

That's what had happened.

I *thought* I had looked for a job; I *thought* I had gone to Kimball to get me straightened out by the straightest guy in town, but all the time I had my eyes screwed shut. I wasn't looking to be straightened out; I wasn't looking for a job. I was in town to do my job on Weylin. And that's what I had done.

And Weylin was right; what difference did it make that I had delayed half a day or even a whole day? What difference did it make if the dame slapped your face when you asked her to put out for two bits, after she'd agreed to do it for a million bucks. No difference: she was a whore and I was a black-mailer.

Mary said, "He wants you to call him back."

I nodded sickly. It was a trap.

"He sounded so nice," Mary said.

I nodded. "Yeah."

"Maybe he'll take you in, after he sees—what a good job you do."

I said, "Maybe he'll adopt me."

Mary looked up from her ironing. She set the iron on its rear, tipped up in the air. She stared at me, trying to tell whether I was kidding her.

I figured I'd help her out. "Maybe he'll take me into the business and see to it I marry his daughter and when he retires he'll say, 'Son, here's a billion dollars, don't save any of it. I want you to blow it on yourself and your eight kids.'"

"What's wrong, Ed?" she said quickly.

"Nothing," I said savagely. "Not a goddam thing. Everything's peachy-pie. A punk shopkeeper says he'll let me watch his paint brushes for a couple of weeks, and you're doing handsprings. Don't you think I can do better than that? Is that all I'm worth? A high-school moron could do that and still smoke his marijuana all day."

"Don't take the job," she said swiftly. "Ed, I don't want you to take it. I only thought—he had said you were in this morning, and I thought you were in looking for the job and he had suddenly decided you'd do, after you left, and I thought you'd want to know, since you had been in there—" She started to cry.

I walked over to her and tried to put my arms around her.

"No," she said, "no, Ed. Don't touch me. Not just now."

I sort of tugged her away from the ironing board and I put my arms around her waist, smelling the steamy smell of the iron and the hot clothes and her own warm body. I held her and we rocked together like that, until she stopped crying. I said, finally, "I'm a heel, hon. I'm a no-good son of a bitch. You ought to conk me with that iron." Her head started to move from side to side under my chin, and some muffled words came out, but I kept talking. "I'll call Kimball, honey. You're right, I *was* in, but I didn't think he'd want me to run the whole show while he was gone. I was surprised by what you

said and by what he said. I guess he changed his mind. I didn't think—I did-
n't want to think I had me a new job so quick. I didn't know how it would
work out; maybe I wouldn't like it, maybe he wouldn't like me. I didn't want
to get your hopes up."

I kept talking like that, soothing her, talking around the point, missing it
every time, but coming so close she didn't know I was missing it. And pretty
soon she stopped moving her head and the muffled words were silent, and I
stopped talking, too, and all that was happening was the two of us rocking
back and forth, and I felt my arms sort of relax from around her back and hang
loose at my sides, and we kept rocking like that, pressed tight together, and
I realized *she* was holding *me*, and she was saying fiercely, "Shh, shh, honey,
shh. Don't, honey, don't...."

I called Kimball half an hour later.

"Hello, Vin," I said. "Mary told me—"

"Yes, yes, Hawkins," he said, the eager beaver slopping right out of the
receiver. "I ran into Carlstrom and he told me how—he told me you weren't
working any more, and I thought, my God, why didn't I think of you, you'd
be perfect for this place. How about it—Hawkins?"

I knew he wanted to call me by my first name but he had forgotten it since
the time he had looked it up in the phone book an hour or so ago, or whenever he had called. His voice was first-naming me all over the place.

"Sounds fine, Vin. When do you want me?"

"Whenever you say—Hawkins," and I swear, I had a vision of him snapping his fingers to that poor gray-eyed wife of his, jabbing his hand at the
phone book so he could find out again what my first name was. "Whenever
you say. We're leaving Thursday night. How about coming in tomorrow and
letting me show you around the place?" Then I knew he had found the book,
because he said very warmly, "How's that sound, Ed?"

"Tomorrow's swell, Vin. First thing in the morning?"

"Whenever you say, Ed. Of course, the sooner the better, but there's no
big hurry the first day. We'll bone up on the price book, eh? Bright boy like
you, it'll be easy as pie."

There was a raw edge to what he was saying. It was as if he was being
forced to offer me this job. Hell, I hadn't asked him for it.

"All right, Vin. Tomorrow morning. And, Vin—"

"What's that, Ed?"

"We didn't mention salary. Of course, whatever you think's fair, Vin—"

"Eighty, Ed? How's eighty a week?" It came out strangled. "And, Ed, I
want you to know that—that this doesn't have anything in the world to do
with—the other. Not a thing. I've forgotten about the other. That was just
nonsense on my part. I've thought it all over, and no matter what, I would-
n't be interested. Understand, Ed? It's just that I need somebody, and that's
the truth. Why, I've had that sign in the window for a week, and you're the

first decent prospect who's walked in."

"Sure, Vin," I said. "That's swell, Vin. I'll see you tomorrow morning."
I hung up while he was thanking me.

"There," I said, turning to Mary. "It's all set." Her eyes were very large
and round. She said, "How—much, Ed?" which shows you how she must
have felt. Mary never asked questions like that; she'd figure. I'd tell her when
I was good and ready.

"Eighty fish," I said. "Eighty simoleons a week." Maybe it doesn't sound
like much, but it's enough for us to get by on. We don't have the expenses I
used to roll up back East. For instance, I haven't bought a suit of clothes in
five years. I spend maybe ten bucks a year on laundry and dry cleaning, as
against a couple of bucks a week back East. Mary has a bunch of those drip-
dry, no-iron clothes. We buy lots of produce—it's cheap as dirt, and the best
I've ever tasted, and we go in for the cheap cuts of meat, and when we buy
liquor we get it from one of the supermarts or big drug chains that bottle their
own—gin at three bucks a fifth, bourbon and rye at three-fifty, Scotch at four-
fifty. The car still hasn't started to burn oil, we buy cheap gas at a serve-your-
self station. What else is there? A four-partyline phone, natural gas fur-
naces—but we use the wood-burning fireplace most of the winter and cut
down there—and light rent. Eighty will get you by.

Mary said, "That's very nice," in a restrained way, and once more, somebody had sneaked a mirror under my face, letting me see what a crumb I was.
Sure, eighty will get you by, if you want to spend your life at the ironing
board, nursing old cars, waiting for somebody to get off the party line so you
can call the doctor to come and look at your kid, soaking meat in tenderizer
and stewing it because if you roasted it you'd break your molars, paying a light
rent—but paying it every year, year after year because it's not your house and
knowing all the time the rent's so light because that way the landlord does-
n't have to apologize for the hollow walls and sagging beams.

That's what she might have been thinking. It didn't seem likely she'd
think eighty was so good that she could hardly let it show on her face.

It had been a crazy, mixed up day. I had walked in knowing I was going
to be getting a hundred bucks a week, and feeling great, whistling all over the
house, figuring I'd do some work around the place with Mary. Then I found
out I was making one hundred and eighty a week, and I felt lousy. I crawled
into the sack and lay on my back, staring up at the ceiling. I didn't feel like
doing anything.

Later, I heard the boy come in. There was some other boy with him,
which was a big change, and I could hear them mumbling in the kitchen, Mary
probably stuffing them with cake and milk; and then I heard them rummaging around in Matt's room, and then they walked out and the house was quiet

for ten minutes. Too quiet.

I got off the bed and found Mary hanging wash on the line, and I said, "Where's Matt?"

"Oh," she said, a clothespin in her hand. "He went—someplace with Tubby."

"Tubby?"

She giggled. "Some big boy from his class. He's a ball player, I think. He had his glove with him. He plays on one of the Little League teams. You should have seen—"

"They went off to play ball?"

"Um." She put the, clothespin in her mouth and stretched a pair of shorts on the line.

"Where?"

She pointed with her head.

"Take that pin out of your mouth."

She did.

"Where, damn it, where?"

Mary looked at me, that sullen look crawling over her face. I was pushing at her, and she didn't know why, so she was hurt.

"There," she said, pointing across the canyon. "To that lot you took him to yesterday. Are you satisfied?"

I was satisfied, all right. I was jumping with joy. I brushed past her and went down the back stairs and stood at the edge of the canyon wall, staring at the two dots, tossing a smaller dot through the air on Weylin's lot.

The canyon is a raw, rough land. You can see most of it this side of the pine thicket, from either this side of the canyon or from Weylin's, but there are blind spots, hidden gullies and dips. You don't know which abandoned gopher hole houses how many sleeping rattlers, waiting for the spring suns to wake them so they can stretch out of their skins and go hunting rabbits. We've had deer, rabbit, bobcat, skunk, opossum, ground squirrel, and weasel down this far; out there it wouldn't surprise anyone to see mountain lion prowling that brown slope, sniffing for food.

So I don't like the boy just taking off by himself, even if he's going straight across the canyon to Weylin's empty lot to have a game of catch. You know kids. They start off for the corner drugstore for a Coke and they end up seeing a movie two miles away, going bowling, and eating pizza, before they hit the Coke counter.

I walked down the slope and through the valley bed and up the other side. It was midafternoon, the sun still high enough and hot enough, and the walk made me feel good, stretching my legs.

The kids saw me come over the lip and Matt ran over, all lit up and smiling. He said, "Hi, Dad. Want to have a catch?" Then he saw my face. He said, "What's the matter, Dad?" The boy with him, a flabby, red-faced kid with a fleshy chest, started to edge away.

I said very quietly, "Matt, who told you to come up here by yourself?"

He said, staring at me, backing up himself a little, "Nobody. Isn't it all right? You and I came—"

"That was different."

He was open-eyed and close to tears—though God knows why. I hadn't said a thing—and he turned to his fat friend. He said, finally, "We—we were just having a catch, weren't we, Tubby?"

Tubby nodded, the wet flesh at his chin folding up from his neck.

"Get your jacket," I said.

Wordlessly, he turned and walked back toward the middle of the lot where his jacket had been home plate, and he picked it up and started back.

Then I heard the car.

For a minute I froze. This was what I had been afraid of. It was one thing using Weylin's lot yesterday, before I turned the screws; today it was something else. That was what I meant when I told Matt it was different.

It wasn't, of course, that I was afraid the boys might wander off in the canyon. A couple of kids with a baseball and two gloves and an empty lot in front of them aren't out looking for sleeping rattlers. They're out to stand on the mound and fog 'em through. They don't see the cactus and the gopher holes; all they see is the Stadium, packed and rolling with sound—even a boy like Matt, who never acted as if he liked the game.

It made me feel better to know that the kid was like the rest of the boys, that he wasn't a damn bit different. Sure, he liked books; that was swell, I take my hat off to him. But books were for reading, and the outside sun was for fogging 'em through. So maybe he flapped his wrist and snapped his elbow; we all can't be Hubbell.

But the car.

I didn't want that bastard Weylin seeing us—me—up there. It was funny. I felt all right about blackmailing him; I didn't like trespassing on his land.

I said, "I'm sorry, boys, but I was worried about you walking across the canyon by yourselves. And I don't know whether Mr. Weylin would want you to come over here so often, without his—"

"Oh," Matt said suddenly, lit up again, "that's all right. I asked Mom before and she said I could call him, so I did—"

I said, "What?"

"So I called him at his office. I looked up the number myself, and he said sure, why not?"

"He said sure?"

"Sure."

I kept looking at the house, around toward the front where the road lies below the raised house. I couldn't see the road, so I hadn't seen the car, but it must have belonged here because nobody else lived up this far. If it had been a car that had followed the road too far by mistake, it would have turned by now and gassed out of there.

No, it had to be Weylin's. It was in the garage now, and whoever had been in it must have gone in the front door.

I said, "Well, then, I guess I'll beat it—"

"Aw, Dad," Matt said. "Stick around. Show us how you throw that curve."

I started to shake my head, and the two boys pressed close, Matt saying, "Come on, Dad, for a few minutes. Please."

The rear door opened on the patio, and a dame came out.

Maybe she had seen us. We were two hundred yards away or so, and she walked out, finally standing next to an umbrella table, and I saw her hand tapping, preparing a cigarette against the table top.

She looked like a thin dame, in slacks and a bright blouse without sleeves, and, from here, her arms and legs looked too long and thin. Her hair was not as dark as it had looked in the picture on Weylin's desk, but more sandy, a dirty blonde. Her blouse was loose and rippled, but not bulgy, so I figured she was pretty small in the chest. Her butt looked lean, too. She wasn't Miss America, but she moved gracefully, nice and loose, like a cat.

I said, "All right, boys, but just for a few minutes. Then we'll beat it."

I walked toward the spot where Matt had had his jacket for home plate, and I inspected the ground very carefully, and finally decided to move the pitching area closer to the house. I wanted a better look at Weylin's wife, who was getting ready to divorce him. Somehow I felt she was on my side.

The boys pitched to me. I didn't have a glove, but it didn't matter. Even Tubby, who played with the Little League, couldn't do more than warm my palms. I fed the boys softly, the uncomfortable feeling fading—lobbing the ball with a flick of the wrist, and they wound like pretzels and flung at me, Tubby pretty close to the target I held up for him, Matt all over the place, but better than I had seen him throw before. The two days in a row had done him good.

Finally I said loudly, "All right boys. Half a dozen more, and that's that. Let's fire 'em up."

I stood up to tell them, and to look past them, and the woman, who had since sat down on a patio lounge, raised her head and then got up. She looked at us and finally decided we were better company than the patio and her magazine.

She walked over and stood near the two boys, forty feet from where I was catching. I gave the boys a target with my hands, up high so she couldn't see my chin—I was saving that—and finally she said, "Who's winning?"

It was a typical dame's remark, figuring she'd be one of the boys and trying to use the right words. Matt turned to her and I could hear him explain how we were only having a game of catch, it wasn't a real game. She stopped listening.

I had dropped my hands when Matt had stopped his wind-up to talk to the dame, and I stood there, the sun hitting my face.

She saw my face, my chin.

And I swear, the pupils of her eyes narrowed to pin heads and her tongue flicked her lips.

She wanted me.

Oh, you'll say I'm reading too fast, and at too great a distance. She looked like one of those who'd end up as nurses in nuthouses where on the q.t. they can get their kicks from some poor gassed-up World War I vet who's maybe crippled up with bursitis, or else they'd set up their stations at bars and pick up winos and slobbering dope addicts, rheumy-eyed old men and spastics and guys whose faces are carved up with fire scars.

She looked like one of those. Maybe she'd have wanted me because I was a big guy with a big body, and she was seeing it the first time, the heat making me look loose and healthy, involved in a physical act only boys and men can do well. But I think it was more. It wasn't her wanting me, it was her wanting my Frankenstein jaw. She was probably wondering how it would feel, kissing me on a mouth that was flesh on the upper lip and plastic on the lower, and she wanted to stroke my jaw, wondering whether I'd feel it.

She said, "Hello. I'm Millie Weylin."

I said, "The boy who's telling you the score is Matt. Matt Hawkins. He's my boy. The other boy is Tubby. Tubby something or other." I grinned.

"And you?" she said.

"I'm Ed Hawkins, ma'am," I said, nodding just a little. "We live across the canyon." I pointed over my shoulder and she looked politely past me, and then back to me.

It was one of those moments when, if I said to her, "Let's get lost," she'd have said yes. Her eyes had swung back to me, and her mouth moved as if it hurt her and then her lower lip hung a little and her eyes clouded up.

Some women wear sex like a badge, like Times Square on Saturday night. It would take a blind monk not to take advantage of it. I'm not blind and I'm not a monk, and I am married, so I kept my eyes on hers and we could feel each other anyway, forty feet apart.

Then she turned away—it ends as it starts, in a split second—and she said, "Well, have fun, boys," and she turned back, made a little wave with her hand and walked off. She looked like a cat, moving away.

I said to the boys, "All right, kids, that's it." They picked up their stuff and followed me across the canyon. I felt washed out.

CHAPTER SIX

I walked into Kimball's paint shop at five minutes past nine, and Kimball was behind the counter, rubbing his dry hands together. He smiled at me as if I was his long-lost brother, and I grinned back.

"You certainly are in early," he said heartily, and I figured I'd have to stop this noise because he'd drive us both nuts in two days.

I said, "Look here, Vin, I'm no baby. Stop conning me, huh? Don't practice your hick-town politics on me. Save it for the convention. Okay?"

He started to frown and tighten his mouth, but that would have meant he wasn't liking me, and a politician just can't not like you; every joker is a potential vote. He said, "You've got me wrong, Ed. I want to talk to you about that." He shot a look toward the back of the store, but it was dark as night back there.

I said, "Your wife's not in yet, is she?"

"No," he said. "I told her—I told her that with you here she probably wouldn't be needed as much these two days."

I grinned, nodding. "Sure, Vin. That was smart. So we could talk. Is that it?"

"Yes," he said quickly, "but not the way you think. I—you caught me at a bad moment yesterday. I won't try to fill you in on all the politics around here, but I just want you to know things look lousy in Laredo and through this part of the county, and I was feeling pretty low when you walked in with—your proposition. Otherwise, I wouldn't—"

"Party bosses on your neck?"

He nodded ruefully.

"Tell them to shove it."

He looked startled, and then he smiled again, a tired, washed-out smile. "Sure," he said. "That's the talk. I wish I could."

The gutless little rabbit, I thought. "Who supports the goddam party down here?"

He said, "I do, I guess."

"Damn right. No guessing about it. What do you do, slip them a couple of grand every campaign?"

He nodded. "But," he said, "they figure it's because they have to run me for office then."

All right, so maybe in a way they were right, and Kimball was twisting their wrists. Nobody else would have run. Nobody else would put in the time and the money. He ran for Congress four years ago, and the state senate two years ago, and this time they'd probably run him for assembly. He was a loser all the way, but people knew him and liked him, and if he were on the other side he'd probably walk in.

"So give 'em the dough next time, and tell 'em you won't run for any-thing. See where that leaves them." He looked shocked. He said, "I—I can't, Ed."

"Why?"

He bit his lip. "Because I—couldn't do that to the party."

"You mean they've got to have a candidate? They'd find one."

"Who?" he said quietly, with a little tough pride in his voice. I liked him better right then than I had ever before.

"That's their problem."

He shook his head decisively. "No, it's not, Ed. It's mine, and yours, and everybody's."

"Count me out. I never register in any party."

"It doesn't matter. You deserve honest representation."

And there it was. Long way around Robinson's barn. Vin Kimball, Hon-est Abe. Yesterday was a mistake, see? Now he was letting me know he was Honest Abe once more. Forget about yesterday.

Sure. I'd forget about it, and maybe one day I'd say somebody's name—like Otto Weylin's—in a tone of voice that would tip him and the sneaky bas-tard would figure I wasn't watching him any more, and Vin Kimball would put the fuse to his earthquake.

Hell, they'd run him for Senator.

So he was softening me up, giving me a job, telling me to forget that slip of the tongue, buttering my crumpets, treating me like a political brother—and what's closer than that!

All right, I'd buy it. It would make it look as though he were off my back, and that was fine with me. I'd just watch my lip, and take my salary.

I said, "What the hell good would honest representation do me?"

And he looked sick. He could play the violin, he could act, the shrewd lit-tle do-gooder. "We all need honest representation," he said stiffly. Oh, you little man, I thought.

"You're right, Vin," I said, and I reached for a plastic showcase of Dupont brushes. "What's the price of these?"

We talked paint the rest of the day. He handled Pittsburgh, Fuller, and Sherwin-Williams, pushed the rubberized wall paints ahead of the oil-bases, the nylon brushes ahead of honest-to-God horsehair. He had his own paint thinner and his own labels, and he'd sell it in any quantity from half a pint to five gallons. He showed me how to work the paint-shimmier, and how to squeeze off the little tubes of color, dropping the emptied tube into the can before putting the whole business on the shimmy. We ran through the color cards, and he removed the cards that were obsolete or out of stock. We took some paint and smeared it on pieces of beaverboard he had in the back, so I'd see how it dried compared to the color card. It went on lighter and an hour later had dried darker, as a rule.

Customers came in dribbles, one and two at a time—forty bucks gross by noon.

I said to him when we started out for lunch, "How much do you net? What's your profit on an eighty-dollar day?"

He shook his head. "First of all, I don't have an eighty-dollar day. We opened early today, and we do more business in the morning than the afternoon. People siesta in Laredo from two o'clock on, except for a last-minute rush when businesses close down. This is still mostly a resort town, even off season."

"What do you gross then?"

"Sixty-five, seventy a day, three-twenty-five a week."

"Which leaves you?"

"After rent, overhead, expenses—forget your salary just now—about a hundred, a hundred twenty-five."

I whistled. The guy was painting Little League posters for kicks; he was selling paint for kicks, too.

I didn't want to ask him why he stayed in the racket, because that would embarrass him more. He'd have to have a helluva imagination to answer that one, and to answer the next one: Why he paid me eighty a week? We'd be back at the same old stand, both of us knowing he was just buttering me in order that I either relented and let him have the dirt, or else forgot to button my lip. I didn't want to hear the other side of the record, how I was the best prospect he'd had in, how he and his wife really needed the vacation, how he just had to go to the convention "for the party—for me and you."

The afternoon droned by, warm, and smelling of paint and turps, and Kimball was right. We grossed sixty-eight dollars and forty-one cents by five-thirty, when he closed shop.

I said, as he ripped out the cash register tape, "How many years you been doing this, Vin?"

He rubbed his nose. "Six years, right here on Sand Street. I've seen lots of—"

I didn't want him to reminisce about the people he'd seen come and go in six years. So I said, "What'd you gross the first week you opened? Throw a big sale that week? Balloons for the kiddies?"

"Why, yes," he said, looking a little surprised, remembering that first week, bunting outside his shop, probably, and people flocking in, wishing him well. "We took in close to three hundred dollars that first day," he said, the pride back in his voice again, but not the same kind of pride. This was damn-fool pride, old man's pride. "Not quite three hundred," he repeated firmly. "Grossed over eight hundred for the whole week."

"So," I said wickedly, the two of us standing outside now, "so what it amounts to is you're losing about five hundred potential bucks a week."

He winced when I said it, the pride gone, and the present day swamping him with the bitter knowledge of what was what.

All right, so Vin Kimball doesn't need the money. He had been a gentleman fruit rancher, sinking lots of money into his orchards and nurseries, but not shaking much out—and apparently it didn't bother him too much. Yet he had quit that line. So there was a limit to how much he threw down a rathole.

He had been told he was throwing five hundred a week away. And you can bet what he was thinking. Sure, the county chiefs had told him he'd better show some results in and around Laredo and this part of the state, or else they'd look elsewhere for their area wheel. They'd probably have to write off Kimball's couple of grand each election year. They'd hurt without that money, but they were hurting with it, so what the hell, the bosses figured, they could always tell Kimball to play across the street.

But with five hundred a week, he could be county leader and captain of every goddam precinct. He could write policy and then run his car up and down the hills of Laredo, knocking on doors and meeting the people face to face. Five hundred a week wasn't going to earthquake the county, but it would whip up a small storm.

We stood there, next to my car, squinting into the sun falling into the ocean at the end of Sand Street. I said, "So long, Vin. We'll give 'em hell tomorrow," and he shook his head, a little shabby grin on his face, dreaming of five hundred a week down the drain for nearly six years now, and he said, "You said it, boy."

I got into my car and watched him through my rearview mirror, plodding toward his own car—a two-year-old Olds. I watched him get in and sit behind the wheel for a long minute, shaking his head, and then he pulled away from the curb and went by. I noticed his license plate; it had a red frame around it, and on the frame it said, "Another Laredo Olds," which meant the poor sucker had bought his car right here in town, which meant he had paid maybe four hundred more for it than he would have if he had gone up to L.A. or down to Dago and shopped around. But that was the sort of jerk Vin Kimball was; he wouldn't dream of buying outside his home town; it wouldn't have been loyal.

I started to laugh at that, and then I sort of pictured the guy again, plodding forward, his eyes on the ground, and the laugh froze in my throat. A guy who believed what he believed, who thought he had to be loyal to the home town that was practically laughing him out of the only racket he cared about, politics—a guy like that might just be the kind who would mean it when he played his violin and went into his song and dance. It was just possible that Vin Kimball had made a mistake yesterday, but in a day's time his conscience had got up on its hind legs and belted him ass over teacup. It was just possible that a guy like Vin Kimball hadn't been buttering me a goddam bit.

I don't know why all this mattered to me, but it did. If he were telling it straight, and was no longer interested in my information, then he was giving me a job because he either liked me or felt sorry for me or thought I was the best prospect who'd walked into his place. And if all that was so—or some of it, anyway—then I had nothing to worry about from Kimball's end. He wouldn't be trying to steal my pigeon.

It should have made me feel better, relieved—if it were true. All it did was send crazy chills up and down my back.

Right after lunch, I had left Kimball to run over to the post office and rent a box. Now, in the car, I pocketed the key. Wednesday. I drove the car south along the ocean highway, toward the canyon turnoff. But before I made the turnoff, I stopped the car and ran into a bar and made a call.

I had checked the number yesterday and the number had stuck. I dropped my dime and dialed it quick, and I waited for Weylin to pick it up.

So I was surprised when the voice was a dame's. She said, "Hello?" and even if I hadn't recognized the voice, I'd have recognized the feel of the voice. She didn't drawl, but she let the word hang out on the line, flowing at me.

I said, "Hello, Mrs. Weylin. Is your husband there?"

There was a pause. "No," she said politely. "Who's calling, please?"

"Ed Hawkins."

There was a pause again. Then she said, "Oh, the baseball man." She laughed a little at that.

"That's right," I said. "Your husband—"

"How's your cute little boy?" she said.

"He's fine—"

"And Tubby?"

All right, I thought, I'd give her another chance. It was a tease act, that was sure. I said, "Fine, Mrs. Weylin. When do you expect your husband?"

This time the little laugh was lower, huskier. "I don't expect him at all, Mr. Hawkins. I haven't expected him for the last two or three years."

I started to laugh politely, to let her know I was just going along with the gag. And then she made a noise. It was, I guess, her way of really laughing. A dirty laugh. I understood what she had meant by the last thing she said.

She said, suddenly, choking off that terrible sound, "Oh, my. I'm awfully sorry, Mr. Hawkins. That was an awful thing to say."

"Well," I said, "I wouldn't say that, Mrs. Weylin. I wouldn't—"

"No," she said. "I guess you wouldn't." There was a bitterness in her voice now, and I was confused. "None of you bastards would. That's why I have to. Go to hell, Mr. Hawkins." And she hung up.

A nasty, hard bitch. Yet I knew something about her. She was a woman divorcing her husband. Yesterday, when I heard this, I figured it gave her husband some reason for getting drunk and chasing a fifteen-year-old girl; now I was wondering. Maybe it worked the other way. Maybe Otto Weylin liked to get drunk and chase little girls all the time. Maybe she wasn't the first. Maybe that was why Mrs. Weylin was hard as nails. For she sure as hell didn't look hard as nails. She looked cat-soft.

I dropped another dime into the slot and I dialed with furious speed. I was chasing the woman. I wanted her. I wanted to grab her and shake that hardness until it dropped off and the cat-sleek softness was under my hands, squirming, alive.

She said dully, "Hello?"

I said, "Listen, I want to know when your husband's going to show up. I've got to talk to him. That's all I want to know." But she had to know I meant more than that. The words were blurted out.

She said, "He'll be home around ten or eleven, I think. He's got a meeting at one of his lodges."

I said, "Millie—listen—Millie, can I come up and see you?" If it had been yesterday, I'd have been able to see her face, those eyes with dagger pupils, clouded over. I wouldn't have had to ask. I would just have told her.

"Sure," she said. But it was tired, uncaring. "Sure," she said. "Come on over." And then she started to laugh again, that gutter noise. "Come on over. Bring the whole team." She was laughing when I hung up, but I was trembling.

Then I made another call. I called Weylin's office, taking the chance he'd still be in.

He was, answering the phone himself, which meant he had sent his girl home.

I said, "Take it down, Weylin. This is Hawkins. Post-office box seven-four-six. That's the address from now on. Got it?"

"Oh," he said. "Yes, yes, I've got it."

I repeated the box number and hung up.

I walked out of the bar, and I picked a newspaper off the stand out front and dropped another dime into another slot. The newspaper stands were run by a bunch of honest johns. You took your paper and threw a dime into a slot on the rack.

I put the paper under my arm and got back into the car, the steering wheel slippery with the sweat of my palms. I felt foolish, like a kid measuring up to a third piece of strawberry shortcake, not sure he wanted any more, knowing, in fact, he ought to shove the whole sticky fluffy mess out of the way, and fast.

I got onto the canyon turnoff and went inland about three-quarters of a mile. Then there is a fork, north up to our side of the canyon, south to Weylin's slope.

The fork came up at me and I never wavered. I goosed the accelerator going north around the curve, and the Chevy just hung as if she was glued to the grade of the curve, gobbling up the yards.

And, Jesus, it was good to be home.

CHAPTER SEVEN

It was funny, getting up early like that the next morning, Thursday morning, eating breakfast with Mary and the boy. Matt has to make an 8:30 bus,
ten minutes away from the house if he walks. I've usually had a nine o'clock
job, which meant I'd pull the Chevy out of the carport at five of.

So Mary and Matt and I wolfed down eggs and bacon, cereal, juice and
coffee—milk for the boy—and the kid wouldn't stop talking about Mr.
Weylin.

"...and yesterday Mr. Weylin showed me his trophy case. He won a hundred cups, at least."

"For chasing ambulances?" I said politely.

"Huh?"

Mary giggled. "Silly," he said. "He plays golf."

"Tennis, too," Matt said. "Yesterday he was telling me...."

Yesterday. Yesterday Weylin was at his office until at least six. Millie
Weylin said her husband was going to a lodge meeting and wouldn't be home
until ten or eleven. Matt came in around seven-thirty. I couldn't remember
whether he had his glove with him or not. When Matt got home, I was in
the living room, watching the Wednesday TV fights. I heard him and Mary
wrangling a bit about coming home late—we don't make a big deal of it, but
it helps Mary with the supper, getting things on and getting the dishes
cleaned up before midnight. But then I had forgotten about it; there was that
Algerian featherweight, bouncing along like a kangaroo, getting the bejeebers
jabbed out of him by a colored boy from Brooklyn for eight rounds, when he
finally connected with one from left field. He starched that colored boy as if
he'd laid him in concrete. I read the paper after that, thinking of that Algerian boy. That feather division is sure as hell a good one nowadays....

So Matt was saying now he had been to Weylin's last evening. He was
lying. But there wasn't a thing I could do about it. I couldn't say, "You
weren't over at Weylin's till seven-thirty, son, because Millie Weylin told me
herself while I was propositioning her over the phone that her husband was-
n't home and wouldn't be home until late that night."

Well, maybe I could. I said, "Did you see Mrs. Weylin? Is she back from
her vacation?"

The boy said, "Huh?" his face blank.

"You didn't see her?"

He shook his head. It was as if he had never heard of her.

So I'm a stupid empty-headed lug. I just plain forgot that Matt and Tubby
were there with me on Weylin's lot yesterday when Mrs. Weylin sashayed
over and gave me the eye.

I got a tight clamp on myself and waited for him to say, "But, Dad, you know she's back. You saw her yourself."

I took a deep breath, and waited.

Mary said, "Drink your milk, Matt," and the boy looked up quickly and picked up his glass, hiding his face.

And that was that.

I was left right where I was before. I still didn't know where the boy was, or why he had been lying. He hadn't seen Mrs. Weylin—at least, he had shaken his head on that one—and he had seen Mr. Weylin, which was all wet. She had been home, not him.

Then I figured to hell with it. The boy had made up a fish story. Maybe he and his fat chum had sneaked a smoke on the beach or maybe they'd met a girl scout, or anything. Boys that age just have to do things they know are not right. Matt wasn't any different.

I drove the boy to the school bus. Just before we got there I said, "Matt, I can drive you to school, if you'd like."

"Uh-uh," he said, shaking his head.

Usually the boy would rather ride the bus. That's how most of the kids got to school. There's something wrong, too protected, about a kid being chauffeured to the school door by his old man.

I nodded. "Okay," I said. Then we pulled up to the stop and I waited for him to open the door. Instead he looked at me, with wide frightened eyes, and he blurted out, "Mrs. Weylin said—she said I should tell you you must have sixth sense."

"What?"

The kid was scared. He was passing on a message he didn't understand, but which he had been told to pass on. He said, "That's what she said."

"When?"

"Last night."

"You *were* up there, then?"

"Huh?"

"Never mind." My hands were shaking. "When did Mr. Weylin get there?"

"Pretty late," he said. "We were finished playing ball—Tubby and me—Tubby wanted to go, but I wanted to wait. He's swell."

"Who? Tubby?"

Matt laughed a little. "Mr. Weylin. He's swell. He had two ice cream bars with him."

"For you and Tubby?"

"No," he said, "for him and me, of course."

I frowned into the windshield. "When did Mrs. Weylin give you that message?" I asked him lightly.

"When—when we heard Mr. Weylin drive up. I was sitting with Mrs.

Weylin, and we heard the car, and she whispered in my ear, so Tubby could-
n't hear, about sixth sense. She said I shouldn't tell anybody else. Not even
Mr. Weylin."

"She said you shouldn't tell Mr. Weylin?"

He opened the door, looking at me peculiarly. "No," he said, "*she* didn't
say that. I mean—she said I shouldn't tell anybody."

"You just added that other part? About not telling Mr. Weylin."

He nodded, standing in the road. The bus was coming up the hill so I'd
have to pull off the shoulder, across the street from where the kids were waiting. Matt started to walk away. I said, "Matt—"

"What, Dad?"

I waved my hand. "Nothing. Have a good day, son." I drove to the side
and let the bus pull in tight to its side, and then I squeezed by.

There were a lot of questions piling up.

Weylin wasn't supposed to be home, yet he had been. How come? A man
like that doesn't just walk out on his lodge chums without a good reason.
When husbands come home unexpectedly, it always looks to me as if they're
spying on their wives. Yet Millie Weylin was divorcing her husband. I can't
figure people getting ready for divorce, but still living under the same roof.
So he couldn't have been sneaking back to catch his wife at anything. Why,
then?

And what the hell was Matt doing over there every day, playing ball? Kids
Matt's age sometimes get crushes on older women who like to mother them
up. Still, you wouldn't figure Millie Weylin for that type of woman. She did-
n't look like the mother type.

And Matt was up there that other afternoon *before* Millie Weylin had got
back from her trip.

There was another question. How come I took that left fork instead of the
right, as I had planned? How come I decided to leave Millie Weylin waiting?
Hell, it wasn't sixth sense; I never gave Weylin a thought. She had said he
wasn't going to be home. That had been enough for me.

I don't like to admit it, but maybe I knew Millie Weylin was over my head.
Not that she wasn't a tramp. She was, but some dames are like that. It was
as I thought yesterday. She was a piece of strawberry shortcake I wasn't sure
I could handle.

Then I grinned. I'd get hungry again, and she'd still be around. So it was-
n't that. It was something else. But I didn't know what.

The Kimballs were all bustle and business that Thursday morning, and
Vin was all smiles. We sold paint and thinner and brushes, he and I, and the
old lady finished the last of the Little League posters—the Laredo Savings one.
She brought it in before lunch, some paint on her cheek and her gray hair all

out of place. She said to Vin, "I finally figured what to put on it," holding the poster behind her.

"You did?" he said. He was grinning at her, trying to look behind her. They had talked about that last one, how they had kept putting it off because they couldn't think of anything jazzy to say about a bank that was sponsoring a baseball team of kids. It wasn't like the VFW or the American Legion that you could decorate with stars and stripes. It was like Kimball had said to me between sales, "You can't paint dollar signs all over a baseball poster."

So now she had it. He said, "Show me."

She said, "Guess, first."

"Golly," he said. He screwed up his face and thought hard. "Let's Go, Laredo Savings?"

She wrinkled her nose. "You already ruined that one. 'Let's Go, Rotary!' —remember?"

"Yeah," he said. "Golly." He stared at the ceiling. I was watching the two of them, getting sort of interested myself.

"Try again," she said. "You've got two guesses left."

"I can't," he said.

She turned to me. She had a playful look on her face. She looked ten years younger. I guess they were really looking forward to that vacation. "How about you, Ed?"

Now she was Ed-ing me, too. But she didn't make it sound as if she was doing me a favor. I said, "Beats me, Mom."

She whirled around and waved the poster high. It read: "Sock it, Savings!" I thought it was awful.

Maybe Kimball did, too, but he didn't let on. He grinned at her and shook his head and repeated, "Sock it, Savings!"

She said, leaning forward, her gray eyes all bright, "Do you get it, Vin?"

"Why, sure," he said. "Sock it, Savings."

"Aw," she said in a disgusted voice. "You don't. Don't you see? Sock it is swell for a ball team. But the bank will like it, too. Sock it away. Get it? Save your money. Sock it, Savings. Now? What do you think?"

Vin shook his head, marveling at her. He was practically speechless, except, of course, no politician is ever speechless. He said, "Why, that's absolute genius, Mom. In all my life, I've never—"

I said, "It sure is, Mom."

And the three of us started to grin and laugh and pretty soon we were doubled over.

I said, "Retire 'em, Rotary. Get it?" And we all howled.

Vin said, "Buy-buy, Byler's." Byler's was the sporting goods store. "Get it? Bye-bye is what the radio announcer says when you hit a home run—you know, it's bye-bye baby! But we spell it b-u-y. Buy-buy. Get it?" And, of course, we howled some more.

Vin insisted we all have lunch together, which was an unnecessary luxury, but I didn't argue, because it was his last day for a few weeks, and we wouldn't be seeing each other, and I was going to miss the long-nosed song-and-dancer.

We went to the Seashell, on the highway, instead of one of the counter joints, and Vin said, "We're celebrating. Let's have a drink."

Mom Kimball said warmly, "What are we celebrating, Vin?"

He frowned. "Darned if I know. What are we celebrating, Ed?"

I said, "For winning the World Series, that's what. Carry on, Kimball. Count on us, Kimball. You can't cork us, Kimball. Get that one? *Cork* us? Caucus."

It was awful, I know, but they loved it.

Vin murmured, "Isn't he great, Mom? Didn't I tell you we had a wonderful boy, here?"

Mom Kimball glowed at me. "Ed," she said, "you don't know how glad we are you're working with us."

We had a drink—they had some sweet rum drink, and I had bourbon on the rocks—and then we had another.

Kimball said, "You know, Ed, I got a feeling there's going to be a big change around here. A very big change."

I said, "On registration day, they're all going to be sick. We're going to outregister them, five to one."

Kimball shook his head. He sighed. "He's still an Easterner, Mom. He doesn't understand. We don't just have one registration day or one week, out here. You can register practically any time. It's permanent. Once you're registered, you're registered for good, unless you move."

Mom Kimball said happily, "Or unless you die."

But I had somehow spoiled it, or rather, Vin Kimball had. He had got too serious, explaining to me about registration. I had known, but I had just wanted to keep the rainbow shining up there. The rest of the lunch was eating and forcing the talk beyond its natural limit.

Except for one item. That was the worst. It showed me how phony the rainbow had been, even before we had spoiled it, and how phony the grin on Kimball's face had been all day.

He said, over coffee, staring down into a tiny whirlpool made by his spoon, "Maybe we ought to fly up there, Mom."

I jerked my head up. "Fly? What for? This is Thursday. The convention opens Monday."

Kimball played with his spoon. "Yeah. I guess you're right. Still, we've just got to get there a day or two early. We've just got to."

Mom Kimball reached out her hand and placed it on top of his. She turned to me. "I never knew a convention, Ed," she said, "that wasn't over before it began. It's all in the dealing, all in those smoke-filled rooms you hear about, and none of it in the actual playing. Once the cards are dealt, the game is over."

I said, "What do you mean, Mom?"

Kimball said slowly, "It's this way, Ed. There are guys coming up to Sacramento from all over the state, some of them like me in positions of some small authority—town, assembly district, county. Then there are other guys who pay the bills, some of them, anyway, and guys who are friends of national committeemen, guys who were once in but now aren't. And there's a scramble, see?"

Mom Kimball said, "Once the cards are dealt the game's over." She was halfway crocked, but I understood her jargon better than I did his. "You got to get a seat in the game, that's all that matters. It's five-man poker, with eight guys wanting to play."

I said lightly, "They wouldn't deal you out, Vin."

He looked up with that little tough grin, the one I liked. "They better not. That's why we're leaving tonight. We'll sleep over on the road, and then hit Sacramento late tomorrow. Maybe we'll shoot over to Frisco first and see some of the boys there. Then we'll be ready." He rubbed his hands together, and winked at me, and the tough grin became a forced bright one, the phony rainbow, and I knew the guy was scared to death.

And it was my fault. I'd had to bring up the realities. I'd had to mention that five-to-one registration that was dogging Kimball and had the party bosses on his neck, and the guys who were out angling to get back in, riding Vin right out of the picture.

I tried my best to make up for it. When the girl brought the check, I grabbed at it and pinned it to the table. Mom said quickly, "No, Ed. That's ours."

I held tight and shook my head. "Uh-uh, Mom. This one's on me."

"Vin," she said, "don't let him."

He said, "Ed, don't be foolish. It was my idea; it's our celebration."

He looked at me with a pleading look in his eyes. It was as if he absolutely couldn't let me do this, it would hurt him. But I felt the same way. He absolutely couldn't pay; it would hurt me.

So we sat that way for half a minute, my hand on the check, his hand over mine, and Mom staring at us. Then I shook my head and pulled the check out from under and said, "Next time, Vin."

Mom Kimball walked to the door ahead of us, and Vin and I stood at the cashier's desk. He was still hoping, I guess, I'd let him pay the charges. I shot a quick look at his wife—she was fumbling with her hair and waiting for us, paying us no attention—and I said harshly, "Quit it, Vin. Don't butter me. I'm not selling anything."

He winced when I said that, and I could have cut my tongue out. "Is that what you think?" he said quietly.

I said, "Jesus, Vin, I'm sorry. I didn't mean—anything."

"You won't believe a guy, will you?" he said.

"I'm sorry, Vin," I said. "Believe me, I'm sorry."

"You don't trust anybody, do you, Ed? It was a mistake, the other day. I don't know what got into me. I don't do that sort of thing. I leave the smear stuff to the other party. Do you understand? You've got to believe me."

I said, "Vin, I'm sorry. I never should have said that."

But it was no go. I had said it, and it had hit him hard. The three of us were quiet the rest of the afternoon, and though I tried to get them to leave around three—they wanted to hit Santa Barbara tonight, and that's a hundred and fifty miles up the coast—Vin refused to leave until five o'clock.

Then they got into their Olds to go home, finish whatever packing they had, and take off. I walked them to their car and I said, "So long, Vin. So long, Mom. Have a good time."

Vin said brightly, "So long, Ed. You're in charge, boy." But it didn't cover it up at all.

I waited until they had driven off, and then I took the key out of my pocket and re-opened the paint shop and called Mary and told her I'd be home in a couple of hours. I kept the shop open for an hour and a half, hoping I'd get some stragglers. I did: three customers, eight dollars and sixty cents.

The last guy complained when I charged him a buck for a nylon brush. He said, "You'd figure by now they'd be able to sell these things for pennies."

I agreed with him, tossing it into a paper sack.

He shook his head and gave me the dollar—and the tax—and he said, "Well, it's only money."

I said cheerfully, "Money isn't everything."

He said, "Guess not," and went out. I closed a few minutes later, thinking hollowly that I was trying to fatten up the gross because I had to apologize to Kimball somehow, and I couldn't think how to do it otherwise.

I told myself, money isn't everything, but it's sure as hell a lot.

I was lying. It wasn't. If Kimball hadn't been giving me a song and dance, eight dollars and sixty cents wasn't going to apologize. I couldn't shake that goddam uncomfortable feeling.

Mary said, "You're tired, honey?"

The boy was in his room, finishing up his homework. Mary had done the dishes, and I was lying on the couch. The radio was on, a Pacific Coast game. It was an out-of-town game, one of those re-created affairs, with artificial fan noises and the announcer putting on a big act. Still, it was a ball game, the first week of the season. I lay there thinking of the old days, how about this time we'd be getting together at night in some back room of a bar, with beer and pretzels, to work out our lineup, to see who was still with the club and who had dropped out and who was a likely prospect from one of the local high-schools or colleges, some kid who didn't mind making a few bucks on weekends and evenings playing under a phony name.

"No," I said. "Well, maybe a little tired."

She sat on the edge of the couch and put her hand on my forehead and stroked my hair. I pulled her down and she settled in my arms, her cheek against mine.

I said, "Honey, you know, I *like* that job."

She laughed quickly, delightedly. "Oh, Ed, I'm glad. I thought just the opposite. I thought you were hating it."

I grunted. "Why did you think that?"

She shrugged. "I don't know. You—seemed that way. Not liking it, I mean. Why, I thought you liked your job with Carlstrom better than this."

I was quiet for a minute. In a way, she was right. I did enjoy driving a tow truck. It's not hard work, and most of the time you just sit around on your butt, gassing with the grease monkeys or playing a hand of cards. And I had never liked selling anything from behind a counter. You weren't yourself back there. You were some sort of smiling joker, glad-handing every stupid son of a bitch who walked in to buy.

This was different. I was working hard for Kimball, hustling my butt for him, selling, straightening out his shelves, re-arranging his windows, helping Mom wrap the big orders, toting packages to customers' cars, delivering orders via my car which meant Kimball wasn't left shorthanded, because, brother, when I deliver I make the delivery and get back before Kimball would have shifted into second. Take today, for instance. Even with that long lunch hour, and even with the Kimballs leaving half an hour early, we took in ninety-five dollars gross. Cancel out that last eight dollars sixty, and it was still a very good day, compared to the usual gross.

"They're pretty nice, the Kimballs. Square, I mean."

"That's good," Mary said.

"Actually," I said, "they're rubes from the word go. But nice."

"Umm," she said.

"The money isn't really so awful, is it, hon?"

She pushed away and looked at me. Her eyes were very close to mine and she stared into my face, studying me. Then she gave me a fierce hug. "Of course it's not awful," she said. "It's fine."

"I think Kimball wants me to stay on, after he gets back."

"I'm sure he does."

"Maybe he'll raise me."

Mary said, "If he does, fine. If he doesn't, fine. We'll get by." And she meant it.

The boy came in from his room a few minutes later and I shut off the game. Matt said politely, "Who's winning, Dad?"

I said, "The Seals. Four-two, sixth inning."

I waited for the boy to ask me who was pitching and if anybody had hit one out of there, but he didn't. Sometimes I can't figure him; either he does or he doesn't like the game. The last few days I was sure he was getting crazy about it. Well, I couldn't blame him not getting hot about a rehashed Pacific Coast game. Still, you'd think he'd have something to say.

Mary said, "You finished with your homework?"

The boy said, "Sure." He was standing there in the living room. It was after nine o'clock and the boy would soon be off to bed. But you could see he didn't want to go yet.

Mary said, "You want something to eat?"

"No, thanks," he said.

"Matt," I said, "what is it, boy?"

He looked sort of embarrassed. Then he said, "Dad, can I go out for a while?"

Well, I thought. The kid's got a girl. Ten years is too young, but he'd have to learn that himself. I said, "Sure. Need some change?"

He looked surprised, his soft brown eyes open and innocent. Maybe he didn't know he could buy her a Coke. I wondered whose kid it was. I didn't know too many kids up on the canyon.

"No, Dad," he said.

Mary said, "Where you going, Matt?"

He said, "Over to Mr. Weylin's."

"Oh," I said. And the room was quiet for a minute. Mary said, "You're going to walk across the canyon at night?"

Matt looked confused. "I could go down to the fork and then up on the south side. I could take a flashlight," he said.

"No," I said.

The boy looked hurt. "Please, Dad," he said. "I'll be careful."

Mary said, "Don't be silly, Matt. That road's pitch black at night. You might fall and break your neck."

"I won't, Mom," he said.

"I'll say he won't," I said.

Matt said, "Please, Dad. *Please.*" He looked close to tears.

Mary said, "Why do you want to go over to Mr. Weylin's at this hour?"

"He invited me over."

"Crazy damn time to invite a kid over," I said.

Mary said slowly, "Well, they don't have any kids, I guess, and they probably don't know— How did he figure you'd get there?"

Matt looked at me. And I froze. The boy said slowly, "Well, I guess he thought Dad would drive me up there. But I can make it all right with a flashlight."

Mary said, "Are you sure he invited you?"

"Honest, Mom," he said. "Honest."

"Well," Mary said. "Well—"

He worked on her. "Please, Mom. I'll be careful."

She said sharply, "Don't be foolish, Matt. Of course you can't walk over there. But maybe your father will drive you."

Sure, I thought. I'll chauffeur the boy. Any time my boy wants to go over there, I'll just drive him over. We're all pals, me and my pigeon, Weylin, and his wife whom I was likely going to bed down before too long, and Mary, who didn't have the slightest idea of what was going on, who didn't know that Weylin was going to be buying our potatoes for two years.

I said, "Well, the boy ought to be able to take care of himself."

Mary said, "Nonsense. If you won't drive him, he can't go." She turned to the boy. "Your father's tired, Matt, and it is pretty late. You can stay up another hour or so, which will be later than you ought to be up. Maybe some other time."

Matt looked at me as if he wanted to stick a knife in my heart.

I said, "Damn it, Matt, I've worked all day and I'm tired. That's that."

And Matt said, the words all crazy in the room, the boy not understanding what he was saying but saying them anyway, "*Mrs.* Weylin will be there! *Mrs.* Weylin will be there!"

I pushed Mary away and got up and clouted the kid one with my open hand.

He staggered back, his hand to his cheek, the white finger marks showing and then filling in with hot blood.

"Now," I said, panting, "now, what the hell does that mean? What the hell do you mean by that?"

"Please, Ed," Mary was saying, her hand on my arm, touching me, holding me, "the boy doesn't know what he's saying."

Matt stood there, shaking his head, too scared to cry.

"Tell me," I said, standing over the boy, "what do you mean by that crack?"

"Please, Ed," Mary said. "Please."

I said, "I won't have my son calling me a skirt-chaser. I won't stand for it. Out with it. What do you mean, Matt?"

But all he could do was shake his head, holding his cheek, dry-eyed, terror-struck.

Mary said, "Matt, go to bed. Now. Go to bed."

The boy turned slowly, and walked away. I kept waiting to hear him cry, but he didn't. I didn't hear a thing from his room. Not a sound.

Mary said to me, "You shouldn't have hit him like that, Ed."

I said, "Nobody talks to me like that. Mrs. Weylin will be there. Who the hell cares? What does it mean to me? I've seen the woman once in my life. What the hell does he mean, accusing me?"

And she said, "When did you see her? Before her vacation?"

Nice?

In bed that night, I said to her, "I swear, honey, I've never been untrue to you. Never. Not once. Believe me, Mrs. Weylin is nothing. It just skipped my mind that I'd seen her when we were playing ball."

She said, "Apparently Matt was pretty impressed by what he saw."

"A kid! What does he know?"

"Enough, apparently, to think you'd care whether she was home or not."

I put my arms around her, but she lay still, neither trying to move away or to come closer. "Honey," I said, "he's dead wrong if he thinks there's anything between me and Millie Weylin."

"Millie?"

"God damn it," I said, "yes, Millie. She does have a first name. Or shall we refer to her as that other woman? Is that what you want?"

"I don't want anything," Mary said. "Just—just—" and she began to cry.

She cried herself to sleep, I guess, because after a long while she was quiet and I could hear her breathing nice and even.

What I was thinking was starting to upset me. First, I thought I was being a damn fool, and I had to stop that right away. There'd be trouble, lots of trouble, big-league trouble if I didn't watch my step. For one thing, I was messing around with ten grand. A lot of money. A man doesn't toss ten grand aside just like that. I'd have to watch my step, or that would be exactly what I'd be doing.

Then, there was the little matter of blackmail. What I was doing was a crime. Maybe nobody would blow the whistle on me, but unless I watched myself and put a gag on my big mouth, I'd be blowing the goddam whistle on me.

And—maybe this came first—there was Matthew. *Mrs. Weylin will be there!*

Did it mean what Mary and I first thought it meant? That the boy figured Millie Weylin meant something to me, and that I'd want to drive him over so I'd be able to see her?

Think it over. Does a kid, a quiet ten-year-old boy who doesn't know girls from jellybeans, does he suddenly start matchmaking his old man and some dame? Especially some dame I had seen only once, and that one time for a couple of minutes? No, a kid doesn't think like that. At least a kid like Matt doesn't.

So it meant something else. It was important that Millie Weylin was going to be home. But important to whom? To me? I think we've settled that. Not to me.

To him?

I wouldn't believe it. It made me sick. It disgusted me. I wanted to forget it. I wanted to crawl away from myself, from Matt, from everything. A ten-year-old boy.

I tried to work up an anger. I tried to be sore, at him, at Weylin, at Millie Weylin. It wouldn't come off. I just felt sick and dirty. A kid like that, *my* kid.

It was so bad, staring me in the face, that I did crawl away from it. I wiped it out of my mind. It was better and easier to think Matt pictured me as a skirt-chaser. What was wrong with that? A hot piece like Millie Weylin? Nothing. Nothing was wrong.

I stuck to that thought, and went to sleep thinking about Millie Weylin, and I did forget the other. When I woke the next morning, I had a gray taste in my mouth, an uncomfortable feeling, but I started thinking of Millie Weylin, the dame everybody—Matt and Mary—knew I wanted, the skirt I was chasing. The uncomfortable feeling went away. I made up my mind I was going to bed down that dame, and fast.

CHAPTER EIGHT

It was raining when I woke. Slow steady straight up-and-down rain, coming out of a lead-gray sky thick as a mountain, with no break in sight.

When it rains here, you talk about it. This was the rainy season—the end of the rainy season, actually—and either this one or the next one would be the last rainfall until November, maybe even until January. It rains several times a year, during periods stretching out over a couple of months. Two or three of those rains are little drippy affairs, two or three are half-day rains, maybe an inch or so at a time, and one or two are floods. This one looked like a flood.

It was beating down when I got up, and when I looked out the kitchen window I could see rivulets cutting down the slope, so it must have been raining half the night. That relieved me; it meant I hadn't been awake as long as I'd thought.

I didn't bother to wake Mary; I let her sleep. Matt and I fixed a breakfast of juice and toast and boiled eggs, and we both drank milk.

The boy was clear-eyed and quiet, looking at me every so often, not hating me any more, not wanting to stick that knife in my belly any more, but trying to figure me. You know kids.

I said—finishing my first glass of milk and pouring myself another and shoving the container toward Matt—"Regular cloudburst."

He said, "Yeah, sure is."

"Looks like one of those all-day rains."

"Yeah," he said, "at least."

"Doesn't do the ground any good, this kind of rain."

He said, "Sure doesn't. Water just runs right off."

I said, "Did you look down the canyon?"

A little look flickered on his face, a wary look. "No," he said, "I didn't."

"A regular flood. Running down there a ton of water a minute. Going to wash out the trail for sure."

He was silent for a second. Then he said, "Guess so."

I said, "No ball playing up on the lot for two or three days. That's for sure."

He made an elaborate shrug. "Who cares?" he said.

"Well," I said stiffly, getting up, clearing the table, "I thought you did. You and Tubby."

He said, "To heck with Tubby. He's just a slob."

I said, "What? What kind of talk is that? I thought he was your pal."

Matt carried his egg dish to the sink and ran water into it and put it down. "Please, Dad, don't mention Tubby. He's—he's just a slob."

"What's the matter with him?" I said slowly.

Matt shook his head. "Oh, nothing. Just the things he says, that's all."

"Like what?"

Matt shook his head, "Dad," he said, "I—I can't tell you. That's not the kind of stuff I can talk about."

I didn't press him. We got ready to leave and I woke Mary, who looked up at me out of great eyes, frowning and frightened for a minute, and then she relaxed. "Oh," she said. "That's nice. You let me sleep. Umm." She yawned and stretched like a kitten and I wanted to sprawl down there with her.

I said, "We're going, hon."

She said, "Is that rain?"

"No," I said gravely, "that's water running down the drainpipe."

"Oh," she said, "I thought— Silly! Listen to that rain!"

I knew she was half-awake then, and I bent down to give her a peck on the cheek, but she turned and I hit her square on the mouth, a soft just-awake mouth, a child's mouth. I thought, You poor sucker, you.

"So long, kid," I said.

She said, "Drive Matt to school?"

I straightened. She was more awake than I had figured. I said, "Sure."

"I mean—all the way to school."

"I know what you mean, hon."

She nodded, her face settling into its firm shape. "Come home early, Ed. Not like—last night."

"Okay," I said. "I'll be home. There won't be much call today. Nobody's going to be downtown."

I went out to the carport and drove up to the front of the house, and then waved the boy down. He ran down, climbed in. He wasn't terribly wet, but he sure wasn't dry.

I said, "I'll drive you all the way today, Matt."

"You don't have to, Dad," he said. "I can wait for the bus."

"Nonsense," I said.

He couldn't have wanted to stand there on the road, waiting for the bus. Of course, he could have waited in the car until the bus arrived, and then run for it. But two seconds would be enough to get soaked. It was a bitch of a rain, steady and a little swifter now. The road was like glass.

We got halfway down the canyon when I brought him around to where we had left it at breakfast.

I said, "You know, sometimes boys say things that sound funny—dirty, sort of—but they're not really. Not when you get to understand a little better, when you get a little older."

Matt shook his head. "It won't change. Not what *he* said."

"About who?" I said lightly, staring through the alternately gushing and clearing windshield.

"About Mr. Weylin and his wife," Matthew said. He said it fast, without thinking, a little indignantly.

"About what—they do?"

"Yeah," he said, starting to hunch down in his seat. It really bothered him. That was funny. I had been sickened last night about—about something totally different, and now he was disgusted with what a fat friend of his had said about a man and his wife. Something that was perfectly normal. Or was it?

How normal was it—if I'm right about Tubby and what he said—how normal was it for a couple about to get a divorce to sleep in the same bed?

And why did it upset Matt so goddam much?

I made the turn onto Bel-Eyre and went past the Congregational Church. Behind it, you could see the high-school ballfield where the Little League played out its schedule. I nodded my head at the field. "You going to try out this year for Little League, Matt?"

He turned to me, his face tilted up to mine. "Me?" he said. "Me? Try out for Little League? Why would I do that, Dad?"

So I spat it out, harshly, angrily. "Why not? It's what normal boys do, isn't it? Or wouldn't you know?"

"Huh?" he said, bewildered.

"Why not?" I said again, but more softly. "Why wouldn't you?"

"I don't like baseball," he said simply. "Gee, I thought you knew *that*, by now."

"Seems like you've been playing up there pretty often for a boy who doesn't like the game."

He hunched back down, silent.

I went up Laredo Street and to the school, and inched up as close to the front gate as possible. He still had a thirty-foot walk, and then up two dozen steps. I said, "Watch your step, boy."

"I will," he said.

"I'm sorry—about last night," I said quickly.

"That's all right," he said, and he ran from the car.

But it wasn't all right, and it wasn't going to be all right, and it was going to get worse. I could see that, and I figured there was still time to stop it, but I didn't know how.

Nobody came into Kimball's the first half-hour I was open. I started to walk around the place, dusting the counter, rearranging the display cases. I fiddled with some paint on pieces of wood Kimball had lying around the back, beaverboard, plywood, redwood, some nice plain straight pine, and some very nice walnut. I found out that the rubberized paint, which Kimball pushed very hard, went on all of them very easily, but while it was drying it sort of spread on the beaverboard and plywood and even a little on the pine. It stayed firm on the walnut and the redwood. On the cheap wood, it stretched, leaving little freckles of bare wood underneath. It sure as hell wasn't a one-coat paint for cheap wood. It probably wasn't even a two-coat paint. The oil-base, on the other hand, went on and stayed put, and even though it dried more slowly, it finished off much better, satiny and neat. You had to be more careful applying it—a brush was better than a roller with the oil-base, whereas with the rubber-base, you could roll it, brush it or shoot it on with a gun, it didn't make the slightest difference.

But what I found out might help Kimball. He wasn't the kind of guy who sold the rubber-base just because in the long run the customer had to come back and buy twice as much if he was painting on beaverboard or that kind of stuff. He sold it because it was cheaper and easier to put on, and he thought he was doing the customer a favor.

Well, I figured he was making a mistake. The guy who was painting beaverboad couldn't afford to buy two quarts of rubber-base, when one quart or even less of oil-base would do. The rubber-base wasn't cheaper; it worked out more expensive.

I started rearranging the shelves, putting some cans of oil-base paint up front, right alongside the rubber-base. It all depended on the customer, and what he was painting.

Two hours had gone by. Still no customers.

I kept busy, or at least I tried to. The rain was making a mess of the front window; I couldn't see anything but an occasional car with its lights on, creeping by. Once, the wind blew the window perfectly clear for a brief second, and I saw a telephone repair truck chugging along. That meant the lines were already down somewhere.

I picked up Kimball's phone, and got a dial tone. Then as I started to put it back on the cradle, I changed my mind. I dialed Weylin's office. It was getting me like an itch.

The girl with the bright superior voice said, "Hello," and I said. "Is Mr. Weylin in?"

She said, "I'll see. Who's calling please?"

That meant he was in. I hung up.

Then I dialed Weylin's house.

Millie Weylin said, "Hello?"

I said, "This is Ed Hawkins."

"Yes?" she said. There was nothing in her voice, no lure, no heat, nothing.

"I thought the rain might be depressing you. I'd like to come up and keep you company."

"That's what you said the other day."

"This time I mean it."

"What's the matter?" she said. "You get chicken last time?"

And again, I was scared. She scared me, I swear. "No," I said, "something came up."

And that dirty laugh.

I said, "You're a pretty dirty-minded little girl, aren't you."

She laughed, and it rose until I thought she'd crack. Then she stopped it. "That's right," she said. "But it seems to me you understand me pretty well."

I forced myself to laugh. "I do," I said. "Birds of a feather. I'll be up in an hour or so."

She hung up without a word.

I had a customer at eleven-thirty, and I managed to talk him into taking an expensive can of oil-base. He and his wife were painting their studio up in Laredo Canyon. That's the canyon on the north end, the worst, poorest part of town. He was a shabby-looking guy, hair too long, shoes curled at the toes. He didn't say it, but I figured his house was made of cardboard.

He frowned, uncertain, weighing the price.

I said, "Tell you what. You take that quart of paint. Just take it. Smear it on one wall. Then if you don't like the way it looks after one coat, bring back what's left, and I'll sell you some rubber-base. If you do like it, come back and pay me. How's that?"

He still frowned, and then he said, "It's not that I can't pay this much. It's—"

"Hell," I said, grinning (and hoping it looked close to a grin and not a snarl), "I'm not worried you're going to rob us. I'm just trying to prove a point. I think you'll save money my way. And if I'm right, maybe I can convince some other people. That's how I—we—make money here, by getting customers."

"Well," he said slowly, "that makes sense, of course."

I tossed the can into a sack and said, "Pay me when you get down here again. And let me know how you like it."

He shook his head and walked out, smiling.

A couple of minutes later I sold a woman a fifty-cent can of natural high-gloss finish for her kid's toy chest. Then just before noon, I sold a guy a one-inch nylon brush.

I closed up and put the cardboard clock inside the window of the front door. It read: *Will be back at*—and I set the hands at two o'clock. Two hours.

I drove the Chevy slowly through the shiny black streets, to the highway instead of Bel-Eyre, because the highway would be much safer on a day like this. Then I turned off at the canyon road and took the right fork this time, and wound slowly up the neat asphalt road that ended in front of Weylin's place. I put the car in the two-door garage and shut the doors and then I walked through the rain to the front door. Before I knocked, I looked around. There wasn't a house in sight. A row of eucalyptus trees rimmed the road.

If it hadn't been so gray, I'd have been able to see down to the ocean, less than two miles away. Instead, I could see the trees and nothing else. Nor could anyone see me.

I knocked and the door opened fast.

I had to kick it shut with my foot, because my hands were very busy.

Later I said, "You know, you really had me scared for a while."

We had worked our way to the bedroom.

She laughed huskily. "I know."

"You know?"

"Sure. I could tell."

"But not any more."

"I know."

Outside the rain made a faint thrum on Weylin's roof, a much fainter noise than on our roof. Insulation. His—theirs—was like a house back East, a house that had been built, not thrown up.

"This is nice," I said.

She murmured.

"I mean—this house."

She moved a little in the bed. She was small, even smaller than Mary, because Mary was rounder and Mary had more bust and more rear end. There wasn't much to her, she wasn't curvy at all. Still, she was pretty good. It was something other than her body. It was her. Mary, well, Mary would lie there, pretty quiet, enjoying it, mind you, but not doing much, receiving her pleasure, I guess, out of mine. With Millie, it was like two different things going on, instead of one. I didn't feel as close, but then I figured that was because we weren't used to each other. Still, I imagine that's how she'd always be.

She moved again and said, "All right, that's enough. Stop it."

"Stop what?"

"Comparing. I don't like it."

I reached for her and dragged her over my body and kissed her mouth, hard.

"Jesus," she said, "take it easy. What are you trying to prove?"

It was after two o'clock when we got back to the living room. I wasn't liking her at all by then, which was another point of comparison. When I finished sex with Mary, I liked her very much.

Millie said, "Well, that was fun, wasn't it?"

"Yes," I said.

"Don't be so wild," she said. "Don't be so enthusiastic. You make me too too happy."

I said, "Shut up."

"And don't tell me to shut up," she said. "Who the hell do you think you are?"

"Tell me," I said. "How come you wanted me to do this?"

She looked at me, at my face, and she shivered.

"That's what I thought," I said. "Have you tried guys in iron lungs? That ought to be down your alley."

I started for the front door.

She said, "Wait a minute. Don't be so smug. You're in a hell of a spot for a guy who's giving advice."

For a second I froze, thinking: Weylin's told her about the blackmail. They're planning to turn me over to the cops, or something like that. *A hell of a spot.*

But it didn't make sense.

I turned around. "What kind of a spot am I in?"

She said, "Why, are you blind? Don't you know? Can't you see what's going on?"

She didn't mean blackmail. I was pretty sure of that. She wouldn't be talking like that. If they were going to call the cops on me, she wouldn't be cueing me.

Besides, I couldn't see Otto Weylin telling his wife about his trouble with a fifteen year old.

"No," I said. "I can't see what's going on. Tell me."

I took a step toward her, and her face washed white. I guess I was starting to get sore, I guess she could see that vein at my temple throbbing now. "Tell me. What's going on?"

"No," she said, backing up. "It's—nothing. I'm just—shooting off my mouth."

I walked forward and grabbed her wrist. I guess I twisted it because she let out a little moan and I let go. She stood there, huddled up a bit, small and frightened.

"Tell me," I said, and I swear I was saying it very gently.

She shook her head.

I hit her. I think I started out to grab her again, but somehow my hand got balled up, and I hooked it under her arm that was across her chest. I raised her up with that left hook and then her legs folded and she went back on her rear.

She sat there, holding her belly, trying to breathe, and looking up at me, yellow fear in her eyes.

I said, "Tell me, kiddo. That was just the beginning."

She sat there, shaking her head, but it wasn't because she didn't want to tell me. She was just trying to get breathing again. So I waited, standing there, and she started sucking air pretty regularly, and then she said quietly, "Why do you think Matthew comes over here every day?"

"Tell me," I said. "Why does he?"

She looked past me. Then she said, "Because Matthew can't stand you."

Now she said this in a tired, leaden voice, sitting there on the floor, still clutching her middle, looking over my shoulder. It came out quickly and without any real feeling behind it, and if it didn't make such good sense, if it didn't add up to an answer to all my questions, I wouldn't have believed a word of it.

I said, "Is that straight?"

She held out her hand and I helped her up. "Sure," she said. Then she looked at my face. Now, I don't know how I looked right at that moment, but I do know most of the ways I can look. Sometimes I've got that Andy Gump look, chinless and almost sad, sort of, like a kid sucking in his lower lip before he begins to bawl.

Millie Weylin's face softened up, and she said, "Oh, I'm sorry, I didn't mean to—to hurt you."

Can you beat it? I had belted her in the gut and twisted her wrist, I had made her tell me something she didn't want to tell me, and *she* was sorry *she* had hurt *me*. Sometimes I can't figure people.

I snarled, "Hurt me? Why, you couldn't—"

She reached up and kissed me. I pulled back, and she slobbered all over my jaw.

"Shut up," she said. "You stupid lug, shut up and grow up. Don't you—can't you see what's happening? Don't you want your own kid? What's the matter with you?"

I gave her a push and walked out.

You understand, of course, that I didn't go on up to Weylin's to see his wife. I went up there to find out why Matt was spending so much time up there. That's all I wanted. It was bothering me. And now she had told me a reason—*the* reason. Now I knew. They were babying him, treating him like a kid prince, filling him with Cokes and ice cream and loving kindness, showing him trophy cases and picture albums and baby shoes. They were making him part of the family. After the kind of treatment I'd been giving the boy, no wonder he was ready to climb down that slope with a flashlight.

That made everything so easy. All I had to do was relax a little. I must have been tight as a ball of yarn these past few days. Just relax around the boy, and he'd soon stop running over there. Not that I cared any more. Let him run. He'd get over it.

I picked my way down the canyon in second, my brights on in case anybody was coming up. The shoulder on my right was starting to crumble and turn to soup from the rain, and I knew that if I skidded I'd be off the road. My hands were around the steering wheel as if I was trying to choke it to death. Relax, I thought, you've driven in these floods before. But I wasn't relaxing; that uncomfortable feeling was gnawing away.

You see, if I skidded off the road, and had to get a tow truck or a car with a winch to get me back on, and word got around, Mary would want to know what I was doing up there. Well, I'd probably be able to figure it. I was delivering paint. That's what I was doing. Still, I couldn't afford any more quizzes; I didn't want more quizzes. I didn't want any more lies, either.

But I didn't skid, because I don't skid on any kind of road, and I turned right on the highway, and crawled along the highway to Sand Street and Kimball's. It wasn't quite three o'clock. There was some mail under the door that I rerouted up to Sacramento, to the hotel they would be staying at for the next week. Then I frowned. The damn rain was going to slow them up. They could have used a couple of hours' start yesterday, to get them even farther than Santa Barbara. Now they'd be stuck there for a day, at least. Kimball wasn't the kind of guy to drive in a flood, and, as a matter of fact, I wouldn't be surprised if they closed the road, what with the water pouring down the sides of the hills and swamping the highways. Up around Santa Barbara the Coast Range presses down close to the ocean, and every year pieces of the road get washed out. This was the kind of rain—if it extended that far north—that would wash out the road.

I turned on Kimball's radio in the back room, and all the local stations were talking about the storm. It was something like five inches in L.A., and over three in San Diego. But the important thing was that it was four-plus inches in Frisco. It was raining all along the coast. The Kimballs were stuck. The radio said there was no letup in sight, which didn't mean a thing because yesterday the papers and the radio had said today was going to be fair and warm, and in L.A. they had said it would be smog-green, which means no eye irritation, clear high weather, and you can burn your rubbish.

I said to myself, in the back room of Kimball's, "They'd better be wrong," and I guess I meant the weathermen.

Nobody came in, and I finally shut up shop at quarter to five. It was night-dark in Laredo, for fog lights or high-beam, the rain like silver spears. The curbs on Sand Street were hidden, and all through the shopping area you could hear running water, which meant the canyons were streaming. Next week the whole town would be up in arms for flood control and for a dam system some place in the eastern hills, but of course it would be too late by then, and the warm dry season would be on us, and everybody would forget the big rain and start worrying about the farmers.

I drove slowly along the Coast Highway, hanging onto the middle of the road because it was higher. I found the canyon turnoff by hit-and-miss, stopping every so often, hoping the jerk behind me wouldn't plow into me while I was staring into the dark for a landmark—the big Ford agency or the supermart or the cheap two-buck-a-night hotel.

I made the turn and crawled up the canyon, glad to be going uphill because I was in first, and the car felt heavy and solid beneath me, gripping the slick asphalt and then making the last jag-off turn onto our dirt street, the wheels churning mud and finally finding purchase.

I had left Kimball's at quarter to five; it was quarter past when I backed the car into the carport; the three-minute ride had taken thirty. I looked around and saw that I had left a sack of ready-mix cement on the floor of the carport. I picked it up and put it on a wooden shelf in the rear. The carport floor was wet, but it wasn't so bad. And the rain was definitely slowing down. It might last out the night, but it didn't look as if it had enough in it to go far into the next day.

The Kimballs could still hit Sacramento some time tomorrow, provided, that is, that the roads would be usable.

I trotted from the carport to the front steps—the back steps are wood and slick as grease when they're wet—and I pounded on the door. Mary answered, white-faced, and I felt sorry for her, up here all by herself without a car, without anybody, the rain probably driving her nuts after a while.

I said, through the closed door and above the wind and the rain, "Give me a big towel," and she nodded and disappeared. She came back with an old towel and a couple of sections of last Sunday's L.A. Times, and she opened the door. I stepped onto the paper and dried myself and patted my clothes and then I took off my shoes and socks and left them by the door.

"It's a river," I said.

She nodded, still white-faced and frightened. She said, "I was worried for you, hon."

I looked at her and wanted to hug her or kiss her, but it was pretty hard, remembering the business with Millie Weylin this afternoon, so I just grinned and said, "Nothing to worry about." Then I looked around. "Where's the kid?" I said sharply.

"Oh, he called me up after school. He's staying the night with Tubby. Tubby lives near the school, and I said it would be all right."

It was. It was smart. The school bus would have had trouble making the canyon hill; it would probably have been forced to let the kids out a quarter of a mile further down the canyon, at the fork, nearer town, where the bus would have room to turn around. Matt would have been half drowned, walking up here.

But Tubby. Tubby was a slob. Tubby was on Matt's list. Tubby had made Matt sore.

Still, that sort of shows you. Kids are like that. They think the world is coming to an end, and then they're back at the same old stand a few minutes later.

I said lightly, "Did you speak to Tubby or to his folks, Mary?"

She cocked her head. "Why, no. I—I didn't think of it. Why?"

The boy had—infrequently—spent the night at a friend's. We would say okay, and that would be that. Mary used to say, "Let the boy alone. Don't pamper him. It's a big deal for a boy his age to sleep away from home. He wants to be on his own. Let him." I did as she said because she was right, and frankly I sure as hell wasn't going to pamper him at any time.

But this time. I shrugged. "No reason. Oh, you know. The boy's got no pajamas with him, and that sort of stuff."

"Well," Mary said thoughtfully, "I could call now. I guess I figured with two boys the same age there wouldn't be any trouble. But they're different sizes. I guess I should call."

I told you how Matt came home late the other night and had us worried. Nothing serious; because he'd done it before, and we don't believe in drawing a line for the kid to follow every minute of the day. It's Mary's theory that the boy should have freedom to come and go, just the way she and I had. It was understood he'd be home for supper, and if he weren't going to make it, he was supposed to call. That's why the other night we were a little worried. He hadn't called, and Mary had supper ready.

But this time he had called—

I said, "Where'd he call from, hon?"

"From school, I think at least that's what I thought. It sounded like a bunch of kids."

"Well, everything's all right, then. If anything had happened, Tubby's folks would have called us. What's Tubby's last name?"

She frowned "Well, I'll be darned. I don't know. He told me the other day, but—Tubby. I don't even know his real first name." She giggled, a little worried, and a little ashamed of herself.

"So that's that," I said. It wasn't, but I was going to let it ride. I could have called around until I had found Tubby's last name. He played on the Laredo Savings, and somebody in Little League would know, or somebody from the bank. Anderson, at Carlstrom's, was the assistant manager of one of the teams, and he'd have known. Matt's teacher probably knew Tubby. I could have called her at home.

But I didn't see the sense in it.

Because—suppose Matt was lying? Suppose he wasn't at Tubby's? We'd have ourselves another scene, like last night's. I wasn't up to anything like that.

I said, "Well, what's the supper situation, hon?"

And Mary and I went into the kitchen and we listened to the rain on the roof while Mary patted some hamburgers into shape, and shoved potatoes into the oven and whipped up a salad. Then we went back into the living room while the potatoes baked and we sat on the couch, listening to the rain.

It lasted about ten minutes, quiet, like that, and then Mary got up and said, "Excuse me, Ed." She went into the hall and I heard her turning the pages of the phone book. Then she picked up the phone, and I waited for her to dial.

But there wasn't any dialing.

She said "Oh, damn. Ed, come here a minute."

I walked into the hall, and she handed me the phone. It was dead.

I depressed the little buttons and dialed Operator. It was still dead. I jig-gled the buttons but there was no answering squawk. It was just dead. The wires were probably down. It was just a question of how long it would take the repair crew to find and fix the trouble.

In a way, I was glad. It took the responsibility off my shoulders.

Mary said, in the hall, her voice bright and a big smile on her face, "Well, that's that, I guess."

"Yeah," I said. "Nothing we can do about it."

"You couldn't go out in weather like *that*," she said, shaking her head.

"Sure as hell couldn't," I said.

"And even if you did," she said. "What good would *that* do?"

"Not a bit of good."

"Of course," she said slowly, walking ahead of me back to the living room, "if it weren't raining so hard, and if the road weren't so terrible, you could just drive over to—well, to anybody's house here on the hill and ask to use the phone." Then she added sharply, "But that's out, of course."

"Honey," I said softly, "I'll go if you want me to."

"Nonsense," she said. "There's nothing to gain by it. The boy's certainly all right. Otherwise we'd have heard. Isn't that what you always tell me? And anyway, the lines are probably down all over the canyon, so what good would it do, using somebody's phone up here?"

"I could try."

She turned to me, in the living room, and I swear her smile wasn't forced, her brightness wasn't phony. "I don't want you to, honey," she said simply. "I want you to stay here with me."

"You could drive with me. You wouldn't drown."

So you see, I tried. I didn't let it lie there, even though the wires were down and the responsibility wasn't mine any more. I asked her, I answered every one of her arguments. I knew it was crazy to drive in that rain—though it wasn't raining as hard as it had been at noon, when I drove up a strange road to visit Millie Weylin—I didn't think we'd be able to prove anything, even if Matt weren't at Tubby's, wherever in hell *that* was. All we'd do would be to make misery for ourselves. But still, I tried.

Mary just shook her head slowly, looking up at me with a soft sort of wist-ful look on her face, under a strain, not liking the rain, not liking having been by herself all afternoon, not liking the situation now with Matt not home. She looked as if she was waiting for something—for me to do something, but I did-n't know what she wanted. What could I do?

So we sat and listened to the rain, and I think if the potatoes hadn't started to smell charred finally, we'd have sat that way until it was time to go to bed. But the potatoes smelled charred, and we ran into the kitchen and fussed around, and I scraped the charred portions of the skin, and we broiled the hamburgers and ate, and with supper, the hobgoblins just disappeared.

Mary said, over salad, "Are you going down to the shop tomorrow?"

I frowned. "Well, maybe. Depends on the weather." We listened for a moment. It was definitely down to a slow drip. "I think so. We didn't take in beans to-day."

"I hope the Kimballs missed most of this rain."

"Me too," I said, knowing they hadn't.

"It must be nice," she said, "just taking off like that, driving halfway up the state, and then drifting for a couple of weeks."

They were going through Yosemite, and then down to Sequoia, and maybe even as far down as Joshua National. If they missed the deal at Sacramento, they'd sure as hell need that vacation.

"We'll do it some day, hon," I said. "Don't worry."

She laughed. "I'm not worrying. I know we will. My, you are the mother hen tonight, aren't you?" She laughed again, delightedly. "If I didn't know you better, I'd think you'd been cheating around and your conscience was making you extra nice to me." She laughed some more, and I laughed, too, right through the rising flush that spread to my ears.

She knew.

Oh, she didn't really know, but she smelled something.

I said, finally, "I thought I was always nice to you."

She nodded quickly, too quickly, up and down, very hard and fast. "Oh, you are. But tonight it's extra special."

I said, "The rain. You being here alone all day. And—" And that was all I could add. She knew, and I was on her hook but she wasn't twisting it or anything.

And it makes you wonder. What kind of dame is this? She smells out her husband's dirty underdrawers and she just takes it. She doesn't rub my face in it, she doesn't badger me or anything. Didn't she even care?

I told you about Mary, how the first time she ever saw me, she didn't wince at the sight of my jaw, and she didn't get slobbering sorry for me.

I said to her, "I'm tired, hon."

"Go to bed," she said quickly. "I'll sit up a while. I'll—read a little, I guess."

So you see, she did care. That was her way. I'd go to bed, and she'd stay up, and she wouldn't have to lie down next to me, the two of us awake and maybe me touching her, reaching for her with the same hand that had— Well. You see it.

I said, "G'night, hon. Don't stay up too late."

She shook her head and that goddam bright smile was there, letting me know how sick I made her, and she said, "I won't."

Just long enough for me to start to snore. Then she'd creep in the other side of the bed and lie on her side, facing out, her back to me, as far away as she could get.

To hell with it. It wasn't my fault. This is the way it was, and the way it was just had to be. I lost my job because four sailor boys got creamed and I hit the old geezer and went to the station and saw how Otto Weylin, drunk, had been picked up for molesting a fifteen-year-old dame. I put the screws on him, and he was kicking in, but it wasn't hurting him a goddam bit, entertaining my boy just to let me know it wasn't bothering him, letting me know what a heel I was compared to him.

Well, I'd showed him. Ask his wife.

And now the rain, making everything so queer, so isolated, the phone dead, and us up here on our slope, nobody within a quarter of a mile, the roads black rivers.

It wasn't my fault, none of it. I was trying, wasn't I?

I was awake when Mary got into bed. She sat on the edge of the bed in the dark, and then she sighed once and got in facing me, and I kept right on breathing long and slow and even, faking it and fooling her, and she crawled right on up to me and sighed again as if she was breaking in half, and then she put her arms around me and laid her cheek against my jaw, and I could feel the tears running down my chest.

The rain stopped in the middle on the night, and I woke as if somebody had screamed. I remember when I shipped back from the Marshalls on a hospital ship, halfway between Hawaii and Frisco the boat stopped in the middle of the night.

We woke up, from the noise of silence. It was ghastly. Guys who didn't have any legs started to get out of their hospital beds, crying, pleading for the goddam boat to start again; guys with their eyes bandaged so that they couldn't see groped in the corridors; everybody was screaming, and a doctor finally grabbing me in the hall and saying, "Hawkins, Hawkins, you're a hero, boy, you held together your platoon until it got all shot up and you carried boys back who couldn't walk and now you're yelling like the rest of them. Come out of it, boy. Help us."

So I was a hero. A guy gets rapped in the jaw, he's a hero. He doesn't remember what's happening except that his platoon was all shot up and three platoon leaders, one right after the other, kept trying to charge a pillbox and getting reamed, everybody getting reamed with them, and me finally taking over, and leading them back, as many as I could find, one by one, off the line because what was the use, it was getting dark and we'd have to dig in soon anyway, so I led them back and dug holes for them and I was digging a hole, finally, for myself, when I got rapped.

But that was nothing compared to the ship's motors breaking down in the middle of the ocean in the middle of the night.

I snarled at the doctor and I said, "Leave me alone. It's not my fault."

But somehow I followed him, and I went back and I led some of the other guys back, and we all stopped yelling, and the motors started up again in an hour or so.

Now it was like that. Nobody screaming, but dead silence.

Then I laughed out loud. It was just that the rain had stopped.

I looked at Mary, but she was curled up, dead to the world. I disentangled myself carefully, and went into the hall and I picked up the phone. There was the reassuring answering buzz. The repair crews had patched the lines. I hung up and went into the kitchen and turned on the light and looked at the wall clock. It was twenty-five to four. I went to the icebox and took out a can of beer and plugged it and drank it slowly, sitting at the kitchen table, nothing on but undershorts because that was a GI habit and I never went back to wearing pajamas.

When I finished the beer, I put the can on the sink top and grabbed the big towel from the kitchen drying line and went to the front door. There wasn't much I could do at this hour and with Mary asleep.... I wouldn't go anyplace, not with Mary asleep, because that would be raw hell on her, in case she woke.

But I could see whether I could go any place if I had to. I opened the door and stepped onto the porch, in bare feet. It was cold and wet on the porch. I turned on the porch light and went down the brick steps—colder and wetter—and onto the dirt road in front of the house, a thick ugly yellow ooze. I dug my foot into it and found bottom about four inches down. It was driveable. The turn at the corner would be bad, but if I made that, I'd be on asphalt the rest of the way down the canyon. That would be the trick.

I went back up the steps and reached to turn off the porch light and go on in the house, when I saw it.

It was the edge of a white envelope, sticking under the door, and shoved into the hall.

I must have missed it going out, but there it was, shoved under the front door and lying on the cheap carpet that we'd cut up ourselves, Mary and me, and laid so it looked like wall-to-wall. Still, it looked pretty good, and people would compliment us on the way we laid it. Why, we laid the rugs in all the rooms. The one in the living room was real tricky because it's a big room, and one piece didn't quite make it, so we had to buy two pieces of carpeting and tack them together near one wall. Then we fixed the furniture so most of it ran along that wall, and you can hardly tell where the two pieces joined.

I went back into the kitchen, holding the envelope, and I dried myself and then I got paper toweling and dried the wet spots on the linoleum where I'd dripped pretty bad, and I took off my undershorts and went into the bathroom and threw them into the hamper. Then I got a fresh pair from the bedroom—mostly to see whether Mary was stirring. She wasn't. I went back and took another can of beer out of the icebox and opened it and started to drink it.

I opened the envelope, sitting there at the kitchen table, and a slip of paper fell out, a thin snipping of yellow paper.

It was a break, of course, that I had found the envelope, and not Mary. It wasn't fair that Mary had to be involved. It wasn't her fault at all. Not that she'd have been likely to understand what was on the paper or what it meant. What it meant to *me*, that is.

I don't know how Weylin had gotten that yellow snipping of paper, but I guess a guy like that can pull off most anything. After all, it didn't mean a damn thing to the Laredo police department. They had seen it and probably they had a record of it in their files, so the piece of paper was useless to them. And even if they wanted it, I guess a guy like Weylin could get it if he wanted it enough.

It was the message I had seen over Sergeant Sakimoto's shoulder in the police station house that day.

There was the same code—letters and numbers—which didn't mean anything to me and after that came the meat of the message: "Otto Weylin picked up drunk susp molesting a minor, fifteen years old. Don Farland."

A boy.

And now my son Matt was spending the night, someplace, with Otto Weylin....

I went to the hall and quietly I dialed Weylin's home. The phone rang and rang, but nobody answered. I didn't think he was home, but I didn't know. It seemed more likely they'd gone off—he and Matt—in Weylin's Caddy, to a hotel room or something like that. A man and his son, that's what it would look like. I knew different.

I knew different now, and I guess I knew different then. I think I had known a long time back that it had been a boy Weylin had been messing around with, and not a girl. I don't know when. But I knew, because though I was shocked when I saw the yellow slip of paper, curling up like party confetti, it wasn't as though I were knocked off my seat. I was shocked that Weylin could pull this thing off, shocked that *he* was blackmailing *me*.

You see what he had done. He was blackmailing me. Ain't it a howl? Ain't it a laugh? He was saying, with a sneer that must have made my own stitched-up sneer look like an angel's smile, "All right, scream. Go to the cops. Yeah, go to the cops. Tell them that Otto Weylin, queer son of a bitch, had gone off with ten-year-old Matthew Hawkins, for a night alone together."

Blow the whistle on him. Sure, that's what he was saying, laughing like a herd of hyenas, laughing, till he burst, laughing because he knew damn well

I couldn't.

Could you?

Could you let it be known that your son was in the company of a queer for a night or two or three? Could you smear your boy for the rest of his life— I almost said the rest of his natural life—could you smear him so he'd soon be known as the town fruit, the little boy who took on older men. Could you? Of course you couldn't.

Weylin knew I couldn't.

That was all there was in the envelope. There didn't have to be anything else. Weylin had sent it, I knew damn well, and he was telling me what he wanted. He wanted me off his neck. He wanted me to shut up anybody else I might have told about Weylin's arrest.

And when you get down to it, he wasn't really asking for much. All I had to say was, "Okay," and hand him back his claim to ten thousand dollars.

Ten thousand dollars for a ten-year-old boy.

Sure it's bad enough if Weylin had got drunk and fingered some cute little teen-age dame. Sure, he was a married man, respectable, a big shot in politics, in the community—so it was wrong, dead wrong. But this was so much worse.

That was why the police message had read: "Doubt family press chg."

That was a fifteen-year-old boy, and the cops doubted the boy's family would try to tie a can to Weylin's tail. How could they without involving the boy?

That was a fifteen-year-old boy, and maybe it wasn't the first time. Maybe the boy *was* the town fruit; maybe he did take the older men and bigger boys into the alley.

My boy was ten years old. He was a kid, a little boy, mind you. A nice little kid with soft dreamy eyes, and floppy hair and a quiet way about him. He wasn't the kind of boy to make trouble, not the kind of boy to set the world on fire the way other boys his age might try—no real skill, no real sport, nothing except maybe he could read better than most kids in his class.

Could I blow the whistle on Weylin—and on Matt? That's why it was so easy for Weylin to ask me for his ten grand back. That's why he was letting me see the whole message.

I took the little slip of paper and held it over the pilot light. When the flame neared my fingers, I crossed the kitchen and dropped the paper in the sink. Then I took the drain out of the sink and washed the ash down the pipe.

Then—and you'll have to take this and not ask questions because I don't know the answer—I went inside to the bedroom and got my wallet and removed Weylin's hundred dollars. I walked back to the kitchen and took each bill, and I burned it, the whole bundle, the whole hundred dollars. And I washed the ashes down the drain.

I went to bed.

CHAPTER NINE

Mary was still in a ball, and I lay on my back, hands folded behind my head, and I started to think.

Otto Weylin had driven his car up this road this very night, while we were asleep. Or else—and this seemed more likely—he had stopped, and thrown the car into gear on the hill, jammed on the emergency, and walked from the asphalt to the dirt road and the couple of hundred yards to our house. He'd get wet; probably he was wet already, but that way nobody would hear him in the rain and wind and nobody would see his car lights pouring into our living-room window. And he wouldn't be taking any chances on a strange, slick road. He must have slipped the envelope under the door and turned around and walked back to the car.

And what about the boy? He probably wasn't too scared at that. He thought Weylin was swell; he was ready to risk a trip down the canyon slope the other night or down to the fork and up Weylin's side, just to see the guy. So being with Weylin—and I know I'm skirting the words, I'm not quite saying the real words, because even just thinking them made my stomach roll—being with Weylin was all right, so far as the boy was concerned. No, he wasn't too scared. Maybe Weylin had told him he'd called us and we said it was all right; or maybe he told the boy that the telephone lines were down, so they'd make the best of it, he and Matt, a couple of men. Then they'd gone off.

They weren't at Weylin's, that was sure. He wasn't that dumb, staying over there where I could find him—them—in a minute's time.

Just Millie Weylin was home, the kind of dame who slept through a telephone ringing at night, probably the kind of dame who took sleeping pills that would knock her blotto.

For a brief moment, panic flared. I was scared gutless. I didn't know where to turn, and for half a second I wanted to shake Mary awake and say, "Listen, kid, Otto Weylin's got Matt, and he's a queer."

I didn't, though, because I knew exactly what Mary would do. She'd call the cops and ring the bell on Weylin. She'd tell the cops exactly what was what, because there'd be only one thing in her mind.

She'd want Matt back home.

That was all she'd think of, and I couldn't afford—for Matt—that kind of thinking. Sure, the cops would toss Weylin into the jug and seal him up for twenty years, and when he got out—if he ever got out—they'd put a tail so close behind him he'd smell cops the rest of his life.

But Matt, he wouldn't go up for twenty years. He'd be down, for life. Maybe the cops would try to hush up the case, keep the kid's name out of the headlines—*doubt family press chg*—but it could leak.

And what do you do, then? You take the kid, and you run to another town as if you were the criminals, not Weylin. You'd be on the run, and all the time, no matter where you'd go, there'd always be the chance that some wise-aleck biddy or some loudmouth cop or somebody would find out.

Everybody knows the treatment sissy boys get. The rest of the gang waves limp wrists at him, yoo-hoos him and the rest of the act. And there's always some joker who plays it straight and makes a practice of eating up sissy boys. So that was out. I wasn't going to let Matt in for that sort of treatment.

It was going to be hell today. Mary was going to go crazy with worry, and it wouldn't be her fault at all. I'd know the score, but she wouldn't, and she'd have to go along not knowing.

I fell asleep.

Saturday.

I woke at eight o'clock, and the sun was sticking a fat yellow head through the gloom. I shook Mary and said, "All right, hon, grab your socks," and she opened her eyes, scared again, but she smiled and stretched and rolled out her side.

Then she remembered, and her chin quivered. She said, "Ed, try the phone."

I walked to the phone, and, of course, I got a dial tone. I grinned at her—it was going to pile on, beginning right now, and I only hoped she wouldn't crack, and when it was over she wouldn't hate me—and I poked the receiver at her. She heard it and nodded her head vigorously.

"Call Tubby," she said.

I grinned again. "We don't know his number, hon."

"Yes, we do," she said. "I remembered his last name. It's McVeigh. There's only one in the phone book. I looked it up last night."

I froze. She had looked it up last night, and got a dead phone. She could have found out last night, except for the dead phone. The sweat was running down my chest.

I reached for the phone book and found the name and dialed it. It rang twice and a woman answered.

I said, "Mrs. McVeigh?"

"Yes?"

"This is—Ed Hawkins. Matt's father."

"Yes?" she said.

"Is—my boy there? Did he spend the night with you folks, with Tubby?"

"Why—no."

"Is—Tubby there? May I speak with him?"

I shook my head at Mary and made a face. She just stood there, leaning back a little, touching the wall, her face white. I could hear Mrs. McVeigh calling, "Theodore, Theodore," and I finally knew Tubby's first name.

The boy answered, his voice weak and wary.

I said, "Tubby—Ted—did Matt mention to you that he wanted to spend the night with you, because he couldn't get home?"

"No, sir."

"You're sure, now?"

"Yes, sir. I'm sure. He didn't. He took the bus and went—"

"*What?*"

"He took—the bus, sir." The boy's voice was wobbly. I was scaring him. "The bus was going up the canyon road to the fork, I guess, and that's where they would have to get out, anybody who lived up there. That's what I heard."

I said "Thanks, Ted," and I hung up.

I told Mary.

She put her knuckles to her mouth and she said, "He started up the hill and fell someplace."

I nodded, my face a mask of pain.

"Oh, Ed," she said, way up high, screaming, sort of, "what will we do?"

"Look for him, I guess," I said. "It shouldn't be hard. It's stopped raining, and there's not too many places he could have fallen."

And then she *did* scream. "He's dead!" she screamed, and I had to hold my heart—that's right it jumped right up through my chest and I grabbed it someplace in my throat—and I almost said, "No he's not, Mary. He's with Otto Weylin."

It would have made Mary feel better—what was worse, a son in trouble or a dead son? The two of us could handle it from there, doing what we'd have to—calling in the cops.

But that's what I was hanging on to, not my heart, but my words, my tongue. I wasn't going to say it. Not yet.

I did say, "No, hon, he's not. He—couldn't be. It's not that dangerous. There're no steep dropoffs or anything. Worst comes to worst, he's twisted his ankle. That's all."

She stared at me, white and trembling. And somehow what I said took root, and she came from the wall.

She said, "Call the police, Ed."

"All right," I said, and I phoned.

It wasn't easy, picking up the phone and calling the cops. I knew what I was doing, bringing them down on me and Mary. I had started this thing, and it was snowballing, and I was scared. But I had to keep at it. In the beginning, it was just a little racket, and it was smooth as Old Grandad. But now I was dragging in the cops—me, the guy who had busted the law, who had walked across the line; me, the criminal.

I had to do it. Hell, I'd had problems before. So the cops would come on up. They'd look all over this damn place, picking up every wet rock. But Matt wasn't here. Matt was with Otto Weylin.

It was a wild-goose chase. I picked up the phone and told myself it was just a wild-goose chase, and then I shook off the fear that came walking up my spine like a tarantula—the fear of getting caught, the fear-shame-guilt feeling I'd had from the first minute. I shook off the fear and I thought, To hell with it, I can get away with it. I've got to get away with it.

The voice was deep and pleasant. "Police department," he said. "Sergeant Sakimoto," and I said, "Ed Hawkins, Sergeant. I want to report—my boy Matt is missing."

"Missing?"

"He didn't come home last night."

At first it seemed as if he was going to laugh quietly and say something reassuring, and then I guess he remembered last night, and the rain. He said, "Well, that's—out all night? What's the boy's name? When was the last time you saw him?"

I told him, and I told him how he'd called, and how he said he was going to spend the night with a friend, but he hadn't—he must have changed his mind—that's what I told him, but I knew that Matt was just trying to fool me, he'd never intended to spend the night with Tubby—and had taken the bus instead.

"The school bus?"

"Right."

"How far is your place from the bus stop?"

"Six or eight city blocks. Maybe even half a mile."

"You up at the end of the canyon?"

"That's right." I gave him the address and he grunted and said he'd check the bus driver and if the bus driver didn't remember letting the boy off, he'd check the other boys on the bus, other boys who lived up the canyon and who might have got off at the same stop.

"What's the name of the friend he was supposed to stay with?"

"Theodore McVeigh."

"Is that Tubby McVeigh?"

"Yes."

"You've checked him?"

"Yes."

"I'll check him. Is he the one who told you your boy took the bus?"

"Yes."

"Did Tubby see Matt get on the bus?"

I stopped. Tubby said Matt took the bus. But did that mean he saw Matt get on? I couldn't imagine that unless it just happened that he was there when Matt actually piled on. Tubby must have lit off for home, or hopped into his folks' car. He wasn't going to stand around in the rain, watching.

"I don't know."

Sakimoto grunted. He said, "I'll check the boy. I'll call you back as soon as I've checked that either he did or didn't take the bus, and whether he got off where he was supposed to. Meanwhile, I'll send a man up. You'll want somebody up around the house. For the wife, I mean. That'll make it possible for you to start looking. Then I'll come up myself."

I stared into the phone. The guy was straight. He was a cop, and he was thinking Mary—he didn't even know her—would be worried stiff, so he'd send company up. And I'd been in bed with another man's wife yesterday afternoon while Mary gnawed her knuckles alone on the hill.

I said, "Thanks, Sergeant. Anything else?"

"Your phone number," he said.

I gave it to him, and hung up.

I told Mary and she grabbed me and hugged me and said, her voice muffled, "Go, Ed. Go on and look. I can wait here." But she was hanging on tight while she said it, and she didn't let go when she finished.

So I led her away from the hall, and we sat on the couch, her hanging on, and she just cried and cried, while I stroked her head and the back of her neck, her lying with her head on my lap. I said, "Hush, honey, don't worry. It will be all right. Don't worry, hon," stroking her gently, loving her so much I thought I'd burst, and pretty soon she quieted down, and then the phone rang.

It was Sakimoto.

"The bus driver—his name's Jerry Cash—says he remembers letting the boy out at the fork. Do you know what fork he means?"

"Yes."

"He remembers dropping your boy and two others. Usually he has eight or nine on that canyon run, but this time most of the boys had lifts or else did stay over with some boys, nearer school."

"He remembers?"

"That's right. I made sure. There's no doubt. Your boy got off the bus at the fork. He places the time at about three-thirty. The boy's someplace in the canyon. Is Larabie there?"

"Larabie?" I said stupidly.

"Larabie," Sakimoto said sharply. "My prowl car cop. I sent him over."

"No, not yet," I said. "The roads—Sergeant, he's got to take it easy."

"Easy?" Sakimoto said—roared, I guess. "Take it easy? For God's sake, man, your boy's lying in some goddam hole out there, in some goddam hole of water, freezing half to death, and—"

"Here he comes now," I said dully. I heard a car on the dirt road, and I saw the big globe on the top, over the windshield.

Sakimoto snorted. "About time. I'll be over myself as soon as I can make it. Begin at the bottom and work your way up."

"All right," I said.

He didn't tell me why and I didn't tell him I knew why, and he hung up.
Bodies, when they fall, fall down. It didn't matter if he'd got halfway up and
then slipped off the side of the road. If he just landed on the shoulder or in a
little draw just off the road, he wouldn't be hurt bad; he'd probably just crawl
out and keep going. But since he hadn't, Sakimoto figured, he'd fallen farther
down than that.

The cop came in, in heavy boots and a poncho. He said, "I'm Jed Larabie," and I said, "Ed Hawkins," and we shook hands. "This is my wife, Mary,"
I said, and Mary nodded.

Larabie was a big-faced paunchy man, even without the poncho, maybe
a shade too genial for me, but I guess Sakimoto picked him out just because
of that. He said, "You go on out, Hawkins. I'll wait here and take care of the
phone in case Saki calls in."

Mary said, "Why don't the three of us go looking?"

Larabie shot me a look and then he shook his head. "No, ma'am. Saki told
me to see to it you stayed here."

They didn't want Mary finding the boy's body.

I said, "I'll make better time myself, hon. It's pretty slick out there. You
stay here." I smiled thinly at her and chucked her under the chin and started
for the door.

Larabie said, "Don't you think you'd better get dressed?" and I looked
down at myself. I was in my drawers, nothing else. We all started to smile and
then Mary giggled way up high and I ran into the bedroom and tossed on some
clothes, heavy-duty shoes but no raincoat or poncho like Larabie's. I didn't
want to be all sweated up in ten minutes. I didn't want to be saddled up like
an ox, either, unable to move fast.

I walked down to the end of the dirt road, and I saw that the tracks of
Larabie's prowl car were already just about washed out by the water running
down the road. So there was no use looking for Weylin's tracks.

I wound down the road, slipping and sliding but not falling, and I remembered the boy walking across the valley the other day, the first day we'd
ever gone to Weylin's lot to have a catch, and I remembered how easily the
boy had made the trip across, even though it was slick from our last rain a day
or two before. I knew that Matt wasn't the boy to fall on his face just because
the valley was a river. He'd have dug in and clung on and waded through,
and if he wanted to get to the top of the other side, he'd have got there. I remembered him walking back that afternoon, straight as an Indian, full of
spring and cat-quick—because Weylin had talked kindly to him, given him a
Coke, invited him up again, man to man.

So now, on his way to see this new friend, he wouldn't let a river of rain
worry him too much.

I got down to the fork in fifteen minutes, hurrying because I wanted this part of it over, so I could get down to the next part. To finding Weylin and Matt.

I stood at the fork and looked up to my right, to the winding hill that rose on the south edge of the slope, heading out east, and then I looked at the winding hill that rose on the north edge, our side, and worked its way east, also. The roads weren't very different—winding asphalt roads, soon out of sight, going in slightly different directions, ending up on different sides of the same valley, but more or less the same general area, the east or inland side of Laredo. I looked for footsteps on both roads and couldn't find any but my own, and I started up on our side, off the road, drenched right on up to my calves, eyes swinging left and right, working my way carefully.

The sun was pretty bright by now, and in places it was thick ooze, but most of it was just slick. The soil is thin out here, and it drinks up the rain until it fills, and then it lets the rest spill over. The rain yesterday and last night had saturated the soil practically immediately, and the rest ran off the top. Now the sun was sucking the water out and fog lay like steam over the canyon. The underfooting was thin mush, and below that was rock. It wasn't hard walking; it wasn't sinking-in kind of walking, just slippery.

So I combed pretty fast, coming up the winding hill, knocking on the door of one of the neighbors we had in this part of the canyon.

She was an old lady, Mrs. Willoughby, who lived alone on her widow's pension and old-age security, a pleasant white-haired old lady who hoed her weeds every summer and watered her front and backyards every evening.

She said, "Well, Mr. Hawkins, won't you come in?"

She smiled up at me, never even noticing that I was by now wet to the hips, my shoes caked with mud. She just opened her door, and I could see inside her little house, a faded loop rug on the floor of her living room, everything neat as a pin.

I said, "I'm sorry, Mrs. Willoughby, but I can't. My boy—have you seen Matt?"

She frowned slightly and smiled slightly. "No-o-o," she said, "I haven't. Should—should I tell him to go home in case I see him?"

I grinned thinly at that. "Well, yes," I said. "He's been gone since yesterday afternoon, since after school. He wasn't home last night."

She sort of fell forward and grabbed my wrist. I looked at her hand; it was like a claw, the fingers long and thin and hooked. She said, "You poor dear," and she let go.

Now, I don't think I've had twenty words with Mrs. Willoughby before in my life. I know who she is; she knows who I am. Or rather, I know her house and she knows ours. She probably doesn't even know what Matt looks like.

"Well," I said, "I'll keep checking around."

She stood in the doorway and she said, "Wait a minute," and she ran—yes, ran—inside and came out again in two minutes, a shawl around her head. She closed the door behind her.

I said, "Now, look here, Mrs. Willoughby. You can't—you're not going to—"

She said, "Let's go, Mr. Hawkins."

It was noon when we hit the top of the hill and turned right angles, to cover the portion of the canyon just off our dirt road.

It wasn't really necessary because Sakimoto was up there, and his cop, Larabie, beating the bushes. There was a whole crowd of people, maybe a couple of dozen, around the front of our house. I couldn't see Mary.

I walked over and Sakimoto said, "Well?"

I shook my head.

He said, "Where've you been?"

"I covered the whole slope, from the fork up, along this side—with Mrs. Willoughby."

Sakimoto nodded briefly to the woman. He said to me, "I've covered this area up here, all around the house and down the valley." He pointed in the direction Matt and I used to go to play ball on Weylin's lot. He said, "Of course, we have to go on up the other side of the slope, too. The boy might have got his signals crossed and got confused. He might have wandered off, you know."

I nodded very solemnly. I said, "Where's—how's Mary?"

He said, "She's all right. She's fine. She's inside, resting. She'll get by, that one." He stared into my face. "You all right?"

"Sure."

"I'm okay."

"You look like hell."

Now that was funny. I knew the boy wasn't down there, so it really wasn't bothering me. But where the boy really was was gnawing away.

"I'm all right."

He grunted. "You'd better be. It's going to get tougher. On your wife, I mean."

I waved my hand. "Who are all those people?"

He shrugged. "They just drove on up."

I had heard cars going by, one at a time, all during the time I was combing the slope. I figured they had been heading for the other roads up here.

I said evenly, "It seems to me you and Larabie ought to have been able to keep them away."

"What for?" he said.

"Bunch of nosy bastards."

"Is that the way you see them?"

"Why, yes," I said. "What else? Goddam vultures."

He shook his head. "They're trying to figure out the best way to comb the whole valley." He waved his hand to the east—toward that bare brown scar that cut a path along the valley floor and headed out toward the eastern ridgeline, fifteen miles away. "They've got maybe fifty square miles to cover, and they're trying to figure it. You call them vultures." He shook his head. I think if it weren't that he was sorry for me, the kid missing and all that, he'd have raked me up and down.

I said, "I'm sorry—I didn't know."

"Well," he said slowly, "when you don't know, don't jump."

I nodded. "You're right. What's next?"

He said, "The valley, I guess." He shook his head.

Another car drove up, and two people jumped out. I'd never seen them before. I pushed past Sakimoto and went up the steps and somebody said, "Tough luck, Ed," and I went inside.

Mary was in the kitchen, busily making two pots of coffee and some sandwiches. There was a pile of cardboard containers on the kitchen sink.

I said, "What the hell is this, Mary?"

She smiled. "I'm fixing coffee and sandwiches."

"Yeah," I said. "But what's the pitch?"

She said. "For the men who go down there." She kept that fixed bright smile on her face, but underneath the trembling had started. "They didn't know how long they'd be out there. So I thought it might help if they had hot coffee, and a sandwich in their pockets." She blinked away tears.

I walked outside. There were thirty people, at least, and Sakimoto was standing off with three of them. The three men had small packs on their backs and one of them was wearing an old leather skull cap with goggles, the kind Lindbergh wore. They had canteens at their hips. When Sakimoto saw me, he waved me over.

He said, "Hawkins, this is Luke Stoddard. He used to be on the force." I shook hands with a white-haired guy, very tall and very thin, but hard-looking. "Stoddard picks up a couple of bucks every so often bounty-hunting."

I looked at the man's feral face, the flat-eyed, hard look. A man who hunted down other men, for pay. I moved back a little, and Sakimoto said sharply, "What's the matter, Hawkins? You don't think it's Stoddard's right to find some escaped con who's maybe got a thirty-year rap on his head? You think a guy like that who'll kill the first damn fool who gets in his way has a right to roam around? Stoddard doesn't."

Stoddard moved his thin lips. His voice was surprisingly mild. "'Course," he said, "there's no pen out here, so there's little call in this neck of the woods. But up around the state pens and the fed pens, you'd be surprised how much they welcome guys like me and my nephews." I looked at the two young men with him, also tall and lean and fox-faced.

I nodded stiffly, but I didn't shake their hands. I still didn't like it.

Sakimoto said, "Stoddard and his boys will take off in advance of the rest of us and go straight east. They like to work by themselves. They'll not bother too much with anything this side of the draw. Out there—" Sakimoto pointed past the gravy-bowl lip of the canyon, past the thicket of pines, and to the unseen scrubland beyond— "they'll work it out by themselves. The rest of us will work up to the draw. Then—we'll see."

"When we going to start?" Stoddard said.

"Whenever you're ready."

One of the nephews said, "We're ready, aren't we?"

Stoddard nodded. "Any time, now."

Sakimoto said, "Take off, then. Good luck. When will you check in—if you don't find anything?"

Stoddard looked at the sky. "Let's see. This is Saturday noon. How's about Thursday?"

Sakimoto nodded. "Fine," he said. "Though I think we'll know by then."

Stoddard stared out at the fifteen-mile-long series of valleys and soft low hills, rising to the eastern ridge. "Can't say for sure. I've seen these things stretch out for two, three weeks. Can't tell with a boy. A girl, she'd be crying, all curled up someplace, waiting to be picked up. A boy, he's just as likely to keep right on walking to Nevada." He chuckled softly. Then he nodded to his nephews, and the three of them strode off and over the lip of the canyon tableland.

I said to Sakimoto, "I don't recognize them. What part of town do they live in?"

Sakimoto said, "They chartered a plane. They live in L.A. Used to live here in Laredo, fifteen years ago."

I said, "They chartered a plane? To come here? What for?"

"To help look for your boy."

"How—how did they know?"

Sakimoto's face hardened. "Every cop in California knows. Every headquarters. It'll be in every paper this afternoon; it's on the radio now. What do you think we do in the stationhonse, read Mickey Spillane all day and sit on our butts? Christ, man, if we can't handle this in a day or so ourselves, the FBI will come in. For all anybody knows—though I doubt it—your kid's been kidnapped."

I guess I gave a little jump at that.

Sakimoto took my arm. He was an inch or two shorter than me, and maybe ten pounds lighter. He had blue-black hair and a thin scar at his right eyebrow. He was the first Japanese—the first Japanese-American—ever hired by the Laredo force. He once got in a scrap with a patrolman here in town—the patrolman said that the next thing would be they'd hire a "nigger." Sakimoto took the cop outside and—in their uniforms—they had it out. Then they fired the patrolman, after he came to, and replaced him with a Negro. Now everybody took Sakimoto for granted. He said, "Hawkins, I don't know much about people, but I think you're pretty shot. I think you're close to shock. Otherwise—" He broke it off, a scowl on his face.

Otherwise he couldn't figure me. All I'd done was fight him, and the men who were out looking for Matt.

He said more softly, "Go inside for a couple of hours. It'll do you some good. Lie down. We can handle this. Your boy's out there and we'll find him. Don't worry." He squeezed my arm and walked away, and I could see him calling everybody over to the flat dead-end parking area just beyond the house, and soon they were standing there, looking down at the canyon bottom, breaking up into small groups, pointing, discussing how they were going to do it. Then they went down, and traipsing behind them were a couple of dames, each carrying a big paper sack. I figured that was Mary's sandwiches and coffee.

Now only Larabie was still up on the slope. He walked over to me and we watched the searching party fan out, some of them heading straight across the canyon toward Weylin's, most of them going down the slope to the valley floor, where they'd spread out and cover the whole valley, going east. Larabie said, "That's okay, Mr. Hawkins. You can join 'em if you want to. I'll cover it from this end."

I shook my head. Another one, wondering why the hell I didn't claw my way down the hill, turning over every blade of grass. I walked away from him and went back inside. Mary said, from a chair in the kitchen, looking out the window, "Oh, Ed, I'm—glad you're still here."

I went into the living room and sprawled out in the big easy chair. Weylin. I had to find the bastard. I had to find him fast. There were forty people, maybe more, down there, giving time and sweat for something that wasn't so. Maybe some of them had knocked off time from their work, which meant they were losing pay.

I started to jitter my right leg up and down. Mary came into the living room and she saw my right leg bouncing and she said, "Go inside and lie down, honey."

I shook my head. Weylin. What was he up to? What did he want? And where was he? I was starting to feel like Mary; maybe the only thing that mattered was getting Matthew back. We could face the rest, once he was back. Then I stopped bouncing my leg. No. That was the wrong way. I couldn't let myself think that way.

But those poor rah-rah bastards out there, up to their noses in mud.

Weylin—he was the ticket.

I won't stretch the day out any more than I can help it. It was bad, and it got worse. By three o'clock there were two hundred more people up there, walking, most of them, because it turned out that the town had posted cops at the canyon fork, sending cars back because there was no place to put them. Still, that didn't stop the people. They kept coming up, spilling over the hill.

One little old guy came up to me some time around two or two-thirty. He said, "Oh, Mr. Hawkins, you don't know how badly I feel about this."

I stared at the old geezer. There was something familiar about him. He was an old guy with plain steel-rimmed eye glasses; he was the old boy I had hit with Carlstrom's tow truck. He had a new pair of glasses.

He went on down the slope.

At five o'clock a new cop came up and relieved Larabie and gave me all the afternoon papers. The boy's picture was on all the front pages.

I said to the cop, Rostelli, "How did they get the picture?"

Rostelli said, "I think it's a school picture. Don't you recognize it?"

That's what it was. A blow-up of a school picture, taken when Matt's class put on a play. There had been a party in school, and a photographer had come around and taken pictures. Now there it was, for two or three million people to look at and file away, in case they saw a little boy wandering around the hills.

And that did it.

Two or three million people, from Frisco down to Dago, and most of the places in between—all of them would have seen Matt's picture. And for all I knew, Weylin had the boy in some hotel or motel or some place like that along the coast here, where the boy had to be seen.

I had to do something myself, and fast. It was boomeranging. The boy was going to be dug up, and in Weylin's company. I had to find him first.

Mary was shuffling about the house. The sun was coming in through the kitchen windows, long flat streams of sunshine. The day was shot. Pretty soon it was going to get chilly and dark. And when night closed down, wet and cold as it always closes down around Laredo this time of year, Mary was going to crack. Last night was one thing—hoping the boy was all right, at Tubby's house—but tonight would be different. The people down there, searching, would start to drift back, discouraged, packed in yellow-black mud, heads down, mumbling their failure. And then they'd go home, back to their families.

Except for guys like Stoddard and his nephews. Throwbacks, that's what they were. Mountain men. Indian scouts. Throwbacks. Or just guys who thought they might help, thought they were pretty good at this sort of thing, so they were volunteering.

But even if they could, there wouldn't be many. The rest would have gone home, to get warm and dry.

And Mary would crack. I had to do something before night, before she cracked.

I said, "Hon, I've got an idea."

She stood at the kitchen sink, washing a juice glass. It was crystal clean. She kept on washing it. She said, "Yes?"

"I've got a hunch. I've got—to go out."

"Don't go down there," Mary said.

"No, honey, I won't."

"I mean it."

She had lost her boy down there. *Down there* was starting to mean something awful to her.

"I do, too, hon. I'm not going down there. I've got a crazy feeling that he's not down there at all, that he's not in trouble like that at all."

She put the glass down. She said, "Where are you going?"

I started to wave my hand, and then I let it drop. "I can't—I don't want to talk about it. Let me try this. I'll either find the boy right away, or I'll be back before it's too dark. Just give me two or three hours."

She nodded dumbly. "Sure," she said. She didn't think I had an idea at all. She thought I was just jittery and had to get out and make a halfhearted stab.

I put my arms around her and pulled her away from the sink. I said into her soft blonde hair, "Don't worry, honey. I'm going out, and when I come back, he'll be with me. You've got to keep your chin up. We'll be back before you know it."

I felt her nod, her head rubbing against my jaw. "Just hurry."

I went out and to the carport. There were people outside in small clusters, looking down the slope. I saw Rostelli and called him over. I said, "Rostelli, watch my wife. When it gets dark she's going to be in trouble. Get what I mean?"

He smiled quickly. "Right, chief. I'll watch her. My wife—my wife said she'd come over later, anyway."

I got into the Chevy. Jesus, all of them. Not just Stoddard and his manhunters. All of them.

I drove slowly through the muck and down the canyon road until I got to the fork. I had to see Millie Weylin.

CHAPTER TEN

I left the Chevy in front. It didn't matter if anybody saw me now. I knocked on the door and heard soft quick noises inside. Then I heard footsteps, from a long way off, it seemed. Millie Weylin opened the door. She wore a robe. Her hair was a mess. She was sallow and her eyes were rimmed with lack of sleep. Her horse pills had worked, but only up to a certain time. She looked like hell.

She stood in the open doorway for a moment, eying me, and for a brief second triumph lit up her face, the pupils shining, ice-bright. I had come back—she figured—for more.

I said, "Can I come in?"

She shrugged with elaborate indifference. The robe fell from one shoulder. I glanced at it and away. "Sure," she said. "Any time."

I walked past her and into the living room, where I had sat with Otto Weylin and Matt a few days ago drinking Cokes and talking baseball and movies.

"Sit down," she said, pointing to the couch. She plunked down and waited for me to sit next to her, and I walked away and over to a big overstuffed chair.

I said, "You've heard about my boy?"

She shook her head, eyes wondering.

I told her that he was missing.

Her lip curled and she leaned back, enjoying herself. "That's too bad," she said. "My, isn't that awful. What did you expect, you stupid jerk. I told you you were losing that kid. So now he's run off." She rubbed her hands together as though she were delighted.

"Millie," I said, "where's your husband?"

Her eyes opened wide. "Why—I don't know, for sure. I told you the other day he comes and goes when he wants." She started to laugh a little.

"Millie," I said, "where is he?"

"I said I don't know," she snapped. "For God's sake, stop pushing me. I feel lousy enough without you throwing your bulk around. Go home, why don't you. Stop bothering me."

"When did you see him last?"

"Yesterday morning. Look. Can I have a drink? If you're going to ask your goddam questions, at least I want to have a drink. Am I allowed to get up and get a drink—or are you going to punch me again?"

I wasn't getting anywhere. "Sure," I said. "Where are the makings? I'll get it."

"No," she said. "I'll do it." She got up and shuffled off, to the kitchen, I guess, and I heard ice cubes spilling into the sink, and then something pour-ing from a bottle. It was a long pour.

She came back with two glasses.

"Rye," she said. "Is that all right?"

"Fine," I said, taking a glass from her. She looked down at me in the big chair, and I could see she was weighing the other approach again, trying to warm me up. But I wasn't having any. She said, "To hell with you, Hawkins," and took a long drink. Then she went back to the couch.

I said, "Didn't you expect him last night?"

She sighed and set the glass down. "Oh, God," she moaned. "On and on. Can't anything shut him up?"

I said, "Don't be so melodramatic. Didn't he call some time yesterday in all that rain to let you know when he was coming home?"

"Yes," she said. "He called. He called and said he'd be home around four or maybe a little earlier. Now. Are you satisfied?"

"He didn't show up?"

"No," she said, "he didn't show up. He said he was coming home, but he didn't show up." I swear she was close to tears.

"You call his office?"

She nodded. "At four-thirty. There was no answer."

So he had started up from the office, probably, and then he had changed his mind, or he had come up to the fork, and there was Matt, climbing up on his, Weylin's, side of the slope. And Weylin had given the kid a lift, and the kid had told him how he didn't want to go home or something, and Weylin figured the kid needed him, somehow, and he took him someplace.

She watched me, thinking it through, and she got it, finally. She said, slowly, "You mean—you think your boy's with Otto?"

I said harshly, "What's wrong with your husband?"

She shook her head. "Nothing, really. He—just likes children. We—he—can't have any kids, and he wants them so bad." She got up and walked past me and then turned. "So do I, God damn it. But we can't, and it's his fault. See?"

"So that's why he's like that, with kids?"

She nodded vigorously. "That's why. That's what's so awful about it. Otto really likes kids, he's crazy about kids. He's always having somebody's little boy or girl over, staying up here, playing tennis with them, or going to the beach with them, taking them to movies. Sometimes he takes them to a place he has—we have—a beach house. He's got it fixed up for kids. We used to live there, in the beginning, and he thought, I guess, that we'd have kids, but he couldn't. So we left that place and came up here. Still, he goes down there every so often. I guess if the divorce goes through I'll keep this place, and he'll take the beach house."

"What do you mean *if* it goes through?"

"He wants to reconcile." The lips curled into a cat's smile. She leaned back, mocking me, letting me know how she could dangle him on a line. He'd go off sometimes, but he always came back.

"Oh," I said. No wonder Tubby had those thoughts. They must have pawed each other that day, in front of the kids. Tubby was wiser than Matt in these things; Tubby would have known, but Matt would just have been disgusted. Matt was just a kid.

I said, "Where's this place he takes kids to?"

She looked at me, the lips curled into that cat's smile, her body leaning back against the bolsters, a tired-looking, unappealing woman, a nasty, hard woman. "Wouldn't you like to know?" she said.

I got up then. "Where?"

She patted the couch, next to her. "Come here," she, said.

I took a step toward her. "Where, God damn it, where?"

She shook her head, the smile even fuller, her mouth parting and the tip of her tongue touching her lips.

"Where?"

She kept her head moving, slowly, and her hand crept to the opening of her robe, at her chest.

"Look," I said. "Stop it. I've got to know and I've got to know fast. Just tell me where your beach house is. If you're trying to tell me that you won't let me know unless I lay you, I'll lay you, but I'll hate it. Tell me where the beach house is, or tell me I've got to lay you first and I'll get it over with and get out of here. Which will it be?"

Her mouth clamped shut and she said, "I hate you. I hate your guts."

I grinned. "I know. I think you're nice, too. Now, where's that beach house."

"I won't tell you."

I moved another step closer. Inside, I was trembling. The kind of trembling that rises up, finally, and spills over. She saw it, but she wasn't backing off, the way she was yesterday afternoon.

I said, "Tell me."

She laughed, then, in my face. "Make me," she said. I reached for her and dragged her from the couch. "Look," I said. "I swear I'll belt you silly. I've got to know. Where did your husband take Matt? Where is this beach house?"

She kept on laughing. I held her wrist tight, and I could see the skin puffing around my hand. She said, "Oh, you're so funny. You're actually trying to make it sound dirty, aren't you? You're trying to make it seem if Otto is— what you think he is. That's very funny." She went right on laughing.

"You know damn well that's what he is," I said. "You know, but you're afraid to admit it."

"No," she said quietly. "No. I don't know anything like that at all. How would I know anything like that? What do you think I am, a Peeping Tom? How would I know? Do you think he'd tell me things like that, even if they were true—which they're not? How would I know?" She frowned. "How do *you* know?"

I let go of her wrist. She was going to tell me. "I know," I said. "I just know. I know what he is. I know that he likes little boys, even better than he likes you. Where is that beach house?"

She turned away, huddled inside her robe. I had whipped her with my words. I had hurt her more this way than with my fists. "On Marguerite Street," she said, in a muffled voice.

"Where's Marguerite?"

"It's south of Laredo, between here and San Loma, about two miles down the highway. There's an underpass—"

"I know the underpass."

"It leads into Marguerite. Marguerite is the no-through street closest to the ocean. You can't miss the house. It's on the left, the ocean side, a little yellow house."

I said, "Thanks."

She turned back. "But you're wrong. He's—not what you think. That's not why he and Matt—spend so much time together."

"No?" I said. "Why, then?"

"Because Otto and I know that Matt can't stand you. We're sorry for the boy. Matt's scared of you, terrified of you. That's why he comes over here, to get away from you. That's why he sits on my lap, and Otto talks to him and—"

Sits on her lap. I remembered the boy's words: *Mrs. Weylin will be there. Mrs. Weylin will be there.* That's what he had said. Matt sensed that I didn't like Weylin, that I didn't want Matt to go over there to see Weylin alone. But Mrs. Weylin would be there, too. So there was nothing for me to worry about. He had seen how I had got along all right with Millie Weylin that day over at the lot. I wouldn't mind his being with Weylin, visiting him at night, *if Mrs. Weylin would be there, too.* Jesus, God, that's all the boy had meant. Nothing else.

And I had walloped him for it.

No wonder he was willing to go off with Otto Weylin, alone. He had been trying to please me by letting me know Mrs. Weylin would be there, too, and I had walloped him. So he'd see Weylin alone. He liked Weylin better than he did Millie, and he'd be seeing him alone, and it was my fault.

"—and Otto always takes to kids, so naturally he'd take to Matt, scared the way Matt was."

I said, "Yeah. That's how it must have been." All right, I'd play it her way. Maybe she didn't know. Maybe, as she said, she never played Peeping Tom. Maybe she smelled things, but she didn't know. She was his wife. She wasn't going to admit it, even if she did know. Hell, it wasn't likely she'd admit it even to herself; it was a blow to any woman, and especially to a woman like Millie Weylin. She thought she could dangle Otto Weylin, but sometimes he spent the night out, away from her. Sometimes with a kid, like Matt, for company. No, she wasn't going to admit it, even to herself.

"Don't think those things about Otto," she said.

"All right," I said.

She came up close to me. "And don't think wrong of me, either. You were the first, you know."

"Yeah," I said, walking to the door. "I bet." I walked out, slamming the door hard, but not fast enough to cut off her laugh.

Marguerite was a pleasant, twisting street, going downhill from the Coast Highway toward the ocean. It was as close to the ocean as you could get without fighting off sand flies.

I got out at the yellow house, small, with a light inside. I rapped on the door and pretty soon it opened.

Otto Weylin said, "Well, Hawkins. Come in."

I felt my fist draw back, slowly, almost mechanically. He said, "Don't." He looked down.

I looked down, too. He had a gun in his right hand, pointed at my belly.

CHAPTER ELEVEN

We walked inside, and he directed me to a rattan sofa. I sat, and he sat across in a sagging rattan chair, the gun in his right hand.

He looked gaunt, and very grim.

I said, "Where's Matt?"

"Inside," he said. "Asleep."

"In bed?" I asked harshly.

He nodded, a thin smile on his face. "Where else, Hawkins? On the floor? He's a tired boy."

"I want to see him."

He waved his head. I walked past Weylin, the gun following me, but I could see how it wavered, how Weylin himself was wavering. I could turn back suddenly, chop down with my left hand, knock the gun to the floor, cold-cock Weylin before he left his chair.

I thought of the boy.

I stepped into the hall and saw a door opposite the rear of the living room. It was slightly ajar and I pushed it open quietly. It was dark in there, the blinds closed, and only a thin orange light from the ocean's rim spilling inside. I could see pennants on the walls, pictures of ball players, tennis stars, fighters, golfers. The boy looked peaceful, and terribly young, more like a baby than a ten year old.

But just my breathing, my movement in the room made him stir. I watched him for half a minute or so, and then I went back to the living room.

"You can put that firecracker away," I said.

He looked at me and pocketed the gun.

I said, "All right, what's next?"

He looked surprised. "Take the boy home, I guess. But I wouldn't let him be too disturbed. I wouldn't make him answer too many questions. I—"

"No," I said, "I guess you wouldn't want him to answer too many questions."

He winced a little, deep in his chair. "He's tired, Hawkins, and I think he hurt his ankle walking up that road yesterday. He must have stumbled; it was awfully slick. He was two-thirds of the way up when I found him. He's been limping since."

Two-thirds of the way up. Nearly half a mile; no wonder he was all in.

"He goes home tonight," I said. Then I had another frightening thought. "Did you have a doctor in?"

Weylin shook his head. "It didn't appear serious. Besides, the phone was out."

That was good. I didn't want Weylin and Matt seen together, spending a night together in an out-of-the-way place like this.

I nodded, thinking, He's still my patsy. He's still my pigeon. The ten grand hadn't flown the coop. Then I looked out the window of the small living room, facing away from the ocean. Night had socked in. I said, "Is the phone working now?"

He nodded. "Off the kitchen." He pointed.

I walked to the phone and dialed our number. A man—Rostelli, the cop, I guess—answered.

I said, "Let me speak with Mary."

"Who is this?"

"Hawkins."

"Just a minute."

Mary came to the phone, a long minute later. She must have been lying down. "Yes, Ed?" she said, anxiety brimming over.

I said it quickly. It had to be done well, with no room for questions. Ten grand, I was thinking; it's still there in neat piles of a hundred bucks each. "He's all right, Mary. I've got him and he's fine. We'll be home pretty soon."

"Where—where are you?"

That one was out. That was the one I couldn't answer, not with the ten gees lying there, begging to be picked up. "No questions," I said. "Not now, Mary. We'll be home soon. He's fine. Not a scratch. Nothing."

"Oh, Ed," she said. "I'm so glad." She was close to tears. "Let me talk to him, hon."

This was it.

I said, "Wait a minute."

I said to Weylin, my hand over the mouthpiece, "Wake him. Tell him his mother wants to speak to him." Weylin walked inside, slowly, to the bedroom.

I said into the phone, "He's resting, but he'll be here in a minute."

"He's not—you're not in a hospital, are you, Ed?"

"No," I said. "We're all right. I'll tell you about it later." Then I laid the phone on the little pine shelf. I didn't want to have to answer any more questions for a while.

The boy walked into the living room, eyes blinking, a couple of minutes later. Then he saw me. He cringed. That's what he did, just looking at me.

I said to him, quietly, walking away from the phone, "Don't tell your mother you're here. Don't tell her you've been with Mr. Weylin."

He looked at me, eyes wide now, scared, uncomprehending eyes. He started to shake his head, shrinking back a little. He wasn't getting me at all. I wasn't getting through.

I said to Weylin, half a step behind Matt, "Tell him. Tell him he's not to tell his mother where he's been. Tell him just to say he's fine and he'll be right home."

Weylin looked at me. His hand slid toward his pocket, but our eyes were locked, and he faltered. The dirty bastard, I thought, the dirty queer bastard. Let's see his guts.

He said, "Matt," and the boy turned slowly. "Matt, boy, your mother just wants to know that you're all right. Tell her you're fine. Understand, Matt?"

Matt nodded. "Sure," he said. "I am fine. I'll tell her."

"And that you'll be right home, that you'll tell her all about it later, but that right now you're kind of tired and you just want to get home—to her. You understand, Matt?"

"Sure, Mr. Weylin," the boy said. "I understand."

"And if she asks you where you've been, tell her you'll explain it all later, but you're kind of tired now and you just want to get back home. Understand? You're not to tell her where you've been."

Matt turned and walked to the phone. He brushed past me as if I wasn't even there, and picked up the phone and said, "Hello, Mom," his voice warm, alive, tender, loving.

He said, "Sure I'm fine, Mom. I'm swell." He was smiling into the phone. "No, Mom. I'll tell you later, Mom. I'm fine. Don't carry on like that, Mom. I'll be right home."

He handed me the phone, hardly seeing me, and stepped back into the living room, near Weylin. That was step number one.

I said into the phone, "Okay, hon. That's it. Thank everybody." And I hung up.

Jesus, yes, thank everybody. The poor suckers who gave me time and sweat, so I could still grab off that ten grand.

I said to Matt, "Go inside, boy, and get dressed." He went, averting his face.

I said to Weylin, "You freak."

Weylin frowned and his hand went back down, toward the pocket.

I said, "Why did you do it?"

"Do what?"

"Take the kid away with you?"

He said with a quiet bitterness, "How would you like to shell out a hundred dollars a week, for absolutely nothing?"

I wouldn't let him con me. I said, "But there's nothing you can do about it, is there?"

"I—I guess not," he said, finally.

I guessed not, too. "You wouldn't let it get out, would you?" I said. "You're too chicken to let it get out, aren't you? You wouldn't even dig up a doctor. You wouldn't let anybody know that you and the boy were here together all night? You don't look forward to any more nights in jail, do you? And brother, you'd have plenty; twenty years of them, that's what you'd have. No, you wouldn't let it out."

"Me?" he said slowly. "You thought I was thinking of myself? I was think-ing of the boy."

"I bet you were thinking of the boy. You freak. You just didn't have the guts, that's all. You couldn't do it." All I had to do now was figure some story—how I found the boy in some hole or other, his ankle hurting, and I had dug him out myself some place or other that wouldn't have been covered by the searching party. It was still pretty early. They couldn't have covered the other side of Weylin's ridge, the south side of his slope. The boy had missed directions and had panicked, or, like that fox-faced Stoddard had said, he'd just kept going, looking for lights or a house or maybe just another hill to climb over. Like a real boy. I laughed inside, it was so easy.

Then I remembered Millie Weylin, and as quickly forgot her. She thought Matt had been with her husband, but she'd be happy to forget about it. She didn't like thinking about those kids who liked Weylin and whom he liked. She didn't like the competition. So she wasn't going to say Matt had been with Weylin.

Otto Weylin wasn't going to admit it either. He wasn't going to let it be known that right on top of an earlier arrest, he had picked on another little boy. They'd seal him up in a cell so deep he wouldn't breathe fresh air for twenty years. He'd be through.

Then Weylin said, "This has nothing to do with guts, Hawkins. You can't see it, but you're wrong on that, just as you've been wrong on the whole busi-ness." He sounded tired, pushing a tired old story at me, hoping I'd buy it but knowing I wouldn't. "I've told you before it was a mistake, all the way down the line. That you were trying to blackmail me for something I'd never done. You were making me pay ten thousand dollars for absolutely nothing."

All right. I'd hear the bastard. He was asking for his hour in court like the Philadelphia lawyer he was. Well, I was judge and jury, and I've give him his hour.

Inside, I could hear the boy rummaging around.

I said, "For nothing! That's great. That's rich. For messing around with a teen-age boy. And you call it nothing!"

He shook his head. "Hawkins, listen to me." He was speaking very care-fully, you could see, his eyes shooting to the bedroom where Matt was dress-ing, speaking as if he didn't want to have to say any of this, and didn't want to have to go for that gun. "Listen to me, please. I didn't do a thing. Do you understand? I didn't do a thing. Not that night when I got picked up, or last night, or any time. Believe me, I didn't do a thing."

"Sure," I said.

"Nothing," he said evenly. "Nothing at all. You've got that police mes-sage. You've read it pretty thoroughly by now. Read it again some time. You keep missing one word."

I didn't tell him I didn't have it any more, that I'd burned it. But I sure as hell remembered.

"Otto Weylin," I said, my voice low in the room, "picked up for molesting a minor, fifteen years old. I thought it was a girl at first. I missed the name, but I'm not missing it any more—and then it says something about doubting that the family will press charges and should they release you to Laredo's jurisdiction. Right?"

"Wrong," he said. "Wrong. You keep missing one word."

I heard the boy moving toward the door, and then going back inside again, probably looking for his tie—he always forgot his tie, that kid—and I knew we didn't have much time.

"What word?" I said dully. "What word am I missing?"

He said almost cheerfully, "Look it up when you get home. I don't think we ought to discuss it with the boy so close."

I moved up to him then and I said, "What word, Weylin?"

"Suspected," he said quietly. "*Suspected*. That's the word you keep missing."

"Suspected?"

He nodded grimly. "The police thought I had done something wrong. They found out different. That's why they released me. That's all."

Matt walked into the living room.

The boy walked in, and we had to stop talking. I guess I could have continued it some other time, but I knew it wasn't going to do any good. I felt as if I had been in one of those amusement-park houses full of crazy mirrors and tilted floors and spooks and screams, and then I had come out the other side to another world, all untilted and unspooky.

The cops had picked up Otto Weylin, drunk, because it was *suspected* that he had molested a young boy. Weylin said he didn't do it, but nobody goes around admitting those things. The family had dropped the whole business, either because it didn't want to get involved in a thing like homosexuality, or else because it wasn't true at all!

Maybe—maybe the fifteen-year-old boy was an old hand at this racket, spotting some drunk, friendly, rich geezer, and the boy figured him for an easy mark, maybe leading the poor drunk to a men's room someplace, and then screaming, grabbing Weylin, hanging on, and screaming until somebody knocked the door down.

Maybe that was the way it had been. And when the cops took over, first arresting the drunken bastard and then finding out he was Weylin and who Weylin was, finding out he was rich and respected, and respectable, too—nothing on his record, no record except that of a law-abiding, decent average citizen, never picked up for anything—when they found out that Weylin was clean and the kid was dirty, why, they could have gladly, happily, in great relief turned him over to Laredo's cops.

It might have been that way—or it might not.

That's where I stood. I could investigate, I knew. I could hire a private dick and have him dredge up all the facts, but suppose the facts were inconclusive, the kind of facts where you might suspect, but you'd never know.

Maybe Weylin had seen Matt on the road and had heard from the boy what a hard time I'd been giving him. Maybe Weylin had decided to let the wet, tired, aching kid have a pleasant evening, talking baseball and tennis and movies. And then maybe Weylin had seen how he could use this pleasant evening to stop my blackmail. I could get me a private dick, and I'd still not know. What could I ask Matt?

I said to Weylin, "None of this matters, you know."

"None of what?" he said foolishly.

"Suspected," I said. "None of this suspected stuff matters. I don't give a damn whether the cops just suspected or if they knew. You're still going to come through."

He looked up, shocked. "You mean," he said, "you're still going to shake me down?"

I shot a look at the boy. I said, "Call it whatever you want."

He said, "You're going to tell the boy to say he wasn't here last night?"

"You catch on fast."

Weylin looked at Matt, a deep, sad smile on his face. The boy smiled back. Weylin kept his eyes on Matt, staring at the boy, and I could see that he was weighing something, making up his mind. Then he turned to me, and his face was set.

His hand slipped inside his pocket. The gun barrel shoved its snub nose of fabric at me. The boy was behind Weylin, so he couldn't see it. Then Weylin walked briskly toward the phone, the gun on me all the way. I moved into the middle of the room. Weylin picked up the phone with one hand and laid it on the pine shelf. I could hear the dial tone.

I said, "You wouldn't dare."

"Watch me."

He was going to call the cops. He was going to risk his reputation, his life, just to get me off his back. No, just to get me off *Matt's* back. And at the same time he was going to ruin Matt.

I said again, my lips dry, my throat tight, "You wouldn't dare. You don't have the guts."

His finger went to the dial. The gun never moved off me. "Watch me. Listen."

I said to Matt, "Matt, get out of here. Go to the car and get in and wait for me." The boy looked at me and his eyes dropped, but he didn't move.

"Matt! Get out of here. Go to the car."

The boy took a step toward the door.

And Weylin broke. He put the phone back on the cradle and he moved a step or two away, and he put his head in his hands and he said, "I can't do it."

I said, "Of course you can't."

The boy stared at us both, confused, tired, three steps from the door.

I said, "Go on, Matt. I'll be with you in a minute."

The boy stood there, transfixed.

"Go on," I said sharply.

The boy went and the door closed gently. Weylin said, "Why do you have to make the boy lie about being here?"

"I can't give you your club back," I said.

"Club?" he said. "Oh!"

It was so simple. If I let it be known that Weylin had been arrested for doing what he was suspected of doing, Weylin would be able to get back at me. My son had been with Weylin last night. But if I could make it look as though Matt hadn't been here, Weylin's club was gone.

"So you'll make him lie," Weylin said, stupidly, slowly. "There's no need to. I'll pay you off—I'll pay you off in a lump. You won't need any club. I'll dig up the ten thousand somewhere, and it will be over. Don't make the boy lie."

I said harshly, "I can't take a chance." Weylin wouldn't talk, but that didn't close the case.

"But nobody knows about the arrest. You're the only one who knows, aren't you?"

"The cops know."

He stared at me. "You don't trust anybody," he said. "Not a living soul."

I said, "It takes just one nosy bastard to spill the whole thing."

He looked at me with a strange look. "You're a crud," he said. "You're just a crud, and you're losing your son. You're just no good."

"That's right," I said. "Song-and-dance me."

"No," he said. "No song and dance. You're just a crud."

"And you're just a sucker," I said. "Tell me, why did you send me the police message? Did you really think I'd let it scare me into dropping this thing?"

He turned away. "You're right," he said. "I'm just a sucker. And now, I suppose, you'll show the thing all over town. The money won't be enough, will it, Hawkins?"

"I burned it."

He turned slowly. He looked at me, closely, moving a step nearer, staring into my face. "You *what?*"

"I burned it. I burned the hundred dollars, too." I walked outside and over to the car. I said, "Okay, Matt, we're going home."

There was no answer. I poked my head in the rear window.

The boy was gone....

I was scared at first. Who wouldn't have been? But then I gave it some thought. Where would he go? I drove the Chevy to the highway and turned in the direction opposite the canyon turnoff. That's how he would have gone, trying to get away from me. And I found him two hundred yards down the highway, walking along limping a little.

"Hop in," I said.

He turned, scared, and just stood there.

"Hop in, son," I said pleasantly. I threw open the front door.

He looked wildly around, and then he crawled in.

I said, "Listen, Matt. When you get home, just tell your mother where you were last night. Tell her everything. Don't worry."

I wanted to reach over and rumple the kid's hair, but he wasn't ready for that.

Why did I do it, why did I change horses right there in midstream? It happened long ago, I guess, and the rest was noise and shouting and playing with a dream of ten thousand bucks. So I had Weylin where I wanted him, from the beginning right to the end.

But what good was he doing me? I felt lousy.

Don't tell me that's not important, no, not when you weigh it against ten grand. I know how important it is. So the kid cringes when you look at him, so he averts his eyes, scared to death of you. That's lousy, but that's not enough.

But when you realize you've got the kid where you can turn him and twist him and make him lie for you—for your ten grand—it starts getting important.

And when it gets so bad he's got to get away, then it's enough.

Twice in two days I had driven my son out of reach. Now I realized this was a boy who might have been in terrible trouble last night. Do you send a boy like that away?

Maybe it's just because I hate queers. Maybe it's because when I was a kid my old lady dressed me in fauntleroy collars and golden curls and short pants, and the bigger kids began to call me names, and one of them made a practice of beating the crap out of me.

Or like Millie Weylin had gasped, "Take it easy! What are you trying to prove?"

That I was better than the next guy—the next man—that it didn't matter that they had me dead to rights at third base, the throw ahead of me, I still had to knock the baseman on his ass, and it didn't matter that a guy like Otto Weylin was king of his hill, I just had to be king of Otto Weylin.

But where are you?

I knew right then. There on the highway with the kid limping out in front of me, a little boy, Jesus God, just a little boy, limping to get away from me, a little boy who maybe had done something and maybe hadn't, but couldn't I even give my own son the benefit of the doubt—I knew right then that I couldn't keep it up, this sneering, pushing, slugging, cutting-him-in-two sort of life, I couldn't keep it up because it was hurting me too damn much, and I hated it.

So I was better than Otto Weylin. I had him trussed up and ready to be carved. I'd laid his wife. I had him and when I told him to cough, he coughed. So what? So my own kid wouldn't look at me, wouldn't talk to me, ran away from me. To hell with the lousy ten grand.

I said to the boy—on the dirt road near the house, a dozen cars up there, lights on, the noise like a circus, everybody celebrating because Matt was coming home —I said, "I'm sorry, son, about everything."

He said, because he trusted me, he gave me the benefit of every doubt, "That's all right, Dad."

I said, "No, it isn't, Matt, but it will be. You don't know what I'm talking about right now, but I've got to tell somebody and it's better I tell somebody who doesn't understand. I burned a hundred bucks because it was dirty money, and I wouldn't have it. Maybe I tried to kid myself that I'd take more, but a guy doesn't burn a hundred bucks when it's money he's after. Understand? And do you know why I burned a police message? Because I didn't want anybody else ever to see it again, because I didn't want to have anything to do with it. Understand? It didn't happen just now, in the car, or at Weylin's door, it was happening all the time. Understand?"

He said, confused as hell, but grinning a little. "Sure, I understand, Dad."

"So what are we waiting for?" I said, throwing the door open. "We're home."

Chapter Twelve

They say one swallow doesn't make a summer. Or, I like I always said, one swallow doesn't quench your thirst. There was still a long way to go.

Vin Kimball came home the next day—he and his good gray wife—because they had heard about it in their Santa Barbara motel room—two bits for half an hour of TV—and there it was, all of Laredo combing that hillside. The rain had held them up and washed out the road, but even if they were halfway to Sacramento, they would have come back.

They came home even though it meant they didn't get to the convention the day before it opened, like all good politicians have to, and Vin Kimball missed out on the dealing and the double-dealing, and when they finally did get back up to Sacramento, he had been dealt out. They had shaken up his congressional district, and he was just a stooge now for another supervisor, working out of the central committee, or whatever it was called; he told me, but it was all Greek. All I knew was that Vin Kimball had come back to lend me a hand, and because he wasn't around when they cut the deck, somebody grabbed his seat at the table.

I went back to work on Monday and he drove back up to the convention because he was a good joe who didn't take his marbles and scram, but he and his wife didn't take their vacation because they felt too lousy, and we all three were working together again, the next week.

It was awful. The poor guy went around, his face long and sick, and every so often he'd shoot me a look. I didn't want to think it, but, as I said, one swallow doesn't make a summer and I still had a long way to go before I learned to trust people—I thought that Vin Kimball was going to snoop around and finally get down to asking me for the dirt I had, so he could work his way back into local power.

I had that thought, and I wouldn't stand for thinking it. His wife was in back, wrapping up quarts of paint, and I jabbed Kimball and said, "Look here, Vin, I forgot to tell you but I made a big mistake the other day about the guy I was telling you about. Mistaken identity or something. It washed me right out of the picture."

And he let his breath out with a long, loud *whoosh*, and he slapped the counter, laughed and slapped my back.

He said, "That's swell, Ed, you don't know how good that makes me feel. I—I was worried for you, I really thought you were going to follow through, and it had me worried all the way out of here and all the way back. You don't know how glad I am to hear it."

So I said, because I wasn't over it all yet, "How come you keep shooting me those bloodhound looks?"

He shook his head as if I had hooked him one on the side of the kisser, and then he said, "Looks? Why—oh, well, that was just—you know, I was sort of sorry. I didn't want to see you getting involved and I felt if I just kept me eye on you—you understand—" And he quit, he broke right down in the middle of that stutter-and-stammer sentence and he got red in the face.

He was sorry for *me*. That's all. Whatever had happened to him in Sacramento still wasn't half as important as the fact I might be doing something dirty, and he was worried about me, sorry for me.

"Sorry?" I said.

He looked at me, helpless-like, as if I had intruded on him somehow, and then we both were grinning, turning away, sort of. It didn't last long, because we were busy these days, busier than I had been in the shop even when Vin was out of town. Business had started to pick up. Nothing big, maybe nothing more than the usual spring cleaning pickup. But whatever it was, we were busy, and the cash register tape read ninety-eight one day and the next day it broke a hundred and on Friday it hit a hundred and fifteen. Nobody had time to be sorry for anybody; Vin was too busy selling and Mom and I were too busy wrapping and running. And that was that.

But still, he had been sorry for *me*. How do you figure people like that? The woods were full of them.

It was a week later that Mary and I went to the ceramic shack, the big one in the middle of town. We had a list a mile long, and if you buy right here in the pottery joints in Laredo, looking for what they call selected seconds, you can get ashtrays, casseroles, glasses, dishes, all that sort of stuff pretty cheap.

Mary pushed a little cart. She looked down, and she said, "That's Sergeant Sakimoto. Let's see." She took out her list. "Sergeant Sakimoto and those other two policemen, and Mr. Stoddard and his two nephews, and—" and she kept rattling off names. We were buying presents for as many people who had helped us out as we could.

I said, "Who's left?"

Matt looked over Mary's arm and read the list. "Mrs. Willoughby and Mrs. McVeigh. That's all."

I said, "There's a little old man I'd like to get something for. I don't know his name, but I guess Sakimoto will. I mean the old geezer whose glasses I had broken the day that I drove the tow truck into him, the guy who started me out of the mess."

"All right," Mary said. It was a lark to her. It was fun. Even Matt—who kept making faces at the ceramic cherubs and nonsensical doodads all over the shelves—seemed to be enjoying himself.

I said, "Let's try this aisle." I pushed ahead. Just then a dame came down another aisle at right angles to me, in red toreador pants so tight you could see—I spun around so fast that I knocked into the arm of one of the young fellows who works in the joint. A dish popped into the air, and we both clutched and dove at it, and it crashed on the floor. He got up, brushing himself off, looking sore, and he said, "Why, of all the clumsy—"

He was one of those guys you always seem to see there, either working or buying. He was tall and very thin, with a soft manner and a faint smell of cologne, and he was upset.

I let him finish.

"—all the clumsy idiots, I'm the worst," he said.

I said, "That was my fault, buster."

He said, "Don't be silly. I work here, and the least thing I can do is look out for the other fellow."

I said, "My fault, all the way." I bent down and Matt bent down at the same time, and our heads bumped. Matt stared at me, a little scared, I guess, scared maybe that I'd be sore, and while he stared, I felt something new happening to me. Matt kept staring at me, staring at my mouth, my face, and I could feel the skin on my face crawling with new muscles, new nerves coming into play.

I grinned, and then the grin broke into a laugh, an easy, pleasant laugh. I laughed, and Matt grinned back and then he laughed, easily and pleasantly, too.

We picked up the pieces together.

THE END

Flint

By Arnold Hano
writing as Gil Dodge

In memory of Jim Thompson, who wrote
this story first and wrote it best, and then
gave me permission to try my own version.

CHAPTER ONE

I had been coughing a lot that past winter—a colder and wetter winter than usual for southwestern Arizona territory—and there were streaks of blood showing in my saliva again, so I stopped drinking. I had a little vegetable patch right in the middle of cattle country and the ranchers used to jolly me about it, but when you've got a hole in your lung that just won't ever seem to plug itself, you've got to figure the easy life.

The vegetables grew. I took enough to eat. The rest I sold in market. And that was that. Arizona isn't much of a vegetable-eating place; they all seem to live on beef and potatoes and I can't say I blame them; but there was enough business to keep my bones together.

More than that I never expected. Not any more. All I wanted was the sun and some dry climate so that the ache in my chest would leave me alone. I hadn't ever taken it to a doctor, no, not in the six years that had gone by. A man doesn't take himself to a doctor and show him a bullet hole in his lung without questions asked.

I couldn't afford that. During the first twenty-five years of my life (I'm thirty-one now), I had killed twenty-eight men.

That's why I couldn't say anything when this stranger came up to my place and put it to me. I don't carry a gun any more, not since I outran a Texas posse out of El Paso in 1869, the hole in my chest leaking blood. I'm finished with that sort of business. I'm a vegetable farmer. That's all.

That's what I told the stranger. He was a cowman, riding a fine sorrel, a big, brawny, shaggy man with a punched-around face and a curving beak of nose. He carried two guns.

I told him I wouldn't do it, that it wasn't my way of life any more.

"That's too bad, Flint," he said. "I'm sure the sheriff will be interested in what I have to say, even if you aren't." His hand wrapped around one of his guns and his lips got thin and tight. He meant every word he had said.

That's how I got hooked.

His name was Hawkins and he was just a messenger on this errand. His boss was a rancher in Colorado, a man named Good. Hiram Good. He had twenty thousand head of cattle and not even Good knew how many thousand acres of land. He owned all but one piece of a sprawling valley, plus all the sloping hill country that squeezed down on the valley, except for one little hill high on the north end.

Good was nearly seventy years old, Hawkins told me—over a bottle of bourbon that I suddenly felt I needed—and he liked his comfort.

But in the last twelve months, his cows had been on occasion rustled and his land subjected to minor depredations. Nothing serious—neither the rustling nor the fence-burning nor the little grass fires—but Good was a peace-loving man who didn't want his last years roiled up any.

That's where I came in. Good had sent Hawkins down to get me. I was to clean up the mess.

"But," I said, "if it's so clearly obvious that this one rancher up on the north slope, this man Thomason, is behind the rustlings and the rest, why don't you just call in the sheriff's office? You have a sheriff nearby?"

Hawkins nodded. "County seat is Dryhock, a little town just on the other side of the north slope. We have a sheriff nearby."

"And?"

Hawkins shook his head. "I'm not supposed to tell you any of this, mind you. I'm just supposed to bring you back, but—well, I guess it won't hurt any. You'll have to know sooner or later. Mr. Good doesn't think the sheriff is on the up-and-up. He thinks he's in cahoots with Thomason."

"Is he?"

"I think he is, yes."

"Why do you think so?"

He looked puzzled for a moment. He shook his shaggy head. "I really don't know. Mr. Good seems to think so. That's enough for me."

"What do you expect me to do?"

Hawkins patted his gun butt. "Mr. Good expects you to follow his orders." His eyes slitted, and he stared hard at me.

I did not like this man. He didn't like me. I did not like the setup. But I had no choice. "And he's prepared to pay me five thousand dollars? Is that right? He's going to pay me this money?"

It was the most money anybody ever had offered me.

Hawkins reached into his back pocket and tossed me a thin sheaf of bills. "There's the first thousand. The rest when you're finished."

"I have no gun."

Hawkins reached to his left holster and removed one of his .44s. "Here," he said. It was a long-barreled model, the barrel filed down until it was a dull black. It would not reflect light. Staring at it, I had the old feeling inside, coming so strong and quickly it surprised me. I took the .44 from Hawkins and when the butt slipped into my palm, riding against the horn of callous on the heel of my hand, the black horn of flesh that tingled ever so gently, I could feel the snakes slithering in my belly.

Hawkins left shortly after. He told me Mr. Good would be expecting me any time in the next six months. Horses were posted for me all along the route. I merely had to follow Hawkins' map—and it was a detailed one—and drop in at the ranches or stables indicated and show a letter Hawkins gave me.

"Just show the letter," he said. "Don't mention Mr. Good's name. Do you understand?"

I understood. Good had purchased ten horses for me. Ten stable-owners and ranchers—and maybe dozens of other people—were to become links between a killer and the man who hired him. Except, they didn't know the identity of the latter. Good was a man who took no chances.

At no time did I question my course of action. It would have been idiotic—and futile—to take the money and run. Hawkins had found me. I had thought there was no conceivable planned way in the world that anybody could have found me, yet Hawkins had. I had had no contact in the past six years with any of the people I had previously known and lived among—nor with any of the places I had ever set foot. Yet Hawkins had come directly to a tiny vegetable farm in Arizona.

I do not pretend any moral compunction on my part. I had killed for money before, many times. Thomason appeared to be a leech, hanging onto his land via another man's labor and riches. He rustled and pillaged. Much has been made of horse- and cow-thieves in this part of the country. It may seem like petty criminality to those back East or down South who do not live off the back of a horse, trying to run down and brand a calf. The horse and the cow made this land out here. Thomason destroyed more than animal-flesh if he butchered calves; he threatened another man's way of living.

And the sheriff? If he stood by, he was more then guilty.

So the prospect of killing these two men could not have deterred me. And killing them for money gave me further chance to find a place in the sun where I might curl up—me and my pitted lung.

But—I told myself—I did not like it. I had buried my guns.

I tilted the bottle of bourbon and drank past a cough that started to crawl up my throat. It was no time to get sick.

My name is Flint. I come from Georgia. When the War Between the States began in 1861, I was seventeen years old, a boy actually, attending school. When it was over in 1865, I was a man of twenty-one, and I had a mission or two in life that had to be fulfilled. You see, when Sherman came on through, one of his soldiers raped my sister in our barn and murdered her when he set fire to the barn. It took me quite a while to find the man who had done this. I thought I would easily remember what he looked like, but I didn't. His face had become vague—and now, as I try to recall it, it has become vaguer still.

Be that as it may, I found the man in my home town. I stabbed—no, I shot him. Yes, I shot him to death. By the time I had finally managed to do this, I was sick of the town.

I set out West. And when people started asking me what I could do real well, I had nothing to tell them. I hired out to punch cows a time or two in Texas. But cowpunching seldom was peaceable in those days at the war's end. Pretty soon somebody found out what I *could* do real well. I got paid ten dollars for the first one (that is, the first one since the man in my home town who had raped my sister), and I did it so well I got twenty for the next. After that I drifted, my gun for hire. My soul? Well, I figured I'd meet that when I had to.

My name is Flint. I'm wanted in ten states and territories. I haven't touched a gun in six years.

It took me a week to finish my business in Arizona. I had two orders from Hawkins. One was to make sure I arrived at Good's ranch within six months. It was implicit what would happen if I failed to meet that date. The second order was not strange. I was told to arrive at night, not daytime.

What Good wanted me to do was his business—and mine. He wanted nobody else to know about it. It was funny. I didn't like Hawkins, who merely was doing his job, carrying out orders from another source. Yet peculiarly, I savored the idea of meeting Hiram Good. I felt I would like the man.

The night before I left I filled my saddlebag with clothes and canned provisions. I had previously deposited seven hundred dollars of Good's money in the town bank. The rest was in my pants pocket.

That night I wandered out over the little farm that was no longer mine—I had sold it, of course, depositing that money, too, in the town bank—and the warm rush of velvet-soft air was like a sister's kiss. As far as the eye could see there was a long table of land, etched in moonlight and starlight, and ending only where the hills of the Chocolatos grew gracefully out of thick, sweet, hip-deep grass, dotted with gold poppy and lupine and desert marigold. I could not feel too sad. It was a temporary place at best, this little vegetable farm. I had never allowed myself the luxury of living more than two years in any one place after the last killing. I would have had to leave anyway, very soon.

And I wondered why I had put the money in the town's bank. I could not imagine ever coming back here. It was as though I had to leave a little piece of me behind, almost as a protest against what the rest of me was going to do.

I went back to the house and opened a fresh bottle of bourbon. My hand went to the .44 on the table where Hawkins and I had sat. And the snakes gathered in my belly.

And I knew then, the gun in my hand, why I had not chosen any other course. I knew why I had not run, for the border, into Mexico. Hawkins had come to ask me to do what I had to do. The snakes, the snakes were crawling, and the feeling was good. They were out and crawling and my belly burned with their silent cries for lust, for blood, for that one thing I could do so well. I stood up and breathed deeply into my lungs and that too felt good,

good.

My sleep that night was long and passionate. I stood in the center of stampeding stallions, and they swerved around me. It was midnight. Lightning and thunder crashed all about me. At the apex of the stampede, coming toward me, was an old man. He was saying things to me, foul things, terrible things, but I laughed at him and grabbed a lightning fork from the sky and drove it deep into his throat.

I was refreshed the next morning. I started out for Hiram Good.

CHAPTER TWO

It was early April when I left. It was late May when I arrived. I hurried. I knew that Good would stand by his word. He would have given me six months. At that rate, I could have taken my time. But that would have meant traveling the long hot months of dead summer. I did not know how my lung would take it. I thought: get there before summer and get it over with and get out. And so I hurried.

It was only in southern Colorado that the going became difficult. Although I have been out west for many years and I had ridden in the Confederate cavalry, I am not much of a horseman. It may be because I must favor one side, my right side, and thus I tire and cramp up easily. But no, that is not quite it. I never rode well even before I was shot.

In Colorado, Hawkins' map left the main routes and took me through passes that sometimes were not passes but laborious direct paths over the tops of great hills. This was the two-hundred-mile-thick Rockies, the silver rivers and creeks rushing down their great green sides. I crossed the Animas where the alpine fir and spruce began to thin out, close to the twelve-thousand foot level of Ealus Mountain—because the map said to. I followed the Iola River toward Gunnison, but then shied away from the town—because the map told me to—and scaled the black-nosed Cachetopas, the scent of ponderosa pine filling my nostrils. I slept up there that night because I was too tired to go any farther, and the chill darkness was filled with the harsh arrogance of jays and Clark nutcrackers, begging food. In the morning I woke, icicle fingers clutching my chest, and I found my horse had slipped his tether and run away. I had to walk the next twenty-two miles, to the next out-of-the-way stable.

It was obvious that Good had taken pains to protect himself. I was chattel. I was not reaching his ranch by a direct route. Nobody who saw me—and few did—would have known where I was headed, even, I think, when I was twenty miles from Good's valley.

I stopped hurrying suddenly. I had come nearly seven hundred miles in forty-five days, and it was as though all the pain I should have felt during that long, rocking, jogging month and a half, and hadn't, had now accumulated — just when I was within sight of the headwaters of the South Platte River, which crawled down the sides of the hills rimming Good's land, twisting rivulets among the scrub oak and piñon.

It was the morning of what I figured to be May 23. In front of me was the town of Dryhock; thin trails of coal smoke cleaved the haze and then added to it. It was not like a morning in Arizona. My chest began to burn, and then before I knew what had happened, I had fallen from my horse, the gagging blood oozing through my mouth. I tried to swallow it, but it made me cough, and then it came out in a pink torrent. It was the first hemorrhage I had had in three years. I lay there until it seemed I had no more blood to bleed and then I rolled to my side and retched drily twice. My face was soaked with sweat and my hand shook as I mopped myself with my bandanna.

I knew I should never have gone into Dryhock that morning until after I had checked in with Good. He had not told me to avoid the town, but I was no child. A man could ride onto a ranch the size of his and be any one of his hundred-or-so hands, no one would know the difference. But a stranger in a small town was a thing apart.

I had a day ahead of me. I could not show on Good's land until dark. Ten hours. I stared at my hand, felt the trembling in my legs. I had to have a drink before the shaking threw me from the horse again. To hell with it, I thought. This is wrong, but to hell with it. I turned slowly toward Dryhock.

It was a conglomerate town, one that had grown out of thin gold mines which still gave up ore and therefore held out the promise of further rich strikes—always the promise, nothing more. At the north end of town was the office of the mine surveyor, claimsman, and gold assayer—one man. He had once been an important man, no doubt—or possibly there had been three men. But now the town was a cattle town. The false fronts were designed to so-licit cowmen. Brands and ornate saddle markings were posted over nearly every store. The saloon was called The Spur. The bank was the Cattleman's Trust and Loan Association. The street of the town was dirt and horse chips watered down by each store owner. Hitching posts leaned into the street.

I stopped at the saloon. It was ten in the morning. I took my time hitch-ing the horse. I could not, must not, drink too much. One or two strong drinks after a bleeding such as the one I had just had would be all right. In fact, it always seemed to help. But too much, no.

When I arrived the saloon was empty, except for the tender, a small wiry man with a red nose and a black mustache. He had a long, rough pine bar, un-finished, but so thickly layered that he would never need to worry. The bar would outlive him. He was at one end with a handful of sawdust and a thick, stiff wire brush, scrubbing away. Judging by the remaining forty feet of bar, I knew that a clean bar was a hope, not an expectation.

He walked over and wiped his hands. He frowned at me. "Pretty early in the day for a drink."

I laughed. "You must be a great businessman."

He grunted. "Come around at night and you'll see. More goddam hands than I can handle. I don't need anybody's business."

Suddenly I didn't want to talk. All I wanted was a drink. "Take my busi-ness, please. What whiskey do you have?" He dragged out a bottle of corn.

I shook my head. "Tell you what, do you have any brandy, good brandy? I'm not feeling very well." I could feel the shaking start in again.

He stared close at me and I tried to smile and then I began to cough. I got my bandanna to my mouth. It wasn't staining, but he could see my trouble. "Holy Christ," he said, "why didn't you say so?" He went down on his knees behind the bar and rummaged and came up with a silver flask. "My own," he said. "Not much left, but—" He spilled some into a shot glass.

It was the best brandy I'd ever tasted, so old and warm it was almost musky, but not quite. It burned evenly, flowing through me. I chewed down on my teeth and kept my head down while the brandy traveled, and then I looked up. He took a quick look at me and poured me another, tilting the flask nearly vertical. "Slow," he said, "that's good stuff."

I knew it was and I knew it should have been sipped, but not yet. I threw it down and held out my glass. He poured me another. I looked about the bar and walked over to a table. I sat down and stared at the brandy. Slow, I thought, slow now. It's done you good, don't spoil it.

I stretched my legs out and leaned back in the chair. I felt drowsy, light-headed. Not from the brandy, of course. From the weakness. My toes tingled and I lingered there, between sleep and wakefulness. The brush-brush on the pine bar as he scrubbed it filled the room with the dry smell of old wood, a good smell. I am a man to whom breathing is so vital that I catch each breath and hold it and taste it. This was good, expunging for the moment the coal smoke and dust and horse chips. The morning went, over that one brandy, my third, and every so often the door banged behind me and feet trampled and muted talk sifted through the room; but none of it involved me.

At noon, I rose and walked to the bar. "How much?" I said.

"One dollar," he said.

I felt myself frowning. "For all that? That's fifty years old if it's a day. No, you've made a mistake."

He leaned forward, mustache bristling. "You don't like the way I run my bar, get the hell out. I set the price. One dollar. Cough it u— I mean, pay me or get out, I don't care."

I removed some bills from my pocket. I stripped off a dollar. "You are a rich man," I said. I don't know if he understood me, but I didn't care. He didn't need me. I walked out.

The heat struck me and I watered my bandanna and tied it across my forehead. I started for my horse.

"Hold on," a voice said.

I turned and stared into the shadows of the sheriff's office.

CHAPTER THREE

My stomach rolled once, and I felt myself tensing. The door was open but I couldn't see inside.

"Come on in," he said.

I walked slowly and when I stepped from the dazzling sun into the stinking filthy office and saw him sitting there, I plunged from tension to terror. He was the fattest man I ever saw, a man of fifty or thereabouts, leaning back on a cot at the end of the room, a tiny orange crate in front of him which he used as a desk. He stared at me out of pig eyes glittering in the shadowy murk. An unshaven man, a gross man. And a sheriff.

"Yes?" I said, standing at the door, half in.

He pointed to my hip. "Your gun?"

"What about it?" I knew I could not give up the gun. It was not mine. It linked me to Hawkins and thus to Good.

"New in town?"

"Yes, sir."

"Staying or heading through?"

"Staying in town, you mean?"

"Now, what did you think I meant? Staying in this room with me?"

"No, sir."

"No, sir, *what?* Staying in town, or no, sir, you didn't think I meant staying in this room with me?"

I had to gamble. "Not staying in town." That was the truth. I wasn't. But I was going to be around the area.

He grunted. He now had the option of asking me the rest of the question—was I heading through?

Instead he pointed to the .44. "We don't allow guns carried in Dryhock. It's a peaceful little town. No trouble. Don't want any." He hesitated. I could see he meant it. He didn't want any trouble. He sure as hell didn't want my gun.

I stepped forward and took the gun from the holster. "Sir, here's my gun. Put it on ice until I'm ready to leave. Right now I'm just giving my horse a breather. Later, I want to feed him. I'm going to get some food. I may want some other provisions. Keep my gun until nightfall."

He waved his hand back and forth in front of his face. "Don't want it. Don't want to clutter my office. Hate guns. Just put it away. Don't let me, anybody, see it. That's all."

I let out my breath silently. I thought I had him figured. A fat man, a slovenly fat man who must have known somebody and had got this job where he did nothing but sit on his cot and fill his office with the stink of his hairy, oily, unwashed body. The smell of the room washed over me. I had to get away.

I put my gun carelessly inside my shirt, tucked into my belt, yet still I was to all intents a man carrying a gun. It was a slap in his face. I had to do it, to test him further, to stack him against the picture vaguely outlined by Hawkins. Was this a man who tolerated the lawless? Was he a man who could be in cahoots with a rustler? I patted the blocky lump inside my shirt and turned and started out.

"Just a minute," he barked. "What's your name?"

Once more, the plunge into the maw of terror. My name is Flint. But not to him. Not to a law man, or to anyone else, except myself—and now, Hawkins and Good. They knew. No one else.

"Flynn," I said, giving him the name I'd been using for the past six years.

Maybe you wonder why I use a name so close to my real one, when my real name could drag me into a noose. It's just—it's just that a man, I guess, can't get too far from his own name. This is who I am, nobody else. I do not feel I am cheating myself when I drop the final consonant sound at the end of my name.

It is not as dangerous as you imagine. There are many Flynns out here, now that the rails are going down. The Irish can work better at laying rails than any other people in the world.

For another thing, though a man named Flint is wanted for murder, that man has not been seen in over six years by anyone who has the remotest interest in him. And Flint, of six years ago, was an inch taller than Flynn, today, stooped and bent slightly to one side. That Flint was ten pounds heavier than the ravaged Flynn of today. Flint wore glasses, but out here, seeing at great distances, Flynn's eyes are strong. Flint had dark brown hair, but Flynn has been under a blazing sun for more than six years and his hair is streaked with red and silver. Flint was a young man. Flynn's face has been crisscrossed with a farmer's thousand tiny wrinkles.

Flynn is just not Flint to the outside world.

"Flynn," he said, his eyes glittering even more brightly. "Flynn. I'll be double-damned. How you fooled me." He started to laugh and the cot shook. His laugh was high-pitched, just short of a shriek, and once he raised his feet and stamped them to the floor, sending up a wave of dust.

"Flynn," he said. "Oh, what a shrewd one, you are. Flynn, you are, eh? Damn, damn, damn." He couldn't go on, choking with laughter and with the dust. I started to choke, too. "Laugh at me. That's right, laugh at me," he said. "Old Barney Slott doesn't get fooled too often, no siree. Hands me his gun pretty as you please. Oh, what a laugh. Flynn, Flynn, you certainly took the old man that time." Then he stopped and pressed his hands to the cot and forced himself to his feet. It was a shocking sight. He stood seven inches taller than I, maybe more. He was twice my breadth across the shoulders. He must have weighed—

"Three hundred pounds," he said, nodding his head, watching my eyes as I took all of him in. "Pity, isn't it? A man's body can run away with him. Now take a young man like you, Flynn—how old are you now, thirty, thirty-one—" His eyes narrowed and he stared down at me.

"Yes, sir, that's right." He had looked through those wrinkles and past the stoop and he knew my age, and I wondered.... But that was silly. He couldn't have known. If he had known who I was, would he be acting this way? I started to turn away again. My head was whirling with the heat and with his words. I did not know what was tickling him so, but he seemed to know me, to have been waiting for me. I had to get out of the office, out of this goddam little stinking hot town, back into the hills, and to Good.

He put a huge hand on my shoulder. His nails were bitten down to the flesh, black-edged. "Now, you'll want to see a bit more of the town, I suppose? Is that it?"

"Why, yes, like I told you," I said. "My horse—" I faltered.

"Been a long trip, hasn't it?" he said.

"Why, yes, it has, as a matter of fact."

"How are all my friends in Arizona, Flynn? Tell me about them?"

I squared my shoulders. Now I had nothing to lose. He was watching my face. My hand crept to my waist. Christ, I thought, even before I get it started, it's all over. Why don't they let me alone? My fingers touched my bare stomach and I quivered. They slid to the butt end of the .44.

"You're tired," he said suddenly. "I'm asking too many questions. You want to get freshened up. Maybe... maybe you want to—" His eyes were a slit through spiky blunt lashes. "Maybe you'll want to see the girls? A long time on the road—a month, hasn't it been, Flynn, a month since you left?"

I nodded. I could not do it. There was something else here, not just cat and mouse. At least, I hoped so.

"Go on then. I'll see you soon.... Tomorrow? Is that long enough, Flynn? Tomorrow?"

I nodded again. I could not talk. He was so close to dying.

And I? Where was I? In a hell where the paving blocks were six and a half feet tall and weighed three hundred pounds, and I had to move them up an unending hill? Was that where I was?

Sometime, somehow, maybe right then, maybe not for another ten minutes, I got out of there. I stumbled out, drenched through to the bone. I swallowed up the dust and the sun of the street eagerly, greedily.

I do not know how I spent the remaining hours of that afternoon, and the first few hours after sundown. I do know that my horse was bathed and fed and rested. I do know that I got a haircut and a shave. These things must have occupied me for two, two and a half hours. But that is all I remember....

Except her. I remember her, and I always shall. I had just come out of the barber's and I was about to mount my horse when she passed me on her horse, a white monster incredibly thick in the thigh and hams, slender as a thistle in the shank. There was white gleaming froth at the horse's mouth and his head moved in anger. But she was unaware of it. I do not like people who hurt their horses. She had hurt hers. The horse's hair was matted down with sweat. His veins stood close to the skin, pressing outward. The branded "T" on his rump was red-edged.

Yet she was oblivious. Her head was high and she was looking past her horse's jerking head. I was standing to her left. She looked down at me; her eyes drifted across my face.

She had thick black hair, and it must have been a hot ride she had just had, because her hair glistened with sweat and her face shone, too, and one thick curl fell over her brow. She put the tip of her tongue to her lips. All the time her eyes were on mine. She seemed tall and she was not a girl, but a woman. I judged her thirty or thereabouts, staring at the fullness of her breasts beneath her checkered shirt and at the heavily sluggish eyes, slumberous in the middle of the day.

Maybe the sheriff had been right. For just at that moment, I do not know what kept me from reaching her heavy thighs and pulling her from her saddle and into the dust, my arms around that waist and my hands sinking into the faint bulge of belly that stretched taut her jeans.

"Well," she said, so low only I could have heard her, though I am sure the street was empty, "another one. That's fine," she said, her tongue going to her upper lip and moving back and forth. "And with a gun inside his shirt. My," she said, "he looks like fun." Then she was past. I watched her until she reached the sheriff's office. She stopped her white horse and pressed her cheek against his neck, and then swung off. She walked into the sheriff's office, her hips rolling gently.

It was eight o'clock. I had walked my horse out of the town and to the hills around Good's valley. I suppose it had a name, but Hawkins had not called it anything but Good's valley. I imagine that was what everybody called it.

An hour later I stared down a dark slope to a huge lighted house that stood well to the north of the center of the valley. About it were the corral, no, two of them, and bunkhouses, four or five, and a large blocky building that was—the barn, I imagined.

Night was coming in fast now, but I waited. If I could stand in this valley and make out corral shapes and bunkhouses, then it wasn't dark enough. That was how Good would think. I waited another hour. Then I tied my horse to a piñon in good grass, gave him thirty feet of rope, and walked to the ranch house.

Chapter Four

"Tell me, Hawk, how did you do it? How did you spot our Flint?" Good asked.

We were seated, the three of us, in Good's library. There were brandy and cigars, but I had waved them away. All I had was a glass of well water which Hawkins had lumbered for and got when Good had curtly ordered him to.

Hiram Good had white hair and piercing blue eyes, but not so pale you'd call them cold. He had a soft white mustache. He was a slender, erect man with hollowed-out temples and one blazing vein over his right eye that leaped when he laughed. He laughed often, apparently.

"Tell us, Hawk," he said, and I looked at Hawkins and saw the curling beak of his nose, the long thin lips and the deep-set eyes. "Did you go around asking everybody you saw? How did you spot our boy? I never would have—" He started to laugh. He took a short drink and then drew on his cigar. "—I never would have, not in a hundred years. Tell us how you did it?"

Hawkins grunted. "You know damn well how I did it, Mr. Good. I went to the farm and there he was."

And Good bent over, laughing so hard that when he looked up his eyes were full of water. I had to laugh, too, looking at his puckish face, the dancing blue eyes and the full, easy laugh. Even Hawkins grunted a couple of times, and then let the grunt break into a chuckle.

"Not," Hawkins went on, "not that I would have known him otherwise. He certainly doesn't look like the way you described him. At least, not too much. If he had denied it more strongly, I might have believed him."

Good waggled a finger at me. "Now, Flint, that's not like you. Letting a man like Hawk here, a good, honest, stupid man like Hawk"—he looked warmly at Hawkins who grinned uncomfortably— "a fool, you might say, walk right up and put his hand on you and say come along, boy. You disappoint me, Flint." And all the time he was laughing.

But suddenly I had a chill. He meant every word he had just said. He meant that Hawkins was a stupid man, a fool. And he was curious why I, Flint, had allowed Hawkins to beat down my denial, to hog-tie me so easily to a proposition that must have rubbed me wrong. If Good knew my background—and it was more and more apparent that he did—then he knew I had quit killing for pay over six years ago. He knew I had buried my past with my guns. And yet here I was, all because Hawkins had walked in on me and told me to come.

What I said now was important. Good was testing me, finding out whether he had not made a mistake in seeking out this man Flint. Maybe six years was too long a period for a man to be away from the sport, maybe I had grown old and rusty. Good's eyes peered out, twinkling, the head tilted back as if expecting a response, nodding now, encouraging.

I breathed in and put my glass down. "Hawkins is kind to me," I said. "He knew who I was. A man doesn't wander six or seven hundred miles to the middle of nowhere unless he knows where he's going, whom he's looking for. Hawkins knew I had to be there." Good was nodding his head, but his eyes were not twinkling. They were serious. "It's the difference," I said, "between the law and the—the others. The people like you and me. The law is limited. But if a man like you, Mr. Good, wants to find somebody, why, then, he'll find him. You've got the money and you've got the men and you've got the time. Three things. Money, men, time. The law's got pennies. It's got fat-assed sheriffs and chicken-hearted deputies, underpaid and scared turdless. And it's got only as much time as its indignant citizenry wants to give it."

Good was grave now, his head still, listening. Hawkins sat there, wondering what it was all about. I had them now. I had turned Good away from his unspoken question: was I still the man for the job? But it didn't matter. I was proving something else to him, and it balanced the other, even if he had wanted to pursue it. Hawkins had made me come because he had made a simple threat—and I hadn't faced up to it. But I was telling Good that behind that simple threat lay terrible power, and even I, Flint, knew what that power could do. I *especially*, because I was part of that power.

"I don't know how much money you've got, Mr. Good," I said, "but twenty thousand head of cattle and a valley this size add up to more than enough. Obviously you've got good men"—I shot a quick look at Hawkins: he had flushed deeply—"though of course even a fool could have taken me the night Hawkins showed up." I thought I could take the chance of belittling myself and at the same time taking Hawkins down a couple of notches. I still didn't like the man. Nor he me. "Hawkins knew I had no gun on me. That made it easy. He must have watched through my window— How long, Hawkins, an hour or two, until you were sure I had no gun?"

Good turned to Hawkins. Hawkins swore once under his breath and ran his hand through his thick hair. "Not that long," he said, and Good howled with laughter.

"How long?" Good asked. "How long, Hawk, forty-five minutes?"

I had done it. I had turned Good away from me to Hawkins. It was his turn to face the test. I had let Good know that he and I were alike—we were "the others" I had talked about, the ones who weren't the law. And Hawkins was one of our men, an obvious underling.

"To hell with it," Hawkins said, tossing down his brandy. "What difference does it make?"

Good got up and walked over to him. "You're right, Hawk. No difference. You had a devilish job to do, and you did it. You found Flinty for us. Didn't he, Flint?"

"He sure did," I said. Hawkins looked from Good to me and back again to Good. We both were nodding our heads, looks of deep appreciation on our faces. He flushed again.

"And now," I said, "I'd like to ask a question."

"Of course," Good said. "You deserve to. Ask all the questions you want to. I know Hawkins told you more or less what I wanted, but there must still be so much you don't understand."

Hawkins started to say something, but Good waved his hand at him. "That's all right, Hawk, I know you did. It wouldn't be human not to spill a little, would it, Flint? And how could Flint have come so willingly unless he knew the fun we had waiting for him. Isn't that so, Flint?"

"He told me terribly little," I said. "That's why I have questions. But really, all I want to know now is why—why you're doing it this way. I know that you want it done right, but look at all the chances you took, doing it this way. Getting me to come up here. Sending Hawkins down there, maybe to his death. No offense, Hawkins. But what would have happened if I'd thought—I mean it, Hawkins, no offense—if I'd thought he was a law man looking into that El Paso killing, that last one? Did either of you think I'd let a law man take me, if I had a gun handy?"

Good shook his head. "No-o-o, I guess we didn't. Did we, Hawkins?"

"You said there'd be no trouble, Mr. Good," Hawkins said.

Good looked at me. "It's just as you put it, Flint. I wanted it done and done right. I went to a lot of bother to find you. I told Hawkins to be careful, to make sure you had no gun on you. I said, if necessary, wait until he's stark naked—didn't I, Hawkins?—before moving in on him.... But I didn't think there'd be trouble. I know your past, Flint. I know what you've done, and I think I know why you've done it. I thought you'd come along, just as you have.... Is that all you want to know, Flint?"

He hadn't answered my question. That was for sure. I wanted to know why all this bother, why five thousand dollars for something one of his hands could have accomplished for a few dollars. I grinned. This was the way he wanted it done.

"That's all, I guess."

Good looked at Hawkins. "Do you see that? Here's a man who's been called nearly seven hundred miles to do a little job on two men he's never seen, a rancher and a sheriff—and he has no questions. Now, there's a man for you, Hawkins."

I thought I was riding high enough to say what would have to be said sooner or later. "That's not quite true, sir."

"Eh?" he said. "What's not quite true, Flint?"

"That I've never seen these men. I saw the sheriff today."

Good walked up to me, away from Hawkins' chair. He peered at my face from close up. "You did?"

"Yes." I told him what happened.

He didn't like it. "Not a goddam bit, boy. You know I didn't want you meandering all over that town."

I felt myself redden. "I wasn't meandering, sir."

"No?" he said, staring at me, "no? What *were* you doing, having some gold ore tested? Getting laid? Having a drink? You tell me you were there *all* day, all day. What in hell would a man like you find in Dryhock to keep you all day?"

"Sir, you didn't tell me not to go to Dryhock. You haven't told me a damn thing. You haven't offered to tell me anything now. I'm supposed to kill a couple of people, and you think enough of me to let me wonder that one through, but now you're sore as a boil because I went into town for a drink or two."

Good shook his head. "No, that's not good enough. Of course I didn't tell you not to go to town. Do I have to tell you everything? Or am I to trust you?"

That was the crux. He had to trust me. Once he didn't... you see what would happen? I carried his guilt around with me. If I made the slightest mistake, spoke the wrong word, turned in the wrong direction, I could drag Good to hell. Good had decided I wouldn't make that mistake. He had trusted me. But now? If I could not now be trusted—Good could not afford it. I took a deep breath. I *had* to be trusted.

"I told you I was sick. I told you I needed a drink. You don't have a hole in your chest. You didn't ride ten goddam different nags over six hundred miles. You didn't have to bleed your guts all over the ground. I *had* to get into town and have a drink." Then I paused and said mildly, "Or would you rather they found me bled white, lying outside your ranch, with Hawkins' map in my pocket and Hawkins' gun in my shirt?"

Good went back to his chair. He said, "Are you going to be all right? That is, well enough to pull this off?"

"I think so, yes."

He nodded. He knew I had been hurt in that Texas posse affair—Christ, he knew every goddam thing about me, in fact—and he could not have been surprised at the seriousness of the injury, its long-lasting effects. "Mind you, Flint. I don't care what happens after it's over. I only care that you do the job."

"I'll do the job."

Good sighed. "I don't know. It had all been planned so well. I suppose you've ruined much of it."

"What do you mean?"

He turned to Hawkins. "Hawk, old boy, would you mind checking the bunkhouses. I'll have a word or two with Flint. We'll be out looking for you in a few minutes. Is that all right, Hawk?"

Hawkins' eyes were shining. He got up swiftly and left. It was obvious he expected Good to chew my rear end some more.

Good pulled his chair closer once Hawkins' footsteps had receded. "Before we go into that, there's one little thing. You've noticed how Hawkins doesn't like you, I suppose?"

"I have."

"I hate to do this... such a loyal man... but he's a man with a grudge and I can't afford that. You remember that Dodge City business? Those three men?"

I remembered the Dodge City business. I had been hired to gun down the foreman of a cattle train that was up from Texas. I found him in a bar and worked him into an argument. He had come all the way from the Stockton Plateau in the hell-to-gone corner of southwest Texas and it had been a dirty drive. It was no problem to rub him up. And naturally he had been drinking pretty heavy, now that the train had arrived. So finally he went for his guns and I drilled him. There were two men with him. They decided that was good odds. They were dead two seconds later.

"I remember," I said.

"One of those men was Hawkins' brother."

"His brother?" I said. "That's why...."

Good nodded. "Any way you want to take care of it. But quickly, it's a painful business to me. He's been—well, you know how dogged these fools are. If you and he do any squabbling, the whole thing might go up in smoke. I can't take any chances. Do it quickly, will you?"

There was something disturbing about this, and I knew I should have known what it was, but I kept missing it. "Well... if you think it has to be done."

"Doesn't it?" Good asked softly. "Doesn't it, Flint?"

"I guess so."

He walked me to the door. "Let's make that the first order of business. Get him away from here, far away. Know what I mean?"

For a brief minute I didn't, but as he stood there looking into my eyes, nodding warmly, it gradually dawned on me. He wanted Hawkins' body on Thomason's land or else near their mutual boundary. "Yes," I said, "that's very good. Shall I come back here when it's finished?"

"Why not? Where else would you stay tonight except among friends? There is more brandy... or bourbon or good corn. We shall talk into the morning, the way friends do when they get together after a long time. With us, it's been a long time, eh, Flint? Forever, you might say."

The two of us went into the night. We found Hawkins coming out of a bunkhouse near the far end of the group of buildings.

"All fine, sir," he said. "Everyone in except the line-campers." I noticed he carried a gun.

"Hawk," Good said, "I hate to bother you any more tonight, but I promise this will be the last time. That's a promise." He kept looking at Hawkins, nodding in that puckish way, soliciting Hawkins' good will.

"What is it, Mr. Good?"

"I want you to take our friend over to the ranch's northern boundaries, especially where we've had that trouble with Thomason. Show him the narrow pass where it appears Thomason grabbed off those calves. And the place where the fence was burned. Will you do that one thing, Hawk?"

"Sure thing, Mr. Good." There was a stiffness in his reply, a pride, I think. He lit a cigarette and I was surprised how white his face was. His hand was shaking. Christ, I thought, how the man hates me. Or was it something else...?

We strode to the corral and Hawkins saddled a horse for me. There were two corrals, one at each end of the buildings that swept out from the center ranch house.

In silence we rode together. It was nearly midnight when we set off, and we worked our way slowly as Hawkins pointed out the tiny draws and creek beds starting to dry under the late spring sun. We reached the north limits at half-past two.

"This is the pass," Hawkins said. It was too dark to see much more than a rocky path up a slight rise that disappeared against the bulkier darkness behind it. This was Thomason's land, in front of us, the only land in the entire valley that Good did not possess.

"No lights up there," I commented.

Hawkins chuckled. "Thomason's in bed at night. You would be too if you had a wife like his." He sucked in his breath noisily.

Idly I said, "Handsome woman?" I thought of the woman in the empty street in Dryhock, her horse branded with a "T."

"I'll say."

"Tallish, black hair? Rides a white horse?"

"Why, yes," he said. "You've seen her, too?"

"I think so," I said. The mission to do in Thomason took on additional relish. "What business would she be having with the sheriff?"

"None that I *know* of."

"She's not laying for him, is she?" I asked sharply.

"Wouldn't put it past her," Hawkins said.

I remembered her words. *Another one.... He looks like fun.* The lazy look in her eyes, her tongue, pink-tipped and moving. I thought of her lying on that filthy cot with the sheriff, his sweating three hundred pounds rolling all over her. Disgust welled through me.

And I thought of another man with a featureless face as he raped my sister and burned down the barn, with her inside. The snakes stirred sluggishly.

"...You won't forget now?" It was Hawkins.

"No," I said, "I'll never forget."

"The pass leads in here, you've got that now? And this is where we can post men so that Thomason could not surprise us. You've got that?"

"Yes," I said, "I've got it all." I turned away from Hawkins and bent my hand to my waist. The moon had ducked behind a cloud. Even if it appeared, my shoulder was hunched high, so there would be no glint of metal to warn him. Actually, moon, shoulder, and cloud be damned, there could be no glint, so dulled-down was the gun. Still, this was my way. I had to be sure. For, in a few minutes now, my own blackness would set in. "...Hawkins?"

"Yes?" he said.

I pointed to the ground between us. "Is that anything there?"

He leaned over. "Where? I don't see—"

I brought the butt of my .44 across the back of his neck. He made a sort of gulping noise and hung there, flapping like a fish out of water, his feet still in the stirrups. I pounded down on his head and, cursing, got off my horse and dragged him to the ground. I flipped him onto his back and with the barrel of the .44 whipped him back and forth across the face. Then I turned him over and, groping in the darkness, caved in the back of his head with the gun butt, just as the pulse-beat thundered wildly in my throat and the snakes screamed in tense agony, and the blackness swallowed me....

It does not always happen, the blackness. That first time, in my home town, yes, the blackness gaped like the pits of hell, and other times in the beginning I stumbled through periods right after the kill which I later could not recall. So it was not a matter of surprise that I should have been so afflicted, after a lapse of six years.

It never lasts long. Seconds, I imagine. And then I am all right.

...Thus, I found myself standing over Hawkins' body, panting, the sweat half-blinding me. Not that I could have seen much in that inky valley. My toe found the body. I lifted it with my foot and let it fall heavily.

The next part posed a problem. I did not know whether Good wanted Hawkins' body left on his land or on Thomason's. If it were found on Good land, then it would appear that Thomason had wantonly crossed over the boundary and murdered Hawkins. On Thomason land, it would make Hawkins look like a marauder himself.

But—if a neutral party found Hawkins on Thomason graze and then investigated and uncovered the marks left by a man being dragged from Good land to the point where the body would lie....

Then it would appear that Hawkins had been murdered on his own land and quickly dragged across to Thomason land in a patent effort to cover up the actual scene of the deed.

I lifted Hawkins' head by his incredibly thick—and blood-matted—hair, looped a rope under his armpits and knotted it securely. Then I tied the other end to my pommel. I walked alongside the horse, urging him over the pass and into the dip between the two ranches. Quickly I unhitched the rope, rolled it up and shoved it into my saddlebags. Then I led my horse back to where Hawkins' horse still stood patiently, and tied the two loosely to a nearby piñon. I went back to Hawkins' body and shoving it, pulling it and rolling it, I got it to one of the twin boulders that marked the pass. Halfway to the boulder I felt his heavy wool shirt rip under my fingers, so I switched my grip to his ankles, grabbing him by his boots. Then I wrestled the body to the top of the boulder, and, from the top of the rock, I used my heels to teeter the boulder forward so that the body fell into the crevice. Then I let the boulder rock back into place. Unless somebody went out of his way to look here for it, the body would probably remain hidden some time.

It was past four o'clock when I once more walked into Good's library. I had killed a man—the first time in six years that I had done such a thing. I had ridden many miles that long night and morning, and I had been forced to wrestle the dead weight of a man up a hill in pitch blackness. I was experiencing the letdown that always follows such an event. I was tired, dull. Inside, the snakes had glided away and were still.

Good waved me to a chair. This time I accepted the brandy, brandy as good as the brandy I had had in town, and inhaled deeply of the cigar. I told him what I had done, how I had felled Hawkins on his—Good's—land and dragged him to the boulder on Thomason's.

He nodded, beaming at me. "Yes," he said, "pure genius. The only way, of course, but how many would have done it that way? You, I, who else?" He chuckled. I could have told him who else, but he must have known himself. The whole goddam territory to the south swarmed with men who could have done it just as well. He went on, "It never leaves you, does it, Flint? It's instinct, isn't it? Something you're born with."

"I don't know," I said. He may have been right; I just didn't know. Christ, I was tired. Drained dry and tired.

"But it must be," he persisted. "Let's see, that's number thirty, isn't it? Thirty people in just a handful of years. You couldn't have learned it that well, that fast, could you? It must have been there all the time, waiting for its chance to—let's say, to blossom forth."

I didn't want to talk about it. "Twenty-nine," I said.

"Twenty-nine? Now that's funny. I thought I knew your record about as well as you did yourself." He gazed off at the far wall, over my head. He flicked his fingers and then he shrugged. "Well, you must know."

"Damn it," I said—I may have shouted—"of course I know. Shall I detail them for you, right from the start?"

He frowned at me. "I'm sorry, Flint. You must be dreadfully spent. And you must be dreadfully bored by an old man such as myself. You see, I crave company. It's a lonely life, a man alone." He sighed and I thought: he ought to have a wife.

I shook my head. "Not bored at all."

"Well," he said, "I hope not. I had hoped by tomorrow to improve your company, but—"

I waited for him to continue. He had mentioned my ruining his plans by my going into town and seeing the sheriff.

"It was so nicely set up," he said. "Well, no bother. We'll get along other ways."

"What was so nicely set up?"

He laughed again. There was now beginning to form in me a dislike of that laugh. "You think I'm a fool, don't you, Flint? Now, don't deny it, you must, and I wouldn't blame you at all. I *am* an old fool, but there are so few pleasures left an old man." He shook his head as I started to answer. "No, don't object. That's the truth."

...Finally he told me. And beyond the complicated madness, there was a simple, slender thread of sense, slender but strong.

He had arranged for my appointment as deputy sheriff in this county, working directly under, and for, Barney Slott, the sheriff. He had done this just as he had found me: pulling a string here and a string there, paying a dozen men more money than they had ever seen. And it was done.

"You see the advantage of it, don't you?" he asked.

"Yes," I said slowly, "I see the advantage, all right. With an entry to Slott's office, I can see how he operates, how closely associated he is with Thomason. But—"

"But what, Flint?"

"Where do I fit in there? What are my qualifications?"

Good chuckled. He said, "Excuse me a moment, will you?" and he left the room. He was back shortly, a bundle of papers under his arm. "Here," he said, spreading them out on a table. "Your dossier. From the Arizona Cattleman's Protection Association. You've been an officer of the Association for four years. Here. Your record. Comments of your superiors attesting to your ability, your loyalty, your dogged devotion to the upholding of law and order."

I said, "What is the Association? A private detection agency?"

"Well," Good said, "you might call it that. If it existed, that is."

"It doesn't exist?"

"Of course not."

I was silent for a minute. Down in Arizona, I had heard on occasion of the Arizona Cattleman's Protection Association. Nobody knew who was in it, exactly, but there always were rumors that this or that former sheriff or ex-captain from the Texas Rangers was in it, and maybe running it. Nobody knew for sure. And all the time it had been a figment of Good's imagination. Yet so strong a figment, and so carefully seeded were the rumors, that there flourished the idea that the Association existed.

I said, "But you said there are testimonials from my superiors."

Good's eyes were mocking. "I am your superiors, under several different names."

I said, "You—you've gone to all this trouble just to establish me in Slott's office?"

Now his eyes were wide, innocent. "Do you know a better way? Because if you do, I'll be delighted to incorporate it into my schemes. This way, as you can see, is dreadfully expensive."

"So why do you do it?"

He sighed. "I've told you, Flint. I want the job to be done and done right. I take no chances. This way I've closed all the avenues to error. I have placed the finest killer in the entire southwest, if not in the nation, right next to one of the two men I want killed. Could anything be more sure of success?"

I felt the frown deepen on my face. "That takes care of Slott," I said. "But what about Thomason?"

"Oh, come now, Flint," Good said. "Can't you see the next step? How it must follow?"

I squinted at him. "No, I guess I don't. I'm tired and I—I just don't go along with this way of thinking."

"I'm not so sure," he said. "Listen, and see if you don't." And the machinations of the man's ice-sharp, yet insane mind took me with him. Once established with Sheriff Slott, I was to volunteer to take a job as hired hand on Thomason's ranch. Slott knew Thomason was shorthanded and he also knew of the rustling, the fence-burning. If he were an honest man, the sheriff would want to keep an eye on Thomason. That's where I came in. I'd be Sheriff Slott's eye, on Thomason.

I broke in on Good. "But if Thomason's shorthanded, why doesn't some hungry cowhand walk in and get himself a job?"

Good shook his head. "Would you, if you were a hungry cowhand? All the trouble brewing in this area between myself and Thomason, and me with a hundred men to Thomason's one? Would you want to get involved in such uneven odds?"

So Thomason would hire me. He'd hire anybody if he came cheap enough. Thomason was a poor man, Good said. Still, he needed somebody, desperately.

And shuttling between Thomason's and the sheriff's office, I would be in perfect position to move against either or both.

Of course, the other way—the way any sane man would have wanted it done—would have been merely to send me over to Thomason's at night and find him working a piece of his land by himself. Then I would gun him down.

Killing the sheriff might introduce the problem of getting him out of his office. But even so, either in or out of his office, it could be done.

I told Good.

He sat there for a long moment staring at me with sober eyes. "I suppose you're right, Flint. It could be done that way. But that way is just cold-blooded, unjustified killing."

I said, "You don't strike me as a man with much of a conscience."

"Conscience?" he frowned. "It has nothing to do with conscience. Surely you must know that. It's just safer this way. If two men are killed, wantonly and with no apparent justification, a cry goes up. The hounds are out. The posse." He glanced at me and I felt a shiver run through. "You don't want to hear a posse pounding after you, do you, Flint? I know I don't. I couldn't stand it. You see that, don't you?"

I nodded, dry-throated.

"But if two men are killed," he went on, "and it is apparent that one is a rustler and a vandal and probably a murderer, and the other is a dishonest sheriff in cahoots with the first man, why, then, nobody cares. And I'm safe. I repeat, Flint. My safety is all that matters to me."

There was something else, and again it was escaping me.

I was tired, but I still should have thought it through. It was there for the asking.

"You're puzzled, Flint?"

"Well—" I said.

He waved a hand impatiently. "All right," he said, "forget all that. It's the truth, and it makes sense, but you seem to be troubled by it, so forget it. I'll bring it to your level. You went out to do a job tonight. You did it. You did it marvelously well. But right now you feel drained, as though there was no real thrill to it. And there wasn't, really. I shoved you out there, told you I wanted it done and done quickly, and you did it. But where's the thrill when something is over even before it has scarcely begun?"

I started in my seat. It was how I felt in Sheriff Barney Slott's office when he asked me about my friends in Arizona. I thought I was going to have to kill him, right then and there, and I didn't want to, even though I knew I'd have to kill him sooner or later. Good was right.

"You see, don't you?" he asked. "With you, it's all in the doing, not in the deed. The means justify the end. The planning is the thing; the delicate, deliberate planning, the weaving of the plot, slender as a cobweb, complex as a cobweb, and just as strong and inevitable. Any lout can go out and butcher these people. But not you. With you, Flint, it becomes an art. *You like it.*"

And this was the truth, though I wanted to deny it, to scream out that it was wrong, that it was insane. I couldn't deny it, because even as Good spoke, the snakes came out from behind their rock.

I wrenched my eyes from Good. The first pale sheen of false dawn stood over the eastern hills. I stood up. "Where do I sleep?" I said.

"But we haven't finished talking," Good said.

"I'm tired of talking."

"You don't want to know how we'll proceed now that you've ruined everything with Sheriff Slott?"

I frowned. "Mr. Good, I haven't ruined anything. You talk a lot, but sometimes you don't listen too well. I've ruined nothing. Go over what I told you. The sheriff doesn't know that I didn't know I am to be his new deputy."

It was the only explanation for Slott's action, his words. When I told him my name, it was as though he had been expecting me—and he had been. "...Flynn, Flynn, how you fooled me." He thought I was the one playing the game. He knew my age because he had all the official facts on me, a duplicate of the dossier Good had just shown me. He knew I had left the Arizona Cattleman's Protection Association more than a month ago. He thought I wore my gun because, as a private range detective and as his new deputy, I was legally entitled to. I was willing to hand him my gun because he was my boss, and he could keep his eye on it until I officially reported for business, when I was through drinking, watering my horse, getting supplies, seeing the local girls.

Good heard me out, staring at his hands. "Can a man—even a man like Slott—can a man be really that stupid?"

I nodded my head vigorously. "Not stupid, Mr. Good. He was expecting me, a man named Flynn. He *knew* who I was, you see. He *knew* I was his deputy."

"I suppose you're right," Good said.

"Mr. Good, the only thing that disturbs you is that now you have to proceed along lines previously agreed upon. You need not be forced to think up a new plot, based on a real blunder on my part in Slott's office—though how you would have done that is beyond me."

"If it would have kept me safe from suspicion, I would have found a way."

"But you don't have to, do you? Not if I'm right. You're still perfectly safe, you and your cobweb."

"Enough of this," Good said. "You've convinced me. Tomorrow—today, actually—you'll check in with Slott. He'll ask you if you've established quarters. You'll tell him, no, not yet. If he asks you where you spent the night, just wink a big fat dirty wink. That's what he understands. Then you'll tell him about your idea—about hiring on at Thomason's. Finally, you'll check in at Thomason's and get yourself that job."

There was little else. The talk had run dry. Good was cranky, I thought, tired, old-man cranky. And I—I did not know what I was, nor did I remember a longer day....

Good showed me my room for the night.

"Do you like it?" he said, standing at the doorway, his eyes twinkling once more, the crankiness gone.

"Yes," I said. I did like it. It reminded me of home.

He left me then. And as I crawled into the huge bed, the first streaks of sun edged through the cracks on the east wall of the room and through a tiny square window high up the wall.

I slept five hours, and in the last little piece of that sleep, the old figures rose up, the old faces hove into view, and I dreamed about them....

Chapter Five

...I dreamed I was once again a young man, dressed in gray. It was early evening, not dark enough to be called twilight, yet the dusk was coming in. And adding to the dusk was a huge, heavy white cloud, in the east, over the sea, and thunder rumbled in the distance.

I was not alone. She was with me. My sister. We stood on a hill near our place and we watched the other men, in blue, go by, and they were laughing. I felt a bitter envy, that they could laugh so. And worse, I felt a nameless rage that my sister was laughing, too. She watched them troop by, swaggering young men, neat and muscular and flush-faced with triumph, and she laughed and once her hand raised in an involuntary greeting.

One of them saw her, and they all stopped and watched for a moment. I was angry and frightened.

"Come," I said, "let's get out of here." She followed, still smiling, her face warm and alive and lovely. She was fourteen years old.

The sky had grown quite dark then, and they couldn't have found us, because we were now in the big barn that was behind our house. Hers and mine, and father's. And while we stayed there, for protection from them and from the storm that had swiftly descended in gigantic raindrops and jagged forks of lightning, her smile remained and her eyes were cloudy as she thought of those men outside, of a life outside the farm and the burned-up South, of a life where people laughed when they walked. At least, that's how she looked to me. It was a habit I had, putting myself in other people's places, thinking like them, making believe I was like them, making believe I was them.

"Don't worry," I said, "I'll take care of you."

She laughed again, a rude laugh, as though I had said a foolish thing.

...And then one of the men in blue came slowly into the barn. The rain must have sent him from the road, looking for shelter, and maybe he remembered the way my sister had smiled and waved her hand. For here he was, suddenly, tall and wiry and gleaming-toothed, eyeing my sister with that wary boldness that spells covetousness.

I rose up and stood off to the side and in my mind I said many things to him. I shouted—in my mind—and I waved my fists and even smashed at his face and wrestled him away from my sister when he started to—to do to her as he pleased. And, oh, yes, there was screaming a-plenty.

But it wasn't mine.

It was hers.

I just stood there the whole time he raped her, frozen with fear and with something else, too, something that rooted me to the barn floor and made me stare bug-eyed as he lay all over her, slobbering and laughing, while she screamed and writhed.

...Then he was gone, running off, the fear in his eyes coming full and yellow now that his passion was spent. And my father, panting and rheumatic and trembling-chinned, came running into the barn. He had heard the screaming, and he had come from the fields where he had been trying to cut a furrow through the river of mud that clogged the plow and sent the veins bursting in his forehead.

He stood there, too, rooted and speechless for a moment. Then he turned to me. I do not know what he thought. Maybe he thought that I had done it. But, no, he couldn't have. He may have seen the man run off or else he guessed, because he didn't seem to be accusing me of that. His eyes were pained and full of scorn and disgust, and I felt myself cringe before him.

He saw my cowardice and my guilt and my shame, and he saw that other thing, too, that had kept my eyes fixed on the northern soldier while he raped my sister.

And I could not stand the way he looked at me.

He said, "You let her—" He got no further. I picked up the pitchfork and drove it through his neck.

...And I found myself out of the barn. And the barn was on fire.

You see, it was the lightning that had struck it. Yes, that was how it was.

Or, maybe, it was that man in blue who had raped her—maybe he came back and burned the barn, to hide from the world the evil thing he had done. That could have been it. He could have burned down the barn and gone off with the other northern soldiers, laughing and talking in that northeastern nasal twang.

Yes, I am sure now that it was he who burned down the barn where my moaning, pain-wracked sister lay, and my father. The northern soldier had done it. Burned the barn.

And them.

It was noon when I woke. I could feel the fever in my head. My lips were on fire. I opened my mouth and the skin around the corners of my mouth was so dry it cracked. I shook my head. The dream dissipated. I had no fever. It was the sun streaming in on me. I was all right. The dream had no meaning. Absolutely none. I knew the truth about what had happened. A northern soldier had raped my sister and burned down our barn. Later, I found him and killed him. He was the first person I ever killed.

And that was that.

CHAPTER SIX

What wakened me was neither the sun, nor the dream, nor my satiation after five hours of sleep. What wakened me was a disturbing thought. Mrs. Thomason—if it indeed were she—had gone into Sheriff Barney Slott's office. Would she have asked him who the new man in town was?

That was the question. But that was not the disturbing thought. Good knew everything I knew. I had told him that I had passed this woman on the street, that I had watched her as she jogged on to Slott's doorway. Good had agreed from my description that it probably was Mrs. Thomason. Cora, her name was.

If she had asked Slott who I was, and Slott had told her that I was his new deputy, then Good's plan was in a snarl. And Good had not even mentioned the possibility. That was the disturbing thought.

I asked Good at breakfast. He sat there, surprised a bit, I thought, fork poised at his mouth, and then he lowered his arm.

"I wouldn't worry," he said finally. "Mrs. Thomason is not a talkative woman."

"Slott is a talkative man."

"Yes," he said, "that's so." He stared over my head. "I just don't think the subject would have come up in any meeting between Slott and Mrs. Thomason."

"It strikes me that that would be the first thing Slott would talk about, his new deputy." I was getting irritated.

"Normally I would agree," Good said. "That is, with any visitor but Mrs. Thomason. I'm afraid when Slott sees Mrs. Thomason, his—his thoughts are not of the mundane problems of administering law and order."

"Hawkins hinted the same thing. What's wrong with her?"

"With her?" His eyes were grave masks, but behind them I thought I detected—anger? "Nothing that I know of. We were not talking about her, but about Sheriff Slott and his thoughts."

I fell into silence.

He cleared his throat. "I—uh—I don't usually ask a man of your ability and temperament to move a bit faster, but if you're right about Slott talking about your being his new deputy, I would suggest you get over there with your idea. That will settle it once and for all. Ask him whether he's told anybody about you. He's an honest man."

I laughed at that—Slott an honest man. An honest man in league with a rustler and vandal. It was amusing.

"All right," I said, moving to the door.

Then I was outside, breathing the smell of piñon and blue grama grass while I mounted my horse and jabbed him with my heels.

I rode into town and strolled into Slott's office late that afternoon. It appeared that he had not even moved. He sat sprawled on the cot, in what must have been the same shirt. At least—I thought—he'd know enough to take it off if he ever beds *her* down. There was a bottle of whiskey next to him.

"Well," Slott said, "Flynn is here, ready to carry on. Welcome to Dryhock, Flynn-ie." He sounded drunk.

I told him of my idea, Good's idea actually. Of working for Thomason, keeping my eye on him in case it was true that the rancher was rustling Good's cows.

At first he shook his head, his pig eyes squinting. "How come," he said, "you know all about the fuss between Thomason and Good?"

"How come?" I said, feigning huge astonishment. "Why, man, isn't that my job? Or would you rather nobody knew about it until it blew sky high and took a couple of lives with it?"

He grumbled to himself and then he said, "Aren't you making a mountain out of a mole hill?"

I grinned. "That's rich," I said. "Did you think of that all by yourself? And do you suggest I look before I leap, because a stitch in time saves nine?"

Slott struggled to his elbows. He said quietly, the alcoholic slur gone from his voice, "Yes, I suggest all those things. I suggest you take it easy around here and don't start beating a dying ember into a brush fire." There was, all through this, a tiny crawling at my back. Here he was, fat and filthy and apparently chained to his bed, a slothful, useless man. And yet he was piercing me with his tiny eyes, looking right into the crux of the matter here in Good's valley. Wasn't it just a pissant I was magnifying into a puma? Then the other feeling took charge and the crawling ceased. Slott was a man who sat by and watched another man steal land and swap brands on calves. Here he was, telling me not to investigate the trouble in the valley. And why wouldn't he act that way? Any trouble I'd find would be of his and Thomason's making.

I leaned forward and waggled a finger in his face. "All right, let's find out who's right. Send me over to Thomason's and we'll know. If the man's stirring up something, if he's the one who burned down that fence and branded those calves, then I'll find out, or at least I'll give it a try. And if I find nothing, I'll come back and apologize to you. How's that?"

"Sounds fair enough," he said, crushing a yawn behind a hand the size of my head. "It's just—it's just that—"

"What's wrong?" I said. "Have you told everybody I'm here?"

"No-o-o," he said, "haven't had the opportunity. Nobody's been here. Seldom have any visitors." He forced himself to his feet. "People don't like the smell. Well, I don't like people."

Good had said Slott was an honest man. Slott had just lied to me. Somebody had been in. Cora Thomason.

"Nobody at all?" I pressed.

"Well," he said, "now that you ask, a lady friend was in for—for a brief while."

I felt the tension leave quickly, and another build up, slowly. I didn't want to hear about Slott and Cora Thomason. The thought disgusted me. "Did you tell her?"

He looked at me out of wounded eyes. "Old Barney doesn't spend his time blabbing away to lady friends. Not—not—" He trailed off into silence.

"You're sure now?"

"See here," he said, getting up. He put his hands on my shoulders and shook me once, lightly. The power behind all that bulk was terrifying. "I think we're starting off wrong. I'm your boss. Oh, I know you're a hot trigger from the Arizona Cattleman's Protection Association, but this isn't Arizona. This is a peaceful little county in a territory that's trying awful hard to grow up into a State. We don't want any fussing around here. And I don't want any fussing around me. You stop pestering me, right now. How I spend my time with lady friends is something between me and the lady friends." He closed his right eye exactly as Good had said: a big fat dirty wink.

"All right, so you haven't told anyone. What's wrong with the idea, then?"

He sat back down. "Who'll run the office?" He sounded petulant.

"You don't need me for that."

"You don't like the smell either. That's why you want to get up on the ranch."

I said patiently, "That's not why at all. I want to keep my eye on Thomason. If he's filching Good's cattle, I want to see him."

"All right," he said finally, "have it your way. Go on up to Thomason's. See if I care. Just make sure you put your gun away."

"I will," I said. "And I'll check in here every so often. That is, if Thomason wants to hire me."

"Thomason?" he said. "What makes you think it matters if Thomason wants you? His missus does the hiring."

I laughed. "No wonder you don't want me to go up there."

He raised himself six inches. The drunken glaze had crumbled away. He looked like a struck ox. "Now what do you mean by that?"

I closed my right eye and thought of all the dirty thoughts I could think of. Then I walked out.

...But I didn't go to Thomason's that evening. When I stepped from Slott's office into the Dryhock main drag, the town had started to hint of its nighttime promise. Cowhands strolled the street on foot or sauntered their horses obliquely through the dust. I figured most of them came from Good's ranch. A crude "G" was branded onto their saddles. Others must have come from the ranches on the other side of Good's south slope, from the graze beyond the valley.

There were women in the street, too. Tired wives of tired punchers or more tired farmers, women going home, women going shopping, women going to work in the two restaurants and in the hotel-restaurant or in the saloon or in that cathouse Slott had referred to.

I saw no reason why Thomason could not wait another day for a hand he did not know he wanted. Though I had slipped into a routine of drinking once again, my chest felt clear. I promised myself I'd quit once the tightness grew and my breath shortened. But right now, right now I needed a drink.

The little mustached bartender in The Spur remembered me. "You'll have to drink corn tonight," he said gruffly. "You killed the last of that brandy."

The bar was crowded. I wedged myself between the end wall and a stocky cowhand who was drinking beer. "Fine," I said. "Corn, then."

It was ugly tasting whiskey, harsh and hot. "Jesus," I said, "what'd you do, piss in it?"

The bartender glowered. The beer drinker next to me said, "See, Jake, now you know why I drink beer."

Jake said, "Best goddam corn in the territory."

I tried sipping it but that way the taste lingered. I drained the oversized shot glass, my face screwed up, squeezing tears out of my eyes. "I take it back," I said. "I wish you *had* pissed in it."

The beer drinker let out a howl and beer came dribbling from his nostrils. He turned to me, wiping his nose on his sleeve. "I'm Perry," he said. "Clint Perry." He held out a thick hand.

...He was not a cowhand at all, but a farmer. We talked crops a while. He had come into town to buy a cultivator that Morse's General Store had a good price on, so he said, a used, slightly defective cultivator, but Perry thought he could get it in good shape. Now he was on the town. His farm was twenty-five miles to the north. Dryhock was the biggest town in the vicinity.

I told him about my Arizona place, how it wasn't much of a farm, more a patch.

"How come you left it?" Perry said. He was on his second beer. I stood by idly. I didn't feel up to another corn.

"Too dry down there. Now if we had the water down there you people have, that'd be a helluva place."

He shook his head. "For cows, maybe. Not for vegetables. The sun down there would just burn 'em up. I don't know why you ever tried produce. You got to go east for that. Or else out to California."

I thought: wouldn't he be surprised if I told him I couldn't go to either place because I had murdered too many people and they had been spread all over creation.

The thought made me grin.

"All right," he said, "so I'm wrong. Do your vegetable farming wherever you damn please."

"That's not it," I said. "I was just thinking I could use another drink, but I'd be damned if I'd try this firewater again."

"And that's funny?" He was a single-minded cuss.

"I was thinking I left the best bottle of corn in my shed back in Arizona to come up here because it was too hot and dry down there. Now that I'm here I'm beginning to think it's worth a dry spell or two, just for that little old bottle."

He grunted. That seemed to satisfy him. "You want a drink that bad?"

"Why, yes, as a matter of plain honest fact, I do."

"I know a place," Perry said.

"Go on."

"That's all there is to it. I know a place."

"You mean the cathouse, don't you." I made it a statement.

He bridled. "I should say not. I wouldn't go near that place ever since Doc Smalley went in there to examine the gals and came out with a dose of clap hisself."

"Where then?"

He acted like it was the biggest secret in the world. He leaned forward. "Little place just outside town. Couple of ladies—seamstress and her kid sister—keep a bottle or two on tap."

"Anything else?" I said.

"W-el-ll—"

"But you wouldn't call it a cathouse?"

"N-not exactly."

"Charge pretty heavy?"

"Come on," he said. "Let's stop talking."

He led me out of the saloon. We mounted and rode slowly to the town's outskirts. It was a cathouse, of course, and probably less safe than the better-known one where Doc Smalley got his case of clap. The way Perry talked, it wasn't known at all, except to a few of the more refined boys in the area. The two women were working-girls by day and tried to supplement their income by night, selling whiskey without labels and going through their little routines without ever having one of the local doctors in for an examination.

But I didn't care. There was a quickening in my belly as we neared the place.

It was a small clapboard house, a modest, tidy affair set off the road a couple of hundred yards, with a hill behind it of trembling white aspen and the dwarflike piñon you see out here in the foothills of the Rockies. The whole place was so neat from the outside that I wondered whether it might not have been Perry's imagination that the girls put out at night. One could imagine the town schoolteacher or the mayor's maiden aunt or—or your own sister taking care of such a house.

Once I saw the girls, though, I knew.

...She was a little girl, actually, no more than five, five-one, and a bit too blocky in the waist to be called well-shaped. But she had an enthusiasm for her sideline that led me to believe she didn't do it because she needed the extra money, but because she liked it.

Her name was Amy.

She was the sister of the seamstress, and she did laundry in the neighboring homes. Sometimes she hired out as a domestic by the week, but never longer than that. She was an orphan, and her only relative was her sister. No, she had nobody else in the world. She—

"Don't ask so many questions," she said. "Land sakes, you're nosey. Is that all—is that what you came here for, to have a drink and make a lot of talk?" She turned to me in the bed and let the sheet slip from her bare shoulder.

She didn't know why I talked so much, or, rather, made her talk. I wanted so desperately to—to do this thing and do it well. By all rights, I should have been able. I hadn't had a woman in at least six weeks and though I appreciate that the more regular you get it, the more regular you can do it, I still felt that my abstinence should have had some cumulative effect on my ability.

"I just don't like to leap in," I said mechanically. "If you do things fast, then they're done," I said. "It's all in the doing."

"So do it," Amy said dryly.

I turned to her and—and then the cloud came along, the blessed cloud that takes me apart from myself and makes me watch a man named Flint. That way, you see, I never feel responsible for what I do. I wasn't Flint; Flint wasn't me. And so I lay in bed with Amy, and I remembered somebody else with my sister, doing something to her while I watched. But it really wasn't me watching. I couldn't have just stood there and watched while he did—

"God," Amy panted. "I guess—I guess I was wrong. Just t-take it easy, honey."

—it wasn't me, ME. It was Flint, a man with my name. And Flint was a man who did things that I had no control over. Flint watched his sister with that other man, that northern soldier, and Flint kept laughing and rubbing his hands together, and saying, "Go on, go on," while she—he screamed....

"What's that?" I said. I pulled away and sat up in bed. Amy giggled. "Don't mind that. That's Perry. He always screams when he—you know—"

That was the end of it for me. The cloud was gone, and I was Flint and everything that had happened just before was a jumble and a lie. I knew who I was and what I had done.

I fell asleep and it was five in the morning when a small hand shook my shoulder and said, "Please get up. You'll have to leave now. It'll be light soon."

I got dressed and gave Amy five dollars. She opened her eyes wide. "Oh, no," she said. "That's too much."

I tucked it in her chemise and she reached up and kissed me on the mouth. "Any time you want to talk," she said in my ear, "you know who to talk to."

I said, "All right, I'll remember," and she gave me a little shove toward the door.

My horse was alone in the back of the house, munching in a patch of fat, spiny ice plants, chock-full of water. Perry had gone before me. For some reason, that made me feel good.

Chapter Seven

I turned my horse up the gently rising slope of the hills that circled Good's valley, and at the crest pointed him north. It was still early morning, sometime around nine, I judged, when I looked down into the valley from the top of Thomason's spread.

Still, it was not so early that there should have been no activity on Thomason's land, directly below me. A dozen head of cattle pawed the air sluggishly, their chesty lowing scarcely audible. It was a muted place, Thomason's land, peaceful and lovely. The ranch house sat high on the hill, higher than any other building in the entire valley, looking down on the thick May-scented grama grass that flowed under his fences and onto Good's great sprawling domain.

It couldn't have been more than a quarter section of land. He had a green alfalfa patch, a tiny corral, a barn, the house with a vegetable garden behind it, some graze, and a piece of plowed-up land, lying idle. And that was all. Enough land for a man, his wife, and maybe a hired hand to run. In time of trouble or during roundup or branding, another hand.

I saw nobody. Just the thick-necked cattle, nuzzling each other, their tails slicing the air, driving off the blood-flies.

I rode the crest until I was directly behind Thomason's house. Nothing had impeded me. Where a fence once had been, there was now a tangle of split wooden rails, charred black. This was the fence-fire Good had mentioned.

From behind the house, and to the far side, the east side, I looked for the pass where Hawkins and I had come the night before last—

And then I began to tremble so hard I almost fell from my horse. It was not the sickness coming on. It was worse. It was the thick-skulled, ox-brained stupidity of a man who acted as though his life was about as vital as a fart in a tornado. I had, until that moment, forgotten that Hawkins was lying behind a boulder down there, and that if he were not soon found, there'd be hell to pay.

I cursed bitterly. The man had been missing from the Good ranch since around midnight the night before last. If he were found—let's say, this morning—and Good had not even previously reported he was missing, somebody was bound to raise his nostrils. That's why Good had wanted me to get down to Slott's in a hurry, and then back up to Thomason's.

That was yesterday, noon. Had Hawkins' body been discovered yesterday—less than a day after he left Good's for the last time—then no one would question why he hadn't as yet been reported missing. A man might be gone for a day without anyone wondering about him. Hawkins could have gone off to the other end of the range and checked fences all day, sleeping in one of the lean-tos in the line camp at the extreme south rim of the valley where right now a yellow haze obscured the sharp-toothed hills that grew from the valley floor. Or he could have gone to town and—and then any place at all, for a day.

Two days was another matter. I felt a crawling uneasiness. Twice now I had managed to botch things. I never, never should have gone into Dryhock that first day. Christ, what was happening to me that I couldn't stay away from a drink for one day? Not even a day—a half-day. And I should have high-tailed it up here yesterday, even if it were evening when I showed. Just to get the body rolled out from under the stone. Just to get the whole bollixed mess over with, and me the hell out of the whole son-of-a-bitching territory.

I pushed the horse down the hill, swerved around the house and started off for the pass and the twin boulders that marked it. I didn't know what I was going to do. But first, I had to make sure that the body hadn't been found—

For that was the real problem. Suppose Thomason or his wife had dug it out? Suppose they put two and two together and spelled Good? I was a dead man.

I was around the front of the house now, and shoving forward when she shouted.

"Hey, where the hell you going? This is private property." Her voice was shriller out here in the open than it had been in town.

I turned. She stood on the porch. She had on a thick sweater, a man's sweater obviously, and a pair of sloppy corduroy trousers. Her legs were spread wide, her hands on her hips, and that tangled black hair hanging over one side of her face. She was barefoot.

"Oh," she said, "it's you. Well." It was not a question.

"I'm looking for Thomason," I said. "I figured he'd be out on the grass."

She stared at me. We were about twenty feet apart. Her eyes were perfectly innocent, her face completely devoid of guile. But something lay back there, a waiting something. She kept looking at me that way, and I thought she was somehow measuring me. Women do not let their eyes travel, the way a man will sweep a woman's body with his full stare. Women—like Cora Thomason—pierce through at one spot, trying to find that single weak spot that uncovers the whole man.

And then I realized how foolish I was. I had said I was seeking out Thomason, and to anybody less than half-blind, it was apparent no human being was on that land.

"Or maybe you can help me," I said.

"Well," she said again. "That's more like it. Thomason isn't one of those cows, you know." Then she laughed, a braying sort of laugh, nasty somehow. "Nor one of those bulls either."

I got off my horse and led him to the side of the house where a spray of silver birch marked the beginning of the garden. "May I?" I asked.

She shrugged. "Unless you want to ride him into the kitchen. That's where I'm working. If you want to talk, come on in."

I followed her through the parlor and into an immense cluttered kitchen. She was making breakfast. Water was boiling for coffee and for the two eggs that sat perilously close to the edge of the big kitchen table. Cloth towels were on the floor, on the table, on the big wooden sink. The bottom of the stove was open and coal smoke was backing into the room.

"Well," she said, following my eyes, "a pretty mess, isn't it?" Her eyes were laughing.

I was embarrassed. She seemed to know how sloppy everything was, and yet she didn't care. "I'm sorry I burst in on you," I said, "just when you were cleaning up."

She looked hard at me. Then she started to giggle, and her face was shiny with tiny beads of sweat. I had to laugh myself, and there we were, standing in the middle of that fantastic kitchen, the water starting to hiss over the edge of one pot and climb the top of the other, standing like a couple of imbeciles, laughing like hell.

Finally she leaned against the table, weak from laughter, and her hand brushed one of the eggs. It rolled forward, hung, and then plunged. I plunged with it, trying to catch it, but I slipped on the greasy floor and went down flat, next to the egg. She looked startled at first, but then gave in once more, doubled-up this time. I sat up and she leaned down with a towel to mop up the floor. A wisp of hair brushed against my cheek, and the fine steam of her body was all around me.

"Let me," I said, reaching for the towel. I gave it a tug, but she didn't release it. Instead she looked at me with huge sober eyes, her face two inches from mine, leaning over me, her fine full bosom rising and falling heavily, slowly, under that many-sizes-too-large sweater. I gave the towel another tug and she came still closer, put her right hand on my shoulder, and then let it creep behind my neck.

Slowly she settled herself onto my lap, easing her way in gently, leaning back so that she lay nearly horizontal in my arms.

"Oh," she said, once.

Then I bent over her and her mouth opened—and I heard the horse coming up the hill.

She dug her nails into my back and shook her head once. "Damn, damn, oh, damn," she whispered, and then she pushed her hands against my shoulders and raised herself. I scrambled to my feet. She took my hand and dug her nails hard into my palm. "Let me," she said. "Let me handle it."

I stood there as Thomason came into the room. If he was surprised by my presence, he didn't let on. He went directly to the stove and roughly pulled the two pots of water away from the fire. Then he looked down at the floor, at the egg, and then at his wife. He shook his head sadly. "Don't you—can't you ever—" He broke it off.

Thomason was in his middle forties. His brow was furrowed and his eyes crinkled with deep crows' feet. His mouth was thin and his lips pale. He had sandy, almost washed-out hair, thin, lank hair that did not quite cover the crown of his skull. He had a mild, thin voice.

"I was busy," she said. There was arrogance in her now, flashing scorn at him, wiping his face with it. I felt dirty.

"Busy?" he queried. He had not, so far as I could gather, once looked at me.

She pointed her thumb at me. "He's looking for work," she said.

I felt my eyes narrow. Did she know anything or was she guessing? Or was she just making a reasonable excuse for my being on Thomason's land? It had been so swift, her remark, as though she were sure I could not deny it.

"Oh," Thomason said, turning to me. His eyes were pale, tired eyes. "I'm sorry," he said, "but I don't think—"

"Twenty a month," she broke in. "Christ, Ed, we're short. You can't ride to market and handle the cows at the same time. Twenty a month," she repeated. "I told him that's all we'd pay."

I marveled at her. She had told me to keep quiet, that she would handle it. She was handling it, too. If looking for work had not been my business, she was giving me the out. I could always say the pay was too little and ride off. If it had, I could either try bargaining or take the job.

Ed Thomason picked up the cue. "You can't do much better around here," he said. "Good"—he waved his hand toward the south window—"Good has all the men he needs, more than enough in fact. And the other ranchers on the other side of the valley—" He broke it off. "Well, you must know about that, you probably rode up from there. They're all full-up, doing no hiring until fall roundup."

I had to step around that. In case he ever spoke to the other ranchers and nobody remembered seeing me, he'd be suspicious. I could not allow Ed Thomason to become suspicious of me. Pretty soon now, I'd have to kill him, and it's always easier when they're not expecting it.

Still, it's also less interesting. There's no thrill when you gun down a man who's got a smile on his face. When they go for their guns, though, that's different. Take, for instance, those boys in Dodge City, those three men I killed in a handful of seconds, their guns in their hands. Most of the men I had killed were pretty vague in my memory by now, and even those three were starting to fade. For some reason, while Thomason and his wife stood by, I found myself thinking of those three men in Dodge City, and—and there was something about them, about who they were, that was bothering me, trying to make me remember better. They were alike, those three, short, husky men, bland and pale and—and that was all I could remember.

I shook my head and they disappeared in my mind, though there was a feeling rubbing at me, prodding me to tie them up better, but I wasn't able to. To hell with it, and with them, I thought. They're dead and buried, and Ed Thomason is alive, and this is my job, thrill or no thrill.

"I wasn't over to the other side of the valley," I said. "I spoke to the sheriff in town yesterday. He advised as you might be shorthanded. Mrs. Thomason has confirmed that."

He stared at me. "Where—where do you—never mind," he said.

"My name's Flynn," I said. They waited. "Just Flynn," I said.

Cora Thomason had a little smile on her face. "Flynn told me his other name," she said, "but I swore I'd never tell anybody else. Poor man, with a name like that."

I looked at her and let myself smile, but I knew it wasn't much of a smile. She acted like she knew something, and yet if she did, if she knew who I was, would she act this way? If I wasn't Flynn, but really Flint, then I was a killer, and she was toying with me. Would she?

"Flynn," Ed Thomason said, sort of putting the word on his tongue. It must have sounded good enough to him. "All right," he said. "Why don't you ride the fences so that you know our land and then check in with us later?"

"Fine," I said. I swung out of the kitchen and made loud footsteps for three strides and then quickly ducked back to the swinging door and pressed my ear close.

"How did Slott know we needed a man?" he was saying. His voice was still mild.

"How would I know?" she said. There was a sulky undertone in her words.

"Where were you yesterday, Cora?"

"Jesus Christ," she said, "take your mind out of the pigpen." Then her voice softened, her words a mumble as though her face were pressed close to—to his body. I stepped out of the house and quickly to my horse.

I did not like what I had seen, or heard. Cora Thomason was a slut. Even her husband knew it. But what was far worse was that Thomason seemed to be a decent man, less like a rustler than any man I could recall. And if Good wanted culpability demonstrated beyond doubt, it would take some doing. Still, if Thomason were a desperate man—a man who had to keep his wife happy, he might have done anything.

I did not know.

I followed the fence from behind the house along the crest and down to the northeast edge of the boundary. Then I cut south and Good's ranch house was now visible. The fence veered sharply after a quarter of a mile and worked its way across the far limits of Thomason's land. I was nearing the pass.

To my right was the patch of plowed-up land that Thomason must have reserved for special planting. You saw more of this, one piece of land unused one year, another the next. Already the farmers were worrying about the soil, and the ranchers were worrying with them. When the winters were mild out here, and the spring rains failed to materialize, it got dry as Arizona desert.

There were the two boulders. There, too, were the heavy scraping marks, partly obliterated, marking the path of something dragged to this point. I let the horse drift lazily to the near boulder, the east boulder, and around it, once. I looked down through the three-inch opening.

My heart leaped and then gave one tremendous beat, and I plunged once more into that deep and black terror.

There was nothing behind the boulder. Hawkins was gone.

I moved to the other one. I knew I couldn't have been wrong. It had been the east boulder. That much I was sure of. But was I? I went around the second boulder, peered down through the tiny slit-like crevice, and, of course, there was the faint flapping of Hawkins' torn shirt, the pale glimmer of his softly polished boots.

I couldn't have been wrong, yet I had to be. There was no alternative, none that made sense. They would not have found the body and moved it fifteen yards and shoved it out of sight, right close to where it had been uncovered. They would not have done this. Or would they? *Why would they?*

And again, I did not know.

So, you see, I had to be right. It had to have been the west boulder all along. It had been dark. I had hit Hawkins while we faced—I felt the frown deepening—while we faced south, heading back to Good's. I had been on his left, to the east. The skin crawled up my back as I remembered. I had hit him and then—had the horses turned as I tugged, his body flapping, held only by the stirrups? Had we somehow spun around, and had I not realized I was crossing over the pass to the far boulder, to the west? Had I blacked-out that long?

It seemed incredible. But it had to be.

I stared down at the boulder, through the tiny crack at the faint color of Hawkins' clothes, and once more the crawling went up my spine. I spun around, and there coming toward me was Thomason, on horseback. I edged my horse up the tiny hill and waited at the crest while Thomason plunged down and then up to meet me.

CHAPTER EIGHT

I had to keep him away from the pass. Until I knew—

"There you are," he said. He rode well, slouching deep in the saddle. I saw that he carried no guns. "You've come a long way."

"It's not that big a spread," I said.

"No," he murmured. "It's not." He pulled past me, toward the pass.

"I've been that far," I said sharply.

He did not seem to have heard. I followed him to the rocky pass. He sat his horse there, his eyes sweeping far out and over Good's land. "Beautiful sight, isn't it?" he said, half-apologetically.

"You get a better view from the top of your hill," I said.

He seemed a bit surprised by that. "Why, yes, that's true. I—I sometimes forget how lovely my own land is. A man gets—gets a bit envious, I guess, about what he doesn't own."

There it was.

He had spoken quietly, from his heart, without thought. Thomason was envious of Good's land. The seed of greed was there. With a woman like Cora Thomason to nourish the seed, it would have to blossom.

And yet, spoken thus, it was an honest man's way of putting things. I worked the words over in my mind. Was he—could this mild, tired man be capable of offering me words so openly just to lure me into the belief that he was honest? Good had pondered whether Barney Slott could have been so stupid as not to understand my words. Now could Ed Thomason be that intelligent, that shrewd?

I thrust the question aside. He had spoken blunt words. I had my first indication of proof. That was what we—Good and I—were after. Even Slott had tacitly admitted the possibility of Thomason's guilt, distorting it in his great thick head so that Good appeared the greedy one for coveting his own land.

...I do not know what else we spoke of. I do know we walked the fence around, leaving the remains of poor Hawkins to rot away behind that—that west boulder. And when we reached the burned-out section of fence, Thomason just frowned and shook his head and turned away.

We ate dinner in the kitchen. Cora—she insisted I call her by her first name; her husband had not seemed unwilling—served us scrambled eggs and I thought I detected a twinkle in her eye when she laid it on my plate.

"Not," I said, "not—not the one that fell?"

She laughed and wiped the thick tangle of hair from her forehead. "No, we're not that up against it."

Ed Thomason stayed out of the conversation. The frown that had deepened the furrows of his brow when he'd seen the charred fence still lingered. Once he sighed, deeply, and in what appeared to be embarrassment or—or guilt—he murmured, "Pardon."

"Bored?" Cora asked him.

He turned toward her and his voice was quite gentle. "You know that could not be," he said, and lapsed again into silence.

I broke the long fretting silence. "The sheriff—Slott, I think?—tells me there's been trouble up here."

Cora was at the stove, reaching for the pot of coffee. She slammed it down on the iron top and whirled around. "That big mouth," she said.

"Now, Cora," Ed Thomason said. "I'm sure he just wanted to warn Flynn here for his own sake. The safe way, you know."

"Who's defending the man now?" she said savagely. I sucked in my breath, just watching her. She was vitriol and flame, her dark eyes raging.

"It's not a question of defending him," he said. "He does have a job to do, and the preserving of law and order is the main element of it. He didn't want to send Flynn into something that might bring harm to him."

I broke in. "Might it?"

"I don't think so," he said. "We had some trouble, *had*, mind you, but I think it's over. We hired a hand last summer who—we think—had a sticky rope. Mr. Good thought maybe it was he who stole a couple of Good's calves and put our brand on them. I must admit that some freshly branded calves were found on our land. I know we hadn't done any branding recently."

"What happened to the hand?"

"I guess he just thought things were getting too warm for him. He disappeared one night."

I thought, I'll bet he disappeared. Wasn't that Good's way, I thought. Having some poor fool of a hungry cowhand do his dirty work, branding a few calves, and then having the puncher hustled off, maybe even killed and buried in this soft land?

I said, "And that was the end of that?"

"Well, not quite," Thomason admitted.

"You're damn right, not quite," Cora said. She still held fury in her eyes.

Thomason went on. Sometime this spring, about two months ago, he thought, a piece of mutual fence—between his and Good's land—put up by Good and to be repaired alternately by the two ranchers, starting with Thomason, had burned down at night. It was Thomason's opinion that the hand, in a fit of spite, had returned for this bit of vandalism.

"Seems like a mighty petty act for a man carrying a grudge for nearly a year," I said.

He nodded. "That's what I thought at first. But nothing else seems to make sense. We know we didn't do it. Naturally, Mr. Good didn't burn his own fence.... So, who else could it have been?"

I let that one pass. "And that is the sum of the trouble?"

"Why, yes," he said.

I looked at Cora Thomason. She shrugged and sat down. She seemed to know more about it than he did. Or than he wished to admit. Once she looked up, and I was still staring at her. Immediately she lowered her eyes.

"No more rustling?" I asked.

"Nope," Thomason said flatly.

"Well," I grinned, "one burned fence doesn't scare me off. I'll stay."

Thomason looked at me queerly. "I didn't think it would," he said. Then he excused himself and got up. "I have to go over to Good's." He seemed uneasy about something.

I thought I knew. "Is it a chore I can handle for you?" I asked.

"Why, yes, as a matter of fact, it probably is. It's that fence. I had allowed it to slip my mind. I know it's up to us to repair it, but—but I just didn't have the time. Now, though, with some help, it should be pretty easy. I want to tell Good not to get his bowels in an uproar—excuse me, Cora—that I hadn't had much chance to do it until now, but I'm sure in a week or so...." He let his words dribble off.

"Be glad to," I said. "Might as well meet Mr. Good, since he'll see me up here from time to time." It was essential that I check in with Good when I had the opportunity. He would want to know how I had progressed with my plans. So far as I could see, we were about ready to move against Thomason.

Cora looked at me. "You've never met Mr. Good?" she said.

"No," I said, "not that I know of."

Thomason grunted. "You'd know if you had."

"Rough character?"

Thomason just shook his head. Cora turned her eyes on him, and for a moment there was pity in them. Then he walked out.

"Well," she said, "here we are, in the kitchen again." She reached out and took my hand, digging her nails in once again. "Oh, I'm so glad, Flynn. He'll be gone so often, for such long periods during the day. Sometimes he's gone for two, three days. And then we can—" Her eyes were bright. Her cheeks were red with excitement. She looked like a schoolgirl. "We can, can't we, Flynn? There's no reason why we can't?" She had come up close to me.

I looked out the window and Thomason was on his horse, riding to that west boundary, to look at the fence undoubtedly. Then I looked down and she was in my arms.

I turned my mouth from hers and put it to her cheek, and with my lips I felt the pulse just below the fine high cheekbone. "Yes," I said, "we can and we will." I reached my hand to her sweater and then ran it quickly underneath and she gasped.

"Flynn, Flynn, my God, Flynn. You don't know how it is, with him. He says he wants to all the time, but even when I let him, it's—not good."

"But you don't let him try too often, do you?" I said.

She pushed me away and stared into my face. She was troubled by what I had said, and she searched my face for—for whatever she could find.

"Because if you do let him, I'll be jealous," I went on. "I don't want to hear about it, if you do. I see no sense in hurting him." I had to say these things. She had a quick instinct, a way of sensing meanings that were not always at the surface.

"You won't have to worry about that," she said. "I know more excuses than he does questions." She pulled away from me and danced a step out of reach. "I get the most splitting headaches sometimes," she said.

I put out my hand, but she avoided it. "Backaches, too," she whispered, "from scrubbing the floors. All sorts of aches." She continued to move away as I pressed forward.

"I'll ache you," I said. And then she was against the far wall and her hands were at her sides. Her face was serious again.

"No," she said, "you won't. You won't hurt me. I can tell by looking at you. Oh, Flynn, please be good to me. You don't know how long I've waited."

At that moment, I had seldom seen a more beautiful woman. Her lip trembled and tears were at her eyes, deep magnificent eyes, dark and throbbing. I could barely stand her sweetness; it had an old, an almost nostalgic quality to it, as though she and I had stood together on some darkened hill years and years ago, a lifetime ago, and there were but the two of us, filling the night with our love. And the love was pure of any taint, of any contact.

"What are you thinking, Flynn?" she asked.

I was thinking, at that moment, pushing aside the old memory that didn't exist, that Cora Thomason was playing her hand too fast. Or was she playing at all? She was asking me to take up with her, and there was, in her words, in her manner, a permanence to our relationship. And suddenly I was excited by the thought that I could use Cora Thomason in the plot to kill her husband. I felt myself nodding, thinking *yes, yes,* she and I, together. It will be surer that way, and Good wants it to be sure.

"—Flynn," she said again, "what are you thinking?"

"I'm thinking," I said with a short laugh, "I'm thinking that if I don't get started for Good's, I never will, and your husband will find us still standing here."

"Here?" she said, and the serious look was gone. "Standing? Oh, how I've overrated you, Flynn! I would have thought by then—we'd at least be sitting," she said, "holding hands. At least."

I had to do it this way. I was in a situation unlike any I had ever been in before. I needed all the help I could find. She had practically committed herself. And with the permanence that I sensed—if it was there—I would gain an ally.

"Cora," I said, "what if—if Thomason weren't—well, if he just weren't?"

"What are you saying, Flynn?"

I was in deep now. Yet hadn't she led me this far? I plunged the rest of the way. "Would you want me around all the time, Cora? Would you like it if Thomason were out of the way?"

"Oh," she said. She walked away from me. I followed her. Now she had the option. She could ask me what I meant. Did I mean divorce or desertion, or what? But if she didn't ask me, then she knew what I meant. And I wondered how she could help not knowing, the way the snakes were screaming inside of me, begging for blood. I raised my hands to her shoulders, but she pulled away.

"Please," she said, "don't touch me. Oh, not that I mind, I don't. I really don't. But now, just now, don't." She looked at me. "Out of the way?" she said. She seemed to be talking more to herself, taking the implicit question and trying to grapple with it. "And you here with me instead of him?" She turned her back on me, hugging her arms to her sides. "Don't touch me while I say this, Flynn." Her voice was strange and muffled. "You've offered me something I've wanted all these years, eleven long years. It's so sudden. I can't face it, I guess. It's too much, too much. Too much for me ever to have hoped for."

"I'm not that much, Cora," I said.

"Oh, yes, you are, you are. But even more than that, you've offered to take *him* away." She shivered when she said that, and I knew that we were talking of the same thing: murder.

I could not help it. I put my hands on her shoulders and gently turned her. She offered no resistance. It was as though she had made up her mind. Her eyes were closed when I kissed her, and I do not know whether they were open while I carried her up the long flight of creaking steps.

"No," she gasped, "not that room. Down the corridor. Your room. The last room on the right."

And I found the room, and the bed, and though I did not think I could do it so soon after Amy, I knew I had to. I was asking her to help me kill her husband. For this, she had to expect to be loved, by a healthy man, as often as a passionate woman desired. I had had little sleep and no rest.

It did not matter. I had found her, and her softness was all the rest I needed, burrowing my head between her breasts, big and bold and pressing against my mouth. And so we did it, and it was as it seldom is, at least seldom to me, long and slow and explosive.

"Darling," she said.

"Yes?"

"Nothing. Just darling." I felt a wetness against my shoulder. And then she slept, in my arms.

I did not know what to do. I knew I had to get out of that room, and get her out of there, too. I had to see Good. Thomason might be back any minute. I started to draw my arm from around her, and she murmured and wriggled toward me, her breasts stirring against my bare chest.

"Flynn," she murmured. She leaned back against the pillow, her eyes open now, expectant.

"I'll have to go now," I said.

"Oh, no, not yet," she said.

"Thomason will be back."

"No," she said, "no, he won't. He stays out all afternoon. He'll nap out on the hill. He won't be in until it's time to bring the mulch cows in. Please."

"You sure?"

"Would I take the chance?"

I drew in a deep breath.

This time it was like pain, long and drawn out, and I was like a man dragging his burning feet through a searing desert, long and unending, stretching before me to a tiny bright oasis, a hundred million miles away, and I crawled on my belly a half-inch at a time.

But I got there.

I got there and I was drenched in my sweat and hers, and each breath tore great holes out of me.

"Oh, darling, darling," she was saying, and her voice was hollow in my ears amid the pounding of blood against my temples.

I had done it and it had cost me. I could not breathe.

...And somehow we were standing together, and she was helping me into my clothes and we were walking, she half-carrying me, down the stairs and out into the air.

"Please," I kept saying.

And she was saying, "Oh, darling, not yet, don't pass out yet."

My face was on the ground and then up to the sky and she was wiping it with a wet rag. I struggled to a sitting position and when she tried to hold me, I thrust her aside. I had to, you see, I had to. I was drowning in my own blood.

It came out, then, in a red gush. I thought it would never stop. And even when it stopped, I kept retching, and that, I knew, would never stop, could never stop. No, not for me who had always made a hell out of what another man would call heaven, who drank water and found salt in his throat, who drew the sweetest air God ever made deep into his lungs and spewed out great thick crimson wads, and who, right in the middle of love, found death.

...Now, in the worst moment of weakness I had known since I nearly died one lonesome night in Texas, with the baying of the hounds bouncing off the stars and my chest oozing blood, now I had so much to do, so fast.

I could not, of course, get on a horse and go to Good's. I would never make it. And yet Good had to know about Hawkins, still lying behind that boulder.

I had to wipe up every speck of blood, on me, on her, on the ground. Thomason must not know.

And I had to act in such a way that Cora Thomason would eventually feel that she had thrown in wisely, that she had waited for the right man to come along. For if she ever became suspicious that I would not be able to kill her husband—now that she had joined forces with me—what good would I be to her? There would be nothing to prevent her from turning me in to Slott, and when Slott started digging....

I would be a man in metal chains, on his way to Texas or Arkansas or Oklahoma or Georgia or God knows where else they were waiting for me, noose in hand.

And if—somehow—if Slott failed to dig deeply enough, it would not matter.

Because Good would not stand for it. If I failed Good, I was a dead man.

And getting to my feet that afternoon, wiping the last trickle of blood from the corner of my mouth, I had to laugh at the predicament.

Because I was a dead man no matter what. If I managed to beat them all— Good and Slott and Thomason and the rest—I would do it only at the expense of my own body. I could not take too much more. That was obvious. Yet I had to take too much more.

Pretty, isn't it?

She helped me clean up the mess. I insisted on doing more than I physically could. It had to be that way. Every so often I found her looking at me, sidewise, a musing, measuring look.

"Is it—?" she finally asked. "Is it like that often?"

"Hell, no," I managed to say. "I must have strained my side riding up here. Not enough sleep. That long trek up from Arizona. Lots of things. You'll see, it won't happen again."

"We'll be able to—" she blushed "—we'll be able to see each other, at times?"

I walked over to her and put my arms around her. She jumped away. "Not here," she said sharply.

"I can't help it," I said. "That's what you do to me.... You bet your sweet life we'll see each other. Lots of times."

...I think she was satisfied. It was the best I could do.

I made myself get up early the next morning. I had retired before supper the night before. I had Cora tell Thomason that I was worn out, that I had seen Good, and that Good had said Thomason needn't worry about the fence.

Cora had looked dubiously at me, then. "I can go offer to tell Good."

"No," I said sharply. I didn't want Good to wonder where I was, as he would if any messenger came from Thomason's other than myself, now that I was sure to be working there. I didn't want Good to suspect there was anything wrong with me. "You entertain Thomason," I said to Cora. "Keep his mind off me."

"Oh, Flynn," she said. "Will it be—soon?"

"Yes," I said.

"H-how will—"

"You leave that to me," I said. "It'll be soon and simple. And nobody'll be the wiser."

She frowned. "I don't see how that will be possible."

I chanced a quick grab and a peck at her cheek. "I said leave it to me. Old Flynn never misses."

Her eyes narrowed. "Never misses? You've done this before? Many times?"

I did not like the way the talk was going. There was something uncanny in her intuition. She always grabbed the wrong—or right—word. And there was something wrong with Cora Thomason. She was at turns slut, school girl, conniving, trusting.

Or was it only wrong with me?

...I had turned the talk away, and she had agreed to tell Thomason what I had instructed her. And I, on legs that were papery, somehow clambered to my room and to that bed where it had started.

I was out of the house before they were up that next morning. I would walk the horse every step of the way to Good's. Even so, the pain was intense. I moved out behind the house and past the burned fence and onto Good's land. An hour and a half later I entered the house.

CHAPTER NINE

Good was in the familiar library. There was on his face when he first saw me a look closer to genuine friendliness than I had ever seen on him before. The face was not puckish but thoughtful, and behind the thought lay concern.

"You're not well," he said finally, after he had studied me for a long minute.

"No," I admitted. "I've had another attack."

And then I told him everything that had gone before. I hurried the business about Amy and I was conscious of the heat in my face when I told him about Cora Thomason and myself, in that end room on the corridor.

He listened quietly and only once did his face seem to yield up any expression other than thoughtfulness. That was when I told him about Hawkins' body being behind the west boulder.

"The west, you say? As I recall, the way you told me the other morning, it was the east boulder."

I did not want to make a point of this. "I must have been mistaken."

"You sure now?"

"It's the west boulder. I'm positive. Anyway, why would—" Then I broke it off.

"Yes," he said, "why would anyone move it?" He started to nod his head in that familiar way, coaxing me to talk, encouraging me.

I saw no reason to continue this conversation, to dwell on the error I had made. I had made enough mistakes already, without this one. "I have no idea," I said.

"Sounds pretty foolish, doesn't it?"

"It does."

"And yet, it never pays to write off the moving of a body some—fifteen, Flint?—some fifteen yards as foolishness. Nobody is quite that foolish."

"So that means," I said, "that it just didn't happen. It means that I got my directions mixed up, and that I originally put Hawkins' body behind the very boulder where he is now."

Now the face was puckish. "That's one alternative. The other would be that it was *not* foolishness that dictated the moving of the body. That it was sense to do such a thing. Isn't that the other alternative, Flinty?"

He was right, of course, but this was the sort of sense I could not understand. This was sense the way his plan of murdering Thomason and Slott was sense, sense laced through with the bright red threads of insanity.

I nodded in mute answer and sat back, waiting.

"Well," he said, "I see no need to change our plans. In fact, I think the order of business demands we execute them promptly."

"My thought exactly," I said.

There was in him a growing graveness that disturbed me more than the previous jocularity. He seemed weary of what was transpiring, and of what would transpire.

"I can't say," he said, "that I'm happy that we must act now."

"Why?"

"I would have liked more, better proof to stack behind us. A butchered calf or two, with Thomason standing nearby and Slott watching, let's say. That's what I would have liked. But—"

"I can wait," I said. I threw in my bluff because I knew he would not take it.

"No need," he said. "Actually, you've done better than—I suppose—I could have expected." There was a mild regret in his words. "You've enlisted Mrs. Thomason's aid—that may have been rash, but it's worked, so you say."

"It has."

"And Thomason has admitted a craving for my land."

"Craving may be too strong a word."

He waved a hand at me. "Thomason is a mild man. That he admits to such a desire is indicative of some storm inside. He craves my land. I think I'm being fair to him, using that word. I think he's indicted himself.... Now, Slott, that's a different matter."

"Have you any ideas on Slott, sir?" I asked.

"I'll go along with your idea, Flint," he said, nodding.

He must have known I had no idea. But now, we were back to the relationship of employer and employee: was I good enough for the job? He was making me delineate the means for killing Slott.

I forced myself to smile. "I'm glad you feel that way." He looked startled for a minute, and I knew why. I was doing that old thing again, putting myself in somebody else's shoes—Good's, this time—and thinking the way he thought. When I thought how Good no longer trusted me, Good was thinking the same thing. I don't know how I knew this, but I did. I didn't like it when I found myself thinking the way somebody else did. It got in my way, made it more difficult to see things clearly, the way I saw them. I would see them the way *they* saw them.

But thinking the way Good did was a help. I was able to keep up with him. At least, part of the time.

A touch of admiration replaced his startlement. (He was thinking— Good was—*Sometimes Flint surprises me. Sometimes he seems to know what's going on in my mind. Oh, he doesn't really, of course, but he seems to.* And I felt like laughing out loud.)

He said, "Tell me about it, Flint. I'm afraid I've been a difficult taskmaster all through this business, but I promise that will change. Right now, in fact. Let's hear your idea. I'm sure you'll put the old man to shame. Just the way you did when you knew how to handle Hawkins' body."

And once more we fell into place. He was Good; I was Flint. I had to think my own thoughts. To hell with the other nonsense. Nobody knows what's going on in another man's mind.

"As I see it," I said crisply (far more crisply than I felt), "it simply entails Slott going over to Thomason's on official business. That's up to me to figure out. Slott has sent me to Thomason's to check on the rustling and the rest. I've been up to my neck in ferreting out facts up there—that's why I've not had the opportunity to check in with Slott before. But now I'm ready to proceed. I've got proof, *the* proof. Hawkins' body." I paused to light up a cigar and I watched Good's face through the thin cloud of smoke. He was rubbing his chin.

"I've got an out-and-out dry-gulching of a Good man, but I'm no damn hero. I want help, and I want it fast. Not from outside. That will take too much time. From him. He's the law enforcement officer of this county.... He does ride, doesn't he?"

Good was smiling. "Why, yes, it's been known to happen, Slott on a horse."

"The rest, then, is terribly simple. Shall I spell it out?"

"Go on," Good said. "No, wait a minute. Let me see if I follow you. You are going to Slott's to tell hi—"

I let out a short sharp laugh. "*I'm* not going," I said. "I'm up at Thomason's, bird-dogging the mess. Cora Thomason is going." I wondered if he would perceive that I had just thought of this angle.

He frowned. "And Cora Thomason is going to tell him that her husband is a killer. Oh, no, Flint, that's nonsense."

Once more, I laughed at him. "I see I do have to spell it out. The *facts* are that Thomason has killed—or seen to it that someone has killed—poor Hawkins. But Mrs. Thomason won't tell him that. She'll tell him, her big eyes brimming over, that something terrible is happening up at the ranch, and won't he—won't he *please* come up, quickly? Of course, I might be able to get Slott up here. But is there any doubt that Cora Thomason *will?*"

His eyes were shining. He let out one long breath through pursed lips. "And then when Slott gets there, you and he and Thomason—"

"And Cora," I broke in.

He nodded. "Of course. Cora, for protection and witness. You all go over to the pass, to the boulder, and there is Hawkins' body. You'll be behind that little rise so that nobody from my ranch will see you—why not do it at night?—and then you'll shoot them both down."

"With two guns," I concluded.

I was pleased with myself. It had gone far better than I ever imagined.

"When this is finished, Flint," he said, "you'll have to go away for a while." Once more, the regret in his voice.

"Until the hue dies down," I said. "In any case, I'll have to reveal myself to the townspeople as a deputy, to explain my role in the tragic occurrence. I suppose Slott has been provided with official papers that will stand scrutiny for a brief time at least?"

"Oh, now, Flint, give the old man credit for something. Of course he has. Not that anyone will want to scrutinize them. You'll be in charge of that office, with Slott dead. Then, after a few days, you'll be off to your superiors, your Arizona Cattleman's Protection Association."

"And later, you'll want me to return?"

"Of course," he said. "I'm an old man. I've got more money than I'll ever need. With Thomason out of the way, I'll have the whole valley. And then"—he chuckled—"who knows?"

The last bit baffled me, but I did not let it turn me from what Good was offering. He was offering me a share in this enormous place, a share of his money, a place to live out my life. A place where—with a decent break from God—I might at last throw this terrible sickness.

He was being to me the father I had not had since—since I left home years ago. My father had died—sometime soon after. I felt the tears course down my cheeks.

"Bosh, Flint," he said, "that's not like you. You're destroying my illusions. I constantly picture you at work, treading like some silent specter, cold and quick and deadly. And here you are, watering my library." He seemed delighted.

I laughed with him. "I won't say much now, sir, except that I think you know my answer. However—"

And the gravity again. "However," he said, "there is much work to be done. Then there must be the decent interval between the burial of Slott, your resignation from the Cattleman's Protection Association, and your return to this area. Yes, I understand. When you can, when you feel completely free, unshackled, you will speak out about your future plans."

"It won't be too long," I said. "We'll set tomorrow night as the target date. Is that all right?"

He nodded his head quite slowly. "Fine," he said, "if you think you can pull it off in that short time."

I wondered whether he knew my own doubts. "I think so, sir," I said. "Tonight would be too soon to hope that Mrs. Thomason could get to Slott and bring him back." I looked out at the range. "By the time I get back to Thomason's, it will be afternoon."

"So late?" His eyes narrowed.

Inwardly, I cursed. Once more I was widening the discussion to embrace more than I intended. I could not let Good know of the pain each jogging step cost, or how slowly I had to maneuver. "I didn't know how long this would take, this talk, so I told Thomason I would go into town. My horse—I told him—needed a front right shoe. I thought you could have it done here. It would save time."

"Flint," he said gently, "if you wanted to save time, you would have told me about the horse as a first matter of business. Now you'll have to wait until it's done."

"How long, Mr. Good," I asked sharply, "does it take to shoe a horse? Ten minutes?"

He let it go at that. He strode through the library and I faintly heard his halloo. Then I heard a horse gallop up, and less swiftly, two horses trot off.

Good returned. "Front right, is that what you told Thomason?"

"Yes, sir," I said.

And that ended that. We sat in silence for less than fifteen minutes until I heard the twin gallopings. I rose and started for the door. Someplace we had lost the rapport of earlier. Once more, I was the hireling, and, I think, a hireling in not complete esteem. I shrugged. I had played my hand as best I could. It was still a pretty good hand.

I mounted slowly and forced the horse to a gallop for forty searing strides. That was in case he was listening. Then I jerked to a halt while the pain flowed through to my toes. We walked straight for the pass, through the heat of Good's valley, and a thought started forming in my head—no, not even a thought, just the kernel of one. It had no handles as yet, no clear lines, just the slightest coating of fuzz. My mind was never the keen instrument that was Good's. But he was forcing it to be.

The thought had to do with Hawkins. Not only his body, but who he was, and why I had been asked to kill him.

I worked at the kernel of thought, and then I was directly before the pass. In a way, I was glad I was so distracted. The pain had not overwhelmed me. Within minutes, I would be headed for Thomason's ranch house, and with luck, with Thomason gone, I would seek out my room and gain precious rest.

The sun was striking the boulders, and an excitement was stirring within me. It was here that I had slugged down Hawkins, and it would be near here that I would shoot down Thomason and Slott. As I dwelled on that, the snakes rolled inside.

For some reason, I edged to the east boulder, where I had previously thought Hawkins had been placed, but where he wasn't. I looked down again at the boulder, and sidled my horse around it. You could see quite clearly through the crevice, a wider crevice than I had at first thought. The relief was a flood of warm perspiration. He was, of course, still not there.

I started through the pass, and then I turned the horse back. In front of me, to my right, I had seen again the freshly-plowed unused land, land where a shovel could sink, two feet in one lunge. I turned to the west boulder and quickly headed the horse to it and around it.

Nothing.

Hawkins was behind neither boulder.

Now it was clearer, though still obscure. I got off my horse and the pain was streaking through me. I lifted my horse's right front foot. He was wearing the same old shoe. I lifted his left front foot.

It had been freshly shod.

I got back on my horse, some minutes after, though not too many. There was no nagging in my head any more. I turned back toward Good's. I rode slowly, in some pain, but not too much. Pain no longer mattered.

I had to go back. There was a question I had to ask Good, and though it would change nothing, it had to be asked.

It should have been asked in the dead of night, in the pass between Good's and Thomason's, but I had no time to wait for night, and I had seen that pass too often. It would be dark enough.

I did not fully expect to make it back to Good's, nor did I ever then expect to make it back to Thomason's. I succeeded in both, and I took with me that scene in Good's library....

He did not seem surprised to see me. Rather, it appeared as though he were expecting me (those were his thoughts, I am sure). Or he may merely have known that it didn't really matter, that I had to continue no matter how deep he dug my hell, how heavy the boulders he put in front of me.

I said to him, in that huge library, "Once I was going to ask you if you thought you were God." I paused. My breath was a hissing sound.

"Go on," he said.

"Now I won't ask you that one. I'm past that point now. What I have to know is—"

"Go on."

"...*are you?*"

He stared down at me, yes, *down*, though he was sitting, and I was standing. And then he started to laugh.

It was more a howl—*whee-hee*—than a laugh, or maybe I wasn't expecting him to react that way. He laughed, *whee-hee*, way up high, catching his breath every so often, *a-whee-hee*, going on and on, like a wailing coyote or a lost ghost, and I turned then and fled through the door and out of that house into the fetid, unmoving heat.

But all the way back—from the time I climbed my horse and moved across the valley, all the way to Thomason's, and to my room—all the way, I thought I heard an unearthly sound of Good laughing, back in that huge library.

Then blackness took me.

Chapter Ten

It was near midnight when I thought I heard a noise, and I woke. This time the heat I felt on my mouth was fever. I was burning up. Yet in a way, I was glad.

It meant I would not be able to do the job on Thomason and Slott that night, the next night, actually. Then I remembered.

I would not be able to do the job ever. Not the way I had it planned. I had been so clever. I had played Good's game, and beaten him. He had listened to me as I outlined it all, about the way I'd use Hawkins' body in the killing of Thomason and Slott. And all the time as I sat there in his library, telling him about it, Good must have known that Hawkins wasn't behind the boulder. How he must have enjoyed that bit.

I stumbled from my bed and put on my clothes. I would ride away from here, now. I had slept nearly nine hours. I would never be so strong again, not in the next few days. And that was all I had. A few days. That was about what Good would give me. If I did not succeed tomorrow night, Good would patiently allow me another day, and possibly another. Then he would move.

I started down the steps, on tiptoe, the same flight of stairs Cora Thomason had half-carried me down a short while back.

And I stopped.

I had just proved—once more—how stupid I was. What good—I reflected—would it do to run away? How far could I get? I had known all the time, hadn't I, that if Good had found me once, he would find me again. A man walking his horse in relatively unfamiliar land, a sick man, a tired, frightened, dullheaded man—would he not be easy pickings?

And damn it, did it have to be? Did this man—this man Flint whom I was looking at more and more from a distance—did Flint have to quit Good? Did Hawkins' body mean that much?

I stepped more firmly down the stairs. There were voices in the kitchen. That must have been the noise that wakened me.

Thomason and Cora were sitting there, drinking coffee, and he was eating a thick slab of white bread.

"Well," he said, with what I had to judge was false heartiness, "our sleeping beauty." He himself looked as though he needed sleep.

Cora stared at me. Her eyes were bright and clear. "Hello," she said. "I told Ed how hard you had worked fixing that fence. He wants to thank you."

"Yes," he said. "Mighty good job. Better than I could have done. Don't know how one man could have done it that fast."

I could have told him. One man hadn't done it.

I smiled wryly. "I may be a bit stiff in the morning."

"Hell, I imagine you will," he said. "A helluva lot stiff."

"Sit down," Cora said. "Have some coffee. You're up because—because you've slept enough?"

"Thanks," I said, sitting down across the table from them. "I've slept enough."

I had, too. Under the rules of the game, I had at least twenty-four hours and at best forty-eight or seventy-two to wipe out Thomason and Slott, and to do it in such a way as to protect Good and myself. And Cora Thomason. Sleep—for the time being—was out of the question.

Thomason looked at me with a mixture of confusion and concern. "Uh—you're sure? I mean, you're up now, at midnight, and you don't intend to go back to bed?"

I felt sorry for him. He was suddenly a man afraid. He was going to bed. Obviously, by the look of her, Cora was not. I wasn't either. We had been together, out of his sight, for nearly two days. I wanted to reach out and pat his shoulder and tell him not to worry. For I simply couldn't, not now, make love to his wife.

"No," I said. "I'd like to have your permission to look over the ranch a bit more."

He looked at me strangely.

"I'm a farmer," I said, "not a cowhand. I think you're not getting the best, most economic use out of your land. If I may—"

He reddened slightly. "Why, sure. That's very kind of you. But isn't it too late, too dark for that sort of thing?"

I wanted to tell him it would never be anything but too late, and that not even the sun shed light for a blind man, and I wanted to tell him that hell was as beautiful as his wife, and heaven as gaping as a man's empty grave. There was so much I wanted to tell him, but, you see, I had so little time. And, perforce, he had even less.

"I don't think so," I said. "You're paying me wages and I've slept too many hours already. I can tell the quality of soil by feeling it just as well as by seeing it. I want to trace the creek bed that starts above the house and see whether it might not be broadened so that more of your land can be reached directly by it. Irrigation is the only way to save this land. In thirty or forty years," I said, "this all will be dry as desert unless something is done about controlling the water. Why, without irrigation—" And I stopped. In thirty or forty years, we would all be dead. In thirty or forty hours, Thomason would be. I started to grin.

"Go to it," he said. "Hell, I never stopped a man from working yet. Especially," he said, with a broad wink, "if the man is working for me. Isn't that right, Cora?"

She forced a smile to her face. She had a wondering look on her face, and

I think she looked less bright-eyed. "That's right, Ed. But I do think, Flynn, you're pushing yourself too hard."

The kernel in my head was acorn-size now, and it had good clean lines and I could almost make out its meaning. "No more than other people are pushing themselves," I said. "Take, for instance, yourself. Why," I said, "you work like a man, like a couple of men. I've seen you," I said, "digging and cleaning up and carrying—things." I let my eyes sweep her and she flinched as though I had whipped her with a switch. Maybe I wouldn't find Hawkins this way, but I'd sure as hell find out how he got out from behind that boulder.

"What do you mean?" she said, in a low voice.

"Why, honey," Thomason said, "he's right, you know. You do work too hard. I always tell you that."

I kept silent. I had reached her.

"What do you mean?" she repeated.

I smiled. "As I recall, the first time I saw you, you were in bare feet, cleaning up the kitchen and cooking a meal at the same time. Since then, I've seen you lugging things down stairs. I've seen you lugging things in the fields. I've seen you around the fence lugging slats just to help me out. Why," I grinned, "if your husband's not careful, you'll probably insist on carrying off all those boulders around here, just to get things all straightened out."

Cora turned to her husband. "Let's go to bed, honey," she said. She let her eyes take on that slumberous look that I had seen on her face so many times now.

He perked up. "Sure," he said. He got up. "Don't work too hard, Flynn. There'll be lots to do in the morning."

"Don't worry about me," I said. I turned to Cora. "Sleep well, Mrs. Thomason."

My sleep had wiped much of the thickness from my thoughts. More and more, I was finding it easy to push Cora Thomason as I wished, to make her think as I dictated. More and more, I was sliding into her mind—making myself her—and knowing what was going on in her head.

I had always been able to do that with Ed Thomason, almost from the first minute I had seen him. But that was easy. Any man could have done that. Cora was tougher, yet she was coming around, fitting into the channels I created, reacting as I demanded.

Not that this was important. It was just helpful. And any help—now—would be duly accepted.

Still, the task remained, with or without help. I had two men to kill, my thirty-first and thirty-sec—no, my thirtieth and thirty-first. The easiest way to accomplish it was the way I had outlined it to Good. With Hawkins' body crying out for vengeance.

There were other ways. But I did not, at the moment, know them, other than my first and simplest plan: cold-bloodedly killing Thomason and then riding to town and doing the same to Slott.

I didn't want to do it that way. But it remained a possibility, a last resort. I had gone too far this way, Good's way, to turn back now. And despite the evil of the man, there was something desperately magnetic about him. There was something unmoral—not immoral—about murder, done this way. It all became a chain, and each link was so delicately forged and with so complex a pattern that all the effort was in forming the chain. That the chain would then be brought shatteringly down on the skulls of two men seemed almost an unfortunate afterthought.

Good—and wasn't this terribly important to me?—had made murder an art.

But, oh, so difficult. If I only had Hawkins' body. That was my immediate task. I had at best a few hours to search for it. Cora Thomason would be down here with me by then.

I went to the boulders on foot and looked, once again, beneath each. No body. I did not expect there would be any. I looked about me. The moon spread a soft glow over the land, Good's land and Thomason's, blending the two into a silken and silvery fusion. It could have been —and, I suppose, it was—a lovely place, this valley. What was happening here was man-made. That was clear enough, even with a man named Good at one end of the string. And the valley, that was surely God-made.

I walked to the freshly-plowed earth that stretched nearly to the pass. It was a patch of dark brown earth, cool to my fingers. I dug my hands into the dirt, up to the wrist, and let my hands clench and unclench. Then I stood and rolled up my sleeves and got down and reached in.

Someplace in this five-acre piece of ground, too big certainly for me to search it all, Hawkins' body was lying. Where else, but here? I continued to walk around the patch and every so often I bent and shoved my hands to the wrists in good cool dirt. Finally, I had walked the perimeter and was back at the pass. I sat on the west boulder and lit a cigarette. Two hours had gone by, much of it spent on my knees. In case—just in case—anybody had been watching me, it must have been apparent that I was searching for something.

...I did not have long to wait. She came by horse, but quietly. It was dangerous, but she had to know.

She had a coat on over her gown, and a pair of shoes. I don't think she wore anything else.

"Flynn," she said. "Flynn?"

"Here," I said. She loomed over me, her face white and questioning. She walked the horse to the far boulder and looped a line about it.

Then she came to me, walking slowly, her arms at her side. She stood next to me and I moved from the boulder to face her.

"Well," she said, "won't you—aren't you going to kiss me?"

"I'm sorry," I said, grinning, "my hands—I'm sort of dirty." I held out my hands and she squinted down at them. "Let me," I said. I scraped a match against the boulder, and she gasped from the sudden flame. "Here," I said. I held the match over my hands. "See?" I said. "I can't possibly touch you this way. At least not with my hands." I let the flame fall to the ground and I put my arms straight out and she came into them. I pressed my elbows into her sides until she gasped. I kissed her. And, I swear, it was fine.

She stepped back, then. "I was so—worried about you. The way you talked in the kitchen." *The hell she was worried about me*, I thought. She was worried about herself. "I thought somehow that you had turned against me, that you weren't interested any more in doing—what you said you'd do."

I hoisted myself to the boulder. "Here," I said, "sit here, next to me. There... that's better. You know I'm interested. Why else would I do it?"

"I don't know," she said. "You seemed to—hate me before."

"Nonsense. I just don't want Thomason jealous. That's the last think I want. I think your coming down here is foolish, in fact."

"You want me to go back... to him?"

"No," I said, and I meant it. "No, I want you here, with me. I knew what I was doing before, turning you to him, but I hated doing it. Soon, though, we won't have to worry."

"How soon, Flynn, how soon?"

"Tomorrow night," I said casually. "Tonight, that is."

It was already the next day.

"Oh, God," she said.

I went on. "It will all be over by this time tomorrow. How's that sound?"

"Wonderful." Her voice was dull, toneless.

"You don't sound as though you mean it."

"Oh, I do, I do. It's just—just that I've waited so long, and now, in a matter of days—"

"Hours," I said flatly.

"Hours," she repeated, and her voice was hollow.

I drew on my cigarette. I had to wait for her. It was her move.

And she knew it, too. "How will you do it, Flynn, or is it still none of my business?"

I got down from the boulder and walked to the field of plowed-up dirt. She followed behind, and I could sense her wonderment.

"It was never none of your business." I stopped and let my foot trail over the dirt, testing the spongy ground. "It just seemed better not to clutter your head with too much in the beginning. But now, now I need your help." I bent down and began to examine the ground, sifting the dirt through my fingers. "Damn," I said.

"What is it, Flynn?" she said. I thought her voice was shrill and strained.

"Nothing. I just dropped my knife. It's here someplace."

I groped about on the ground, the knife held tight in my hand. I reached under the ground, clawing with my fingers. "Wha—what's THIS?" I exclaimed.

A thin scream came out of her mouth. She had tried so hard to control it. I had to admire her. She was doing so well. "*What's what, Flynn?*" she said.

I got up. I laughed, uneasily. "Nothing, I guess. Just a lot of mud, *or something.* My hand's all wet and sticky." I reached into my pocket for another match and swiftly I scratched it against the stone edge of my knife. I looked at Cora.

Her eyes were popping out of her head, staring at my hand. And then she sagged to the ground.

I don't blame her. I'd have fainted, too. She had to see if it was blood that was all over my hand. It wasn't, of course. It was just some water that I had noticed lying stagnant in a hollow at the base of the boulder. I had dipped my hand in it.

That's what relief will do to a person, I guess. I remember the time I fainted after I killed those three men in Dodge City. I had never been forced to do it like that, three times in a handful of seconds. And when it was over and they lay in a heap, I had all I could do to get the hell out of there before the weakening relief washed all over me. I staggered into an alley and dropped.

Let's see, I thought, that was Dodge City. That was where I had to kill the foreman, Sprague, after he had brought the cattle train through from the Stockton Plateau. And his brothers had not liked it. They had gone for their gu—

Sprague. And his brothers.

Nobody named Hawkins. Nobody who was Hawkins' brother. Not unless Hawkins once had been Sprague. And he hadn't. You could tell that. He had been Hawkins all his life. There had never been reason for Hawkins to change his name. He was, as Good had put it, a dogged fool, a good stupid man who walked straight lines. And anyway, I remembered. Sprague was the name, Al Sprague, and it turned out he and his brothers came from New England. Hawkins was a southerner.

Then why had Good told me?

Beneath me, Cora Thomason was stirring. I reached down and massaged her hand. She sat up and shuddered and then huddled against me.

(*And a far-off thought was saying,* "If I were to make believe I had fainted, this is how I'd do it.")

"T-take me back, Flynn," Cora Thomason said.

"Are you all right?"

"I'm fine," she said. "It was so—so silly. I was frightened for you."

I helped her to her feet, or, rather, I held out my hand and she pulled herself erect. I had felt her in my arms and I recalled how she had helped me down the stairs that day I got sick, and now I once again witnessed her lithe strength as she stood up. For a woman who had just fainted—*or had she faked it?*—she was incredibly strong.

Strong enough to—to do many things.

I walked her to her horse and helped her mount and walked alongside.

"You'll have to be careful when you get inside," I said. "My hands were filthy, and your gown—"

"I'll soak it tonight," she said. Her voice was thin and terribly distant.

"I'm sorry," I said, "that I got you so dirty, but—"

"Please, Flynn, stop talking."

"I just want you to understand," I said. "I was reaching around in that plowed-up field, testing the soil. I was all over it, digging my hands in. I—"

"Flynn, stop it. I—I don't want to hear any more. I'm so tired."

A sob broke from her. She hit her horse once on the neck and he reared and then came down, and she was gone, her coat streaming behind her.

I thought: if there is time, she will drag Hawkins out of there for me. If there is time.

Unless she had been faking.

Now it was no longer night. Not yet morning, but the blade of blackness had dulled. I had dozed for an hour, lying on the ground under the open sky, breathing good fresh air. It was going to be a good day.

I walked to the house and took the day-old coffee from the washboard and fired up the stove. I scribbled a note and put it on the kitchen table, and then drank the coffee in huge gulps. Then I wrote out a longer note, a careful note, and I slipped it into an envelope, and drew a stamp out of a glass jar in the cupboard, filled with knicknacks, spools of thread and a nail file. I addressed the letter to the seamstress's sister, Amy. ("*Any time you want to talk,*" Amy had said, "*you know who to talk to.*" Well, I wasn't going to get a chance to talk to her. But it wouldn't make any difference. The letter would be just as good.) I did not know Amy's last name, but in a town the size of Dryhock, it should not matter. I slipped the letter into my belt and left the house.

The note on the table told Thomason that I was going to town to buy a few supplies, that I thought I would be back early and that I had some items of interest to talk to him about.

The letter to Amy (she was the only person I knew in town outside of the bartender, Jake, and there is in the bartender the natural reluctance to be-lieve the unbelievable; not so with the prostitute who—needs be—lives in a world of long sweet dreams)—the letter to Amy told everything. It was my only real hope in the short time left. I told her of my thir—twenty-nine killings, and of this assignment, of Hawkins and his body, of Cora Thomason, and of how Slott and Thomason were going to be murdered in cold blood. I suppose I should have written to a law office, but I knew how crank letters are received, and I knew, too, how incredibly much of the world I inhabited seemed to be owned by Good. I did not think it likely—although I did not know—that Good owned Amy.

By horseback, and moving slowly because the pain was still there, although much dulled, I got to Sheriff Slott's office a bit before nine o'clock that morning. He was asleep on his cot.

I jostled him and he snorted and then his pig eyes opened. "Well," he said, surprisingly alert, "the prodigal son."

"Wake up," I said curtly.

"And how are all the Thomasons?" he said.

"Fine," I said. "Wake up."

"Goddammit," he said, "stop telling me to wake up. What do you expect me to do, sitting-up exercises?"

I sat on the crate. "I wanted to report in. I think you'd better listen hard."

He sat up on the cot. "I'm listening."

"You know about Hawkins?" I said.

He sank back down again. "Hell, yes," he said. "If that's what you came here to talk about, to wake me up in the middle of the night, then I think you've got a goddam nerve. Of course I know about Hawkins."

"What do you know about him?" I said.

"Missing two, three days," he mumbled. His eyes were closed.

"I think I know where he is," I said.

"So do I," Slott said. "He's out drunk someplace or else in the cathouse and they won't let him go home. I remember the time I—"

"He's dead," I said flatly.

He rolled to one side so that he could see me by opening one eye. "What are you talking about?"

I told him what I thought. That Hawkins had somehow learned about the rustling and the burned-down fence, had learned that Thomason had done it. That he had one night tried to post himself on Thomason's land to see what he could see, and that he had seen enough and—"Just a minute," he said, rubbing his eyes. "What could he have seen?"

This was the weakest part of it all, but in the end I knew it wouldn't matter. Not with Cora Thomason as the final bait.

I shrugged. "Maybe—maybe he saw Thomason getting ready to cut fence or to hustle off another calf. Hell, I don't know what he saw. I'm just telling you how I think it probably went."

"Go on," he said.

"In any event, he saw enough to make him confront Thomason. And Thomason, in a panic, gunned him down and buried him someplace on his land."

He groaned. "You've been reading too many dime novels. Hawkins is dead, all right, dead drunk. Or else he's in the cathouse."

"That's easy enough to find out," I snapped. "Check the cathouse. You'll enjoy doing that anyway. And check the saloon. Check the hotel. Check the seamstress. Check—"

"Check the seamstress?" he said. "Why?"

"You think he might be in a cathouse, you said. What do you think those two girls do all night, sew and wash clothes?"

"Well," he said, staring long at me, "you sure do get around. Regular l'il detective, aren't you? All right, I will," he said. "I'll check this whole god-dam town. And when I find Hawkins, I'm going back to sleep, and you ain't going to wake me for a week. Is that clear?"

"Listen," I said. "I didn't wake you to show you up. I woke you because I think there's going to be trouble. And I don't want to stick my nose in a binder just to be a hero. If I'm right, there're going to be guns waving, and I'm not taking it by my lonesome."

"I said all right, didn't I?" he said. He stood up, finally, and reached into a burlap bag lying next to his cot. He came up with a long-barreled .44, in astonishingly good shape, gleaming with a thin coat of oil. He broke it open and stared inside and flicked away a speck of dust. He frowned down the barrel and then slipped the gun into his belt. He seemed, for a moment at least, a far more formidable man than I had imagined.

He was watching me now, nodding. "Didn't think old Barney even had a gun, did you? Don't think old Barney can shoot it, do you? Clean the flies off a horse's nose with this l'il old son-of-a-bitch."

"Good," I said. "Now clean the cathouse and the bar and the hotel and every damn alley in town. Meanwhile, I'm going up to that target range. I don't expect to be by myself too long."

"Don't worry," he said. "If I don't find Hawkins by late afternoon, I'll hustle up there and we'll rip up the whole spread."

"You won't have to," I said. "If he's buried anyplace, he's in that plowed-up field."

Slott grunted. I kept watching him as he brushed his hair back with his hands. There was a little cracked mirror propped against the window and he stared in it, in evident fascination.

"Pretty horrible, isn't it, Flynn?" he said, looking at me through the mirror.

I felt uncomfortable.

"Not exactly the face—or the body—to sweep a lady off her feet, is it?"

I didn't say anything.

"Now, look at yourself, for instance," he said. "Good-looking young fellow like yourself, why, you could ride up to a woman, let's say, like Mrs. Thomason, and before you know it, she's looking daggers at her husband."

"What do you mean, Slott?"

"Nothing. I'm just talking general talk. A man with a face like mine—well, he sort of dreams about women like Mrs. Thomason, but a man like you, there's no need for dreaming. No offense, of course. I know you wouldn't try anything like that."

"Like what, Slott?"

"Like what I'm talking about, Flynn," he said. "Let's suppose, for instance, you decided this here is a nice place to settle down, and that the old Cattleman's Protection Association of yours doesn't need you any more... or maybe, for some reason you don't want to go back. Well, what would be nicer than a quarter-section of nice land on a hill, and a little woman like Mrs. Thomason to help tend it with you." He turned around. "It wouldn't be so strange, then, for a man to figure some way of knocking off such a woman's husband, would it?"

I forced myself to chuckle. "It wouldn't be strange if the man had a mind like yours."

He laughed with me, shaking his head. "Except," he said, "my mind is only what my face and my body won't let me be. So it would be pretty foolish for a man like me to try anything like that... even if I had a mind to. I *know* it wouldn't do me any good. But you—now that's different story."

"You're insane, Slott."

He laughed again. "You're probably right. But when you *do* have a face like mine, well, you've got to *talk* about having fun."

I relaxed. It was over. He was putting in the needle, but nothing was coming out.

"Maybe," he continued, "maybe you wonder, Flynn, why I live like this, in this office, on this cot, smelling like this? Don't you ever wonder about it?"

"I've had no time to think about it, Slott," I said.

"Sure you've had time, Flynn, you must have.... Shall I tell you, Flynn?"

I shrugged. "Suit yourself."

"Because, Flynn," he said, "what difference would it make, looking like this, fat and ugly, even if I were neat and clean and smelled pretty? Would it honestly make any difference to, say, a woman like—like Cora Thomason—if I washed my clothes?"

"Wouldn't it make any difference to yourself?"

He sighed. "I knew you'd say that. You're smart, do you know that, Flynn? You ought to be running things, not taking orders.... Myself? Maybe it would make some difference. But then, you see, it would be like admitting I cared, admitting that I wanted to get a woman—like Mrs. Thomason—if I preened and strutted around like a crow in peacock feathers. This way I just make believe I don't give a good damn. Sometimes I do believe it." He walked to the door, looked out and then strode through.

I went my way and he went his. I watched him walk to the stable and come out with a powerful-looking, thick-bellied brown horse, and I saw him wrap both hands around the pommel and hoist himself up. And then he rode off. Once again I had figured him wrong. He was a magnificent rider.

Chapter Eleven

I had four chores to do.

First I went to the post office and found out that Amy's last name was Smith. I wrote it on the envelope and gave it to the postmaster.

"When will she get this?" I asked.

He scratched his head. "Tomorrow, the next day," he said. "I'll probably be riding out that way tomorrow."

"Not any earlier?"

He bristled. "See here, young fellow, don't try to tell me how to run my mails. Tomorrow's the soonest. That's final."

I rode off. That was all I had to know. Tomorrow was the very earliest I wanted the letter to arrive. Everything had to be over by tomorrow.

Next I went to the general store and bought two heavy shovels. I had them strapped to the sides of my saddle.

Then I started off for Thomason's. I had been in town less than an hour.

Once, I would have enjoyed working this way. I had no plan, no idea as to exactly *how* it would come off, but I was acting on it. I was doing the forcing. Things were falling into line, only because I was leading. I had not seen Good since—since the morning I had grandiloquently detailed my formula for eliminating Thomason and Slott, using Hawkins' body as the catalyst. That was only yesterday, I realized, but the length of time was unimportant. So much had occurred. And I had come out of the morass.

At least, I thought so.

At noon, the shirt sticking to my chest, and my legs aching from the tension of gripping my horse, I pulled up to the house. Thomason hailed me from inside the screen door. He came out, carrying a glass of water.

"Thanks," I said. "It's a scorcher, all right."

We sat on the ground against the house, in the north shade. "Did you find anything last night?" he said.

"I did," I said. I drank from the glass slowly. The water was already tepid.

"Well?" he said.

"Thomason," I said, "we'll have time for that later. There's something far more important just about ready to pop."

He searched my face. "What do you mean?"

I looked around. "Where's Cora?"

"Upstairs," he said stiffly.

"Well—" I began.

"Spill it, Flynn. What are you talking about?"

"I'd rather Cora heard it at the same time. Can we wait for her?"

He got up. "I'll get her," he said. "And right quick, too. There's some-

thing fishy and I want to know about it.... Has it got to do with you and—
Mrs. Thomason?"

I laughed. "Bad guess, Mr. Thomason. It involves you, I'm afraid, more
than anybody else. It doesn't have anything at all to do with me."

He stamped inside and I heard him calling, "Cora? Cora? Come on down
here."

There was a pause and some words from upstairs that I could not catch.
Then he came out again. "She'll be down shortly," he said. His face was dark.
He did not believe me. He was sure what I had to say had to do with his wife
and myself. He was thinking: *that Flynn and Cora, they've been laying. I swear,
they have.* That's what Thomason was thinking.

We sat in silence, with our thoughts, I with the empty glass pressed
against my brow to ward off the heat, and he motionless, a bandana tied
loosely about his throat. And I thought this might be the only time left for
him and for me where we might find some common understanding, here in
the slim piece of shade while all about a fevered sun burned down. All I had
to do was make up a quick lie... tell Thomason that the word in town was that
a severe drought was headed this way this summer, or something else of interest to him. And that night, I could go my way.

It would do me no good, but then nothing would.

Then I remembered the letter to Amy. If I did not now do the job, my
letter would be merely the ramblings of a mad drifter. But if I did the job, as
outlined in the letter, it would lend credence to all other matters listed
therein. Good would be linked to the murders, and that would be reward
enough for the rest.

And so we sat there, silent, a man who would be dead by midnight, and
his murderer. I felt like telling him he ought not to worry. Sometimes there
just was no difference between being dead and alive. I knew.

He cleared his throat. "Ah, Flynn—" and just then the screen door
banged open and shut.

She was wearing a white dress, and she looked cool and lovely. Her hair
was brushed back from her forehead, and there was a regal quality about her.
She moved through the heat, but not a part of it. She seemed to have gone
through some ordeal within and come out again, either unscathed or else for-
tified for further ordeals.

"Well," she said to me, "what is it?"

"I've come from town," I said, "and from Mr. Good's." At this last she
raised her eyebrows.

"There's a lot of talk in town about Hawkins." I stopped and turned to
Thomason. "You've heard about Hawkins?" I asked.

"Only that he's been missing for three, four days," he said.

I nodded. "That's the report. But—and I hesitate telling you, except that
it's getting pretty hot in Dryhock—it doesn't end there. A man in the gen-

eral store—I don't know his name, of course—asked me if I was Thomason's new hand. I told him I was. He shook his head and said I ought to get the hell out as fast as I could. So, naturally, I asked him what he was talking about." I paused to light a cigarette.

"Yes, Flynn," Cora asked gently, "what the hell are you talking about?"

"Good is up in arms, Mr. Thomason. He thinks the fence and the stolen stock are bad enough, but he's accusing you—or me or Cora or somebody associated with you—of killing Hawkins."

Thomason gasped. "K-killing Hawkins?"

I nodded. I let my lips set into thin lines and my eyes search out the horizon.

Thomason laughed hoarsely. "And you expect me to be worried because some loudmouth in the general store is peddling filthy rot?"

I nodded solemnly. "That's just the way I felt, Mr. Thomason. But he wasn't the only one. There was a man in the bar"—I turned to him apologetically—"I stopped down there for a beer, and this man said more or less the same thing."

Thomason's Adam's apple bobbed. "But that's—that's nonsense. Everybody knows I didn't—wouldn't kill Hawkins. Wouldn't kill anybody, as a matter of fact. A-and you, why, you've just been in town a few days. What right would anybody have—" He stopped talking and looked to his wife beseechingly.

Her lips were pursed in thought. "I don't know, honey. Of course, you or I or Flynn wouldn't do a thing like that, but... but suppose they really thought so, what would we do?"

His voice was nearly a screech. "Do?" he said. "Do? Why, we'll just flatly deny it. We'll tell them to take their filthy tongues off our land and go home. That's—that's what we'll tell them."

"And if they don't believe you?" she said.

"W-why, what's the matter with you?" he asked. His eyes were terrorbright now. "Why wouldn't they believe me?"

She shook her head. "That's not within me to say," she told him gently, her hand on his upper arm. "The important thing is—what will we do?"

He turned to me. "B-but you said, Flynn, that you were over to see Good. Surely—surely *he* doesn't believe this talk?"

I bit my lower lip. "I'm afraid he does, Mr. Thomason. That's why I'm so upset. I went over there soon as I could, figuring to mollify him some. I told him how we'd put that fence back and we'd sure keep our eyes on it now—and—and he just waved me quiet. He was in a white rage, Mr. Thomason. He says he knows why we fixed that fence all of a sudden, all right. He says it's because we've got much more to hide than a burned fence, and we're trying to make things look peaceful on the surface. He says it looks mighty damn strange to him that that fence lay in ruins for two months and now it's been fixed in one day. He says—"

"But he knows I've had no help until now," Thomason said. "What does he expe—"

"I don't know," I said. "All I know is what he said. He says he knows you killed Hawkins and he's going to get you. He says you've buried him some-place on your land and that—these were his words—and that, by God, he'd dig him up and shake his bones in your face."

Thomason looked as though he'd been whipped white. Fear flamed wildly in his eyes, but I had to admire him. He was trying so hard.

"Let him," he said in a low voice. "Let him come and let him dig. I'm ready."

"That's the way," I said. "That's how I thought you'd react. I picked up a couple of shovels in town. I want Good to see us digging. I want the whole world to see us digging. If there's anything rotten on this land, I want to help uncover it." I coughed into my hand. "Of course, I know there's no—" And then I let my words trail off.

"What is it, Flynn?" Cora asked sharply.

"Nothing," I said. "It's—nothing." I got up and started to walk away.

"Flynn!" It was Thomason. "Goddammit, Flynn, come back here. Some-thing's biting you. What is it?"

I turned slowly, and slowly I retraced my steps. I let my shoulders sag and my face muscles relax so that the skin at my jaw hung slack. The pain was nib-bling away at my right side, so it was easy to stoop a bit more.

"What is it?" he asked again.

"Suppose," I said uneasily, "let's just suppose that Hawkins *was* killed"— I raised my hand for silence—"not by you or me or anybody here, but by—by somebody else. Suppose Good wanted him dead"—I felt Cora's eyes nar-row as she tried to follow me—"for God knows what reason. Suppose he just wants to get you, Mr. Thomason, for some long-standing grudge or other." I turned to him. "Is there any grudge between you two?"

He hesitated. "W-why no, nothing other than talk about the fence and the stolen stock."

"Heated talk?"

"Why, yes, pretty heated at times."

I opened my arms. "There you are."

"That's not enough of a grudge to turn a man to murder, Flynn."

"No," I admitted. "But maybe there's something else, something you don't know about. Suppose Good wants something you've got, Mr. Thoma-son, and you don't want to part with it. Something you wouldn't part with, except over your dead body. Maybe that's it."

He looked around at me and then at his wife. He was bewildered by it all.

"Nothing you've got he wants?" I said. "Your land, let's say. How about that? Has he ever tried to buy you out?"

Thomason's face cleared momentarily. "Why, yes, he's often mentioned buying this piece of land."

"And?"

"I turned him down naturally."

"Price wasn't right?"

"Not nearly right," he said. "Besides, I just didn't want to sell."

"Turned him down flat? Didn't even give him a chance to name a new price? Got pretty curt with him?"

"No," he shouted. "Nothing like that. It was all quite friendly. I just said no, and that was that."

I dropped the subject. "Well, maybe you own something else, or he thinks you do. Maybe it's water rights or—"

"Hell, you've seen our creek. Half-dry all summer. He's got fifteen, twenty times the water I've got."

Cora Thomason said, "I don't understand, Flynn. Let's say he does have a grudge against Ed. Then what?"

Now she was ready to go the whole way. I saw it in her eyes. She was cool again.

"If the grudge is deep enough, if he's capable of a murderous mood, then *this* is what: Good has had Hawkins murdered, and when none of us was around (you were in town, Mr. Thomason, and I was at the north fence, and Mrs. Thomason was in the kitchen), or more likely, at night, when we all slept, he buried the body on your land. That means he, Mr. Good, knows where the body is. All he's got to do is what you said you wanted him to do—'let him come,' you said, 'let him come and let him dig.' If he does have Hawkins buried out there to incriminate you"—I swept my arm to the plowed-up field—"it will be no problem to dig him up. And when he does—if he does—there'll be hell to pay."

Thomason stared long at me. "There's something funny about y—about this whole business. Why is everybody, suddenly, trying to—"

Cora squeezed his arm. "Nobody is trying anything, honey. Flynn just posed a possibility, that's all. He may be all wet. Probably he is. But—"

"But," I said, "we've got to think of every angle."

He turned to me. "All right, so we've got to think. I've thought. You know what? I think the whole thing is a lot of rot. I'm going to do just what I said: let him come and let him dig."

I smiled. "You're a brave man, Mr. Thomason. Far braver than I'd be in this mess."

"What would you do, Flynn?" Cora asked. Her voice was husky and her eyes grave.

I stood up. "I'd dig like one—if you'll pardon me—like one son-of-a-bitch. I'd dig until I dropped. Just to show the whole goddam world I wasn't afraid, that I'd dig instead of waiting for anybody else to come here first."

Her eyes were shining now. "Let's," she said, "let's dig."

Thomason looked at us as though we were insane. "I'm going upstairs. I'm going to dig, all right. I'm going to dig out my best bottle of bourbon, and I'm going to drink every last drop. Dig!" he said, in disgust. He tramped into the house.

She looked at me, amusement riding high in her eyes. The coolness was gone and her cheeks were etched in color. She stepped forward and put her arms around my waist and her head against my chest. "Oh, Flynn," she said. "What you've done to that man!"

I slowly released her. "Seems to me he's a pretty good man, at that. He took it pretty well. I wasn't fooling when I said he was brave."

Her mouth was scornful. "Brave? If he were brave, he'd be out here, watching. He's afraid, Flynn. He's scared to death. He's going upstairs to hide. That's what he's doing."

I said to her casually, "I don't know why he's afraid. I haven't the slight-est idea where Hawkins' body is.... Have you?"

She danced away. "Ah," she said, "wouldn't you like to know?"

"I know enough," I said.

She mocked me. She was enjoying herself. "Oh, you do, do you? I don't think you do."

I decided to show her. I nodded my head very slowly. "Yes, I do. I know Hawkins is dead," I said. "I know they buried him under that west boulder." I waved my hand toward the spot where she had ridden to meet me the night before. Her face was still, stiff. "I know—"

"No, that's not—" she said, but I broke through.

"I know he's not buried there any more. He's been moved."

She stared at me. "How do you know all this?" she asked.

"It's very simple," I said. "It all adds up. Though," I said, feeling my frown come, though, "I don't quite know why—"

She was shaking her head. "B-but you're wrong. He's not buried—"

"I know," I said harshly. "I told you that. They've moved him from the boulder. Shall I tell you where he is now?"

She nodded wordlessly.

I walked over to the patch of plowed-up dirt. I held the shovel high. "He's—right—here!" I said. And I drove the shovel ten inches into the soil.

She gasped and stared at me, still shaking her head. "I'm not supposed to—I can't—"

"Not *exactly* here," I went on. "But around here." I waved my hand over the field.

"But how can you prove it?" she said. "Is it important you dig him up? Can't you do what you have to do without him?"

Then I laughed. Whoever was behind her—and that wasn't hard to fig-ure out—had taught her well. But they hadn't figured I would stay with them this long, hanging on every time they buried me under a ton of rock.

"Of course I can."

And she surprised me. She should have been stunned. It should have shocked her. Instead she seemed relieved. A long sigh shuddered its way through her body. "Oh," she whispered, "I'm so glad. I was afraid you wouldn't be able to—do it."

"You really want me to, don't you?" I said.

"Yes," she said, "yes, yes, yes. More than anything else in the whole world."

"Then why—"

"Why what?" she asked, coming close again, staring up at me.

I felt foolish. She was leading me, now. "Nothing," I said. "Forget it."

"But I want to know," she said. She seemed sincere. She was, in fact, pleading with me. "Last night you said you'd tell me what you'd want me to do. You never did. It's going to come off tonight, and I still don't know. Don't you trust me?"

"No," I said, "should I?"

She bit her lip. "I guess I deserve that," she said. "But some day you'll know, and then you'll understand.... If—if you don't trust me, does that mean you won't tell me what you want?"

"Do I have a choice?" I said. I put the shovel down. "In two hours, get on your horse and ride into town. Get in there around five or so. Make sure Slott is still in town. He probably won't be in his office. He'll be out looking for Hawkins. He thinks Hawkins is alive, drunk someplace, or maybe with some woman. He's out checking." I stopped. "Do you have that so far?"

"Yes."

"Fine. All you have to do is persuade him to come on up here, tonight. Tell him to wait until it's dark, the later the better. Certainly no earlier than ten or so. Let him know there's something in it for him." She let out a small shudder. "Oh, you can do it. You know damn well you can.... If I were you, I'd tell him that *I* sent you. That's right, I sent you. Tell him Flynn says come sometime tonight. Flynn thinks the trouble that's been brewing is ready to explode, tonight.... Understand?"

"Yes," she said in a small voice.

"Don't mention Ed Thomason's name once. Don't let him know that you, in any way, think your husband has committed a wrongdoing. Or, if you want, tell him your husband is acting funny and he's up in his room getting drunk and abusive.... I have a feeling that's not going to be too far from the truth.... You got that?"

"Yes."

"Good. After you find him, come back here by yourself and keep on digging. But *don't* find Hawkins' body. Understand?"

"No," she said, "I don't."

"Because it doesn't matter. I don't want anything to foul us up. We don't need Hawkins. I'm going over to Good's after you leave. Good has a hundred men over there. Any one of them could fill in for Hawkins."

She let out a gasp. "Y-you'd kill somebody else and bring him over here?"

"Why not?" I said. "If you and Good want to play games with me, I'll play them with you." I turned to her and I grabbed her shoulders and gave her a shake, hard, her hair flying. "Listen. I've got a job to do and I'm going to do it. I'm getting paid well for it and I can use the money. Nothing is going to stop me. Two men are going to die tonight. If somebody's not careful, maybe more. You've played me for a sucker this past couple of days, you and Good both. I don't know what your game is, but whatever it is, it's all over now. What I say goes. I'm going over to Good's and I'm going to tell him the same thing. Do you get me?"

She nodded. All the fight had leaked out of her. That was a break, of course. I was running the sheerest of bluffs.

"But what if Slott isn't in town? Suppose I can't find him?"

"Don't spend too much time looking. If you don't find him by—let's say, six o'clock—come on back and start digging. He'll be on his way. If he gets here early, I'll take care of that. All right?"

She looked up at me and her lip trembled. "All right," she whispered. "Oh, Flynn," she said, "don't hate me. I've done nothing wrong. When it's over, I'll prove it to you. You'll see. Oh, Flynn, Flynn, make it like it was the other day."

I didn't care that it was the middle of the day. I put my arms around her and drew her in tight and in the middle of a sob—maybe hers, maybe mine—our mouths met. We clung together and I thought of another woman—a girl, actually—and another time like this when we stood on a hill and all about the thunderclouds were piling up. They were piling up even now, the edge of the sky turning thick and gray, and if this was the last tiny bit of love and warmth I'd ever give a human being, I wanted it to be good.

And it was. We parted and her eyes were closed and then the tears formed. She turned and ran off and two minutes later she was on that white horse, tearing great holes out of the earth.

...And I tore holes out of the earth, frantic shovelfuls. I knew I would not find Hawkins, but it seemed only decent that I try. He was lying here, three, four days now, the most abused and vilified corpse I'd ever known, and the least I owed him was the right to be dug up once more and then decently buried.

But, as I said, I was not going to find him, nor did I try for too long. I had that fourth chore to do. I had to see Good.

Chapter Twelve

The strands of the puzzle lay like a tangle of untamed black hair. I was not the man to sort out each hair, identify it, and put it in its proper place. But—as I rode to Good's on that last day—I had to try. There was much that Good could tell me if there was much that I knew. He had all the answers. I had perhaps half.

I knew, for instance, that Good had hired me to kill Thomason and Slott. I had to fall back on this as a starting place.

I knew my job. To kill two men. Good and I had agreed—implicitly—to plant Hawkins' body on Thomason's land, to frame the rancher. And with Sheriff Slott on hand, we would dig up the body from behind the boulder. If Slott made a move to arrest Thomason, the rancher would pull a gun on him (so we would later say). In the melee of fire and return fire, two men would die.

I knew this was the master plan. When I first had heard it, it seemed so complex. But now, after I had seen complexity multiply until each single deed took on more shades than these mountains had colors, that complex plan was simplicity personified.

I had, as a second known fact, taken Cora Thomason into my confidence. It seemed wise, using a person close by, a person who could reach either of the two intended victims by the sheer animal force of her sex. Good had not seemed happy about it (which surprised me); yet he had not seemed unduly unhappy.

And then the facts became woozy. Hawkins' body had been buried behind one boulder. It had—or maybe it hadn't—been moved to another boulder. Then it had disappeared.

That Good was behind these acts—or this act—was probable, though, of course, not a known, provable fact. That he had Cora Thomason as an ally (*why had he?*) seemed nearly as likely, but equally unprovable.

I wondered about this business of Good and Cora Thomason. Had he demanded her help because she was already dragged in—by me? Or was she in it from the start? Had she come around to my suggestion to do in her husband because it meant a way out, a new life—or because she had been thus schooled? Had I suggested something to her that she had already resolved?

I felt Good knew this.

But even if I knew also, the questions kept plaguing me. They came in waves. And they were not in order, not sorted (though slowly, surely, I felt myself stepping away from the character and person of Flint, and viewing him from a distance, watching him, studying him, seeing the whole affair laid out before me, seeing Good, and Cora Thomason, and Slott and Thomason, and, yes, even Flint).

Why—the questions kept coming, and I looked at them from this new per-spective—why had Good shod the left front foot of my horse, instead of the right? Why had he told me Hawkins was the brother of a man I had killed in Dodge City? This last I knew to be a lie, and that made me feel better. I had another fact, and facts were ammunition. But—why had he done it? And why, if Hawkins were not the brother of a man I had killed and thus bore me no great blood grudge, why did I have to kill him, a man Good obviously liked? The answer to that one was near, I knew. I felt it sweep by, teasing me like some heard voice that remains tantalizingly unrecognized.

And still the questions came. Was it a game or was it a fiendishly com-plicated and dead-serious business? Or was it both? And was Good, therefore, a chuckling madman or the coldest, most calculating killer I had ever met—or was he both?

...And that was all that I had time for. There was the house.

As I neared the house, I saw a man leave the front door, carrying a black satchel. He mounted his horse and rode off, away from me. He seemed a man in middle age. The satchel, the size of a doctor's bag, hung from the pommel. Then he was a dwindling figure, and gone.

Good stood in the doorway, watching me come on. He stood motionless, erect. He did not acknowledge my presence until my horse had been tied to a post and I was five feet away. Then he broke into a warm smile.

"Flint," he said. "I'm glad you came. Soon, it will be over. Now, for a while, we can soothe each other."

"You can soothe me," I said. "I'm here to lay down the law."

"Ah," he said, still smiling, "that's good. Appropriate, too. A man with thirty—excuse me, twenty-nine murders to his name, laying down the law."

"Pretty funny, isn't it, Mr. Good?"

"No," he said, serious now, "not really." He turned and we went into the cool, dark library. The curtains were drawn across the windows and it seemed as though the heat had been ordered to exclude this one spot. We sat with half the room between us, and the ever-growing chasm of distrust and fear.

"Well," he said mildly, "what is it?"

"I don't want any trouble tonight. I'm making my move tonight, and I will not stand for any obstacles placed in front of me. Is that understood?"

He nodded as though it were the most obvious thing in the world. "Why, of course, Flint. How else would it be?"

I stood up. "Please," I said. "Don't do it. Don't rile me. Ever since I've been here, you've—you've made it tough for me to operate."

He nodded. "Yes, it's been tough. As you say. But you don't really believe I've made it that way, do you? I thought we understood the way I worked. Long, complicated, maybe—but a sure way. We move not too fast (but not too slowly either) and we cover our tracks. Isn't that the way? Has it been any other way?"

"Please," I said. "Don't. I beg of you, Mr. Good. Don't. I've got it lined up tonight. Don't make it any more difficult." I sat down, perspiration bathing me.

"It's been pretty difficult, hasn't it, Flint?" His voice was warm, sympathetic, his eyes generous.

"You're damn right," I said.

"It was a mistake, wasn't it?" he said. "Bringing you up here to do this job?"

"It's not that, goddammit. It's just the way you do things."

"Undo them, you might say," he said. His voice had taken on an edge.

"Yes," I said, "that's it. Undo them. Everything I line up, you erase. It's—it's impossible—"

"I know," he said. "That's what's so bad about it all. You can't. You can't do it any more, can you?" He stared at me, sad-eyed.

He was turning me again, away from what I was talking about. And I had to give in to his force, though I knew I had to turn him back eventually if I ever were to know any of the answers. "Can't do what any more?" I said.

He seemed surprised. "Why, I thought that was what we were talking about. How difficult it was for you to leave that farm in Arizona and come up here and do those things you had laid aside, years ago. I thought that was what you meant by 'impossible' and 'making it tough' on you. I thought you were saying that was why you keep botching things up so."

Now I felt the rage rise like gorge. "Me?" I said, my voice low and carrying all the white hatred I could bear. "I didn't botch things. You did. Hawkins' body. You moved it from the east boulder to the west, didn't you? And then you moved it from the west boulder, didn't you? You buried it under that patch of soil, didn't you? You and that bitch in heat."

"Wait a minute," he said. "Let's leave Mrs. Thomason out of this."

"So forget her. But I didn't move Hawkins' body, did I?" I glared at him.

"No," he said. "And that's the great pity of this all. If you only had. Well—that's over with." He sighed.

"Sure. That would have been smart," I said. "Killing the man and then moving his body and then moving it again."

"No," he said. "That would have been stupid."

The room whirled. Blind alleys sprang all around me, long, gray, hollow corridors that came around and formed a circle, and I was in each corridor, looking for its end.

"You don't understand," he said. His voice was gentle. "It's a bit too much for you, isn't it?"

I nodded. I could not speak.

"It's as I said. We shouldn't have dragged you away from that little place down there. You could have lived a few more years in some sort of peace. But I do want you to know that I admit it's my fault. I really believed the talent you had was inborn, that it never left, that it came leaping out in all its glory whenever you called it.... I was wrong."

I found my voice. "No you weren't. Take that Hawkins thing. The way I handled that. Why, that night when I returned you said it was genius, the way only a handful of people could have done it. You said it. Was that just a lure, too?"

"Oh, no," he said. "When I said it, I meant it. If only I had reason to say it."

"Mr. Good," I said, "what are you talking about?"

He paused and looked directly at me. "All right," he said, "let's get it done with. I'll tell you what I'm talking about. I've dreaded this moment ever since—ever since I found out how badly you had handled the Hawkins affair. Now, we have no time to gloss it over. My only problem, now, is whether you'll be able to face the facts of your own incompetence. Incompetence, you know, could send us all to our graves."

I said, tight-voiced, "Go on."

He shrugged and sighed deeply. "You remember how I suggested there were alternatives to your answer to the west-east boulder riddle? How you thought that either you became confused and never put him under the east boulder at all, or else it was sheer insanity that dictated moving Hawkins from the east to the west boulder? Wasn't that what you said?"

I nodded, and found myself walking to the window, drawing the heavy curtains and looking out across Good's spread, toward Thomason's, my mind's eye focusing on the boulders between the two ranches.

Good said, standing by my side, "There was an alternative, a good simple one. Do you know what it was, now?" His voice was low and encouraging.

I stared out at the land. And all I saw was the hot yellow ball of fire scorching the valley. I stood in that cool room and looked out on hell, where a man came out from behind boulders and walked the under-face of the earth, begging for me to uncover him. *Hawkins, crying out—*

"Do you know now?" Good said softly.

I began to piece together the night Hawkins and I had ridden out together, and only I had returned. I remembered how confounded dark it was, and how I had blacked out for an instant, and how I had gripped Hawkins by his thick, thick hair and pulled him to the boulder—

"You see it now?" Good said.

—and how later, Hawkins was missing from that boulder. And how— oh, so conveniently—I saw a piece of shirt, the gleam of his boots under that other boulder. And then how he was gone from both.

I turned to Good and nodded. "Yes," I said, "I see." I saw, too, how I had nearly carried Good and myself (and Cora Thomason probably) to a quick grave. How I was doing everything to us that I should have done—and failed to do—to Hawkins.

"God," I said, "no wonder you say I botched things!"

He nodded and chuckled. "You see now, don't you? All I did was to undo what you had done. You'll agree now that I had to."

"Yes," I said. "Is he—it upstairs?"

Good nodded. He got up. I followed him. We went up to that room where I had slept the night after shoving Hawkins behind the boulder.

Good put his finger to his lips. Then he opened the door, so slowly the creaking sounded like the drawn-out moan of a dying coyote, ten miles away. The room was dark. The shades were pulled shut. But I could make out the figure on the bed, his chest moving beneath the sheet in slow shallow breaths.

It was Hawkins.

...We were downstairs again.

"W-will he live?" I asked.

"Now," Good said, chiding me, "you mean 'would' he live, don't you?"

"Y-you're not going to—"

He spread his hands. "Do I have a choice?"

I shook my head. "But why have you kept him alive this long?"

"At first," Good said, "it was essential. That next morning, when Cora and I came across him, moaning loud enough to be heard by anybody ten feet away—and pretty easily seen, too, through the three-inch space—we knew we had to get him out from behind that east boulder. I didn't know how badly hurt he was—compound skull fractures, Doc Smalley says—until we had him upstairs. Then it became obvious he probably wouldn't live too long anyway. Still, I thought it possible we—you or I—would have some idea as to how we might use him, even this way. Otherwise, I'll have to let him die. Doc Smalley says he'd most likely linger another week or so."

"But why didn't you just wring his neck when you found him behind the boulder?"

His face hardened. "And risk being seen by any one of my men, or by Thomason, or by anybody riding on up to either of the two ranges? I *don't* think we were seen, Cora and I, but I didn't know for sure then. If anybody saw us, I'd rather they saw us picking a man up from the ground and putting him on a horse and taking him back to my house. You can't hang a man for doing that."

"But how can you let him die now?" I said. "Doc Smalley knows it's Hawkins. You can't just kill him. He'll talk."

"I can't kill whom, Hawkins or Doc Smalley?" Good asked, his eyes staring at me blandly.

And I knew he could kill Hawkins *and* the doctor.

"Not that I'd want to," Good went on. "Killing does not give me any pleasure. I'm not you, in that respect. But I will kill, if I have to. Because—who knows—if the doctor gets home and talks to his wife, and she talks to her neighbors, why, then, I'd be in trouble. Eventually the talk would reach Slott or some other lawman, and I might be implicated. Though, right now, Doc Smalley has been told—and paid—to keep his mouth shut. He knows that Mr. Good does not want any talk about Hawkins' being brutally beaten this way. You see, Doc Smalley is convinced that Mr. Good is a man who wants peace on the range. If nobody knows that Hawkins was beaten by somebody—probably Thomason or somebody hired by Thomason—then there'll be peace on the range. And if Hawkins dies in bed, of injuries suffered from a fall from his horse, there'll be no outcry. Of course, if Hawkins has to be carried back out there, and laid behind a boulder, or on Thomason's land, and the word gets back, *then* Doc Smalley might talk about what he knows."

"Well," I said, "so that leaves Hawkins out of it."

"Unless you have an idea," he said.

I shook my head. "Not with a doctor and his wife and neighbors involved. Too much."

"Squeamish, Flint?"

"No," I said sharply. "It's not that. Why spend time gunning three, four more people? We can handle Thomason and Slott without Hawkins. We—I wonder...."

"Yes?" Good said.

"Who knows Hawkins is alive?"

Good started to smile. "You know he's alive. I do. Cora Thomason. Doc Smalley. Maybe his wife."

"Nobody else?"

"Probably not."

"Thomason doesn't know, does he?"

Good's smile broke open. "No."

"Nor Slott?"

"Well, I don't think so. No, probably not Slott."

"Nobody else on this ranch? No other hand, no servant, nobody?"

"So far as I know," Good said, "nobody. Nobody on God's green earth, other than the people we've mentioned."

"When is the doctor returning?"

Good shrugged. "When I want him."

"Certainly not before tomorrow?"

"Certainly."

"Then if we want to use Hawkins, we can?"

"Why not?"

I grinned. "I don't know what's wrong with me," I said. "Now you've got me doing it again. The long haul. The roundabout method. The complicated—"

He held up his hand. "Don't," he said sharply. "If it's too tough that way, I'd rather you did it your own way. Just try to protect me, that's all." His voice softened, took on a thin, whining quality. "Try to keep my name out of it. The other way, with Hawkins' body the way we wanted it, that would have been perfect. I was protected. That's my method, Flint. You know that by now, I'm sure."

He had filled me with confidence again. I did not have a plan. There were six hours or so left. It was plenty of time. Good had asked that I protect him. I felt good inside. For once, I was going to outfox him. The important thing was to protect myself.

"You won't forget, will you, Flint? About me, I mean?" The man was almost cringing. I soared. "I'm putting so much trust in you. You'll play it carefully, won't you? Keep the tracks covered up, so to speak?"

I could barely control the lift to my upper lip. "Don't worry," I said. "I'll protect you as if you were my own father."

He gasped, and pulled back. His face had gone white. He looked as though I had slapped him. "Now that's a very strange thing to say, Flint. I don't appreciate your sense of humor, I must say. It's far too grisly for my taste."

I did not know what he was talking about. "Let's not worry about humor," I said. "This is business, not comedy."

A frown bit into his brow. "Well, I dare say you're right. But still.... Never mind. I'm just a complaining old man."

I did not bother denying it.

"And it's my life at stake. Just these few years. I don't want them hounded. It must be awful, Flint, having those men at your throat all these years." His eyes clouded. "On the run since 1865. I don't know how you stood it."

"It's not been that long," I said. "That first man I killed—in my home town—that happened quite a while after the war had ended. The Yankee soldier."

He stared at me. "Oh," he said. "Oh. So now I see. That's why."

"Why what?"

"Nothing," he said. "It doesn't matter.... We have other things to concern us."

I frowned into space. Something was bothering me.... Something... that Good was hinting at. My thoughts were getting thick again, confused. "Listen," I said harshly, trying to think it through, this plan, any plan to get it over with, "this is how we'll do it. You and Cora Thomason will start out

from here around nine o'clock, or as soon after as it appears good and dark."
I looked out the window. The clouds were creeping from the horizon toward
the sun, black clouds. It would be a dark night, unless this was to be a brief
thunderstorm readying itself and soon to be dissipated. "Take Hawkins with
you. Remove the bandage. Go straight to the pass, to the little dip between
your land and Thomason's. Get him back behind the boulder." Good started
to break in. I waved my hand curtly. "I don't give a damn which one. I'm not
you. I don't play games."

Now he did interrupt. "That was no game, changing boulders. We did-
n't move *Hawkins*, as you know now. Just some of his clothes. A bit of his
shirt that was torn, and one of his boots that had become loosened. The boulder you had chosen was dreadful, you realize. That three-inch gap. Why, you
might as well have left him in plain sight."

"But why did you later remove that bit of clothing and put it under the
west boulder?"

"Well," Good said, "we had to get Hawkins out of there, of course, and
back to the ranch house before somebody else came across him. But we decided
to leave some fragment that would tell you he was still there. I did not want
to disturb you with the knowledge—then—that you hadn't killed Hawkins,
that you had botched the job. I didn't want to ruin your confidence so early
in the game. So we left the torn scrap of shirt and the loosened boot."

I nodded.

"The other boulder—the west boulder—was the better spot. By looking
through the tiny crevice, you could see these things, but no more. Not unless you insisted on digging behind the boulder. And in daylight you would-
n't be likely to take such a chance. In fact, from my studies of your past, you're
not the criminal who returns too willingly to the locale of his crime. I
doubted you'd do more than make a cursory check. I was right."

"You figured I would think I had become confused the night I clubbed
Hawkins and wouldn't really remember which boulder I had used?"

"That's right," he said.

"But why did you *then* remove the piece of shirt and the boot from the
west boulder, so that there was no trace at all of Hawkins?"

"For exactly that reason," Good said. "You weren't the only person
likely to ride on up to that pass. Thomason was constantly working around
that area. Putting the pieces of clothing behind the west boulder was only an
expedient, to keep you thinking you had more or less done the job on
Hawkins. But the important thing was to keep anybody else from finding any
hint of Hawkins. So Cora and I—when we had the opportunity—removed
them."

"And," I said, "like the dimwitted fool that I was, I assumed you had now
buried Hawkins in that nearby field. You figured I'd think that, didn't you?
It was so convenient."

He nodded. "It would be the likely place, if we had wanted to bury him nearby."

I remembered how Cora had fainted—*the hell she had*, I knew now; *it was pure fakery*—when I pretended I saw blood on that field. She had been coached to make me believe Hawkins was there. "You still didn't want me to lose my confidence. Was that it? If I thought—*if I were sure*—Hawkins was in that field, then I could proceed as we had previously agreed, and dig him up when we needed him. That's how you figured I would react."

"How else would any man act?" Good asked gently.

"Any fool, you mean," I said.

He shook his head. "Now you know, and it's not so serious. You made a few mistakes, but we've lived through them. Your confidence hasn't been destroyed, and we can proceed.... You were telling me, Flint, about putting Hawkins behind one of those boulders?"

I laughed. Again I was doing it. Botching things. How could we say that Thomason and Slott shot themselves over Hawkins' body? Doc Smalley would know it was a lie.

Christ, what a hired killer I had been. If I had only done that one simple job! Hired killer, hell. I was just a cheap hired hand, deserving no more than the twenty-a-month Thomason was paying me. That's all I deser—

"Oh," I said. And I thought it all the way through, past the doctor's knowledge (and that was whipped) and past Amy's letter (and I think that was whipped), past all the endless questions that would have to be answered. And it held up.

"The only problem, as I see it," I said, "is my involvement."

"What do you mean, Flint?" Good asked sharply.

I gathered in all my thoughts. They would have to hold together. "Nothing," I said, "just thinking aloud. Now listen to me carefully...."

I told him three times. It was necessary. He was angry the first time. "I won't stand for it," he said. "All the work you've done, at least you deserve some reward for it."

"You're paying me well," I said patiently.

"Nonsense," he said. "I could pay you ten times that and you'd still be underpaid for what you're suggesting. I won't let them do this to you."

"Yes, you will," I said. "Remember, you asked that I protect you. This does the job. Now listen to me again...."

The second time he was dubious. "I don't know, Flint, I just don't know. So much to swallow, so suddenly." He shook his head.

"No different from swallowing the fact that I was brought in from your non-existent Cattleman's Protection Association to be a deputy sheriff and to act out being a hired hand to Thomason and then to stay on at Thomason's until the job was done, and then to return to your place later. No more difficult than swallowing *that*. A helluva lot easier, in fact. Listen, you'll see it...."

The third time he did. "I've got to hand it to you," he said finally. "It's perfect. Not a flaw. But more than that, the utter kindness of the act."

I returned his warm smile, and inside my soul was laughing, too, but its laugh was mocking. "No more than I'd have done for my own father."

And again he had his strange *(or was it so strange?)* reaction. The face was stunned into immobility, and then the craft left the eyes and shocked disbe-lief replaced it. "You don't really know what you're saying," he said. "You just don't remember, do you? You don't know what happened to your father at all, do you?" His voice was thin and his body had sagged. The erect line had broken. He seemed older than his nearly seventy years.

"Yes," I said quite distinctly, "my father died sometime after the war had ended."

He nodded. "Do you remember *how* he died?"

I felt my hand *(no, it wasn't mine, it was Flint's)* go to my eyes, brushing. "W-why yes," I-Flint said, "he just got sick—his heart, I think—and he died. It was after the barn had burned down, and after a Union soldier had raped my sister and burned her, with the barn. It seemed to take the life right out of the old man. He just wilted, I guess. It h-happened pretty fast." The first thunder rumbled off in the distance, and though it was clouding up, I felt new thoughts edging into my head.

"And," Good said, "you left home after your father—died?"

"Why, yes," I said, "after that, and after I had found that soldier and killed him. He was the first, you see. Then I *had* to leave. That's why I told you it wasn't in 1865 I left, but later. When I found that soldier. It took—some time."

He shook his head. "Go away now," he said. "It's getting late. There is-n't much time left. You've done a wonderful job. I'm glad it's working out this way. I would have hated disturbing Hawkins again. We'll be able to leave him here... and let him die in peace. That's better."

"Much better," I said. The best, in fact, that could happen to a man.

I left Good then. He gave me the remaining four thousand dollars. I did not say goodbye, nor did he, though I never would see him again. He would not be needed tonight. Later, when they came and asked him questions, he would answer them briefly and in dignity. Even the doctor was his witness.

I had scrapped all our previous plans. Good had given me the idea, and from it, I had developed a new one. Hawkins, poor Hawkins, could remain in that upstairs bed. He could—and would—die there. No more hauling, no more desecrating of his battered body.

He had been found by Good one night or early morning this past week behind a boulder marking the boundary between Good's and Thomason's. Good had heard the man's groans. Good had pushed aside the boulder and hauled him back himself. Using a rope, he had hoisted Hawkins to a horse. That was in case anybody wondered how an old man, as tiny as Good, could have lifted him and brought him back to the ranch house. Good had wanted desperately to keep the savage beating quiet. He knew the temper of the town-folk. He had no proof—mind you—that Thomason had done in Hawkins, so he was not going to start the spread of ugly rumors. He was an old man. He wanted to be left alone, in peace.

Thomason, of course, would have denied it. But he wouldn't have any op-portunity. Nor would Slott. They'd be dead. Cora Thomason would be alive. And she would have heard me say—that night—in boasting explanation as I ravaged her before I left, that I was a hired killer, not a man named Flynn, but a man wanted in ten states and territories, a man named Flint. Her hus-band, Ed Thomason, had hired me. That's right, *Thomason* had hired me, to do in Good. I hadn't been able to get to Good. But his man Hawkins, when he got in the way, I had clubbed him to death. No? Not dead, you say? Frac-tured skull, but not quite dead? Next time I'd be sure. Hawkins didn't really matter, of course. It was Good I was after.

And why then were Slott and Thomason dead? Slott must have gotten wind of my being Flint. He had been suspicious from the first. The good town-folk of Dryhock would attest to that. Hadn't Slott had me in his office a time or two? And finally, he had ridden up to Thomason's to accost me. When he did, Thomason, to protect himself, had gone for his gun. So had I. So had Slott. When it was over, Slott had killed Thomason. Slott lay dead. Cora Thomason—in near shock—did not know who had killed Slott—her hus-band or this man named Flint. It didn't matter.

And, of course, the man named Flint would be gone that next morning, unable to bear down on Good because of this wild shooting spree, and because, with Thomason dead, the hired killer was without a boss, and therefore, with-out a job. So Flint would run.

That's what I told Good.

The only hitch was Good, and the weight of Hawkins' body. How had he moved the boulder, and how had he raised Hawkins—those were the snags in the thread of my story. But if the story were not closely scrutinized, it would hang together. And there was no reason on the face of it for careful scrutiny. I would have made what amounted to a confession to Cora Thoma-son. Enough people had seen me in town and riding to Thomason's. Piece by piece, the descriptions would dovetail. Flynn would be Flint.

On the face of it, there was no reason for careful scrutiny of Good's and Cora Thomason's story. I was the only person in the world who knew that there would probably be careful scrutiny, however. When Amy got the let-ter, and the facts therein did not jibe completely with those given out by Mrs. Thomason, she would in turn pass the letter on to the proper authorities.

I could see them confronting Good now, at first gentle with him, and then more and more biting, sarcastic....

"Let's see, Mr. Good, you weigh... about one hundred and thirty pounds?"

And Good would be silent. (*But his thoughts, oh, how I knew what his thoughts would be!*)

"You're not quite seventy years old... that is, not until November?"

And the silent reply.

"Hawkins... he was a big man, wasn't he, Mr. Good? Two hundred pounds?"

Silence.

"You just shoved that boulder aside?... You lifted him with a rope?... Let's see how you did it.... Here's the boulder, and here's a rope just like the one you say you used. . . . Here's a dummy of a man, properly weighted.... Move the boulder, Mr. Good. Lift the body, Mr. Good. Lift him. LIFT HIM!"

And, of course, he couldn't.

It was a fine thought.

I was not sure it would all follow this way. But it would lead to the same end. There'd be the body of a man hanging from a rope, all right. Good's body.

I left Good's and mounted my horse, moving him at a walk towards Thomason's. And there in the pass between the two spreads, a change occurred that had been on the verge of occurring for the past couple of days. I found myself at a great height (in my mind's eye, of course) looking down on the horseman named Flint, moving slowly toward Thomason's, to begin the events that would end in the killing of two men. I watched, as Flint kicked his horse lightly and every so often bent his head to spit or once in a while rubbed his hand along his ribs.

I watched this man named Flint, and I knew his thoughts, and, yes, from this height, from this vantage point, I knew everyone's thoughts. I knew what Cora Thomason was doing; I could guess what Slott was doing even though I couldn't see him. Good, too. He was getting easier to read.

I watched them all.

Chapter Thirteen

The sky had gone black by the time Flint reached Thomason's. It was—he noted—a few minutes past six o'clock. He was a man more tired than he would have admitted, even to himself. The pain in his right lung, or, rather, in the area of his chest and his back just right of center, had been present from the moment he got onto his horse to ride to Good's a few hours before. There was a growing, rising quality to the pain, one which Flint had long ago learned to associate with an impending hemorrhage. His breath was shortened slightly and every so often he stopped and stood still and placed his hands to his rib cage.

He was a terribly sick man.

Very slowly, he moved his horse to the corral and dismounted. Thomason's horse was there. Cora's wasn't. Nor was Cora herself anywhere around. She would be, Flint reflected, entering town soon. Flint let his mind idle over her mission. Slott would have finished his fruitless task of ferreting out a drunken Hawkins. He'd have asked questions all over town. He'd have—

Flint swore softly to himself. *Slott would have found out.* The doctor knew Hawkins was alive. The sheriff would find out. And when he did, he'd go back to his cot and go to sleep.

And then Flint seemed to relax. In his mind he saw Cora Thomason finding Slott in his office. It didn't matter that the sheriff knew Hawkins was alive. In fact, it was better. He was sure not to leave town too early. Cora Thomason could get him to follow her back to the ranch for no better excuse than just that: being with her.

Flint walked to the house. As he entered, lightning flashed briefly in the distance....

Upstairs, with a sly expression gliding over his face, Ed Thomason left his room and started downstairs. He had seen Flint through his window and he had taken one more drink from the two-thirds empty bottle of bourbon that stood on the floor next to the bed.

He felt good. He scarcely noticed the irregular bump-bump of his feet on the stairs. He walked into the kitchen.

"Well," he said, "the little digger. Been digging like a son-of-a-bitch, Flynn?"

"You're drunk," Flint said flatly.

"Naturally," he said. "I did what I said I'd do." He peered closely at Flint. "But did you?"

"You ought to know," Flint said. "You were watching me."

Thomason sat heavily across the table from Flint. He shook his head hard. "Not all the time," he said. "Not all the time. That's my big mistake, Flynnie."

Flint squinted his eyes. "What was your big mistake?"

"Not watching you *all* the time," he said.

"You'd better go upstairs and straighten yourself out," Flint said.

"What for?" Thomason said. "Need me to dig like a son-of-a-bitch, too?"

"There may be hell to pay tonight."

"Doesn't concern me," Thomason said. "Don't owe hell any money." He laughed shrilly at that. Flint stared hard him. "What's the matter, Flynn? Don't I have the right attitude for you?"

"No," Flint said shortly.

"S'matter, Flynn? Getting mad at ol' Thomason? Don't like ol' Thomason? Wish he'd go 'way?"

"I wish you'd go upstairs and pull yourself together."

"What for, Flynn? I'd just come apart later on again. What's the use? Eh, Flynn-ie, what's the use?" Suddenly Thomason buried his head in his arms on the kitchen table. Flint could see the growing bald spot at the crown, covered thinly with pale wisps of dry hair. Thomason lifted his head and caught Flint's eye.

"Pretty disgusted with me, aren't you, Flynn?"

Flint made no answer.

"And that's funny, if you ask me, Flynn-ie. Because I'm pretty disgusted with you."

"Why are you disgusted with me, Ed?" Flint said quietly.

"Ah," Thomason said, "not *Mr.* or *sir?*" He clucked. "That's not the proper attitude for a hired hand."

"You said to call you by your first name," Flint said.

"You're wrong, I didn't. That was Mrs. Thomason. She—as I recall—*insisted* you call her Cora. You're confusing me with Cora. 'N that's pretty funny. Because you wouldn't really confuse me with Cora, would you, Flynn-ie?"

"What are you talking about?"

"Talking about you and Cora."

"What about me and Cora?"

"Wouldn't you like to know?" Thomason said. He laughed shrilly again, pleased with himself.

Flint got up from the kitchen table and walked outside. The night was going to come in fast. The rain was holding off, just at the lip of the clouds hovering mountain-peak high over the valley. The thunder was clearer now, and the lightning bolts took on jagged definition, rather than lightning in distant white flashes.

Thomason followed him outside. A lopsided smile was fastened to his face. He walked up to Flint and tugged at his sleeve. "Show me where he is," he said, in an exaggerated whisper. "Let's, let's dig him up. Let's surprise Cora when she comes back." Then he cocked his head at Flint. "W-where is Cora? Where—where's she hiding?"

Flint grinned. He said in mimicry, "Wouldn't *you* like to know?"

The lopsided smile fell from Thomason's face. "Yes," he said quietly, "yes, I would. Tell me, Flynn."

Flint turned away. "I don't know," he said.

Thomason followed him around. "Yes, you do, Flynn. What's going on around here? Who—what are you doing? There's something fishy—" He stared at Flint and then started to back away, his eyes wide open.

"Go on," Flint said.

"No," he said. His voice was thick. "No." He spun away, and in heavy lurching strides made his way back to the house. Above the grumbling thunder, Flint heard his crashing steps up the stairs.

He shrugged and kept staring at the thunderclouds.

CHAPTER FOURTEEN

Cora Thomason single-stepped her horse down the main drag of Dryhock. The street was nearly deserted. It was seven-thirty. Big scattered drops of warm rain splashed into the dust. At the far end of town, a wagon pulled heavily onto the road and started moving to the north. Cora watched it as it creaked out of sight.

She pulled up at the hitching post in front of Barney Slott's office. Flint had said Barney would not be in his office. She smiled. Above the muted thunder, she could hear the sound of Barney's snoring. And—more positive than that—she could smell him. She looped her horse to the post and walked in.

Slott was lying on his back, on the cot, his great legs straddling the sides of the cot, his feet firmly planted on the floor. She looked at his gross body and there was, as always, a faint prickle running along her spine. She no longer was horrified by the impulse that came involuntarily every time she saw him like this: the impulse to strip her clothes and lie next to him. She wondered how it would be. So big, she thought, he's so big.

Then her lip curled. Impulse be damned. If she obeyed every impulse to crawl under a man's sheets, she'd have bed sores the rest of her life. And the rest of her life was a very important thing. She had to be careful, oh, so careful, for so short a time. Soon it would be over. And her life would begin anew.

But before it was over, there was much to do. There was this poor, slobbering, faithful dog lying here who had to be prodded and slapped into mobility. And there was that—that business tonight, with Flint. Then, and only then, it would be over.

Soon it would be eight o'clock. Flint wanted Barney no earlier than ten. If she woke him now, pleaded with him to hurry, and he agreed, then it would be too early. But Flint must have been thinking in terms of darkness. With the storm brewing, he might want it earlier. Flint had that about him. He kept changing things. The way Good sometimes was. Men—she thought—they were such fools. Take herself. She had a wish. It was a simple little wish, the wish every woman, has. Usually by the time you're thirty, she thought, the wish has taken on dust, long-neglected. That was the difference between herself and other women. Her wish stayed shiny, through all those dull terrible years with Ed. Now she could bring it to fulfillment.

Poor Ed, she thought, and as quickly as the thought came, she brushed it aside.

Poor Barney, she thought, and she dwelled on that. He had no reason to die tonight. It was no real business of his. Just because Hiram thought the sheriff was a wiser man than he really was. Hiram was, in a way, a coward. He always had to be sure. Suppose, Hiram had once told her, suppose Slott knows that he, Good, is behind the fence burning, behind the branded calves. Suppose he doesn't know, but he suspects. There might be trouble. So wipe it out before it develops.

Poor Barney.

Instinctively she had drawn closer to the cot. A hand strayed to his shoulder, and then she drew it back. She studied his face in repose. It was not a bad face, she thought. The bones were good, big, strong bones. She felt a shiver run through her. If she were a surgeon, she'd carve away at that body, slice off great rolling mountains of fat, until the big broad frame stood stripped to the bone. She did not mind ugly men. There was an essence of manhood about ugliness.

This time she did not stop her hand. It went to his shoulder and gently jostled him.

He groaned once and then opened his eyes. Instantly he was awake.

"Cora," he said, struggling to his feet. His hands went to his hair, trying to brush it into place. He ran his hands down his shirt front. "You'll have to—you'll have to excuse my appearance," he said.

She smiled at him. "You're a funny man," she said. "You always say the same thing."

"That makes it worse, my dear," he said. "I wish I didn't have to say it every time."

She let the smile slowly fade from her face. She could not forget why she was here. "Barney," she said, "I want to ask a favor."

"And why not?" he said. "Who else would you ask?"

She nodded vigorously. "That's what I told Flynn," she said.

The sheriff's face became stern. "What's Flynn got to do with it?"

"I don't know," she said, staring at him, letting her eyes fill as she moved them slowly across his face. "I really don't know. But Flynn said it was a serious matter and I thought—I thought if it was that serious, you ought to know about it." Intuitively she had shied away from telling Barney that Flint had told her to go to him. She wanted it to seem that her being here was her own idea. The thought warmed her. She was glad she had done it this way. Now she could watch Barney react to her charms. "So here I am."

But he did not react as she expected. Instead, his eyes narrowed. "What was a serious matter?" he said.

"It's—it's Thomason," she said. "He's drunk and—and he's saying horrible things about Flynn."

"About Flynn and you?" the sheriff asked.

"N-no," she said. "Just about Flynn. That Flynn is a liar and is starting trouble, and that if he doesn't watch himself, he's going to—"

"Going to what?"

"I don't know. He never says more than just that."

"And because of that, you decided to come to me? Just because Thomason and Flynn are having words?"

She took a breath and she watched his eyes as they flicked down to her bosom. Then she let the breath out slowly. His eyes stayed a long second before they met hers. "But he's drunk. And he never gets drunk," she said. "I'm—I'm afraid."

His voice was gentle. "Flynn can take care of himself."

"I don't know," she said. "Look at poor Hawkins."

He smiled. "What about poor Hawkins?"

"Why," she said. "Everybody is saying somebody killed him. They—they even say Ed did it, to get at Good, or else Good did it to get at Ed. I'm afraid."

"No need," he said. "Nobody killed Hawkins."

She gasped. "How do you know?"

He winked at her. "I know." Then he stopped and looked past her. "Not that I don't think you're pretty close to the truth."

"What do you mean?"

"I'm afraid, my dear, it's not really your business."

Her eyes blazed. "Thanks," she said. "I come here to you because I need help. And you tell me a riddle." She turned and started out.

"Please," Slott said. The voice was low and pained.

She knew now that she was in control. It would not change. She stopped but did not turn. "Well?" she said. "Am I to be ridiculed for coming here, or will you help me?"

"Cora," he said, the voice still low, "you know I'll always help you. All you have to do is ask."

"I'm not so sure," she said. "You tell me Hawkins hasn't been killed, but that he was almost killed. Is that what you're telling me? Or am I to guess while you keep quiet?"

"You're right," he said. "At least, I think so. Doc Smalley's been treating Hawkins at Good's. Smalley says Hawkins fell from his horse and smashed up his head pretty bad. But from the way Smalley tells it, I can't for the life of me picture a rider like Hawkins falling from his horse and getting his skull caved in. It doesn't add up. I get the feeling Smalley has agreed to tell the story about the fall from a horse. I just don't believe it, though. It looks as though somebody slugged Hawkins."

"So," Cora said, "am I not to worry? Or am I to feel relieved because Hawkins isn't dead but only half-dead?"

"Cora," the sheriff said, "I don't understand you. Who are you worried about? Flynn? You're worried about Flynn, that your husband is going to hurt him?"

Now she turned. "No," she said, her eyes wounded. "I'm worrying about myself. If there's a killer loose around here—if that hired hand we had last year is back again—then naturally I'm worried. Who knows whom he might strike?"

"Cora, Cora," he said, "how you confuse me. First you tell me your husband is drunk and is saying nasty things about your new hired hand, Flynn. Now you drag in the hired hand of last year, who, I feel, is a much maligned man. Now, Cora, what's bothering you?"

Once more she drew in a deep breath. Then she took one tentative step toward him, and as she let the breath out, she broke it so that a trembling sob escaped her lips. "Oh, Barney, Barney," she said, "I don't know. I'm so frightened, so terribly frightened."

She felt his arms go slowly to her shoulders and then creepingly about her. A heavy hand patted her back with terrible care.

"Now," he said, "now, Cora, don't carry on so. Everything will be all right. Old Barney will take care of everything...."

Chapter Fifteen

Hiram Good sat slumped in his great easy chair, sipping his brandy. Ten o'clock. It would be happening any time now. Now it was out of his hands, and the thought saddened him.

No matter how often he denied it to Flint, or to himself, it was true that he liked the difficulty of his plan almost as much as he cared for the results. The means justify the end, he had said, and it was true. How dull it would have been to grab the nearest drifting drunk who applied for a month's work just to get enough money for two more days of drink—how dull to use a tool like that for the utterly delightful job of erasing Thomason and Slott. Thirty dollars and it would have been over.

But this way was so right. That Flint, he was a wonder. Half the time stumbling along like a clumsy boy trying to filch from his mother's cookie jar; the other half matching Good thought for thought, hurdling each obstacle that had been thrown in his path, trumping each ace, sometimes even tearing up the whole deck and, like a magician, producing another one from his sleeve. It *had* been brilliant to plant Hawkins the way he had; it *had* been wise and daring to gauge Cora Thomason so coolly and know she'd throw in with a plot to gun down her own husband (though, of course, unnecessary since Cora had been in from the beginning); it *had* been pure genius to use the old master-plan by just twisting Flint's role so that he became *Thomason's* hired killer.

And yet, there was a growing disaffection between them. Good stared into his brandy, rotated the glass slowly against his cupped hand, and sighed. Flint had killed his father and burned his sister to death, and would not admit it, even to himself. Though Good was sure Flint was fighting a losing battle here. The knowledge of those two murders was swamping the man, and soon, very soon, he'd realize what he'd done. Maybe he already did. The way he kept saying to Good, "I'll protect you as if you were my own father"; there was more to this than platitude.

Good knew why the disaffection had grown. Flint—great as he was at times—simply wasn't good enough. They never were, Good knew, but he'd had such hopes for Flint. Well, maybe the next one would have it.

Flint didn't. Good wondered whether Flint now understood the business about shoeing the wrong foot of the horse. Contempt, that was what he was showing Flint then. Good knew Flint had lied to him when he said he'd told Thomason he had to have his horse shod. Such a patent fabrication.

Good had sensed the scrambling lie, the quick coverup. He had seen through Flint. He had had the wrong foot shod, just to show Flint that he, Good, knew Flint had never told Thomason a blasted thing about the horse.

It was Good's contempt for the inferior. And Good knew how it would work on Flint, gnaw at him. The time had come to put Flint entirely in Good's hands, entirely a puppet on Good's strings. Flint was botching things, right and left. He must not botch any more. So remove his faith in himself, and thrust him blindly into Good's own more clever hands.

Good sipped from his brandy. The night was blackening. He wondered how Flint planned his escape. He had no doubt Flint would first pull off the double-killing tonight. He even imagined Flint would drag Cora into the Thomason bedroom and make love to her. And then before morning, while his lady love slept, Flint would step out of the house and onto his horse, and away. That's how Flint would have it planned, no doubt.

Too bad for him, Good thought. It just wouldn't be that way. That's where Flint was at his stupidest. He could not (or was it *would not?*) make himself understand that the same reason dictating the killing of Hawkins would apply to him. Like Hawkins, Flint now knew too much. Good thought he had made it clear to Flint, what with the business of Doc Smalley and Smalley's wife and even a half-dozen neighbors. If necessary, they all would have to go. Like Flint, Good, too, had lost count of the number of people he had killed. Unlike Flint, he had good sound reason. There had been far, far too many.

Good let his fingers run about the delicate curve of the brandy glass. It had been—he reflected—a good life. If it ended now, which it wouldn't, he would have few regrets. Still—there was so much to do.

There was, for instance, Flint's body, once the night was over. That would not be difficult. The plowed-up field that Flint kept digging up, looking for Hawkins' grave. Well, he'd find a grave, all right. His own.

And then there was Good's own prosaic work, right here in Dryhock. The simple business of running things, day after day. The postmaster would bring him his mail tomorrow, Jake the bartender would collect the receipts from the town cathouse, the bank would let him know where the railroad was building so that Good might buy up the land and then refuse to sell. There was talk of eminent domain back east, but until they made Colorado a state, it would be pretty tough to force him to sell, even to the federal government. And, of course, Good was not yet ready to make Colorado a state.

So much, so much to do.

Outside the thunder clapped like doom, or like hearty applause, and lightning crackled so close you could smell the heat of it. It was a magnificent night Flint had chosen for them. The brandy was warm inside, a gentle glow. He must remember, Good thought, to bring some more to Jake. The bartender said he had used his last flaskful.

Good hoped whoever it was that had had it was a man of good taste. He wished the man long life.

Chapter Sixteen

Flint stood on the sagging porch of Thomason's house and cursed the night. The rain pelted down in silver streaks. Thunder crashed about the house. Lightning bolts stunned his sight. Off on the horizon, one bolt lit up a naked pine tree at the crest of a hill, and then before it had vanished, a second bolt had struck it.

He went inside and to his room. He sat on his bed and removed his .44 from his belt. From a small square wooden box he took out a bottle of oil, a thin brush and some rags. He worked an oily rag down the seven-and-a-half-inch barrel, stared through it in the flickering kerosene light. Then he wiped off the excess oil and once more slipped it into his belt. Five rounds. More than enough. Two more than enough.

He lay back on his bed. He thought he'd be able to hear them, even above the storm. It was eleven o'clock. He stared at the shadows playing on the ceiling. He wondered how he would do it. First Thomason, he thought. Get Thomason out of the way, out of his misery. And then he remembered two things: what the sheriff had said about shooting flies off a horse's nose with his gun, and the way Slott had ridden his thick-bellied brown horse. He was a more capable man than he had given him credit for. Slott was a dangerous man. It would be wiser to kill him first.

Flint shrugged. It really didn't matter. They'd both be dead. He let his tongue go over his lips. He could feel the hot crackling of the skin around his mouth. The fever had returned. He stood up. His breathing was too short for lying this way.

He walked down the corridor to the first room. He put his ear to the door. There was no sound at first. Then he heard the quiet gurgling of a man drinking. That was good.

Flint walked down the stairs, not caring how much noise he made. Sooner or later, Thomason would have to be roused.

He stood on the porch. The rain was letting up. It was as though with the storm directly overhead, something had to abate. Each peal of thunder overlapped the last. The lightning had once again lost its individual jagged shape. The bolts came too frequently to identify any one shaft. But the rain slowed down. It gave the storm a hollow, boastful quality. So much noise, such gaudy display. It was, Flint thought, like that other night, years and years ago. Careful, he thought, forget about that night. He knew what had happened that night, and he must not think about it. It was too terrible to think about. When that night had ended, he was alone, dreadfully alone, except for that crushing weight on his soul. The weight, he suddenly realized, had never left him, after that night.

Tonight would be different. Tonight he wouldn't be alone, and the weight would finally leave. First, he'd have Cora Thomason. That was sure. For the remainder of the night. And after that, he had—he had *this*, he thought, patting the gun that dug into his waist. It was the thing that would remove the weight from his soul, at long last.

His hand wandered inside his shirt and he stroked the gun, first the butt and then down the long barrel. It was a good, clean thing, he thought, a real honey. It was his peacemaker.

It would be Thomason's peacemaker, too. Thomason would not mind. His had been a struggle, his life. First he had tried to make a go of his marriage. That had obviously failed. Now he wanted to get the most out of his land, and somebody else was taking it away from him. No, Thomason would not mind. Not if he knew what was going on.

And Slott. The man lived a sad life, staring into a cracked mirror and looking on the ruin of his body with a curious detachment that must have come only after long years of intense misery. Slott was a man who knew what a gun could do. He would appreciate his end, good and clean, his face in the good, clean spring mud.

...Flint heard them coming, the horses splashing through the mud half a mile away. He raced upstairs and hammered on Thomason's door.

"Wake up, man!" he shouted. "She's coming. And there's a man right behind her. Strap on your gun." He heard a scrambling inside and a choked oath. Then Flint went downstairs.

At first it seemed as though it was one figure on two horses. Then he realized what it was. The horses were side by side, and Slott had thrown a huge poncho over Cora. He held it in place with his left arm. He leaned toward her. They came on, terribly slowly, slipping and sloshing in the bog underfoot.

"There," Slott was saying, "there. Old Barney got you here all right, didn't he? Nothing to worry about any more."

Flint looked at Cora through the flashing lightning.

There was on her face that quiet regal look she had had once before, during the afternoon they had thrown white terror into her husband. This was somewhat different. It had a tired quality to it. It seemed more natural. God, Flint thought, what an artist.

"Thank you, Barney," she said simply. She slipped from her horse, and stumbled when she essayed her first step. Instantly Slott was off his horse.

"There's no hurry, my dear," he said. "Just rest here for a moment."

Flint waited for the next flash of lightning. When it came he searched out Slott's gun. It hung from his right hip. Flint knew instantly how he would do it.

He stepped around to Cora and took her right arm.

He stood next to her, on her right side. Slott moved to her left. His own right arm went protectingly about Cora's shoulders. His gun hung useless between himself and Cora's left side. Cora looked at Flint and nodded, imperceptibly.

"Take it easy," Flint warned. "It's slippery as hell out here. The creek's overflown—"

They all heard Thomason at the same time, but only Flint knew what it was. He came smashing down the stairs and into the brief hall. The porch door swung open and cracked against the wall of the house. It came bouncing back and Thomason cursed wildly as it struck him. Then he lurched to the edge of the porch and stood there.

"It's—it's Ed," Cora said. "What's wrong—"

"It must be like you said," Slott said. "He's drunk."

They were seventy-five yards away from the house, the three of them, and when lightning broke close by, they could see Thomason standing there, peering into the dark, his mouth slack and wet, his legs spread wide, and his body swaying.

"H-he's carrying a gun," Cora said.

"Let me handle this," Slott said. His voice was mild. "I'll take care of him."

"No!" Cora screamed. "No, no! I'm afraid. Don't leave me." She clung to his right arm.

"Please, my dear," he said, trying gently to release her. "I can take care of this in a moment's time. Then everything will be fine."

"No!" she screamed again. "He'll kill you!"

"She's right," Flint said. "He's been like this all night. Swearing and drinking and threatening just about everybody."

"Keep out of this, Flynn," Slott said sharply. "I'll take care of Thomason."

"I'm telling you," Flint said. "He's dangerous. He'll use that gun."

Thomason had heard most of this but it had not made too much sense. He had come out expecting—what, he knew not. He certainly did not expect to see the sheriff and Flynn leading his wife to the front door. There was something incongruous about this, after he had heard Flynn's urgent shouts through the bedroom door. And he knew they were trying to trick him.

The sly look once more stole over his face. He bounded down the porch stairs, the gun flapping in his hand. He started in a straight line for the three of them.

"Look out!" Flint yelled. "He's coming." He tugged at his waist.

"Easy, man!" Slott called. "We're not going to hurt you." He shoved himself free of Cora Thomason and stood in front of her.

But at that moment, Thomason cut sharply away from them and ran in staggering strides toward the south boundary. Lightning illuminated his path. He was on his way to the pass between his land and Good's, the only part of the range where there would be no fence to impede him.

"I'll cut him off," Flynn said, racing for the pass.

Thomason stumbled once, went down, and then got up, the gun still in his hand. He had slowed terribly, the effects of the alcohol suddenly catching up with him. But he had had the advantage of surprise and the darkness swallowed him again.

Flint could hear Slott cursing behind him, panting as he struggled to keep from falling too far to the rear. "Wait," he cried, "let him go, Flynn. He'll cause no trouble."

Flint ran on, his own breath coming out in heavy pain-filled sobs. Thomason was in the dip before the pass. Flint ran through the shoveled-up field, to the east of Thomason. He planned on swinging wide in a half-circle and coming back on Thomason as he emerged from the pass.

It worked that way. He was around the east boulder and onto the first fringe of Good's land before he stopped. Now he turned and stepped quietly back. Thomason came trampling through the pass, straight toward Flint. A blinding bolt of lightning struck nearby, and the smell of smoke filled the night.

A tree, Flint thought. It must have been a big one. And then he raised his gun. Thomason stopped ten feet away. He blinked through the flashing light.

"W-wha—" he said. The gun dangled loose at his knee.

Flint shot him through the head. Then he stepped quickly to one side, inching his way to the boulder and waited, in ambush. Nobody was coming. He looked out from behind the rock. He could see clearly now.

And then he saw the reason he could see so well, and why he had smelled wood smoke. Why, too, it had seemed as though the lightning bolts had merged, one literally on top of the other, until they had added up to a second sun. Why, too, nobody was coming this way.

The Thomason ranch house was on fire.

In front of the house, Flint could see the sheriff and Cora standing together, staring at the blaze that raced unheeded through the upper story and now seemed to be licking its way down the stairs. Flint walked toward the house. He was terribly tired. Half the job was done. The other half was so fiendishly easy. All he had to do was walk up on Slott, make some noise until the sheriff wheeled around, and then shoot him as he had done Thomason.

It was not like the Hawkins business. No doubts this time. No backing out, either. Every move stood clear in silhouette. He knew what he was doing. Thomason lay where he should lie. Slott would die right here, in front of the house. Then he and Cora would drag him to the pass.

It was so easy he couldn't do it. He put the gun into his waistband.

He walked up to them. They did not seem to notice him. He said, "Don't suppose anything can be done about it, do you?"

Slott didn't even turn toward him. He shook his mammoth head. "A miracle," he said. "Think—think of what would have happened if you had been in there, asleep. A miracle, that you came to me tonight."

Cora's voice was strained. "Please, Barney, don't talk about it."

Suddenly Slott remembered. He turned on Flint.

"Where's Thomason?" His eyes were lit with rage and suspicion.

Flint felt the strength of the man, and he felt fear with it. "He's gone," he said, waving his hand to the pass.

"Gone?" Cora said sharply.

"You mean he got away from you?" Slott said.

Flint nodded. "Last I saw of him, he was running pell-mell for Good's."

Cora stared. "But he'll hurt—"

Slott shook his head. "No, he won't, Cora. He won't hurt anybody. I doubt that he'll make it all the way. He'll fall down someplace and pass out. Tomorrow he'll have the granddaddy of all headaches. That's all. He'll only hurt himself. And that won't be any tragedy." He sounded a bit sad to Flint, as though he, too, wanted the whole thing over with.

Flint put his arm on Slott. "Come on away from here," he said. "The whole goddam house is going to cave in in a minute."

Slott nodded. "That's the first wise thing I've heard tonight. Come, my dear," he said to Cora. He took her arm and they moved away. They walked a hundred steps and turned around. With the abatement of the storm, a wind had risen, and the flames were whipped through the dying house at a fantastic rate. The thunder had trailed off to a puppy's whimper and only an occasional distant flash of lightning remained. They stared at the house—what remained of it—in hypnotic fascination. And as they watched, it came down. A hissing, spark-filled, flame-tongued bellow of smoke rose from the crashing ruins and within fifty yards of them pieces of burning wood fell to the ground where they sizzled out. A steady fire chewed away, lighting up the whole area.

Slott turned to Cora. "Where will you stay tonight?"

She shook her head. "I d-don't know," she said. Her voice was a whisper. She avoided Flint's eyes.

"You can come back with me," Slott said. She let a little shiver run through her body.

"No," she said. He stared down at her, and then turned away.

"And you, Flynn," he said, "where will you sleep?"

Flint hunched his shoulders. Everything was fine again. The fire had bothered him at first, but he was getting over it now. "I don't care," he said. "Out in the open. I'll have to pull out of here tomorrow. Job's over, I guess."

"What job?" Cora asked. The sharpness was returning to her voice.

"Here. With you and Mr. Thomason."

Slott looked at him through the speckled night. "Why is it over, Flynn? There ought to be more than enough work these next few weeks." He waved his hand toward the burning wreck of the house.

Flint tried to make out Cora. She stood there, her head cast down.

"Thomason doesn't trust me," he said. "I'll have to leave." Then, as though in afterthought, he turned to Cora. "You can go over to Good's yourself tonight."

"Good's?" she said, her voice full of amazement. "Are you insane? After all that talk about his thinking we had killed Hawkins?"

"Nothing to worry about," Flint said. "Mr. Good was over here this evening, while you were in town. He told me that Hawkins wasn't dead. He had hurt himself, but that was all."

"How'd Good say it happened?" Slott asked idly.

Instantly Flint froze. Slott had talked with Doc Smalley; he could tell. "Good didn't say too much," Flint said. "Something about Hawkins falling from his horse and cracking his head against one of those boulders out there. Pretty badly hurt, I understand, but nobody's fault but his own."

Slott said, "That's how Good tells it, eh?"

Cora Thomason said, "Don't you believe Mr. Good?"

Slott sounded dubious. "That's a shrewd old man, that Good. I've always felt, for instance, he knew more about that fence being burned down than anybody here...."

Cora sucked in her breath. "What do you mean, Barney?"

"Well," he said, "I hate to hang an old man without evidence, but when that fence burned down, I rode over here that night—" he waved his hand "—yes, I did, that very night, and from what I could see, whoever had done it, had come *from* Good's side of the fence, and had gone back that way. At least, if I can read track any. And," he paused, "I think I can."

"But why," Cora said, "why would Good burn down his fence?"

"Why indeed," Slott said. "But for that matter, why would Thomason? It was his fence, too."

There was silence. Then Slott broke it. "Well," he said, "if you're sure, Flynn."

"I'm sure," Flint said. "Good was telling the truth. You can trust him."

Cora had caught the spirit back in Flint again. "It's so much closer, Barney, than going back to town."

"And so much cleaner," he said.

"Don't be foolish," she said. "I'll never forget... your kindness."

"Nor I yours," he said.

Flint smiled grimly to himself. Well, he thought, so Slott finally bedded her down.

"Let's go," Flint said. He led the way to their horses. In the still flickering light cast by the dying fire, Flint stood by Cora's horse. Slott came over and the two men stared at each other. Cora looked at the sheriff and then touched Flint's arm. "Please," she said. He helped her on her horse and flashed a look of scorn at the sheriff. Slott's face was taking on the sagging collapsed quality that Flint had known before tonight.

The three of them rode straight for the pass, Flint in the lead, Cora riding at Slott's right side. Flint felt no love for her, no affection, nothing but the utmost admiration. She was so cool about it all, he thought. They were riding to where her husband lay dead, and she must know it, and to where her latest lover would soon lie dead, and this, too, she must know.

Cora was thinking, poor Flint. He couldn't do it quick and clean, as it should have been done. She pressed closer to Slott's right side, and her left hand strayed to his gun butt.

Slott was thinking, it's over. I had her for a moment, and I shouldn't complain, because no man will ever have more or better, but it's over, and I have to complain. I never should have done it. That way I'd never have known how good it could be. Now, every time I look at that scabby bed, that cesspool of a room, I'll miss her. God, he thought, I never should have done it.

Flint rode into the pass. He drove his spurs cruelly into his horse's side, raking down. The horse screamed and reared up, and then he swiftly brought her down.

Behind him, the other two horses collided for a moment, and then sprang apart, trumpeting.

"Easy," Cora said sharply, "easy, boy."

Slott simply reached to his horse's mouth and ripped down at the bit. His horse stopped dead.

Flint said hoarsely, "There's something there, down there." He pointed into the darkness below and in front of them.

"Where?" Slott shouted.

"There, dammit, there!" Flint said. He leaped from his horse and strode forward. "Slott," he called, "come down here."

Slott slipped from his horse. He walked toward Flint's voice. Cora got down from her horse and faded into the darkness.

Flint walked forward confidently, his gun held in his right hand. And then his foot stumbled over something—Thomason's body, he knew in a terror-struck instant—and he lost his balance, slid forward, regained it with a swift, drenching feeling of relief, and then skidded suddenly to the side and fell heavily, painfully on his left hip. He threw up his right hand for balance, and as the pain ripped through him, he knew in horror that he no longer held his gun. He sobbed once, and started to crawl away in the darkness.

Behind him he heard Slott scratch a matchhead with his thumbnail. "Flynn," he said, "Flynn, where are—*my God....*"

Flint got to his feet and went down again. At the very end, he thought, right here at the very end, I'm not going to make it.

"Flynn," Slott called out. "You won't get away with it, I'll—" and then the voice stopped and Flint heard a broken curse come from the sheriff.

Flint turned. The sheriff lit another match. Flint could see his huge bulk, his head down, searching the ground. And Flint felt the strength come back again. Slott did not have his gun either.

He stood there while the sheriff lit match after match. There was a scrabbling frenzy in Slott's movements, and finally, comprehension. He turned behind him, to where Cora should have been, but wasn't. He stumbled back and then to the side. "Cora," he said hoarsely, "where are you?"

And from Flint's side, came the answer, "Here, Barney, right here. Just twenty feet in front of you."

"Cora," the sheriff said, and his voice was a slobbering animal's now, "Cora, why, why did you do it?" He lurched forward.

Flint kept dead quiet. Slott came forward. The moon had slipped out now, and the dark was no longer complete.

The man's bulk was frightening. And Cora stood there, immobile.

"Here," she said, "here I am, Barney."

The sheriff came up to her, five feet away, and then he sank to his knees. "Please, Cora, tell me why."

Four shots ripped the night, each one a second apart. Slott stayed there, swaying on his knees, and his eyes were bulging out of his head. Then he screamed, "Cora, don't!" and fell forward.

She turned to Flint, Slott's gun still in her hand. He opened his arms and pressed his mouth against hers, but all he felt was complete, irrevocable horror.

Then the fifth bullet ripped into Flint's stomach.

Chapter Seventeen

...And that's how it had to end, I knew. Not just yet, because it's more difficult for a dead man to die. I crawled away from her, and she watched me— I couldn't see her, but she watched me, all right, as she had been watching me all the time. For that was the real beauty of Good's plan. Put me over at Thomason's so that I could keep my eye on him and on Slott (though there was no reason to do this, since Good had been behind the fence-burning and branding), and so Cora Thomason could keep her eye on me.

She was in Good's pocket, too.

But I didn't care. I had planned to kill Thomason with one bullet and Slott with another. The third was for me. That was my final escape. It didn't matter that I was crawling on my belly, my blood mixing with the rushing waters.

Still, I had expected one more night, and there was so much I didn't know.

She walked behind me. I stopped and turned my head. "Cora," I said, "Cora."

She bent down. "What is it, Flint?" Her voice was soft and sweet. Sad, too, I think. But what I heard was "Flint."

"You know who I am? You knew it all the time?" It was easy to talk, lying on my stomach. So much easier to breathe this way. I had to remind myself never to lie on my back again. It hurt too much. "You knew I was Flint, didn't you?" I guess I knew that she did. I guess I knew it all along.

"Of course," she said. "Where—where are you going?"

"To the barn," I said. "Where else?"

She bent over me. There were tears in her eyes. "Shall I help you?"

"Yes," I said, "if you can." Then I remembered how she had half-carried me down the stairs. And how she had helped Good lug Hawkins around. "Tell Good that Hawkins can die now. It's all right."

"Hush," she said. She put her arm around my waist and lifted my arm and placed it around her neck. Then she straightened up. I felt something tear, and the blood bubbled down my mouth, but it didn't hurt.

...And we made it somehow. She propped me against a wooden beam and scurried off. She came back with a flickering lantern and a heavy woollen horse blanket. She wrapped the blanket loosely about me. She sat next to me, and put a wet kerchief to my lips.

It felt good being in the barn again. I was wrong. It had never burned down. That meant none of it was true. I hadn't killed my father in the barn or burned the barn down, with my sister inside, because here was the barn. It hadn't burned at all. They were just trying to fool me.

But I had fooled them instead.

"What are you smiling about, Flint?" she asked.

"It's funny," I said.

"Aren't you angry, Flint?"

I shook my head. "Why should I be? I've beaten you all." The weight inside me was starting to lift.

"Oh, Flint, Flint," she said, "don't talk that way."

I smiled. "Why shouldn't I?" I said. "It's the truth. You thought you'd fool me, but I fooled you instead."

She shook her head and the tears rolled down her cheeks.

"Don't cry," I said. "There's not much time."

"I know," she said in a choked voice. "Poor, poor Flint."

"Oh," I said, feeling my smile come on again, very brightly, I think. "Not poor Flint. Poor Cora. She's not got much time."

"What do you mean, Flint?" she said. "Why don't I have much time?"

I raised my hand and tried to wave a finger in front of her face. "Good says he likes to take his time. But he moves pretty fast."

"What are you talking about?"

"Hawkins," I said, "and then poor Flint, and now poor, poor Cora. You're next."

Her lip curled. "That's where you're wrong," she said. "Hiram and I will be married once—once a decent time interval has passed."

And that gave me nearly all the other answers. That was why Cora was involved. Her husband had said he'd never give Cora up to another man. That was why Good had never tried seriously to buy out Thomason. Good knew—if he wanted Cora, and I knew now that he did want her—Good knew he'd have to kill Thomason to get his wife.

Slott, too. Oh, sure Slott was a suspicious man and would have to go. But even if he weren't, Slott would have been killed. Because Good—in his old withered jealousy—must have sensed the dormant flame that existed when Cora and Slott came together. Good was an old man, with that most terrible sickness—he lusted after a young woman. And so Cora was right. She wasn't like me or Hawkins. She knew all about Good's guilt, but he couldn't kill her for that. He would have to have more than that to disillusion him, to turn him back to his old methods.

It made me angry that Cora was going to get away with everything.

"I thought you guessed it once," she went on. "That day you asked Thomason whether he owned anything Good wanted, his land or his water rights or what. Whether Good held a grudge against Thomason for anything. He did. Thomason did own something Good wanted. Me."

I coughed and some more blood spilled to her kerchief. Damn it, I thought, it's not fair. She can't get away with it. "Is that how he hooked you?" I said, my eyes guileless. If I could only get her to show some fear, even some uncertainty. "Promised you marriage? Half his land? His money? Is that it?"

"Why, yes," she said. I could see a flicker of something in her eyes. It might only have been contempt. Then it was gone. "He didn't hook me. He's told me how lonely he is. And how much work he has to do, all by himself."

"Work?" I said. "He never raises a finger on that ranch."

"Oh," she said, "not the ranch. He has so many projects. He says there's a valley a hundred miles north of here that he'd—like to own."

"This valley isn't big enough?"

Once more, the lip curled. "No valley is big enough for Hiram Good."

She was right. And there was my hope. That owning valleys meant more to Good than owning Cora Thomason.

"Does he own other valleys?" I asked.

She nodded. Her eyes were bright. Half of that wealth, she was thinking, that immense wealth would be *hers*.

"Many," she said. "So, so many."

And I thought, a dozen men here, a dozen there. He must have killed fifty by now.

"He'll never own another one," I said.

Her eyes narrowed and her voice was hard. Christ, she was much better than I ever was. Good had a jewel here. No wonder he hadn't lumped her with me and Hawkins. "What do you mean," she said, "he won't own another valley?"

I slid away from that. I couldn't tell her yet about my letter to Amy. Instead I said, "Why didn't you wait until we had made love, before shooting me?"

She frowned and stared down at me and then she shook her head. "I couldn't," she said. A tangle of black hair fell over her cheek. I wanted to touch it. "Not after—after being with Slott."

I didn't care. I remembered what had happened last time we had made love. I remembered what happened to people who slept with her. Ed Thomason. Slott. Myself. Soon, Good.

"I'll never forget," she said, "how brave you were."

"You knew how sick I was then?"

She nodded. "Good had told me. He said to watch you. To let him know if I thought you wouldn't be able to make it."

"You didn't have to tell him, did you?" I felt good about that. It's not easy for a dead man to stay alive as long as I had. Just a little longer and I wouldn't have to any more. And after that, I'd have somebody working for me. Even after I was no longer alive. Amy.

"No," she said, "I didn't tell him. You were wonderful all the way."

"Not at the end," I said. "Don't tell Good how I dropped my gun. He'd laugh." But he'll not laugh too long. Not with Amy working for me.

"I won't," she said. "Not that he'd laugh. You made it all possible, you know. You showed me what to do, making me walk on Slott's right side.

That's what you were saying, wasn't it? Stay on his right and get his gun?"

"That's right," I said. "I—" The coughing started then. I had been talking too much. But it didn't hurt. In fact, it felt pretty good. There was a light-headed quality about it, like the aftermath of love-making. Drained and tired, but fine. Christ, I didn't know I had that much blood left.

She waited patiently for me to stop coughing. She still wanted to know why Good would never own another valley.

The answer came out before I could stop it. "Amy...."

"What did you say, Flint?"

"Nothing," I said. "I just said Amy."

"You liked her, didn't you, Flint?"

"Yes," I said. "She's—a nice girl."

Cora laughed again. "Oh, yes," she said, "very nice. Barney was telling me about her."

"Slott? Slott didn't know anything about Amy."

"Maybe he didn't before today. But he sure as hell found out plenty this evening."

"What do you mean?" There was a spreading cold fever now that had chased away the last of the pain, and I felt myself slipping though I hadn't moved.

She said, "Barney went looking for Hawkins all over. He got to the seamstress and your Amy. They were entertaining. The two girls and half a dozen punchers all on the floor. He said it was the most disgusting thing he ever saw—"

I didn't care. It didn't matter. I liked Amy.

"—so Barney just pitched them all out the door."

"The girls?"

"No," she said. I felt relieved. She giggled. "Not just then," she said. "After he kicked the punchers out, he—he took his strap to the girls, his belt, and he whipped the bejabbers out of them."

"And?"

"He sent them packing, pronto. They had orders to be gone by nightfall." She nodded a couple of times. "They went, all right. They were out of town an hour later."

"They left?" I said. "No address where they—they can be reached? Just gone, like that?"

She bent down and stroked my cheek. "Poor Flint. You really did like her, didn't you?"

There it was. I had done it to myself. Nobody was to blame. Not Slott, not Amy, not the cowpunchers who had thrown the orgy. Just me. If I hadn't mentioned the place to Slott, he never would have known about it. All the time, I was cutting my own throat.

"Well," I laughed, "I guess I'll be going now."

She frowned at me. "N-not yet, Flint. The valley, what about the valley?"

"Nothing," I said. "I was just teasing you. Good will own lots of valleys. Thousands of them. He'll live forever. But," I said, "not you. You're dead, like me, Cora, and like Hawkins. You know too much."

She sneered at me. "Not Cora Thomason."

She said, "He worships me."

She said, "He won't touch me."

All the time I kept smiling at her.

"No," she said, "you're wrong. Not me. I'm protected."

Just like me, I thought. The letter will lie in the rusting postbox until somebody remembers to look there, and then it will end up in the dead letter pile. Finally, like everything else that's already dead, they'll destroy it.

She kept talking and shaking her head, very seriously, and I tried to listen, but it was getting difficult.

"...he mentioned this organization, this association established for the protection of cattlemen against rustlers and the like, and how they do all sorts of odd jobs. Good said how much he admired the organization, how efficient it was, how he envied the way it operated...."

And I started to laugh. He *was* suspicious of her. He doubted her. Above and beyond the call of lust, there always was Good's method: never trust anybody.

"...so I wrote to them, down in Arizona, and they said they'd have an investigator up here within a few days, to keep his eye on me in case Good started any trouble—like you mentioned. In case Good ever did put me in the same category as you and Hawkins. Not that he will," she said hastily. "He loves me. But still—"

I spoke through the laughter, bubbling happy words, "The Cattleman's Protection Association?"

"Yes," she said eagerly, "you've heard of it?"

"Yes," I said. "They do a good job."

"So you see," she said, "I'm protected just in case Good...."

I saw. "Do you know the name of the investigator they're sending up?"

"Yes," she said. "A man named Bonney. He's pretty young, they said, but I shouldn't mind. He's very good, they said."

"Bill Bonney?" I said.

"Why, yes," she said. "I think that's his first name. Do you know of him?"

"Well," I said, "not too much. He used to deal monte in a place near Fort Bowie." Billy Bonney, I thought. It would be the right end for Cora Thomason.

And Hiram Good? Good had always wanted the very best men to do the job. He was getting the best. I wondered what would happen when the job was done, and Hiram Good decided that Billy Bonney—like me and Hawkins and Cora Thomason—would have to go.

And I knew the answer. Hiram Good was getting old. Billy Bonney was as good as anybody alive, and he was just a kid....

Suddenly I felt very, very happy. The weight inside me lifted and was gone. And so was everything else.

THE END

The Big Out

By Arnold Hano

To
SHOELESS JOE JACKSON
Who Batted .375
in the 1919 World Series

Chapter I

"It's a young man's game," Brick Palmer thought, as he came off his haunches into a low crouch, the big mitt out and steady, the right hand clenched, and the sweat scalding his eyes.

It was August, eighth inning August, six outs away from the clubhouse, cokes, and a rubdown, six outs away from the shower, the wisecracks, and the blessed end of another brutal day.

He spat dust from his throat. "Leading lady, Ken," he barked, "nobody hits, six to go." The infield picked up the pepper, racing it around the horn, from stocky Nick Rizzo, the solid third baseman with the rifle for an arm and the frog for a voice, "Lottsa time, ba-bee;" to lean Marv Martin, fidgety at short, a real whistle and holler guy; across the keystone sack to Lew Kerrick, the fleet rookie second baseman, "Easy out, Kenny boy, easy out, boy;" and finally to husky Moe Rosen, the Blues' phlegmatic first sacker, "Knock 'im down, Kenny boy, right between the eyes, kid," in a solemn monotone that nobody knew for sure wasn't to be taken seriously.

And Ken Riley, the league's leading pitcher, nodded, stiffened, bent low, kicked, and poured his fast one through.

The score was 3-2, Blues, and the Tuesday afternoon crowd sat easy. For the champion Blues were leading the league, with a month and a half to go, five games up on the Tigers, and another pennant, another World Series loomed in full view. A one run lead was all the Blues had needed all season against tougher clubs than the lowly Jaybirds, firmly entrenched in sixth place and going nowhere fast.

But Brick Palmer, the Blues' catcher, thirty-eight years old and feeling every year sitting on his back like a nearsighted umpire, knew better. Riley's fast one was coming in heavy as lead, with the hop gone, and the August sun was sucking the strength out of the big hurler's flailing right arm. While out in right-center field, 460 feet away, a Blue relief pitcher toiled, keeping sharp and warm, just in case.

Brick, working his pitcher slowly, called for the change-up, and Riley jumped out ahead, no balls and two strikes. "One pitch and we're five outs away," Brick thought, and then, "how much does he have left?"

He squatted, signaled for the jug-handle curve, at the hands. No waste pitches now, nothing but strikes. Strikes or base hits, and the dust was a cloud in Brick's throat as he waited.

But Riley's curve forgot how, the pitch big and fat on the inside corner. The hungry Jaybird fell away and pulled the ball down the third base line, past Rizzo and skidding to the left field corner for a two base hit.

Brick called time, trotting out to the mound, every step a torment draining away his energy, jarring the ache that never left his thighs from July on, every year since he turned thirty. He squinted at the big pitcher, saw the sag of Riley's shoulders, the tight mouth, the jaw going stubborn. The man had guts, and just so long as there was an arm hanging from the socket, he'd throw. Riley never quit, Brick knew, they had to jerk him out. "How's it?" he asked, hoping the reliefer was using his time well, there wasn't much to spare.

Riley shrugged and half turned away. "All right, I guess," he said, but the sweat had crept into his voice, and the lift had gone, just as an inning ago it had left his fast ball.

"This guy's a bum," Brick said, waving his thumb over his shoulder at the Jaybird who stood outside the batter's box, hefting two clubs.

"They're all bums," Riley said, his sleeve wiping sweat from his brow. "I'll strike him out."

But back on the Blues' bench, manager Bras Watkins knew what Palmer's thumb had meant. Through three long seasons Watkins, and, for that matter, most of the Blues, had learned to rely on Brick's judgment. If Brick jerked his thumb, well, old Brick knew best. Riley was through. Take him out. And Watkins was on the field, making the slow walk to the mound, more time being wasted while the relief pitcher out in the bullpen lobbed them in.

An umpire moved in from first base, and Rizzo, playing the game, somehow got in his way and they exchanged polite words, while the conference at the hill went on, and the seconds crept by on fading August legs.

"What's it to be, Watkins?" the umpire asked.

"Don't rush us," said Rizzo, his voice low and soft.

"Nobody's rushing you, Nick," the umpire said, "we got a game to finish. What's it to be, Riley or the reliefer?"

Watkins frowned as though the question were a tough one, something he had not anticipated, and then he turned to Riley and said, "All right, Ken, we'll see you in ten minutes," and he took the ball from the right-hander who had failed to go the route only five other times all season. Riley walked off, out to the clubhouse runway between the right- and left-center field bleachers, the long miserable walk that rankled, and the crowd was silent, all but the bleacherites who were too far away to see the pain on the pitcher's face but who knew it had to be there. And the applause swelled, even while the loudspeaker crackled, "Vollner, number 27, now pitching for the Blues. Vollner, number 27, now pitching."

Vollner was the butterfly boy with all the tricks, and control that brushed the corners, Vollner who never served up the fat one. Two innings was as far as he could go, three maybe, before the hitters got wise to the wrinkle, the knuckler, and the occasional fast one that was strictly for waste.

Brick was back of the plate now, standing straight up, taking the routine warmup pitches mechanically, rubbing up the ball finally, and lobbing it out to the mound. And his mind crept to the locker room. "A young man's game," he thought again, shaking his head, his broken-fingered right hand pounding the mitt, kneading the pocket, flexing his fingers that always bent involuntarily. Six outs to go, he thought, and he felt cheated, for time gone by, yet two full innings still remained, and if this run came in, who knows how many more.

This was the third game in three days for the Blues, and two of them had gone extra frames. Brick Palmer, older now than he thought he'd ever be, had worn the shin guards and mask for all of them, playing his three hundred and forty-fourth consecutive game for the Blues. Iron man Palmer, the newspapermen were affectionately calling him. And the iron man bent down for Vollner's first serving, feeling the metal turn to rubber in his thighs.

The Jaybird batter, hitless all day before Riley's smoke, dug in and found a toehold, and Vollner's pitch, a slider on the outside, went rocketing back through the box, on a line to center field. Brick had the mask off, his eyes catching the runner turn third and start for the plate, carrying the potential tying run on his spikes.

The throw from short center field was true, a hump-backed line drive that bounced once between the plate and the pitcher's box, but that bounce was freakish, hitting a soft dirt incline and rising fifteen feet in the air, slowly settling while Brick braced himself, a foot in front of the plate, blocking it off, waiting for the ball to drop into his mitt so he could sweep into the tag that meant an out or a run.

But the tag never came. The runner, desperate to find the plate, threw himself into the air, a football block that smashed the waiting backstop, the ball still a devilish foot away from the clawing mitt, and then runner, catcher and ball went flying in three directions. And while Brick clambered to his feet, the sticky blood already creeping down his thigh, the Jaybird runner reached out a flat palm and slapped the plate.

Two pitches later, Vollner, shaken by the rude reception accorded him by the scrappy Birds, tried to waste a fast ball, and instead came in with his nothing pitch, right over the middle, belt high. And the bat's crack, the rising flight of the ball left no doubt as to the result. The Birds had, in four pitches, wiped out a one run lead and gone ahead. And the Blues, with the six outs now left to them, failed to lift the ball out of the infield, dropping a 5-3 decision, while out in left field the scoreboard showed the second place Tigers, snarling and eager, ripping out a big win over the Titans. The lead dwindled to four games.

And, as the team trooped through the clipped grass of the outfield, they clustered around Brick, seeking in him what they always found ever since the blocky backstop had joined the club. Here was bedrock. With Palmer went the Blues.

"Tough one, Brick," said Vollner, his voice embittered by the knowledge that his stuff had gone wrong. But he knew that with Brick he could talk, for there would be no criticism.

"It happens, Volly," Brick said. "Can't win them all." Have to, he thought, we're not that far ahead.

Murphy, the little relief catcher who spent his days in the bullpen, threw an arm around Brick as they went up the iron stairs. "That Myers!" he said. "Glad it wasn't me he decided to break in two."

"Part of the game," Brick said, automatically, realizing these men wanted comfort.

"Part of the game my eye!" Murphy snorted. "Maybe the game's football, then it's part of the game."

"Forget it," Brick said. "We'll get it back tomorrow."

Murphy brightened, and so did Vollner. From behind someplace Brick heard a voice calling him. It was Rosen. "Hey, Brick boy, whatcha doing tonight? The wife says come on over for chicken paprike."

Brick grinned back at the big first sacker. "Not tonight, Moe, got a heavy date." He winked broadly. "With the wife. Thanks anyway, maybe later in the week." When we're winning again, he thought.

And memories of 1934 came floating across the diamond while the beaten Blues trudged off, whispering of another snarling, eager club, the Cardinals, who had wiped out an even bigger lead at a later date and gone on to win the pennant and Series.

In the clubhouse, the cokes were there, and trainer Lefty Fisher's able hands were there, kneading Brick's tired back and legs, but mostly the invisible dust was there, old and defeat-coated. And the men were silent, undressing in the fumes of sweat and wintergreen while lockers banged shut and the echo was tinny and mocking as tomorrow's sports page.

Brick Palmer walked the eleven blocks from the side exit of the stadium to the apartment house where he and Cathy lived in three rooms, overlooking the courthouse and the inky green river. He always walked, wet weather or dry, letting the high tension drift down his legs, easing out onto the steaming pavement, feeling the tight clamp around his muscles slowly loosen until he could breathe fully, pushing the iron band out through his clothes, out into the muggy, sun-yellow August air.

He walked, too, because he knew that every step took him further from the stadium where each day he left a little bit of his life on the spike-flecked grass and dirt of the ball diamond. He walked off and out of the game.

Not that Brick Palmer didn't like baseball. He loved it; loved the sweat and pain and contact; loved the calls, good and bad; loved the fast, blinding pitchers he caught, the tricky ones he batted against. He loved baseball because it was the only thing he really knew, and without it, he'd be lost. But still, at thirty-eight, with ten scrambling years in the minors and three and a half more in the Navy, a big league catcher doesn't have much to hold him once the last out is recorded, and the flags start coming down. And each day, when the hits, runs, and errors were part of everyman's history, Brick Palmer called it quits.

For he loved the freedom from the game just as much, even more, than he loved the sport. He loved his home, his wife, his leisure, earned with broken fingers and charley-horsed thighs and split, bloody nails. He walked away from the playing field to claim his rest so that he could walk tomorrow to the playing field and earn it all over again.

The routine was the same every day. For three blocks, east from the stadium, he replayed the game, conducting a postmortem that was more often a joy than not. The Blues usually won—two out of every three, it seemed—and on those two days Brick was like a fan who sees the game and insists on buying tomorrow's paper to read all about it. He remembered the big runs, he felt the sting of his palms as hits poured off his bat, he lived again the jarring crunch at home plate as he put the ball on a sliding rival runner.

And when that other day came around, like today, the day the Blues were beaten, Brick squirmed through his own fourth inning strikeout with runners on, and that decisive play in the eighth inning, the tricky bounce on the throw to the plate, the oncoming runner, the tag that never came about.

But when he swung his legs north, he shifted from today's game to tomorrow's. He called the pitchers as he figured they'd go, the Blues' and their opponent's; he listed rival hitters' strengths and weaknesses—"Jones lays off the first pitch, easy to get out ahead of him; Telliat crowds, pitch him tight; Sumner likes to run and hit on the three-and-one pitch; Adamick's still weak on the big curve up around the shoulders, and he bites at the high stuff...."

And after two blocks of this projected thought, he quit the game altogether. Always the same, five blocks of baseball and six of Cathy.

The six blocks of Cathy were rambling and ill-directed. There were no signals to guide him, no batting averages to prove a point, no third base coach to wave him on, no base lines to keep him in check. Sometimes he thought of the way she looked, yellow and fluffy and solemn-eyed, and he wondered how a big mug could win such a prize. He saw himself chinked and dented and half caved-in, wrinkled from the sun and from the steady squint through the mask. He looked down at the twisted hams he called his hands and thought of Cathy, so light and fragile.

He thought sometimes of the way she puckered up and frowned when they got out the bankbook and held it against the blueprint of the home they were going to buy in Brick's native Wisconsin when the season was over. And he remembered how she glowed, fresh and golden, when the telegram came from Massina Junior College, ten miles out in suburban Milwaukee where Lake Michigan kisses the grass and the air is immune to dust. The telegram that read, TWO YEAR CONTRACT COACHING BASEBALL TEACHING PHYSICAL ED AT 7500 PER BEGINNING NEXT YEAR AWAITS YOUR SIGNATURE KY NORRIS DIR. OF ATH.

He remembered the long talks that night and how they had finally worded the answer, asking, pleading that Norris postpone action until after the season had closed, until he and Cathy knew for certain that the time had come for Brick to hang up his playing uniform. Until he and Cathy had the money for that home for themselves, and for the children they wanted desperately.

And walking that last block, he recalled the answer, yes, they'd wait, and good luck. The good luck that might mean the pennant and maybe the Series, another line or two in the record books and an inch to his stature as a memory and a few thousand dollars extra in the bank.

As he turned into the apartment house and rode the self service elevator, he wiped thought from his mind, for Cathy was just a half-minute away and his arms started to widen, even before the door opened and he saw her.

CHAPTER II

Supper was an easy delight. Cathy stepped quickly and silently to the kitchen and returned with the steak, broiled and juicy, charred outside and pink within. And all the time the chatter was a soothing flow, like Lefty Fisher's hands, and Brick marveled at the therapy the woman could perform.

"Here you are, butterfingers," she said, sliding the plate in front of Brick. "Eat. You need your strength, my ninety-eight pound darling."

He grunted, his mouth working rhythmically.

"Don't talk with your mouth full," she said, her fingers reaching to his hand where the hair bunched on the bony gnarled knuckles. "I'll throw you out of the game."

"I said," Brick finally said, "why 'butterfingers'?"

Cathy looked up at him. "Oh," she said, "don't you know? You're today's goat, voted so by all the leading radio play-by-play announcers and the official scorer. That throw, the eighth inning one, the one you made the error on. Butterfingers."

He laughed. Weird scoring by the pressbox no longer nettled him. Like umpires, except worse, official scorers miss them. Only thing, when an ump misses them, it hurts somebody on the field. When the scorer goes error-happy, it hurts only in the Sunday papers where they print the teams' fielding averages. "Error my eye. Never had a chance. Myers took me out like I was a tackling dummy. Wonderful block. Have the adhesive tape to prove it."

"That's what I thought," said Cathy, evenly, not looking up from her own more modest plate. "Butterfingers." And that ended the baseball for the evening.

When the telephone rang, an hour later, they were wrapped into a corner of the living room couch, and the talk had concerned the size of bathrooms and kitchens and whether Brick's contemplated trophy room-study would convert to a nursery, if one was ever needed. The home was beginning to be their life, the home and the college and the promise of grass and sun instead of arc lights, dust and rosin.

"I'll get it," he said, stretching to a sitting position, dropping his size elevens to the floor. Cathy was, by this time, halfway across the room to the insistent phone that pealed and pealed and never gave the slightest hint of the doom that lay at the other end of the wire.

"Hello," she said, though the word should have been "goodbye." "Yes, he's here, just a minute." She walked towards him, a frown quivering at her brow. "It's for you." She shook her head, and maybe, years later, she'd almost remember that, for no reason at all, she shuddered once.

He cradled the phone. The voice that answered him was nasal, and Brick recoiled a scant half inch from the receiver. "Yes, this is Palmer." A pause. "Yes," Brick said again, "Johnny Palmer is my brother." Another pause. Then Brick's voice exploded. "What the hell for?" He leaned into the phone, and Cathy watched him, fearfully, as he listened, and his body seemed to shake in a peculiar rhythm. The cracklings from the phone reached her, but the words did not. Finally they stopped, and Brick breathed in once, deeply, and straightened his body, his eyes staring through Cathy, a million miles off. He started to talk into the mouthpiece and stopped and started again, and then his hand, as though divorced from the rest of his body, took the phone and placed it back on its cradle.

He walked over to the window and looked out. Cathy watched him and waited; she knew he'd tell her. When he spoke again, his voice was flat and full of dust.

"It's Johnny," he said. "Some sort of trouble. Again," he added, like a painful afterthought.

"He's not drunk someplace and you've got to get him home?" she said, almost hopefully. Johnny Palmer was Brick's brother, twelve years younger, brilliant, grinning, reckless. A kid who would be a man some day, but not until he laid off the bottle, the ponies, and the inside straights.

"No, not drunk. At least, I don't think so. Worse. It's a gambling note. A big one. He can't meet it. He forged my name as cosigner. He—" he paused, and rubbed the back of his hand across his jaw.

"How big, honey?" she asked, her voice still soft, belying the fear that raced to her throat.

"Ten thousand," he said, and he grinned, a white-faced grin that showed his anxiety more than would a grimace. "Ten thousand dollars. To the old Capone syndicate."

"You're not going to pay it, are you?" she asked, and now her voice started to break, the fear storming through.

He spread his hands. "What else? The kid can't. And if I don't, they'll spread a stink about him that will bounce him right out of internship, and right out of any decent hospital residency. He can't take stuff like that; it'd kill him."

She shook her head, the loose blond hair falling in front of her eyes, for which she was thankful. The tears were already there. "Oh, you boob," she whispered, "you big, stupid, beautiful boob. It's not the kid who's in trouble. It's you. Your name's on the note. You can't afford stuff like that. Don't worry about Johnny. It's you."

"Me?" he said. "I'm all right. I'm no kid. I can always make out. But the boy, he's not— he's not bad, hon. You know that."

"Sure," she said, and the bitterness crept in, while her life lay unguarded, "sure, I know that. He's fine. He drinks himself into the gutter and he's going to be a surgeon someday. He gambles every cent he's got, money you give him, and now he's forged your name like a petty crook. Or isn't forgery petty?"

Brick stood in the middle of the room. Everything she had said was true. Yet he felt the kid could pull through, somehow, if he kept his face out of the mud. A year, two maybe, and he'd be older, his position more responsible. They'd have another talk, maybe the kid would appreciate the situation.

And then the enormity of the whole thing came smashing down on him, not against his thighs, toppling his body into the dust the way Myers had this afternoon, but thundering down on his head, neck, back, hips, an enveloping weight that squeezed the guts out of him for a terrifying second before he shook his head and released the weight. But he knew. He knew where he stood, behind the eight ball of a crooked pool table, and the light overhead, yellow and accusing, was like the gleam of a police floodlight, and the heat of the room was a wave of shame and guilt. Guilt for a crime he hadn't committed, but who would ever know that? For he suddenly knew what Cathy had known immediately. He was through in baseball if he failed to pay, or if the money somehow was not handed over. Ball players don't even go to the racetracks any more, not since Commissioner Landis hauled Rogers Hornsby to the rack and proceeded to make a future managerial career practically impossible for the great Rajah. Or if they gambled, it was on the q.t. and the tickets were the two buck ones.

Whereas the record read that he, Brick Palmer, in the heat of an August baseball drive, had gambled with a filthy syndicate, and now owed that syndicate of racketeers, crooks, and killers a mere ten thousand dollars. The kid couldn't pay it, and when Cathy had said, "You're not going to pay it," it was a prayer, not an opinion. Who else?

It was as easy—and hard—as that. Who else. It was the kid's career and his own, against a flat ten grand. And with the ten grand went the home. Brick, his career—two-thirds of it in Class B, A and Double-A ball—had never made the money the easy way. Nor was it cheap sending the kid brother to college, medical school, paying the tuition right along with the liquor bills.

Cathy turned to the coffee table in front of the couch and looked at the blueprint of the Wisconsin home, five million miles and a century away, and even as she stared, the corners of the long square sheet started to curl up, hiding the fine clean white lines that spoke of room to live in. Fine clean white lines straight as a surgeon's incision.

Brick walked back to the phone, and dialed a number, his hand again acting as a separate thing. "Hello," he said, "Presbyterian Hospital? I want Johnny Palmer, interne." He waited, waited for Johnny to get on the phone and confirm what he already knew to be true. And while he waited he remembered something their mother had said, oh so many years ago, now. "Watch him," she had said, "watch him, he needs watching." All these years, he had been watching.

"Hello, kid," he said, "this is Brick...."

The lobby of the Statler, at 10:28 that evening, was alive with white linen suits and girls in color-sprayed prints. The noise was pitched way up high, the talk fast and punctuated with laughter. Brick Palmer, two steps inside the revolving door, stopped and squinted into the false light and hilarity. He thought, for a foolish second, "What am I doing here?" and then he remembered.

He did not know the face that was at his elbow, long and white and gaunt, nor the manicured hand that tugged at his sleeve. But the voice was nasal.

"Palmer," it said. There was satisfaction and finality in the word; half a chore was over, the victim had arrived.

"Yes," Brick said, staring at the thin, seersuckered racketeer in front of him, memorizing the smell of cologne, the orange and black tie, the slumped shoulders, the voice, the leaping eyes. "What do you want?"

The voice was patient. "Nothing, Palmer, nothing at all. Here's something you may want." He slipped a long white envelope from the right inside pocket of his suit jacket, turned it over to check for any inadvertent markings, and elaborately handed it to Brick. The envelope was sealed with a strip of scotch tape.

"Like I said on the phone. Sealed."

Brick frowned down at the envelope, turning it over, fumbling it once and almost dropping it.

"What's the matter, Palmer, butterfingers?"

The word was a cold shock to Brick and he stiffened, his right hand balling into a fist, crawling up his hip, the elbow crooking. *Easy,* he thought, *easy. Just take it, keep taking it. Don't let a punk like this throw you.*

Brick slit the tape with his left thumb nail, the right clipped short to cut down the possibility of mangling his throwing hand with splintered nail slivers. He flapped open the sheet. It was the original, so far as Brick could see, the two names, his and Johnny's, scrawled in easy flowing, dissimilar strokes. The note was for $10,000, made out to a loan company, fronting for the syndicate. There also was a slip of paper with the words, "Thanks, sucker."

Brick balled up the paper and dropped it at his feet, his eyes pale and hard. "Some day—" he started, and then stopped. "The kid," he said, after swallowing a breath that seemed to hurt, "you'll drop him as a customer, from now on."

The seersucker go-between shrugged his shoulders. "I'll tell the boss what you said. It's his business, not mine."

Brick reached out a hand and gripped the punk's sleeve. "I said," the words spaced evenly and coming out so slowly there was room for an exclamation point between every two, "I said you'll drop the kid from now on. If he shows at your joint, you'll throw him out. Every time. If you don't, I'll come up myself. I'll beat the living hell out of you every time I see you, and I'll see you plenty. You'll leave the kid alone."

"Okay," seersucker said, but his face flushed beneath the waxy skin, "okay, I'll keep him out." And then his own face went hard and he straightened his shoulders. "But don't throw your weight around, playboy. I don't like anybody mauling me. Especially guys whose rent is overdue." He held his stare.

Brick fished into his pocket and pulled out the check. He felt foolish once more, like a kid with a finger in the peanut butter jar.

The punk loosened up. "I thought maybe you forgot," he said, and he laughed noiselessly. "No hurry, though. We know you're good for it. Let's have it over a drink, less like business that way. And the boss told me to pass the good word to you. He tugged at Brick's arm. "How to make your ten grand back, quick and easy." He started out.

Brick grabbed him, and the punk swung around, the hate for Brick leaping back into his eyes, hate for any man who could spin him around like a top. "Tell me here," Brick said. "I don't drink. How."

The punk wiped off his sleeve. "All you got to do is let a few more throws get away at the plate. Call 'em wrong behind the dish. Stop hitting with them runners on. Get your ten gees back in no time, by next week maybe."

Brick's voice filled with poison. "Are you trying to bribe me? Why, you little punk." Once more the fist reached the hip, the whole body edged forward ready to uncoil.

"Bribe?" nasal voice said. "Don't be a chump. That's a dirty word. Just a favor between two friends. You treat the boss right, he treats you right. Think it over, Palmer. I understand you're looking at property out in the Milwaukee sticks."

Jesus, Brick thought, *how do they work?* And the bribe offer, what could he do about it, without exposing the gambling debt, the kid brother? Well, one thing he had to do, besides take his lumps and pay the house its cut of life's blood. One little luxury he maybe couldn't afford.

"Come on," Brick said, laughing a short nervous laugh, "don't mind me. I'm upset. Let's have that quick drink."

The gaunt man stared, his eyes suspicion-lit. "I thought you didn't drink, Palmer."

Brick laughed again, more heartily. "Don't drink? There ain't a ball player in the league who don't drink, skinny. Let's go." He tugged at the racketeer's arm. "Across the street, too hot in here."

They went out, through the revolving door. *Gamble*, Brick thought, *it's a gamble*. Just this once, he'd gamble. Gamble that the syndicate wanted the ten grand and silence more than they cared about the health of a two-bit messenger boy.

Across the street, in the obscurity of an alleyway, Brick turned quickly and grabbed a handful of jacket and shirt, around the chest. The punk started to squeal, just as Brick's right hand smashed down his nose, breaking the bone, turning the short scream into a liquid squish of blood. And then Brick let go, the man folding to the pavement lying like a damp bag of rags in the shadows of the night. Brick leaned down and slipped the check into the punk's pocket.

"Don't get rolled now, sucker," he said, softly, and spun on his heel, towards home and Cathy. One for the money, he thought, while his lips formed a whistle that floated along with him.

The Statler lobby had been filled with noise while Brick and the Capone punk conducted their business, but not so much noise that a keen-eared newspaperman sitting thirty feet away, his memory alive with names of ball players and racketeers, couldn't hear a word or two. And the swirling colors in front of him didn't so obstruct the newspaperman's vision that he couldn't see an envelope pass from the gunny to the backstop.

Nor does it take much brains to put together the words, "ten grand... bribe... let a few more throws get away... call 'em wrong..." and come to a conclusion as eye-popping as a newspaper headline.

By the time Randy York, by-line columnist for the *Herald*, reached the sidewalk outside the Statler, pushing slowly through the crowd that congregated outside, there was no sign of Palmer and his companion. Only the sound of quick, heavy feet moving up the street, and the thin, piercing whistling of "The St. Louis Blues" reached York's ears.

Better, he thought, better this way. No time would be wasted chasing the two around. They were off for a drink, to seal their dirty bargain, and he, York, was off to a telephone booth, the coins jingling, the words pouring out of his brain, click-clacking to the imagined audience of scandal-lovers. This was big, he thought, the White Sox deal of 1919 all over again, but even bigger, because he, Randy York, was in on it from its very inception. And the *Herald*, unlike the *New York Evening World* which had pooh-poohed and played down Hugh Fullerton's story of the White Sox scandal some thirty years ago, loved its dirt. York's lips were moist as he traced the blazing red-lettered headline in the sky, BLUES' CATCHER INVOLVED IN BRIBE with the subheads dangling below, "Brick Palmer Charged with Throwing Games for Ten Grand," "Eyewitness Sees Money Change Hands in Statler Lobby."

Oh, yes, and York's hands rubbed together as the coin dropped into the phone box, oh, yes, this would be big. Big as baseball, big as life. Big as Life, in fact, he chuckled.

"Rogers?" he said to the bored voice that answered his call to glory, "give me Nichols." He waited, a brief, impatient handful of seconds.

"Nick? This is Randy. Hold on to your hat, as they say in the movies, and tear up that front page. This, my boy, is hot...."

Just as Randy York finished his call, a half-mile away Brick Palmer turned the key to his apartment and walked in. Cathy was reading in the big chair, the light on her face showing the white tension. "It's all right, kid," he said, "nothing to worry about. It's all over."

CHAPTER III

Dream, it must be a dream, that ringing, nobody rings a ball player at night, a dream, just a bell in his head, calling the team out for infield practice, ringing, stopping, ringing, stopping, ringing, now it will stop, now, now, but on and on ringing. But it was the phone, and he was awake in an instant; the phone had rung just four times.

"Hello," he said, and the sick feeling of dread stole over him, remembering the evening hours of yesterday. "Hello," he said again, foolishly, for the voice on the other end was going ahead, words coming out a million a minute, too fast for an old catcher to follow, nothing but fast balls, where was the change-up, he was waiting.

"Yes," he said, "this is Palmer."

"I know," said the speedball. "Do you understand what I'm saying?"

"Yes," said Brick, doggedly, shaking his head.

"Well, get down here as soon as you can. I'm in my office on West Shoreham. Get me?"

"Yes, Mr. Stutz," Brick said, and the speedball pitcher started to take on a paunch, the letters of the uniform fading, the uniform itself changing to white linen, and Brick knew it was Malcolm Stutz, the owner of the Blues. "Yes, Mr. Stutz, I'll be right down. What's it all about?" he asked, but in his head, the sweat band tight against the temples, he knew it had to do with the gambling debt.

"No time for questions, now, Palmer, just get on down here. Christ, man, the papers have gone crazy. The Commissioner will be down at noon. There's no time to lose."

"No sir," Brick said, dutifully, "I'll be down." The phone dropped to its cradle. He turned to face a wide-awake Cathy. "What time is it, hon?"

"Six thirty," she said, her voice small and frightened.

He was dressed in five minutes, unshaven and wanting a shower, but no time to lose. "I'll call you when I know what it's all about," he said, and he was out, going down the stairs, no time to lose, a self-service elevator's too slow, and two flights down couldn't take *that* much out of tired legs.

The sleepy cabby drove skillfully, testily cursing the milk trucks that parked four feet from the curb. Outside the West Shoreham Boulevard office building Brick could see a small crowd gathering, and he knew, automatically, *newspapermen.* "Drive around to the rear," he directed the cabby, "there's a freight landing ramp back there someplace."

He shoved a dollar into the cabby's hand and went in through the freight entrance and up the stairs, no time to lose. But outside Malcolm Stutz's office on the sixth floor stood another group of newspapermen, trained to be where all good reporters should be, face to face with the accused.

"Brick," yelled one, who had never before addressed Palmer in his life, "Brick, look over here," and a flashbulb went off. "Over here," howled another, and another, and the timeless call of the photographers, look over here so we can hang you properly.

Only one of them was silent, and for that Brick was glad. It was Timmons, the *Herald* photog, and Brick felt that there was a friend, though he didn't know why he needed friends. It was something he'd always had, on the team and with a newspaperman or two, friends. He smiled at Timmons and the little eye-glassed photographer smiled back and then shook his head.

The rest of the men with pads and pencils were around Brick, and his shoulder was to them, pushing back the crowd that sucked and sniped at him, "What've ya got to say, Palmer? Have you heard from the Commissioner? Is York right? Can we get a denial? Give us a break, Brick... a break, Brick... a break, Brick...." And he drove through the gaping mouths, the meaningless words, the pencils held aloft like spears.

Behind the door, he breathed once, deeply, and then he turned to Stutz. "Now," he said, "now, tell me what the blazes this is all about." For by this time Brick knew it was not a mere gambling debt that had jerked the reporters out of bed, and interested the Commissioner of all baseball.

Stutz, his white hair like a mane down his neck, his baby blue eyes, and his healthy pink skin only slightly mottled by the rich life of the baseball owner and automobile magnate, held out a copy of the morning *Herald* and Brick took it, and sat down.

He read the story slowly, skipping not a drop of juice, his eyes even taking in the gravy, pictures of members of that Chicago White Sox team, Shoeless Joe Jackson, Ed Cicotte, Chick Gandil and the others; pictures of himself, at bat, in the field, even one of the play at home plate yesterday, with Myers diving for Brick's legs, the ball scant inches away, and the caption, "Did Palmer start letting them get away yesterday?"

And, in a sense, he admired the story. It was perfect, the circumstances a chain of firm, alloyed links—the fourth inning strikeout; the "error" in the eighth, letting in the tying run; the night rendezvous in the downtown hotel lobby; the envelope passing hands; the word "bribe" in the conversation; the presence of a positively identified tool of the old Capone syndicate; the going-off for a drink; the quick disappearance of the two conspirators. It was perfect, except that all the links could be broken, the chain shattered into so many useless bits, and a new chain—a libel suit—forged around newshawk Randy York's neck. The alibi was there; all Brick had to do was call its name. Johnny Palmer.

But he couldn't.

He laughed, a mirthless sound coming from the top of his mouth. Stutz looked up and snapped out his words. "The story. Is it true?"

Brick shook his head and mouthed a noiseless, "No."

Stutz leaned back, his whole body relaxing into folds of fat, the pressure off. He smiled and mopped his florid face. "You'll have to excuse me, Brick," he said apologetically, "these things are tough on an old man."

Brick nodded. It's a young man's game, he thought.

"Well then," Stutz said, leaning forward once more. "We'll have to call in the papers and give them the denial. What're you going to say? Don't forget, the Commissioner's coming down from Boston by plane. He's going to want you and York. Let's hear your story, just to make sure." He waved a hand at Brick.

Brick sat quietly. His eyes searched the room, looking for a familiar something, an anything. He saw the plaques on the wall, the portraits on the desk, the baseball, autographed by the Blues, his own name presumably there, the humidor, the row of buttons on the phone under Stutz's finger, the finger tapping, waiting. "Mr. Stutz," he said finally, "I've got nothing to say." His eyes were cast to the floor, but the foul lines had been scuffed away, and he was ashamed of himself for the first time in his life. And not knowing why.

There was a change in Stutz's voice. "Brick," the old man said, heavily, "you don't understand. We like you here, the Blues, everybody on the team. Why, man, there isn't a ball player on the team—in the whole blasted league for that matter—who's better liked. Why, man—" Stutz stopped and looked around, at his office, at the brightness and expense of it. "Why, there isn't a man on the club wouldn't give you the shirt off his back, anything you wanted. But—" and again he stopped, and the new thing in the voice was bewilderment. Brick could hear it now, and he could see it in Stutz's flustered movements.

"Yes, Mr. Stutz?" Brick urged, softly, wanting the man to get it over with.

The club owner stared at Brick, and the contempt started to come to his eyes.

"Palmer, I'm going to let the newspapermen in here in five minutes. You'll have a story for them, true or false, or you're through. York's story's not true?"

Brick colored. "No," he said shortly.

"You weren't at the Statler last night?"

Brick licked his lips. He nodded, "Yes."

"You didn't speak to this Capone gangster?"

"I did."

"He didn't give you an envelope that was sealed and you didn't break the seal, look at the contents, put the envelope in your pocket?"

"He did. I did."

"He didn't offer you an additional ten-thousand-dollar bribe for letting some more get away?"

Brick exploded from his chair. "Damn it, sir, that's enough. The punk offered me a bribe, for ten grand, and I turned it down. That's the only thing that's true. The rest is a lot of bull."

"You received a bribe offer and didn't report it?"

"No."

"Why not?" Stutz was toying with his victim, for the honor of the game.

"I couldn't, that's all."

"Why not?" And there was a small smile on Stutz's face.

"I couldn't. It's—it's personal, sir, and I can't talk. There's somebody else's reputation at stake in this. More than that I can't say. You'll have to believe me." Brick held his voice even, but his heart sank to his cleats. If Stutz stood behind him, the whole thing could be beat to death by high-sounding denials and reputation.

Stutz laughed once more. "*I* have to believe *you*? Palmer, I wouldn't believe you if you broke down and confessed the whole thing. You admit every element of the story, yet you say it's not true. You deny it, yet won't tell me where it goes wrong. Palmer, one last time, can you prove your end of it?"

Brick walked to the door, his face ashen. "I can prove it, but I won't. Shall I let the dogs in?"

Stutz was by him, standing with his back to the door. "Why you fool! You think I'd let those men in, with their filthy scalpels? Stop thinking of yourself, Palmer. There's more than you involved in this mess. I'm in it, the whole team's in it, the pennant, the Series, the future of every man on the club. And you won't talk!"

"I'm sorry, I can't help it."

"Sorry! Don't be sorry. We'll get by. But you, you cheap crook, I'll crucify you. Do you hear? I'll crucify you." Stutz's voice was low and hissing. "You're suspended, Palmer, do you hear? Suspended. From this day on, until I lift it. And when the Commissioner gets through with you, you'll think my suspension was a blessing. Palmer, I'm telling you this right now. The Commissioner is top dog, but he's top dog because I, me alone, insisted on it. When they wanted Trautman, when they wanted Frick, when they wanted Brannum, when they wanted that senator from Tennessee, I kept plugging Shephard. He's top dog, but I hold his leash." He stopped for a breath, and then plunged on. "You'll never play ball again, Palmer, you'll never play ball again."

For a second the two men stood face to face, their heads six inches apart, the only sound the hoarse breathing of Stutz. And through Brick's brain went those words, stamping down the last corridor of life, "You'll never play ball again."

Never play ball! You'll never enter a clubhouse, steamy and acrid, hot with players' breaths and sweat. You'll never feel the heavy pound of Moe Rosen's hand, nearly breaking your back, and his foghorn voice an inch from your ear, "Oh, you Brick boy, how we murdered them, you and me," and always adding, "and I went 0-for-5."

Never play ball! You'll never put on the mask, the shin guards, the spikes. You'll never fondle the bat and feel the good wood.

Never play ball! You'll never rip off that mask and stand jaw to jaw with an umpire, fighting for a strike that can never be had. You'll never hear the roar of the crowd, the call from the bleachers floating across the diamond the way it did that silent moment one day a couple of years ago, spinning freakishly from a seat 500 feet away in dead center field, "That's it, Brick, play the game."

Never play ball! You'll never rise from your haunches for the snap throw to second on the attempted steal; you'll never scramble down the third base line for the dribbling bunt, pluck the ball from the grass, whirl, and peg, in time; you'll never take the throw from the outfield, feel the crunch of oncoming spikes, yet make the tag, make the tag, for the big out.

And as Brick opened the door, he heard, yet did not hear, the yelping reporters, the wailing photographers, "Just once more, look over here, over here, just once more. What's the story, a break, Brick, a break, Brick, break Brick, break Brick...."

All he heard and heard were the words, "You'll never play ball again."

In the street it was morning; people were going to work.

Brick walked slowly, skirting the activity, afraid each face would look into his and fill with hate. And then there was a touch on his shoulder, and Brick pulled away before he turned around. It was Timmons.

"Hello, Tim," Brick said, "want a good picture, me and my bankbook?"

Timmons shook his head, sharply. "Don't be a fool, boy, I know better." They walked along, in silence, and Brick wondered how many Timmonses there were.

The photographer finally broke the silence, and Brick knew what he was going to say and wondered why he had not prepared an answer. He'd need one, for Timmons. "Well, Brick, what's the real story? You didn't lie down for any gambler. What's it all about?"

Brick shrugged. "What's the difference. The thing is stacked a mile high. I can't do anything."

Timmons breathed out, loudly, once. "Ah, that's good. That's something, at least. I thought maybe, somehow, you needed money and—" he broke off, embarrassed.

Brick laughed. "No, I need it all right, but not that bad. I didn't throw that game, any game for that matter."

The little man took off his glasses and blew on them and forgot to wipe them and replaced them on his nose. "Well, how come then? There's got to be an explanation."

There has to be, Brick thought, and there is, but I can't say it. "There is one, and if I ever tell it, I'll tell you first."

Timmons turned on him. "Don't get silly, boy, I'm too old for that sort of stuff. If you don't want to tell, that's your business, not mine. I don't need any explanation, I believe you. It's the rest of them, Stutz and the Commissioner and the others, they need an explanation. And somebody else, too...."

"Who?" Brick said.

Timmons laughed. "Now it's my turn to get silly. The fans, that's who. They need an explanation."

And Brick could not answer, for he knew this was so. They walked along, again wrapped in their own thoughts, and Brick realized if he couldn't talk to Timmons, a friend through long hard years, he'd be leading a pretty silent life from now on. Well, he thought, it'll work out. He stopped at a drugstore entrance. "Have to make some calls, Tim," he said, "I'll be seeing you."

Timmons looked at Brick, and held him for a terrible moment. "Brick," he said, "remember, I work for the *Herald*. A newspaper can do a lot of harm. It can also do a lot of good. If you ever want to talk, call on me and I'll see it gets good play. That's a promise, Randy York or no."

Brick reached out and placed his hand on the little man's shoulder and gently squeezed. "Thanks, Tim," he said, and disappeared inside the drugstore, where he drank two cups of coffee before he started on again.

"You've got a visitor," Cathy said, her voice lifeless. Brick looked past her shoulder into the living room. There, standing in front of the window, his face still as death, was Johnny Palmer.

Brick's brother was tall and slender, blond and long-limbed. An outfielder, Brick thought automatically every time he saw the kid, just a bit too good-looking for a ball player, though.

"Hello, Johnny," Brick said mildly. He sat down on the couch and removed his shoes, raised his legs to the cushions, and waved a hand to Johnny. "Sit down, kid."

Johnny took a half-step towards the older man, and Brick saw that he was not the grinning boy this time, not the perpetual sophomore. *Good*, he thought, *maybe he's learned something*. And a touch of light flared in Brick's tired mind, just a candle flicker, though, blown out by Cathy's half-heard sob from across the room.

"Brick," said Johnny, "I don't know— I can't tell you—"

Brick waved his hand again. "Sit down, boy, you make me nervous. Too many people crowding me all day. Sit down."

Johnny looked bewildered, turned to Cathy, who turned away. He sat down, then rose six inches with an explosive start. "Look," he said, "I'm going crazy. I've got to do something. You can't take this by yourself."

"Grow up, boy," Brick said, and all the meaning of his life was in the order. "What can you do?"

"I'll go to the baseball Commissioner, I'll go to your boss, I'll go to the syndicate, make them tell the truth."

"The truth?" Brick asked. "Which truth? That I didn't take a bribe offer, that I really signed an IOU for $10,000 for missing an inside straight? Or was it a four-card flush? The truth that you forged my name, Johnny?" Brick said, his voice mild as ever. "Talk sense, boy. No matter what you say, unless you admit forgery, I'm washed up. And you're not going to say you're a forger."

"Why not?" Johnny asked, his voice strained and thin.

Brick spread his hands and shrugged. "I don't know. You just won't. I guess I wouldn't let you."

"But you—what's going to happen?"

Brick's voice took on an edge. "I'm thirty-eight, I'm slow as a truck, I'm a half-step slow on foul pops, I'm careful not to run into the railing, I don't like to play doubleheaders. I'm finished." And then he remembered Stutz's words. "But I'll get by, old soldiers always do. I got some dough in the bank. Cathy and I will go someplace and grow tomatoes. Always wanted to eat tomatoes from a tree."

Cathy laughed. "Vines, you fool, not trees." And, surprised by his complexity, she realized suddenly he was making silly conversation so that she wouldn't take issue with him concerning the "dough in the bank." She knew that the ten thousand dollars was all they had had, and in some gambler's darkened safe a garden was dying and a house caving in.

Brick went on, smoothly, not looking at either his wife whom he loved, or his brother, whom he loved as he would a child. "But you, you've got a debt now. Not ten thousand bucks, I don't give a damn about that. You owe me more, and you're going to pay. I won't be corny if I tell you I saved your reputation, your career, your whole life's future. You know it as well as I do. But it's all down the stinking old drain if this happens again, because I'll never bail you out a second time. Or is it a second hundredth?"

Johnny came to his feet. He walked to Brick's side, and leaned over his brother. "I'll never forget this, Brick."

Neither will I, thought Cathy. *I'm watching him commit suicide, for a snot-nosed kid who'll never be anything.* And she dug her nails into her palms, hurting herself so that she wouldn't cry for love; it would seem so futile now.

Johnny's voice was near the blubbering point. "You'll see, Brick, I'll never let you down again. And someday if you want something, you'll be able to call on me. I swear to you, I'll be the solid guy from now on." He was being swept away by his own melodrama, built on a tin-legged dream. "Whatever you want, I'll be there."

And Brick thought, *Whatever I want? The poor fool. All I want is my mask and a handful of dirt.*

Instead, he said, "All right, kid. That's fine. I'm glad to hear it. Now beat it, they need you at the hospital." The boy walked out, with one look over his shoulder, his eyes lit with his promises, and maybe with the easy sentence his brother had imposed.

Cathy looked at the door, the lock's click in her ears just a period. "Well?" she said, breathing deeply. "What did the Commissioner say?"

"What we expected," Brick said, easily, "what Stutz said he'd say. 'You are from this day on barred from formal and legal association with any team or group of teams coming under the jurisdiction of this office.' Then he asked me if I understood what he meant. I told him I did, and that was that."

"What *does* it mean?" Cathy asked, hoping it didn't mean exactly what she knew it meant.

"I'll never be allowed to play organized ball—not even Class D—in the United States and in parts of Canada. Wherever the Commissioner can step in and make a ruling, I can't play. And that's on every team you or I ever saw or heard of. National League, American, International, American Association, Pacific Coast, Eastern, Texas, Southern Association. And so on, right down the line."

"Never?" she said. "Anywhere?" The leagues, the teams were meaningless to her although she knew them well. All over America she knew where the stadiums grew, where the buses and railroads carried the tired players and their wives.

"Nowhere," he said, half in answer to her question, half in growing amazement at the extent of the sentence. "Not even the semi-pros would have me."

"No?" she said, the word suddenly sounding like a slogan, so used to "no" were they now.

He shook his head. "Too much risk. There's nothing official about the relationship between the semis and the pros, but they deal to each other. They wouldn't gamble on me; it might ruin their cozy little family tie." He leaned over and clicked on the radio. "Let's see what the ball players are doing."

And while the radio hummed and warmed up, Brick thought of what he had just said, what the Commissioner had said, what Stutz had said. A crook, he had been called, and a crook he was, on the record. What was he to do, he thought, learn a trade, become a farmer, go to school? He looked at his hands and he laughed.

Red Allen's Ozark drawl broke through the laugh and ended the self-torture. The syrup-smooth voice of the play-by-play announcer handed him a quick answer to the question, what to do. Keep your eye on the ball, from a hidden spot in the far-off stands, or better still, where no one would recognize him, from a perch in front of a television set. And again Brick laughed. Television sets cost money.

"... and the score, at the end of the fifth, the Jaybirds six, the Blues three. There'll be a new pitcher for the Blues, Walt Traylor, husky right-hander with an eleven-and-seven record for the season, two-and-one against the Birds...."

Traylor, thought Brick. Big, fast, wild, make him take his time, opening innings. Not to steady him down, but just to bring on the shadows faster, call in the dusk as a tenth man on the field. You couldn't see Traylor's low quick stuff when the light was dim, and the slower Walt worked, the better his control. So maybe the game drags on two hours fifty minutes, three hours, and the legs give out in the fifth inning, it's worth it.

"... misses outside, and Bellerton walks to open the sixth...."

Bellerton walks, thought Brick, and that brings up Myers, and how they love to hit and run, especially when they're winning, especially with a guy like Traylor who has a big slow stretch, plenty of time to get the jump on him. Call for the pitch-out, high and inside at Myers' head, make the left-handed batter fall away from the plate and give you plenty of room for the throw down to second.

The throw to second! Brick's body tensed, the knuckles white and balled. The secret of big league catching, the throw to second that wipes out the steal and takes the sting out of anybody's rally, gives you the big out and flips the game right over on its face. Can you do it? Can you be there, waiting for the pitch, the weight back on the right leg, left leg forward, glove pointed in toward the clenched right hand, can you keep that right hand closed until the ball touches leather (Dickey couldn't, and it cost him fingers), can the hand fly open, take the ball, cock for the briefest flash of a second while the eyes see Martin scurrying over from short to cover the bag (left-handed hitter, remember), and then the throw? Is it there, on the bag, ankle-high, thrown from the elbow light as a feather, swift and true as an arrow, no, truer than that, true as a throw to second by a catcher who can throw to second?

And then the smash of the play. Now you're the spectator, no different from the guy in the bleachers, watching with your heart up there mingling with your parched lungs, while the base runner is stretched in the air, then spitting up dust and dirt with his spikes and trouser legs, the man with the ball pinwheeling over him, the glove on the spiked under-foot, the ankle, the calf, the thigh, the face. And out of the dust, the man in blue, imperious, arrogant, often stupid, often wrong, more often keen-eyed, right. What does he say to that throw to second? Does it meet with his approval, his honor the umpire? Does he wave assent to it, pitching the thumb into the air, twisting his body to the sky, roaring the final stamp of authority, "Yer out!" Or does he wig-wag the throw to second, his hands open and palms pointed to the dirt, spread low and derogatory, burying the throw to second in the ground where it belongs, because the man is "Safe"?

"... and around the circuit, at the Polo Grounds, the Giants and the Dodgers are tearing up the pea patch...."

At the Polo Grounds! Where it seemed to Brick baseball had been invented, with Matty and McGraw, Eddie Roush and Frisch. Where the fans somehow don't seem to root for the Giants (except they do, down in the dank dugouts of the soul where men pray for base hits like kids but are ashamed of letting it be seen). Where the fans just seem to root for baseball, the Cards yesterday, the Phils today, the Cubs tomorrow. And always, the Giants.

Where he, Brick Palmer, so many times squatted against the center field bleacher background of white and colored shirts, his eyes searching for the ball against the blessed green screen built to protect batters and near-sighted catchers, but never doing it well enough. Where he, Brick Palmer, would never again squat, where he'd never again walk through the visiting team's runway past the friendly bleacherites who knew you before they saw the number.

"... while over in Beantown, Ted Williams has put the Red Sox out in front...."

Williams! How to pitch to him? Low and outside, and watch the line drives fly into center and left-center field? Feed to the shift, on the inside, so he'll hit in the direction of the defensive strength, and he will, in the direction, all right, fifty feet over the right fielder's head, and still going?

"... for the Blues, it will be Rosen, Kerrick, and young Fletcher, replacing the suspended Brick Palmer...."

And Brick stiffened, his whole body rising to meet the challenge of the words, and then falling back with a silent groan as the truth came driving home, a memory with spikes.

Gone were the thoughts. What difference did it make whether his call on Williams was right? What difference did it make that he knew it took him eight running steps straight back to go from sun to shadow at four o'clock this time of month at the Polo Grounds, fourteen steps at Ebbets Field, twelve at Municipal Stadium? Who'd ever call on him for the throw to second? Let the pitchers pitch, the runners run, the batters bat, while an outlaw catcher whisks the dust off his life and starts forgetting the misery of a game that was no longer a game, but an alien land.

T'hell with the game. Three hundred and forty-four games without missing one, callused and broken-boned, his feet so flat he rocked on the middles, thighs on fire. T'hell with the game. Let the fans roar, he'd have none of it. The good wood had turned rotten, the throw to second wound up in center field, and the big out had not been made.

And Brick Palmer turned his head into his arms and cried, while Red Allen drawled on, "... that's two in a row for the skidding Blues. And the Tigers, by virtue of today's win, are only three games behind the league leaders who played their first game this season without the services of Brick Palmer. Palmer, you know, has been barred for life by the baseball Commissioner just this afternoon...."

Cathy clicked off the radio and looked down at her husband. *Why,* she thought, *don't they know what they're doing?*

CHAPTER IV

Brick drove the old Chevvy slowly, along the White Mountain route, avoiding the speedier Vermont-Maine Turnpike. It was better this way, they knew, giving the car its head, but not dropping the reins altogether. Smooth and unfettered, the engine droned on, the late August air alive with the whisper of oncoming autumn. It was their first summer vacation together, their first after fourteen married years.

For two days they had traveled this way, stopping at the $3-a-night motels just off the road, eating at the chuck wagons between towns, their hands alternating at the wheel, the rest of themselves a single motionless being.

It was an enforced vacation. Not merely because of Brick's suspension, now five days old, but because baseball players have few friends during the season, except other ball players on the same team. And ball players' wives have few friends, except other players' wives. Three days in New York, four in Philly, two in Boston, a day on the road, three in St. Louis, four in Chicago—such is the life of the ball player, sometimes with his wife, sometimes without. And a scramble of hotel rooms, restaurants, sleeping daytime after a long night contest, all these result in choosing your friends by the uniform they wear, the same uniform as your own.

But, still, Brick knew, he could have called on them, that handful of friends, the Rosens, Vollner, Watkins, Timmons, little Murphy whose job Brick had usurped and who now was just third string. They'd have answered, he knew, but he couldn't. Let the lines be steady and straight, he thought. Let the crooks find new friends, on the other side of the line, and leave the decent people alone. Why plague them, their consciences, their loyalties? No, thank you, Brick thought, there's too many been dragged in as it is, him and Cathy and the kid brother, all for a hungry gambling syndicate.

Brick was out of uniform, forever. So, too, was Cathy. They had been convicted, out of court, of a crime against the public. They fled that public.

But not before the public had marked them both. Outside the stadium, where he had gone one morning to claim his spikes, glove, and mask from his locker, Brick had been approached by an innocent-eyed boy of twelve, an autograph book in his hand. "Please, Mr. Palmer, may I have your autograph?" the kid pleaded. And Brick, secretly pleased, scrawled his name quickly on the proffered sheet. The boy looked at the signature, and then with scorn and hate blazing in his undefeated eyes, he ripped out the page and flung it into the gutter. And stood there, a skinny twelve-year-old, his little hands balled into bony fists, his chin sticking out, itching to let the ex-major leaguer have one.

Cathy got it, too. In the elevator, neighbors clammed up; in stores, her order was politely but silently filled. One insolent clerk in the local grocery asked her whether she'd pay cash or "write out a check?"

The news columnists, leading off with the irrepressible Randy York, made mincemeat of their already dead victims. Gleefully they seized upon the opportunity to give nicknames to Brick, calling him "Goldbrick" Palmer, "Trick" Palmer, and "Itching" Palmer.

But it fell to baseball itself to inflict the worst hurt on Brick, in the form of a solemn clubhouse meeting after the most recent Blues' defeat, and the incident was reported in the *Herald*.

The Blues, wrote York to his eager readers, *in a locked clubhouse scene open only to this correspondent, burned Itching Palmer in effigy yesterday afternoon, just after the players trooped in, downcast, defeated, but still determined. Not a likeness of Palmer's crooked body, but instead, the uniform shirt the goldbrick catcher wore. Stuffed into a tin trash receptacle, the shirt with the big number 33 was soaked in gasoline (to remove the foul odor) and lit with a match. And every man on the Blues watched while the uniform flared up, and was no more. Never again will "33" be worn by a Blues' player. It is hoped that the Blues will now snap their losing string that began with Palmer's deliberate eighth inning muff against the Jaybirds. At least, the last vestige of Palmer's existence with the Blues has been snuffed out.*

In their apartment, Brick and Cathy read the paragraph and looked at each other, the cold dread of the future in each other's face. A few miles away, in a hospital rest room, interne Johnny Palmer read the same paragraph, swore his revenge, and promptly forgot all about it.

But Brick and Cathy could not forget it, had they even tried, and a charred "33" was burned into their souls, a twisted useless hunk of a thing that would not go down or wash away, and which tasted bitter. Out of uniform they were, but inside, a couple of lucky 3's rattled and rotted.

And so they fled, headed for a lake in Maine where the only noise is the laughter of loons and the dipping of canoe paddles into bottomless water.

And where Brick and Cathy Palmer would be not Mr. and Mrs. Goldbrick, Trick or Itching Palmer, but William and Catherine Palmer, Milwaukee, summer vacationing after too strenuous a sales season.

"Tired?" Cathy asked, the car moving across the New Hampshire border, into Maine.

He shook his head, his eyes clear and untroubled. "No," he said, and then added, "a bit restless, though."

"That will pass," she said, glad he could speak so easily of his inactivity. He nodded. "Hungry?" he asked.

"H-mm, well, yes," she said, slowly, thoughtfully, and he was glad she could give time and attention to such small things.

And each, unknown to the other, reached out gnawing fingers of pity, for they knew the talk was desperate, the casual slowness a studied thing, the thoughtfulness a shallow cover-up for the hammer at their hearts.

But time, and a Chevvy's drone, and a ribbon of road, and New England were on their side, siphoning off the misery as each mile slipped by, leaving it mixed with the rubber-tire marks and the dark, unending stain of oil, trailing back to a horizon behind them. And the sun reached down and melted a bit of the hammer's iron end.

"How much further?" she murmured.

"See on the map? About two inches north of Augusta, just off Belgrade Lakes? That's how far. We're still an inch and a half south of Augusta. Forty miles to the inch. Figure it yourself."

"Can't," she said, "too much multiplying."

"Add 'em, then."

"Can't, too much addition."

"You never could figure batting averages."

"Yours I could. Nothing for three, nothing for two, nothing for four. .000."

And the hammer in each other's throat beat feebly, and subsided.

The sun was hot, and baseball was a game kids play.

The Chevvy pulled into the adult camp, rousing neither more nor less interest than that of any car with any other couple. The camp owner-clerk registered them in his battered looseleaf notebook, Mr. and Mrs. W. Palmer (Cathy's idea, using the initial alone), and they swung down the graveled walk to the housekeeping cabin forty feet from the lake. They unpacked slowly from the one valise, a handful of summer clothes, bathing suits, and toilet articles.

Brick sucked on a cigarette, sitting on the edge of the big iron bed with the old wool comforter at one end, promising an evening chill. "Like it?" he asked.

"So far. The lake is lovely."

"I was just a kid when I was here last."

"I know," she said. "Twenty years ago. Is it much different?"

"I don't think so," he said, "but I'm probably cheating. I think I remember everything I see, the shape of the lake, the little store where we got the groceries, the color of the sky. It feels the same, even if I don't remember anything actually."

Cathy folded the last sunsuit into a cedar drawer and got up, leggy and young. "Why don't you take a nap? I'll walk around a bit and let everybody know you're a liquor salesman."

"Better make it athletic equipment," he said, grinning. "At least I'll know a little what I'm talking about."

"Liquor," she said, firmly. "I always wanted to be married to a liquor salesman."

"What firm?" he asked. "Just to keep the stories straight."

"Schenley's," she said, "or one of the Walker boys."

"Johnny," he said, "if I drank, I'd drink Scotch."

"Johnny it is, William." She bent down and kissed him lightly on the cheek, her hand resting for a moment on his back. "Sweet dreams."

But it was no nap for Brick. He finished his cigarette and got to his feet. Across the lake a loon sent up his eerie laugh, and Brick decided he'd go visiting the bird, if he could. He walked down the gravel path, a shirtless, stocky, nearly-forty-year-old liquor salesman, going out for his afternoon nap on the lake.

He stepped into a canoe at the edge of the water, teetering unsteadily for a second, frowning as he stared down trying to remember how he used to sit, and then kicking loose of the sandy floor and paddling out, straight across the mile-wide lake. The stroke came back to his shoulders, long and easy, the boat drifting water after each pull, his hands shifting clumsily at first, and then remembering how, as the rhythm of years ago came back to him. No hurry, he thought, the sun bending to the west, the air soft as velvet. Time to lose, he thought, and grinned at the memory.

Ahead of him, a half-mile or so, he saw the loon family, three of them, swimming in a tight circle, round and round, a sort of tag with each other's tail. He slowed his strokes and hoped they wouldn't hear or see him until he got much closer.

The sun was baking him and he saw droplets of sweat on the hair of his chest. Seventh inning, he thought, but where was the pain?

In your heart, he answered, but when he probed for it, he could not find it. Good, he thought, now let's do some thinking, now that I can face it without tears. He remembered the way he had cried on the living room couch, and he wondered whether that had happened five days ago or five years. So soon, he thought, satisfied. So soon to lose the pain. Maybe it will pass for good. And he looked up and saw the loons, large black and gray versions of Groucho Marx, just three hundred yards away.

He felt the quickening inside, and pulled once on the paddle, and drifted. The circle they swam in, he saw now, was about fifteen feet in diameter, not as cozy as it had looked from a distance, but still obviously a game.

Like a kid, I am, he thought excitedly and laughed aloud. The laugh broke up the game. The loons went in three directions, the largest into the air, flying and squawking across the lake, at a ninety-degree angle to Brick. The second in size flew away from Brick straight to the trees a quarter of a mile away. And the baby—well, smaller, anyway—gulped once, and went underwater.

The game had started for Brick. Which way, he thought, paddling towards the spot where he saw the loon go diving? There he swung the canoe around, his eyes searching for a black spot beneath the water, knowing he'd never see the loon until the animal wanted to give in. The same game as always, he thought. And his mind wondered, "Why always the same game? Why must I play at something I know?"

"Because," he answered, "I'm thirty-eight years old, and I only know a few games. Old catchers, like old dogs, don't learn new games. A liquor salesman! *I'm a catcher.*"

And behind him, at that very moment, nature's most cynical playmate laughed his special laugh. Brick whirled, in time to see the bird go splashing under once more, three feet from the bow of the canoe.

He waited patiently, unmoving. "Where is it taking me?" he wondered. "Away, away," he whispered, fiercely. And he sat, unmoving. For Brick Palmer wanted to run away, but he knew it was even harder to escape than to stick around and take it. Let the laughter come, let the jeers roll down from the stands, he'd never run.

Why had he come up here? To think. Where no one would crowd him, where hatred would slip away and where he could figure his life from here on out, with baseball or without. Running away from the game he knew and loved, or staying? Bucking edict, somehow or other, finding the loophole, finding the out, or accepting the decision based on gossip, unproved, circumstantial, emotional?

But how? By squealing to the Commissioner that it was no bribe, that it was a gambling debt, not his own, but his brother's? That the signature on the IOU was not his own, but a forgery, by his brother?

Even had there been a chance his story might have been believed, Brick knew he'd never spill it. Himself or Johnny Palmer; it always came down to that.

How about the check stub for $10,000 that he had paid, that had not been paid to him, but that *he* had paid the syndicate. For a flashing sunlit second his pulse sped, and then he saw the flaw there, too. The canceled stub was too pat, they'd say. "So you wrote out a check for ten grand," they'd say, unblinking, "maybe you got in return fifty grand. Or else you gave them ten grand, to bet for you, against the Blues." With millions riding on a ball game each day, a token payment of ten thousand dollars to the syndicate could be explained in a dozen ways.

And, anyway, he had consorted with gamblers. He had not reported it. There, always, was the final crushing word.

So what, the critics, the judges, the commissioners, the fans said, so what, the Grand Jury had failed to indict Brick Palmer. Hadn't Grand Juries been in gamblers' pockets before? Wasn't Capone the original owner of jury lists? A thousand bucks here, a thousand there, and a gentle warning as to what might happen to a juror who thinks—wasn't that the formula for failure to indict obvious criminals?

No, that way was down the drain. He sat there, slumped in the canoe, a man of tired bronze, black-browed and square-jawed, thinking, slowly, his mind covering every square inch of the situation.

The shrill cry of the loon turned him automatically, his arms and paddle reacting, but his mind still plodding the sixty feet, six inches from mound to plate, wondering what to do now, with all the power on the other side, the cleanup man coming up, his own pitcher tiring and the bullpen empty.

What to do, barred for life. Catch the laughing loon.

What to do, barred for life. Follow the laugh and trap it.

What to do, barred for life. Cram the laugh down their throats, and play. Play the only game he knew.

But barred, barred for life from organized ball. Plod along, wear out the grass on rocking-chair feet, plod along back to the plate and call for the pitch, as best he could.

Barred for life, from organized ball. But still, he had to play. What to do. Barred for life, from organized ball—from *organized* ball!

Why the hell hadn't he thought of it before? From *organized* ball. If he had to play ball, he'd play. Not organized ball, but unorganized, independent ball. Or, if you prefer, and at that moment Brick Palmer preferred, outlaw ball. No jurisdiction over its activities by major league teams, owners, or by the czar himself, the Commissioner. Free of formal regulations issuing out of Carew Tower, Cincinnati, where the Commissioner set up his headquarters, or from New York, Boston, Cleveland, wherever His Honor decided to register in a hotel and make his court. Free, he'd be, free as a sandlot kid.

Outlaw leagues, Brick knew, still existed. Like the Mexican League, on its last legs, maybe, but still extant. Not that he'd go there, he'd turned down a lucrative offer four years before, when the gold was waving in every decent ball player's face. Now he'd not go begging.

But where, then? Industrial leagues, maybe, but no, the pay was based on your job, and he was a ball player, not a machinist or a clerk or a watchman. Someplace in Montana there used to be a good independent league, he recalled, growing out of the Chicago White Sox scandal, grabbing the suspended-for-lifers with the pale hose. Probably not in existence any more, he thought, but he'd get in touch. Who else, where else?

He'd get the record books, the *Who's Who*, the J. G. Taylor Spink tomes. They'd take the Chevvy back, along the Turnpike this time, burning the guts out of it, back to the city where he'd send telegrams scattering all over the country, who'll buy an unwanted ball player, with a name guaranteed to draw a tomato-laden crowd? An outlaw they'd made him, an outlaw he'd be, making his peace with outlaws, but playing the game.

His own laugh, triumphant and soaring, whipped to the sky, and for an instant he held the paddle aloft, his body straight as a boy's, unaching. Then down went the blade, biting the green water, down deep he bent into his stroke, and straight for the shore he pulled.

Cathy was in the cabin when he entered, his eyes betraying the excitement.

"What is it?" she asked, but she knew; *he's thought it out.*

"We're leaving," he said. "We're going home."

Good, she thought, good. He's found something, he's found himself. No, not himself, that's always been there. "Why?" she asked. "Afraid you'll confuse rye with gin?"

"Rye? Oh, liquor salesman. No, not afraid. I'm going to play ball."

"New name?" she baited him. "Use an alias, wear a false goatee?"

"Neither, my own name. In big black letters, black as my fame," he leered, laughing. "Independent ball, outlaw ball, anything where they think my name will draw the fans, and where the Commissioner has to pay to get inside."

He explained it to her, as well as his little information allowed him. But both knew, when he had finished, they had to go and try it; it combined the two things that had always remained steadfast these last five days. He had to continue playing ball. And he had to play outside the jurisdiction of the Commissioner's office. It was so simple they both wondered how it had escaped this long.

"Oh," Cathy said, "I'm glad."

He frowned. "Me too, hon. But we don't know where, when, for how much."

She stood against him, pressing inside his arms. "Where? With you. When? Any time. For how much? For peanuts and love. What difference does it make?"

And just like that, it was settled. They left the puzzled owner-clerk thirty minutes later, paying for the day, and sending the Chevvy storming down the side road to the main highway, and thence forty miles to the Turnpike, and home.

"A loon," he said, out on the road, "a laughing loon did the trick. Playing with him, liking it, while he laughed at me. The way it's going to be, from now on, getting laughed at, jeered, mocked, but liking it."

Cathy nodded. But not liking it too much, she prayed. You're too decent to like it while they're hating you. While your hits bounce off the fences, and the crowd is silent, and while the foul pops land a foot away from your glove, and they laugh. Don't like it, too much. You're a man, she thought, the most man I ever knew, and you can't like playing the toad.

They rode in silence, the night coming in swift and cool, and Brick's arms started getting heavy, the back began to ache, and the broken fingers stiffened on the wheel. Old, he thought, to begin a new life, and he wondered if he could keep fooling Cathy into thinking he really liked it.

Chapter V

The heat in the city was frightful. The streets were narrower than they were the day Brick and Cathy left, compressed by the still fresh memory of wide-open farm land and rolling hills. The city crowds, sheeplike and plodding, were more dense than ever, the tar softer, the pavement hotter, the air thicker.

And the flags at the stadium hung draped about the poles as if in need of support, while the river below stirred only slightly as the tugs and barges heaved past. The city was sullen, immobile and lifeless, grudgingly swallowed by the heat of itself, heat that came shimmering off the streets in dancing waves.

To Brick and Cathy, however, it all was a blessed sight. They breathed in the heat, feeling their bodies swell and quicken before the challenge of the city. They watched the still waters of the river and longed to hold out their hands for the precious stuff. They passed the stadium and Cathy's eyes misted.

A patch quilt of impossible patterns had smothered them, but now they could breathe again. In the elevator, their fingers strayed together and they entered their home, not as fearful aliens, but as returning conquerors.

The door closed behind them, and in an instant Brick had folded Cathy within his arms, and the tremble that shook his body was not from fear, but eagerness.

And in the night the dream returned to Brick, the dream he had not dreamed in years, not since his smoking bat and sure hands had won him the security baseball granted only to the select. It was a dream of empty grandstands, mud-coated baseballs, splintered bats, bumpy diamonds, bus rides by night on ill-lit, ill-kept roads. It was the dream of Class B baseball.

It was easy for Brick to remember such a dream the next morning; he merely reached back twelve years and there was the reality of it....

The city is nameless, for it was so many cities. It was a piece of Waterbury where an old major league pitcher, desperate and sick, resorted to a spitter, and sent Brick to the hospital with a brain concussion, and a half-year of headaches. It was a hunk of Cedar Rapids where a losing pitcher crossed Brick's signals, and chipped a bone in the catcher's wrist with a fast ball while the mitt kept waiting for the curve. And it was a ditch outside Fayetteville where a burning bus lay on its side, and seventeen ball players pounded at rusty old doors that jammed shut and kicked at unbreakable glass windows that finally gave way before the bludgeoning of baseball bats. And the scars that criss-crossed Brick's back were there for life, in dreams and awake.

The scouts that never showed up, the torn bags that snarled the spikes and snapped ligaments, the pail of drinking water that was warm and oily, the money that was late, the teams that folded (as they're folding today, before the ravages of TV), the fights that erupted, the hate that hung over the dugouts....

And always the same, this dream. Always it ended in a hotel room of dirty linen and dust, with Cathy sitting in a moaning chair, while he lay on his stomach trying to disbelieve the pain that had already settled in his back, even before his career had had a chance to start. And always, when he looked up at Cathy, she was old.

The dream was Class B baseball, twelve years old the dream, and when Brick awakened this August morning, he knew the dream was more than the past. It was also the future.

And Brick looked over at Cathy, lying small and still in the bed, looked over at her, searching for lines at the corners of her eyes, for furrows on her brow, for gray in her hair, for a sag of jawline, a fold of fat at her throat. And thanked God. For none was there.

His eyes, as though a voice, stirred Cathy, and she turned to him and yawned, and smiled. The dream was over.

"Coffee?" she said.

He nodded. "By me; you lie there."

"Well," she said, "the luxury of unemployment."

He frowned. Guilt, a thing he had scarcely known before, was now constantly with him. He dreamed of an aging Cathy—and offered coffee in bed. More, much more, was needed.

"What's the matter, hon?" she asked lightly.

"Nothing," he grinned. "I just hate the idea of pulling stakes."

She snorted. "Don't sound so primitive. This is no pioneer trek. We've done it before."

"That's what I mean," he said. "Why can't we settle down, like human beings?"

She turned back, and her voice was gentle as a whisper. "We chose this life because we love it." And somewhere in her soul, she found the words he needed. "I'd rather we do the tramp leagues, never knowing where we'll sleep tomorrow, than stay home and fret."

And the surge of life returned to him, while the water on the stove boiled briskly and the air was alive with Cathy's humming.

After breakfast, he piled the dishes in the sink and cleared the kitchen table. He pulled pencil and paper from a mahogany desk drawer and started to write.

The telegram they decided on, an hour later, was simple. It was just three Words. AM IMMEDIATELY AVAILABLE. He signed it Brick Palmer.

Pride rejected the words WANT JOB; humility eliminated NEED EX-MAJOR LEAGUE CATCHER? No words were needed to explain the paradox of Brick Palmer's seeking a berth with an outcast ball club. No batting averages were necessary; Brick's name was still in the record books, as just a week before it was up there with the league's leading hitters.

"How about 'reply collect'?" Cathy suggested.

"No," he said. "I don't know why, but no. I guess it's too cocky. Suppose you got a wire like that, from a guy who's just made a wad of dough for tossing a ball game. You'd say, 'Sure, he can afford paying for collect telegrams. T'hell with him.' Wouldn't you?"

"I don't know," she said after a moment of silence. "Why would you want a cheap job if you had a wad?"

He laughed. "Don't be consistent. They're just going to look for a way out. That is, if they don't want me messing up their lily-white team."

She knew he was right. "Okay," she said. "I'd say t'hell with him."

He looked down at the scattered sheets. "Now," he said, "where do we send this thing?"

"To the independent leagues," she said, brightly.

"Sure," he said, "just like that." He picked up the papers and went into the living room, to the bookshelves where he kept his modest row of sports reference volumes. They sat together on the couch, the books piled on the coffee table before them, and the pages slipped by their searching fingers, while a list of towns took form on a piece of yellow scrap paper.

"The Negro league signed a couple of white high school boys last month," Brick said, scrawling down the names of the towns that housed the teams.

"I wonder why," Cathy said.

"Why not," Brick answered. "The majors raid their rosters for the top talent, Robinson, Doby, Paige. The league's probably taking a financial beating, with the fans sucked over to Brooklyn, Cleveland, New York to see the better Negro ball players. So the Negro league grabs a couple of white boys for box office attractions. And anyway, there's no reason why they wouldn't, even if I'm wrong about the money angle."

Wherever Brick or Cathy remembered seeing a decent ball field that no organized league claimed, they jotted down the town's name, and next to it, unless the dust lay too thick on their memories, went the name of the team or of any man either could recall. Wherever Brick had played for side bets (anywhere from ten to fifty bucks a man) and for a 70-30 split of the day's take, that town was noted.

And there on a slip of paper was the backyard of American baseball, where some men played for kicks, others for tomorrow's groceries, and a few, for yesterday's. There was a team in Cedarhurst out on Long Island; another in Warren, Ohio.

The towns zigzagged crazily across the nation: Fayetteville, North Carolina; Waco, Texas; Watertown, New York; Fresno California. When they had finished, there were thirty towns from twenty-two states, and a couple of potshots up in Canada where Brick knew baseball was played independent of major league rule. Thirty-two telegrams went off, for a cool twenty-five bucks, and out over the wires three words click-clacked their strange story: Brick Palmer, major league catcher (and crook), with fifteen years experience (and ten grand in bribes), is immediately available to play ball (and draw crowds) for the first decent offer (and rotten fruit).

Am immediately available. Like the time, fifteen years ago, in Class D ball in Texas, Brick's first play-for-pay job, when he had caught eighteen innings with the temperature at 110 degrees, a doubleheader he'd never forget. And complained to the manager in the seventh inning of the second game, only to be canned the next day. And never complained again.

Am immediately available. Cathy remembered the time they took Brick to the hospital in Elmira, with a finger so broken no one expected it ever to bend. They called, apologetically, the next day, could Brick hurry it up, they were down to one backstop, and he wasn't hitting. Could Brick make it back, let's say, inside a week. And he did.

Am immediately available. There was the exhibition game just a couple of months ago, the Blues giving the reserves a chance to cavort before a big minor league crowd, the regulars sitting on the bench. Until the bushers started rapping the ball all over the field, and manager Bras Watkins asked Brick to put on the shinguards and see what was wrong with the Blues pitching. And he did, although that day he had skipped the pre-game rubdown and warm-up, and his back kicked up in the eighth inning and an inside scream tore out of his pain every time he went into the squat.

Except this time, it was even more important. For Cathy told Brick what he had feared was true, that the twenty-five bucks handed over to Western Union cut their total bank balance to a couple of uncashed war bonds, which they just wouldn't touch, and two hundred and forty dollars and twenty-eight cents.

He stood up. "I think there's a pretty good movie down the block, beginning today. What do you say, shall we celebrate?"

"I think that's a fine idea," Cathy said, evenly, "but don't you think we should wait until the theatre opens. It's only eleven o'clock. A.M., that is."

He looked down at his watch, in disbelief. "Why—" he started and then stopped. For he knew what had gone wrong with his thinking. He was pushing too hard. Those telegrams, singing their lonely message over the wires, *had* to get somewhere, soon, and the answer—answers, maybe—*had* to be back, soon, and Brick was sending the hour hands of his mind spinning from morning to evening, in the same time it took a man (a strong-legged one) to circle the bases. *Easy,* he thought, *take it easy, you'll live.* And then he thought, *how?*

"Well, then," he said, "I think I'll read a book."

She nodded. "And I'll start lunch."

He stood over the shelves once more, his eyes passing by the titles he knew so well, unseeing eyes that were far off, detached from the reality of a too-small living room, a too-small bank balance, and a much too-small future. Up from the dust he had come, to know the glory of pennant flags and Most Valuable Player awards, and down into the dust he had fallen. And the dream that had become reality was a dream once more, only this time he was no longer a kid, and he knew what the morning line had to quote on such dreams.

But on he dreamed, a book in his hand, his wife in the kitchen, and his life in the trash can. He dreamed of all the old box scores, the clubhouse cele-brations, the winter banquet circuit, and the feel of hard rubber under the spikes, as the winning run came trotting home. He dreamed of Feller's fast ball and Sain's curve and Leonard's knuckler, and how he could hit them all.

He dreamed of Robinson's speed, of DiMaggio's unbelievable grace (and how the man could run bases!), of Reiser's foolish bravery, of Hubbell's cun-ning. And as he dreamed, the minutes silently slipped by....

Out in Montana, it was just middle morning. A tall, gray-haired man sat at the lunch counter diagonally across from the Esso station, in the center of Butte's business district. He ate his buttered toast slowly, sipping his coffee, reading the county's daily paper. On the counter, slowly absorbing the multi-odored grease, lay a yellow envelope, untouched. The gray-haired man did his three chores automatically, each at the same speed, a bite, a sip, a read. Finally he finished. He wiped his mouth with a napkin pulled from a rusting metal upright container, belched nearly silently, lit a cigarette, and opened the yellow envelope.

He would have said, "Well, I'll be damned," had he been less cryptic. In-stead he grunted and dropped the telegram into the sugary bottom of the cof-fee cup. He belched again, as he left the counter, with more satisfaction this time.

They ate lunch, Brick and Cathy, and the electric clock in the kitchen kept drawing their eyes away from the plates.

"Take some more butter," Cathy said, "your spud is dry."

"Sure," he said, slicing off a tiny piece. "How come no milk for you?"

"I'm a big girl now," she answered.

Twelve-fifteen.

The talk was sporadic, just filling in the gaps of silence until there was something to talk about. The food was tasteless to the two. The room was quiet. The sun had climbed to the roof of the sky where it hung, before starting its plunge through the west. And only the electric clock was alive, its second hand whirring around noiselessly, a bright mechanical fixture that told a bright mechanical lie. For while the second hand sped, the minute hand crawled, and the hour hand moved not at all.

And down in Virginia a bony, freckle-faced youngster vaulted from his bike seat, strode the dirt walk to the paint-peeling door of the two-story private house at the corner, and rattled the outside knocker.

A tired-faced woman with a scarf around her hair opened the door. "Yes?" she said dumbly, staring at the messenger boy.

"Telegram for the coach, ma'am."

"Oh," she said, fingering the envelope. "Well, I'll tell you." She stopped and looked down, her fingers still worrying the envelope. "You might find him at the ball field. Said he might go on down early." She frowned at the envelope. "Something about fixing up the white lines, or something. Yes," she said, more quickly, "yes, that's where he is, down at the field." She handed the boy the telegram, glad to be rid of it. She went back to her cleaning.

At the field, Bill Henry tidied up the white lines, but his mind was elsewhere. The crowds were small, everyone was talking about the leagues folding up all over the country, and if the war came, where would they get ball players. Glory be if they'd have to use those weak-armed high school lads again, nobody'd ever show up to see a game.

The boy handed him the telegram and Henry's reaction was like his wife's. He wished the wire, unopened, had never been sent. But he opened it without worrying it further, and for a brief moment he felt something stir in his middle. Just for a moment, though.

"Got enough worries," he said, giving the boy a nickel. "Now the crooks want to play for me. First lame babies, now crooks." He tore the wilted telegram and dropped the pieces on the field. And bent down and picked them up and looked around for a trash basket, and dropped them again....

The afternoon wobbled by in the city. Outside, a paper man sat in the shade of his stand, too hot to hawk the headlines, or maybe too troubled to read them. The shirtsleeve brigades went by, handkerchiefs to foreheads, and the banal chatter drew the usual responses. "Hot enough for you?" "You said it, brother." "Going up to the game?" "Hell, no, see it for a dime at a bar." And the bartenders cursed the day television was invented, sending in the cheap nickel-nursers, loud-voiced, rough with the elbows, stingy with the tips.

And while they cursed, and the deadbeats nursed, and the handkerchiefs mopped, and the listless ball players performed, Brick and Cathy sat upstairs, and stared at each other, their faces wan and their souls dormant. But in each beat the knowledge that now it was four o'clock, whereas before it was noon. And in four hours something might have happened. Something had to happen....

The life of a telegram is a dreary thing. Take the one that sped out of the city, up into the big state, winged by teletype perforator, straight to Buffalo, and then jumping the border to Montreal. Here it changed from words to the old-fashioned International Morse, and as such it fled along the wires banking the St. Lawrence River, to Osage, a few miles away, *di-dah dah-dah di-di dah-dah dah-dah....*

There it lay, translated from dots and dashes to words, on a hardwood desk, a message that once had wings and now had to wait for a bicycle to take it to its wheezing completion. It lay thus for exactly forty-two minutes, until the boy arrived. It was shuffled into a small pile of other similar messages and stuffed into a leather knapsack that hung from the handlebars of the WU bike. And through the wind-blown, bumpy streets went Brick Palmer's three words, addressed to OWNER OSAGE BALL CLUB OSAGE PROVINCE OF QUEBEC CANADA.

OWNER wasn't in, so across the street trudged the boy to leave the missive with the barber who was a friend of OWNER and who promised to deliver it as soon as OWNER showed. And back to the office on the other side of the road went the boy to slip a message under OWNER'S door telling him that barber had his telegram, delivered at 4:46 P.M., August 24.

OWNER wasn't in until two hours later, for the simple reason that he also was MGR of the Osage ball club, playing a game twelve miles away (winning it) and returning to his home stadium office, just in case somebody had wired him, which had happened only twice during the present season.

OWNER walked into the barber shop at seven o'clock, and the evening chill had whipped in from the north.

"Hello, Max," the barber said, "win it?"

Max nodded. "Yeah," he said, "got a wire for me?" His voice was corn belt, USA.

The barber handed him the envelope and watched Max as he opened it, while a lathered customer fidgeted for the blade to come down and go to work again.

Like all the rest in twenty-two states and two places in Canada, the reader of Brick's three words frowned. It seemed, actually, to the barber that Max winced slightly.

"Bad news?" he said, starting his rhythmic stroke.

Max looked up in surprise. "Oh," he said, "no, not bad. Not for me, anyway. For somebody else, maybe." And he left the barber shop, to pile his way into the '37 Pontiac outside the stadium office, and drive, slowly, to the WU office. When his pencil finished its chore, the time was 7:45....

And Brick and Cathy Palmer were in the movies. Like shy lovers they sat, his hand in her lap, her hand resting on his wrist.

The film was the usual pleasant fare dished out by Hollywood, the eighty-two-minute struggle on celluloid of a young lawyer to get his secretary to marry him, and her struggle to repress her desire to say *yes* before the eighty-first minute. The last minute, of course, showed the two of them beaming at their child, born a year later.

Even in this Brick found some solace. The problem, as presented on the screen, seemed in its initial reel to be completely impossible of solution. The lawyer had, in his very first case, won a smart decision that cost the girl's father several thousand dollars needed for an operation for the girl's mother. And the girl liked her parents. So you see.

But somehow, it all worked out. The young man won a case for a sentimental millionaire whose pet rabbit had destroyed some neighbor's vegetable garden, and, as a reward, received several thousand dollars which he in turn handed over to the girl who in turn handed her mother over to a super-surgeon, and everybody, except the spinster whose vegetable garden was ruined, was happy. And she was a mean old woman who hated children and pets.

Brick sat there, his wife's hand stroking his wrist, and wondered where he could find a sentimental millionaire—or an unsentimental baseball club owner—who would hand him, not several thousand dollars, but a glove and a mask. And let all the child-hating, pet-hating spinsters of the world turn their wrath on him, he wouldn't mind.

But I'm not pretty, Brick thought. And I'm not young, at least not young like that fellow. Not young at all, he decided, sitting there, the memories of the past week crowding the images on the screen from his sight and replacing them with the kind of a road Charlie Chaplin always used to walk, long and dusty and endless. And, he grinned, at least Charlie had a cane.

But always, the hand at his wrist kept him there, balanced between a heart that ached and fingers that itched to squeeze the juice out of a baseball.

And when the curtain closed and reopened, and the coming attractions promised another unforgettable film event, Brick tugged at Cathy's arm. Quickly they filed out.

They walked through the muggy August evening, down to the edge of the river where sweethearts sat on benches, and watched in silence the lights dance on the water.

"Cathy," he said, "I'm a coward."

She turned to him and laid her fingers on his mouth. "Hush, darling, you're not, and you know it."

"I should be doing something, trying something else, in case."

"In case what, darling?"

"In case nothing happens, nobody answers the wires." He sat stiff, his back held away from the moist, hard stone bench.

"Time enough," she said. "Light me a cigarette, hon."

His fingers fumbled with the pack, cupped a match, and then handed the lighted cigarette to Cathy. Their hands touched for an instant, message of love and bondage. "But," he insisted, "if they don't answer, what then? How long do we wait? What do I do?" He waited, for the millionaire to saunter over.

Cathy's mind searched. In a way she was glad for moments like these. Too often he was all rock, bearing each wave, breaking it, giving up a chip, a splinter, but standing firm. Now the rock was mush, and he rested, while she took over.

"These telegrams, they went to people," she said softly. "People are good, most of them anyway. They'll read the telegram, most of them, and they'll see behind the words." She went on, as though reciting a lesson to fourth-grade children. He listened, gravely, lapping up the words as the shore received the water.

"They will want to help—these good people—not that you need help," she added a bit hastily, and they will write to you. It may take a long time. The good people never see badness, and they won't understand why baseball has done this to you. But by the same standard they won't understand how you could have done this to baseball; they won't understand it and they won't believe it."

Her voice wandered off into the night, and she was afraid her words sounded too much like prayer. Prayer now might be taken for desperation, and he must not know how desperate she was.

Once again he marveled at her. He studied her as she sat there, unmoving, her eyes fastened at some invisible spot across the river, her brow unwrinkled. He marveled for he knew the fear was there, as strong as his, stronger even, because she could do nothing to rid them of the actual burden—that of getting back into the game. The weight she carried could not be flipped off as a catcher tosses off his harness at the end of each inning. No bat, no gift of strength, no daring on the base paths, nothing but a constant heart.

And so he did not ask the next question, for she had done enough. He did not ask, "And if the good people don't want to help, or can't help, what then?" He was a man, with a man's back—he grinned to himself, an old man's back—and what was this load he was crying about? Just a start in life. Some people might complain if they were thirty-eight and had to start all over again, but—and this time his grin broke into a laugh—when a man's on his knees, with a bat waving in his face and an umpire behind him, when this goes on year after grinding year, then he can get up and walk off if he's got to. He'd even be a liquor salesman, memorize all those percentages about grain neutral spirits or something, or tote ice or haul coal. What was a round back for, any-way, except to bend and dig and carry.

"Thank you," he said, and he leaned over and kissed her lips. She hid the tremble at her lips, but a tear escaped and touched his cheek and clung there. "Why," he said, "why, honey, don't—"

She shook her head, soft hair brushing his neck. "You don't understand," she said, "I'm so glad, I'm so glad."

And they sat there, thus, in the embrace of lovers.

It was nearly midnight when they reached home. Cathy saw it first, a slip under the door, a piece of whiteness extending into the hall an inch or two, just a break in the shadows. She picked it up and read the words left by the WU messenger.

"Come," she said, "we have a call to make. There's a wire for us at the Western Union office."

Inside, she walked to the window, far from the phone, and looked out. It was to be his victory, she thought, or, God forbid, his setback. She would share it, later, but now he must do it himself.

"Yes," he said, into the mouthpiece, "you may read it." He stood there, a hulk of a man waiting in the darkness. "Thank you. I'll be down to pick it up tomorrow morning," he said simply, and hung up. He turned to Cathy, and his face was grave and the dignity of what they had accomplished was in his voice. "Yes," he said, "they want me."

She nodded, there at the window, the pale August moon striking her throat, and he watched her, wondering why she did not sob out, and think-ing, my God, all through this she's trusted me. And thinking, I'd tote ice for her, yes, and more. I'd die for her.

Chapter VI

The route to Osage, in the province of Quebec, Canada, goes along the Hudson to Albany, bends west to Utica, cuts north through the Adirondacks straight for the border. The last decent town on the United States side is Malone, where Brick gassed up as night swooped down on the road.

"Pretty cool," he said to the gas attendant, "for this time of year, isn't it?"

The attendant said, "Nope, real seasonable," and walked off to make change.

Brick looked at Cathy. "Maybe it just blows up like this at night," she said. "Do you feel it?"

He shrugged his shoulders, bunched the muscles behind his neck and let his head loll. "A bit," he said.

They drove on, stopping at the border for five minutes, and then across, on the northern bank of the St. Lawrence, aimed a bit east to hit Montreal. Cathy held the road map in one hand. The other clutched the telegram that had called them to Canada.

FIVE HUNDRED REMAINDER OF SEASON REPORT IMMEDIATELY HOTEL BRETAGNE OSAGE MAX ADDISON.

She held the wire in her hand, but she could have thrown it out the car window, so well had each memorized the message. The words still burned in Brick's ears, *five hundred... report immediately.* And the thrill of playing again was back in his bones, even in the aching ones, like a spring season charley horse that hurts like the very blazes but means nothing. He was on fire with playing again, and not even the cold weather blowing in from the north, not even the complete remoteness of his new home, not even the countless unknowns that lay ahead could quench the fire.

"Five hundred for the remainder of the season," he said aloud. "I wonder how come?"

"How come what, hon?" Cathy asked, her head on his shoulder.

"How come that much? Maybe," he added, with a chuckle, "their season lasts until Christmas."

"Could be," she said, shivering. "It certainly doesn't get any colder in December."

"Real seasonable," Brick said, mimicking the station attendant. "Some kidder."

But, still, he wondered, maybe it will be this cool (he meant cold, but hope made it cool) during the day. And September is just around the corner.

They rolled slowly through Montreal and Brick thought, "Well, I can't kick. Robinson made good up here, and he really had the problems."

Back across the river they went, midnight throwing its cloak on the waters, and Cathy dozed contentedly, while Brick's mind raced with questions.

Osage... what place were they in? Last, he figured, or near the bottom somewhere, why else call up a man who was sure to be big box office, and bigger question mark every place else. Max Addison... what kind of a man was he? How did he manage, from the field, from the bench, from a front office? Was he a scrapper, like Muggsy or the Lip, or cold and shrewd like Mc-Carthy? And the men... what were they like? Ex-loggers who wanted something softer? Minor leaguers who wouldn't take it or make it?

And, always, how would he go? His hands clenched on the steering wheel, and while an oncoming car blinded him for a fraction of a second, he saw himself in the batter's box, gripping his club, waving it, once, twice, poising, striding with the left leg, and whooshing out his breath as the bat—as the bat—and that's where the picture stopped.

For Brick Palmer, as confident as any man who ever faced a pitcher, was also just as unsure. He knew he could hit anybody who ever lived—sometimes—and that there wasn't a pitcher in the world who couldn't stop him dead—sometimes. The picture stopped just there, the bat coming forward, nearing the ball, but going no further.

What was it to be? A lead pipe cinch, this independent ball, where his base hits would rain all over the league, or a fouled-up mess, failing in the clutch, weak at the plate, jittery behind it?

But tough or easy, a .350 hitter or an automatic out, he'd give it a whirl, for five hundred bucks or for nothing, just so he could crawl into harness and eat the dirt off skidding foul balls. And cram down the throat of Malcolm Stutz those words that had been seared into his memory. "You'll never play ball again!"

He wouldn't, eh? Sleep tonight or not, if Osage had a game scheduled tomorrow, he'd be in the lineup. Report immediately, Max Addison had ordered, not for tea and crumpets, but for balls and strikes and a hunk of glory.

A hunk of glory? Where did he get that, he thought. A hunk of pain, more likely, and who was going to glorify an aging ape in harness who was apt to throw a ball game just as quick as peg one to second?

And that was the question that lay behind them all. Not what kind of man was Addison, what place Osage, how would he go... but how would the fans take him, this ball player whose shirt had been burned by his own teammates? What would it be, jeers or silence, tomatoes or disdain?

And then, how would he go under pressure like that? It was one thing, playing ball for a run, for a buck, for a pennant, for the championship of the whole baseball world. But how to play for the fans' hatred, that was another.

Brick turned and shook Cathy's shoulder with a touch so gentle she barely stirred. And then his fingers gripped her arm more firmly, and she wakened, just as the pain from his own grip traveled up the back of his hand.

"We're here, honey," he said, and she tossed her head and rubbed her eyes, and smiled at him.

"I've had the nicest dream," she said. "I dreamed you hit a home run."

And, he wondered, as they got out of the car and walked their luggage into the Hotel Brittany's lounge, and what did the fans do when I hit the home run, get up and leave?

L'Hôtel Bretagne was an anachronism, just as was Osage itself. A hundred years ago, before the rail chiefs decided it was more important to be closer to the States and to the Lakes, Osage boomed with raw industry. For a radius of twenty miles (and before rails were laid, how much bigger a radius could be imagined?) it was the feeding agent for lumber and manpower. Like a town in the American West it had boomed, flourishing with fabled muscle-men and dancing-girls. A hotel, a newspaper, a dozen lumber camps, and a couple of dozen saloons, that was Osage. And the hotel was the Brittany.

Built with the finest lumber in the world, it stood a magnificent four stories, with cutbacks, eaves, colonial pillars, and balconies all chopped and sawed and finished from the great forests just outside the town. A hundred years old, and it looked every minute of it, while in Montreal, a handful of miles away, brick and steel told the story of the rise of another civilization.

Dust came boiling up from the aged carpeting. A sleeping clerk somehow opened one eye and summoned a sleeping bellhop who somehow clawed his way through the dust to Brick and Cathy.

"No," Brick said, holding tight to the bags, "not yet, anyway." He turned to the clerk. "Is Max Addison registered here? He's expecting me." He looked at the clock on the desk, twenty minutes to two.

"Max?" the clerk said. "Where else would he be? Room 202," and turned back to his chair.

"Would you ring him, please," Brick asked, wondering what was wrong with the man, and then knowing what. He had been beaten by it all, and sometime, long ago, he had died and didn't know it.

"Oh," the clerk said, dully, "ring him. Yeah, sure." He turned the crank of the house telephone once, and then his finger pressed a little button wired to the phone, and pressed again. He listened, mild regret on his face. "No," he said finally, "not you, I'm ringing Max." He turned to Brick. "Party line. Rings the whole hotel. Three rings for the third— Yeah, Max? Party down here to see you." He listened for a second, and turned once more to Brick. "Name?"

"Palmer," Brick said.

"Brick Palmer," Cathy added.

"Palmer," the clerk said into the mouthpiece, "and the missus. All right, send 'em up."

He hung up and faced the two. He pointed behind them. "Elevator's not working. One flight up, to your right. Number's on the door. Two-oh-two."

"Thank you," Brick said. "I hope nobody minds about the telephone."

"They mind," the clerk said stiffly, "but can't do nothing about it. Stay here and you'll find out, yourself."

The flight was long and dark, and creaky as old shoes. At the landing above, a tiny red bulb threw out its light, for the stairs and for the whole second floor. They wheeled right and peered at the numbers painted above the doors. Max's room was the second one down the aisle, and Brick paused in front of it, his hand drawn back, knuckles high for rapping.

But while he paused, the door jerked open and a lean gray-haired man with high shoulders like Lon Warneke's stood there, his faded blue eyes traveling from Brick to Cathy and back.

"Come in," he said, and Brick's ears caught the familiar midwest in the voice, and he came in, his hand on Cathy's arm.

"I'm Addison," the gray-haired man said, and he extended a hand to Brick. He had scarcely looked at Cathy.

"This is my wife," Brick said, and Addison nodded once, stiffly.

"Sit down," he said, waving them to two old simulated-leather chairs. They sat, the dust assailing them once more. "What do you think of our town?" he asked Brick.

"A town," Brick answered. And wondered why the question, and why Addison seemed nettled at the answer.

"I slept through it, Mr. Addison," Cathy said, her voice clear and a trifle too loud for the room.

Addison grunted and lowered himself onto his bed, the springs crying out in protest. He reached over to the night table and picked up a piece of paper. His eyes raced down it and then he turned to Brick. "You two got room 301, upstairs, just off the landing. There's a bathroom end of the corridor. Hall lights go out at 9:30 every night, stair lights, them red ones, stay on all night. No training rules. Just be at the park at 12:30 tomorrow." He pulled out a pocket watch. "Today, I mean. We play at 2:05.

"Won't bother you with signs and stuff now, you both look tired. But—" he broke off, and looked at Cathy. "I didn't know you was coming, I—" He was plainly embarrassed.

Cathy's voice broke in, clear and loud, and Brick wondered whether she was scared. "I'm afraid I'm the one that's really tired. I'll go down and have the bags sent up to our room, and then I'll start unpacking." She got up, and then quickly bent and kissed Brick on the cheek. "Good night, hon, I may be asleep when you get in."

The door closed behind her, and Addison wiped his forehead. "Well, Palmer," Addison started again, "I guess we better talk for awhile, if you don't mind. I didn't want to say too much in front of the little lady."

Brick waited.

Addison stood up, and paced the tiny length of room and then he whirled to face Brick. "They throw at your head, what do you do?" he snapped.

"I duck," Brick said. *Now, what the hell*, he thought.

"They keep throwing," Addison insisted.

"I set a league record for bases on balls," Brick answered.

"They ride you from the bench, from the side lines. Real personal stuff, what do you do?"

"Personal? I thought that stuff was illegal," Brick answered, and then he understood. "Oh, you mean the bribe. I take it," he said. "I take anything they throw."

Addison leaned forward. "You take everything they throw," he said slowly, "and you don't throw back. The umps, they'll lay for you. They call 'em wrong enough, without you, but with you, they'll miss twice as many. And they'll be itching for you to kick. The strike zone on you will be from cap to toes, and then some. And when you're catching, they won't give you the corners, the knees, the shoulders. You're out on every close play, the runner's safe at home even if you block him out. That's the umps."

Brick nodded, his face white and his hands gripping his knees. "The men in the league, the other guys. They'll be out for blood. On the basepaths, if you slide, they'll tag you in the face, they'll drop their knees in your guts. They'll spike your hands. They'll murder you, when you're running. And when they're coming home, they won't slide. If they do, it's hip high. And they'll never stop grinding your ears with abuse." He stopped, and mopped his face again, while outside the wind whistled and battered at the old foundations.

"That's the players on the other teams. Us guys, now. They burned your shirt down in the States. Here, I dunno. Maybe the same sort of stuff. Maybe silence. Maybe nothing. They don't like crooks."

"Neither do I," Brick said.

Addison frowned and shook his head, and then went on. "The umps, the other guys, us, that's all bad, but my guess is, the fans will be the worst."

"I've been ridden," Brick said. "They got grandstand jockeys in the majors."

"Ha," Addison laughed, "that's what you think. Why, twenty fans up here is worth ten thousand at Ebbets Field when it comes to letting loose. If they want to, they'll skin you alive."

Brick shrugged. "Okay, it'll be rugged. Is that all?" He got up.

Addison stood up like a shot. "Sit down," he barked, "I know you're tough, but sit down. I ain't near finished."

Brick sat. Like a puppet, he thought, and then he was too tired to care.

"I say it'll be murder, what they do to you up here, but you don't care. And if you don't care, neither do I. I'm taking a chance on you, Palmer, but I think it'll work. All you got to do is keep your mouth shut and your hands open." He looked down at Brick's fists, resting on his knees. The fingers slowly opened.

"You're a major league catcher, the best in the business, maybe. I ain't seen better since Cochrane." His eyes misted a bit, and Brick wondered how much baseball the old man really knew.

"You haven't seen Campanella?" Brick asked.

Addison shook his head.

"I thought not," Brick said. "The best there is."

"No matter," Addison said, "you're good. You can hit and you can catch. You got bum legs, but they ought to last another month. Your back's stiff, we ain't got no diathermy, but I'll rub you down every day. Last year you had arm trouble in April. Is that gone?"

"No," Brick said, figuring he'd better keep it straight, the old man would know anyway. "No, it's not gone, won't ever be. But I'll throw."

"Yes," Addison said, "I believe you will." And then his tone sharpened again, and he was the bully boy once more. "You'll throw every day for a month, that's what I want you for, every blinking ball game until September 30. My catcher, Krakauer, busted his ankle. He's in the hospital in Montreal. Be there two months. I think he's through. So far I've had a fourth outfielder, guy named Lukas, doing my catching." He stopped for a moment and shook his head. "We're in second place, eight-team league, four games out, with twenty-eight to go. We win twenty of 'em, maybe we can take it all. We got to take it all." He stopped and sat down, exhausted suddenly by all the words and by the feeling behind them. His voice, when he went on, was dull and lifeless. "I sunk money into four ball players, new seats, better arcs. I'm broke unless we draw crowds. That's why you're here. But I can't figure on crowds next year, too, even with you, unless we win. We got to win, you understand?"

"Yes sir," Brick said, and for a moment he was torn between hating this man who bought a man about to be flayed alive and admiring him for his purpose.

"That's all for now," Addison said. "Go to bed. See you tomorrow at twelve-thirty, at the park. Can't miss it, down the street, opposite direction you must of come, out a quarter-mile or so." He waved his hand in dismissal and started tugging off his shoes, laces still tied.

Brick stood up. "About the bribe, I think I'd better tell you now."

The hand waved again. "Forget it. Some other time. Too tired."

"But—"

Addison straightened up, the blood in his forehead, a wormy vein twisting at his temple. "Forget it," he barked. "I don't want to hear about it."

Brick turned to go, opened the door and stepped into the darkness. Just before the door closed behind him, he heard Addison call out, "Look me up a bit early. We got more to talk about."

Brick nodded in the dim light and went slowly up the stairs. Worse than he figured, he thought, living in a rat hole of a hotel, in a town that died years back, working for a man without a heart, for a team that hated him, before fans that wanted his skin. Well, skin he'd give them, and guts too, if they insisted, it was all part of the game. Game? He snorted as he stepped through the doorway of 301, they call this a game, this nine-man murder. What was he doing it for, he asked. Why, he realized, with a wonder that lightened his heart, for Cathy, of course, and he sank into bed beside her.

He left Cathy at the hotel at noon and started out, walking, for the ball field, carrying a small valise of spikes, mitt and mask. The air was raw, the sun so high and tiny it seemed in another universe. A wind whipped the dust in spirals before him, filling his mouth and nose. Dust, he thought, always dust, a catcher's oxygen.

The walk was half a mile, and Brick tried to relax his legs, to give the muscles a chance to move beneath the tight skin. But the chill and the handful of hours of sleep had bunched them above the knee in a hammerlock that would not be broken. He saw the stands before him, newly painted green steel girders supporting open bleachers extending down each foul line, the benches running a dozen rows back. Six hundred feet of benches, he figured, times a dozen. Seven thousand two hundred feet of sitting room, maybe enough for five to six thousand people. He wondered if they'd ever filled the place, with the International League just a few miles way.

He walked through the untended gate to the dugout with the sign on the door at one end, Osage. He dropped into the dugout, walked the boards and pushed open the door. Inside was a dank underpass, with two doors off that. He entered the right-hand one; it was locker room and shower. He closed the door, his nostrils quivering at the stale odor of male bodies, sweat and arnica, and went through the other. It was Addison's office, bare except for a big wooden desk, a swivel chair behind it and a plain upright chair in front, one locker, a mirror on the wall, an Osage banner, blue with yellow letters, like a kid's camp pennant, and a picture of a ball player at bat. Brick leaned forward and saw the signature below, Joe Jackson, and he realized the uniform was a White Sox flannel. He was about to step outside when he heard quick steps along the wooden planks. He settled, instead, in the chair in front of the desk.

Addison came in, nodded curtly to Brick and swung around to the other chair. He lit a cigar, placing the bit-off end in the desk's ash tray. He opened a bottom drawer and pulled out a brown paper bag, stuffed full.

"Your unie," he said, handing the bag to Brick. "Shirt, pants, socks, undershirt, two each." He looked at Brick's valise. "Got your spikes in there?"

"Yes," Brick said. "Glove and mask, too."

Outside in the underpass he heard the scuffle of shoes and the opening and shutting of the door. The players, he guessed, were trooping in for dress and practice.

"About the signs," Addison said, "we'll keep 'em simple for a week. I relay all the signals to third base coaching box. Runners touch flesh for confirmation if we're ahead, touch cloth if we're behind. If score's tied at home, we're ahead; away, we're behind. Hands on hips, fingers spread means take. Ditto, fingers tight together, bunt. Touch grass, no talk means steal. Touch grass, hands on hips means hit and run. Got 'em?"

Brick nodded. It was the same sort of stuff. "Behind the plate?" he asked.

"Check the dugout on every batter, man on opposite end of bench from me will give you signals. After a week, I'll let you call 'em yourself. Cupped hands, fast ball; hands on knees, curve; hands out of sight, change-up. Check with individual pitcher for special stuff. Adcock, our lefty, throws a screwball; Pennington, a knuckler. Everything else just about the same. Don't let nobody throw a slider, can't stand 'em. O.K., tell 'em back to me." He leaned back and studied Brick, while the big ex-major leaguer patiently retold the signals to his new manager.

"All right," Addison said, "let's go inside and meet the gang." He looked sharply at Brick. "You all right? Remember what I told you last night."

Brick nodded wearily. Let's go, he thought, step number one. He picked up the paper bag and the spikes and followed Addison into the locker room.

At first glance it was the same as any other locker room, full of men in various stages of undress; crude, natural talk, always a trifle too loud; the swinging, creaking of locker doors. But before Brick could gather more than that, the room stopped being the same as any other. It clammed up as faces turned to meet his, one at a time, and then turned away. Like air leaving a balloon, the noise hissed to silence.

"This is Brick Palmer," Addison said. "Don't bother with names now, you'll learn 'em soon enough. This here, though, is Joe Adcock, he goes today. You two get together after I rub down Palmer," and Addison moved away, chatting in a low voice to the players.

Brick stood inside the door, taking it all in, counting them, feeling their reactions, measuring them. Seventeen of them, not as young as major leaguers, he realized with a shock. They'd been around, knobby-kneed and scarred, their skins white except for the rim of brown necks and lower arms and faces. He moved the paper bag for a more comfortable grip and raised it slightly. "Where do I chuck 'em?" he asked, his voice unnaturally harsh.

Adcock, flexing his left arm in front of Brick, jerked a thumb over his shoulder. "There, number eight," and turned away.

Silence, he thought, that's what it's going to be. Well, it could be worse, and he shouldered his way through, to the too-much space on the bench in front of number eight. He pulled open the locker, and stopped short. There, on the inside of the door, was a yellow slip of paper, with the words, "Greet-ings, Itching Palmer," printed in crude black crayon.

Behind him he felt the rustle of bodies and heard a sharp whisper, and nothing else. A couple of men changed positions, getting up off the bench to stand. Brick fingered the paper, staring at the words.

He could, he knew, whip around and smash the first face he saw. And the inevitable pile-on would follow, the beating that would end the month before it began. That was out, and his hand twitched at his side, in furious frustra-tion.

He could remove the paper, tear it up, and say nothing. And the men would know, by that, he admitted his guilt. Once more his right hand balled up, opened, balled up, and then hung open, fingers shaking in a spasm of rage.

Behind him not a thing changed, and then he moved. One hand went flash-ing up and the paper came ripping off, wadded into his palm in a startling splinter of time. One second it was there, yellow and accusing, the next it was gone. He spun on his heels, and faced the men, and there was a spontaneous intake of breath from a half dozen. His face, he knew, had drained white, his eyes had slitted, his mouth a grim line.

He spoke, at last, his stomach muscles convulsing to keep his breathing even, his words unhurried. "Thank you," he said, "I'm just as glad to see you." And then he stopped and looked from face to face, as if trying to see the guilt that lay behind a pair of eyes, and still nobody moved.

"Who knows," Brick went on, "how good my arm is any more? Maybe in fielding practice some day I'll forget, and throw to the wrong base," and he brought his hand up and grabbed the steam pipe that ran overhead. "Who knows how fast I throw any more?" He pulled himself up, suddenly, just with his right hand and arm, chinning his 190 pounds with just one arm, unsup-ported even at the wrist, and with satisfaction he heard a second intake of breath, this time more unanimous. He dropped lightly to the floor. "In case you don't know, I throw pretty good, straighter'n hell, and fast. Wouldn't be surprised if I threw a ball a hundred miles an hour." He turned to the man next to him, a tall, lean, blond stringbean whose hair was carefully parted to cover the encroaching bald spot. "Did you ever see a guy's head, hit over the ear by a baseball thrown a hundred miles an hour?"

And then he sat down and pulled off his shoes and started getting ready for the game, his hands trembling as they changed him once again to a ball player. Socks and spikes, supporter and jockey shorts, cheap flannel trousers and belt. He stood up, bare-chested and walked through the room, and they moved to let him pass. He stepped out into the hall and knocked on Addison's door.

"I'm ready," he called. "Want to rub me?"

Addison came out, in uniform, and his eyes ran over Brick's shoulders and chest, the flat, ridged stomach and heavy arms. He nodded, less in answer to

Brick's question than in manifesting approval of what he saw before him, purchased for five hundred dollars.

They went back into the room, the still room that was already emptied of some of its men. In the center was a long table, padded with cotton and covered with white cloth. On a shelf underneath were the bottles of the trade, a green liniment bottle that gave off escaping wintergreen fumes, a couple of bottles of iodine, a bottle of rubbing alcohol. Also, a box of cotton, some white-tipped sticks for cleaning out spike wounds or removing dirt from a player's eye. And rolls of adhesive tape and gauze.

Brick flattened himself and Addison leaned over, his hands going down to the big catcher's legs.

Brick kicked once, slightly. "Forget the legs, a waste of time. The neck, right shoulder, and sacroiliac, just a couple of minutes on each." He tried to relax, but he couldn't, the hands were strange, and he missed the soothing flow of chatter that used to fill the room when Lefty Fisher rubbed him.

Addison was good, he admitted, the hands were right, kneading, pulling, drawing, but nothing was giving. The locker room was empty and outside he could hear a pepper game in progress, the faint click of bat against ball, the noise of the men talking it up. And his body tensed, resenting that he couldn't indulge, knowing that when he went out, he'd take his place in a silent row of men who wished he had never showed up.

"That's enough," he said, and rolled over. "Thanks. That feels fine," and he smiled at his new manager.

"Fine, hell!" Addison snapped. "Don't kid me. You're worse now than you were five minutes ago. Go on out and run around a bit, maybe you'll loosen up."

Brick pulled on his sweatshirt and then his unie shirt, buttoned it carefully and looked down to see that it was straight. Like a Yankee, he thought, and he grinned and went out, walking slowly, letting his spikes grip the wooden floor, and then tiptoeing over the gravel two steps onto the sparse grass.

Hard, he thought, and cold. He wet a finger and felt the wind coming in from right center field, blowing a good ten miles an hour, damp and chilly. The sun was over in left field, high and yellow and useless. He started out, around the field, at a slow trot, and winced at the pain traveling up his legs. Hard, not quite as hard as St. Louis in August, but neither was there the heat to loosen the muscles.

He went past first, along the right field foul line, his eyes straight ahead, refusing to admit the presence of the nearby grandstands. To the fence he went, marked 315' at the line, and then he bent left, following the fence to deepest center field, puffing a bit now where the number 435' was marked, and veering further left, into the sun and coming back in sharply when he passed the number 330'. Big, he thought, and built right. Foul lines more than a pop fly away, but still close enough to reach with a healthy belt, the center field fence, practically an impossibility in the face of that wind, making the game more wide open with chances to poke one for three bases over the center fielder's head.

He was even with third base when they spotted him. The stands were nine-tenths empty, an hour before game time, but the word had gone around that the bulky, graceless man trotting off by himself was Brick Palmer. The first words lashed him like a whip, so quiet was the field.

"Banks close at three, you bum, you'd better hurry."

And then they were on him. Like eager dogs at a feast they closed in, and Brick looked once, and turned away. What he saw revolted him, the sun shining down on wet-lipped people, their mouths open, their eyes glinting, their faces twisted in smiles that looked like snarls. He stopped and put his hands on his hips, and looked at a dim spot on the horizon, directly over the center field fence.

"Goldbrick," they called out. "Trick. The Itcher. Go home, we don't want you."

A child's high-pitched voice came to him, "How'd you get across the border, Palmer, bribe a guard?" And the laughter shrilled out at him. The noise grew louder as the fans tumbled into their seats, still forty minutes before game time, but now it was no longer just a handful, but a small crowd, and growing.

He spun on his heels, eyes now aimed at the dugout, and he walked over, his slowness a studied thing. "Addison," he called out, "when do I get my licks?"

"Just pick up a bat and follow Muller, number five, up there now. He bats three in the line-up, you're clean-up." Addison stood at the edge of the dugout, his eyes on the crowd. Already, Brick thought, he thinks it's paying off.

He went over to the bat rack and hefted a half dozen clubs before he selected one he liked. At the cage he stood and waited for Muller, the tall blond stringbean who looked like a first baseman, to take his three. He watched Muller as he stepped in, too heavily, Brick thought, and hit three lofting shots to center.

He stepped in and dug a quick little hole, well back in the box, and with satisfaction he heard the silence fall. At least they're going to watch, he thought, and the fast ball came wheeling in and he went around, and missed it.

The laughing roar came out of the stands, not half-full, and Brick stepped out, frowning. The fools, he thought, don't they know. Away from the plate for more than a week, and nobody hits right off.

He took a medium fast ball, down in the dirt at his ankles, skipping away. *Careless*, he thought, *they wouldn't throw at me.* The next pitch was inside, around the chin, but he pulled his left leg away, and fell on the ball, driving a long curving foul towards the fence, and over. And listened for the crowd. And heard nothing.

The batting practice pitcher tossed again, and even before Brick started to swing he knew he had been curved. His bat limped around, fooled badly, and he went down, his ankles crossed under him. "I thought you was Brick," some wag yelled. "Look more like straw to me." And again the laughing whoosh barreled from the open mouths.

He walked back to the bench and over to Addison. "Tell your boy to stop playing games," he said, his eyes blazing. "I want straight fast stuff, like everybody else." Addison nodded, and walked out to the mound, and took the ball from the pitcher.

The crowd fell silent as they watched the gray-haired manager rub the ball against his trouser leg, his shoulders rising and falling as he tried to loosen old muscles. "All right," he said to Brick, "climb in there."

Brick got back into the box, the bat held motionless at his ear, while Addison went into a jerky windup and came out of it, the ball a blur on its way to the plate. At the chest it was, on the inside corner, fast but without any hop, and Brick exploded into it, lashing his bat with a joy he hadn't felt since he'd driven a winning Blue across the plate. His palms stung right on up to his shoulders, but his eyes were on the ball as it streaked into left-center field and dented the fence, on the line, 375 feet from home plate, a bullet drive that scarcely lifted twelve feet from the ground the whole way out.

Again Addison wheeled in the fast one, and again Brick brought his power to bear, snapping his thick wrists as he powdered the ball, and again there was the streak of white, this time lofted a bit, climbing and clearing the fence at the 360-foot mark, and still showing no sign of quitting.

Addison's third pitch was at the belt, splitting the plate, and for the briefest flash of time, Brick held up, and then he came around, drilling the ball to dead center, testing his power against the wind, and winning the test. At the base of the wall, 420 feet away, the ball kicked up dust and then larruped the fence on the first short bounce, an awesome drive with a cold, damp bat and a scuffed-up ball. Brick nodded his head once to Addison and said a short, "Thanks," and dropped the bat.

And from the stands came just one call, "Oh, you mama's boy," followed by the same ape-ish laughter as before, and Brick knew he hadn't won an inch of his fight.

Addison walked off the mound and caught up with Brick, steering him to the dugout. "Here," he said, "I want to talk to you and Adcock. I'll give you quick book on these bums," jerking his thumb at the rival Victoria Victors, who were starting their hitting practice.

And for a moment everything became normal. The chore was routine, pitcher and catcher and manager discussing the strength of the opposing batters, while out on the field the cries of normal fans, friendly, bantering, could be heard as the Victors teed off on a helpful batting practice hurler.

"Adcock," the manager explained, "throws soft stuff, lots of slow curves, a big roundhouse, and an occasional screwball. He throws this off his fast ball, they look alike only the regular fast one don't break."

Brick wondered how fast the fast one was if it looked like the screwball. Well, he couldn't kick, apparently the lefty had a repertoire.

"Lefty likes to work fast, but sometimes he hurries too much and he loses his control. When he does, good night!"

Adcock sat there, on the other side of the manager, and said not a word.

"The Victors, they're bums, down in the cellar. They can't do anything right, so they try everything. They bunt with two strikes, they hit and run every time a man gets on, they poke, they punch, they get in the way of pitched balls. They can talk it up, too." Addison looked at Brick, to make sure he understood.

"Don't worry," Brick said, "I'm deaf."

"Good," Addison said, and he went on, down the line-up of the visitors, and Brick once again felt the man must have seen some good baseball to be this astute.

Out in the field, the teams swapped again, the Outlaws taking their spots on the diamond, and Brick started to get up. "Easy," Addison said, "just sit here. We got a catcher for fielding practice. I want you to start warming up Lefty, he needs lots of time in this cool weather."

Adcock got up silently and walked out to the practice slab while Brick stood with his back close to the stands, the big mitt on again, warm and leathery and oily. Adcock twisted and let loose the first one, just a lob, thrown with a tiny jerk from the elbow.

While behind him, the monotony of the cries became evident as the fans settled into a routine assortment of name-callings. "Oh, Trick," they shouted, or, "Hey, Goldbrick, look up here." And if Brick looked up, he saw a fan waving a dollar bill. And he wondered if he'd ever get immune, and if he did, would they know it, and invent new insults.

A pitch came in too low, bouncing in front of him and kicking up against his thigh, and he danced in pain, and then stopped. For the crowd laughed, it actually laughed, and the pain drained off as astonishment replaced it. Oh no, he thought, not that. They're not really going to wait for me to bleed. And from his memory surged the thought of two nights ago when he heard the words of the telegram over the phone, and he knew Cathy was across the room.... *I'd die for her....*

For Cathy, he'd die, but first for these brutes with rain-checks, he might have to bleed, and that hurt. He whipped the ball back to Adcock, a blistering throw that stung the pitcher, and Brick could see the snarl form on his face. Three pitches later Brick got his answer, as a "straight" ball suddenly veered in toward his meat hand. Brick took it full in the palm, getting his hand open the very last second, and the pain jolted him to the elbow.

"Cut it," he snapped, and threw the ball back.

Adcock shrugged. "Slipped," he said. And threw again, this time straight.

But Brick knew it had started, and when no one was on base, and the count was no balls and something, Adcock might try it again, and there was nothing he could do. Except take it....

Five minutes later, at two o'clock on the nose, the Outlaws trotted out to take their positions on the field, and Brick snapped on the harness, pulling it tight, feeling it up against his ribs, and closeting his calves. A whistle blew from the dugout, and across a cheap PA system came first the recording of *God Save the King* and then *The Star-Spangled Banner* while the players stood at attention and the crowd got to its feet. And then, as in the old days before stadiums became mechanized, a short, bald-headed man went around the field, holding a megaphone and pointing his voice to the crowd. "The batteries for today's game," he yelled. "For Victoria, Hillsdale, number 27, pitching, Kuno, number 9, catching." There was a spasm of applause, and then silence. "For Osage, Adcock, number 24, pitching, Palmer, number 33, catching."

And Brick froze, the words *thirty-three* piercing his ears and reaching his brain, and he whirled trying to see his uniform shirt. Why, they wouldn't, he thought, and then he knew they would, and did. His old number, a number that meant treachery and shame, burned in a trash can of pungent gasoline, burned forever into the memory of baseball fans as a symbol of degradation. And once again it rode his back.

Somewhere he heard a man behind him call, "Play ball," and he saw the shadow of a batter approach him, go by, and stop. And Brick Palmer sank into a crouch behind the plate, trying to adjust his mask so he could see, but it wasn't the bars of the mask, it was the tears that stung and filled his eyes, and blinded him. Automatically he turned his head to look to the dugout for instructions, finding Addison first in a swimming haze, and then the man opposite on the bench, and he somehow forced the tears to dissolve so that he could see the hands on the knees, *curve.*

He pivoted back and he gave Adcock a target, and while his mind remained back there with the number 33, his mouth opened, and from his throat came tumbling the old words, "Put 'er there, baby, nobody hits, nobody hits." And he waited, steady as a rock, the glove unmoving, under the batter's hands, while Adcock wound and threw and the ball came up like a kid's balloon and the bat hitched back a couple of inches and then lashed around and missed, and the voice behind him said, "Stuh-rike." The game had started....

Chapter VII

And right away he went to work, dusting off the flecks of rust, putting things where they belonged in his mind. An unknown batter from a two-bit team named Victoria hitched two inches before he stepped forward... *he'll never hit the fast ball.* A southpaw who threw from his arm and not from his hip... *he'll go six, maybe seven, but that's all.* A curve ball that came dancing in slowly and broke big and round... *he'll have to have more than that, nobody'll miss that pitch second time around.*

Brick turned for his signal, got it, the straight fast ball, and once again he put his target on the inside corner. The pitch came in, medium fast, right across the center of the plate, and once more the batter hitched, swung, and missed. And the crowd, four thousand of them, roared its approval.

A lead-off man, Brick thought, what must the rest of the club look like? Once more he faced the dugout, once more the signal came flashing out to him, the screwball. Addison knew he did not need to tell Brick how to use the signals, Palmer had been around. Brick gave the left-hander the sign and held his glove an inch or two off the outside corner. Let the pitch come in, looking like the straight one aimed to nick the outer edge of the plate, and then watch it break away from the right-handed batter for a swinging strikeout.

The strategy was perfect, except Adcock didn't have that kind of control, his toss coming in at the hands, and then breaking for the center of the dish, and Brick started to freeze behind the plate, waiting for the hitter to tee off on the little curve. And instead, with two strikes on him, the lead-off man slid his right hand up his bat and delicately bunted the ball out in front of the plate.

Brick was off his haunches and out onto the grass, his left hand held up, warding off Adcock who had come lumbering from the hill, and then his right scooped up the ball, twenty feet from the plate, and he whirled, cocked his arm, and started to throw.

At that very moment, Adcock blasted him, running him down, groping for the ball as though he had a play on it, and the two went rolling, Brick underneath. And Brick's first thought was, "Did I throw it away?" and then he felt the ball still in his grip, and he rolled free, to keep the runner from taking an extra base.

It wasn't until then that Brick realized what had happened. Adcock, he knew, had deliberately blasted him, and the crowd heaped its abuse on Brick as though it had been he who erred. He turned to the plate ump and called for time and walked out to the mound. Adcock was at the rosin, unconcerned, his back to Brick.

"Don't," Brick said, his mouth six inches away from Adcock's ear, "don't, or I'll break you in two."

Adcock turned on him. "What do you mean?" he said. "You looked like you was losing the ball."

"That's why I had it in my hand even after you rolled me?" Brick said, his voice low and drenched in all the sarcasm he could bring to bear.

Adcock started to turn away, but Brick tapped his arm, and he came back. "Well," the pitcher said, "that's how it looked to me."

"No wonder your control's so lousy," Brick said, "you can't see so good," and he walked back to his position.

The second Victoria batter stepped in, a burly left-hander, with legs like trees. Brick remembered what Addison had said, "They hit and run every time they get a man on base," and he got the signal, his mitt on the outside to keep the man from pulling to right field. The Outlaws had shifted to the right, all but the first baseman, holding the bag.

Brick wondered as Adcock lowered his arms to the balk position whether they'd be running with the pitch, or waiting, and as Adcock kicked suddenly, Brick got his answer. The Victor was on his way, streaking for second, and Brick started to shift his feet, the ball coming for the outside corner. But before a play could be made, the batter stepped back, hitched decisively to the rear and rapped Brick's bare hand with the willow.

The catcher managed to flap his glove at the ball and drop it at his feet, but there was no time for the play, and Brick turned to the umpire, once again calling time. "Look," he said, "I know I'm not going to get anywhere with this, but let's not be so obvious. He interfered with me and you saw it and I got the welt on my knuckles to prove it, but I don't figure anything's going to be done, now. But let's make believe we're playing a game of ball, huh?"

And the umpire opened his mouth and spat into the dust, "Turn around, Palmer," he said. "Suppose we make the rules around here." He fidgeted with his ball and strike indicator, and Brick knew it was to be a pattern. Anything went, so long as it hurt him. He moved back into position, and he thought, with a grin, "Five hundred bucks for a month, and I bet I don't last an inning of it." And a second later, he was saying, "All right, baby, put 'er there, nothing to worry about, baby boy."

Adcock threw the curve, and the left-hander fell away from it, and then lunged at it as the ball started to wheel over. A foul pop went skittering off the end of his bat, Brick spotting the ball arching for the railing between home and third, and he was on his way, the mask flung off with a single jerk of the head, his head up, on the ball as it started to come down. It would be the railing, he figured, his memory trying to tell him how close he was, for he knew no fan would yell warning. The railing, a couple of feet either way, maybe, but somewhere around the railing.

And then it was coming down with a rushing swish and he could see the blur of faces and just as he felt the breath of the front row fans he hit the rail at the waist and started to catapult over, his glove twisted above his head in a frantic last stab at the ball. He heard the intake of air once more, and even a fraction of a roar from the fans, and then he was down, face buried into the cold wooden benches.

But he couldn't stay there, he knew, for the ball was in his glove and two things were clicking in his mind... the runner on second breaking for third after the catch... and, who knows, they might say he picked the ball from the ground or never had it long enough for a fair catch. And so he twisted away, the roar still in his ears, and he turned and threw to third base and saw the dust kick up as the Victor ploughed in, and then he saw the ball spinning three feet away from the third sacker, and Brick retreated to the plate, just in case.

The action was over, the dust slowly settling on the hard ground, before Brick rebuilt the play. He had caught the foul fly for the first out, and his throw had eluded the third baseman on the attempted double play, but more than that, he had wrung a cheer from a few fans caught off guard by the catch. And also, he felt the stiff pain jolt his ribs and beneath his cap he could feel a lump forming on his skull, over the right ear, and he knew he had banged his head on the bench. But though the pain was there, ribs, head, and forever legs, he didn't hurt.

Baseball, he thought, it's wonderful, and he crouched and let his peppery tongue throw out encouragement to the stolid-faced left-hander on the hill. But nobody answered, the blond stringbean at first silent and unmoving, the second baseman bending for some invisible pebble, the shortstop staring at his glove, the third baseman wetting the fingers of his right hand. And nobody saying a word, letting Brick's words bleat out empty and hollow, one man trying to sound like a team, and sounding like less than one man.

And he knew the fans were miserable, but the team, the team, not even a semblance of a cheer could he shake from their tongue-tied souls. It was the fans he could count on—oh, not for adulation—but for the instinctive reaction to the thing of daring and beauty. They came to abuse a man they hated, but when they saw his graceless courage as he teetered on the railing edge, even their cheap tinhorn hearts could not help but leap.

He shook his head, and waited for Adcock to throw, and he hoped the lefty's arm was already aching, and he hoped at the same time the lefty's arm would fog the ball through, and to his amazement, it was the second thought that was the more solid.

The infield had drawn in, hoping to chop down the run at the plate, and Brick grinned at the irony of it. At least now they'd have to play with him, rely on his blocky body, his glove, his hands. Their throw had to be true, or it was nothing. And Brick looked out at each face, close enough now to be studied, and his grin froze, for he saw the indecision weighing on each of them, *how far could they go?*

Would they sacrifice runs, Brick thought? Would they kick away a ball game just to make their fellow Outlaw look bad? He straightened a bit, leaned forward under the bat and came off his heels, balanced for Adcock's pitch. The fast one it was, to the number three man, big and rangy with *hitter* written all over him. And the Victor took all the pressure off the fidgety Osage infield. He stepped smoothly and swung easily, hitting off the hips and letting his wrists break as he met the ball, and he cast his head just briefly towards left field before he started running. And at first base he slowed down to a trot, the inexorable trot of the home run hitter who has cleared the wall and who knows it. The Victors led 2-0, in a third of an inning.

Brick started out to the mound, but already the infield had clustered around Adcock, their backs forming a semicircle that would have forced Brick to come around by first or third to break into the conference. Instead he turned and looked into the dugout. But there he got no warmer reception. Addison stared out stonily, and Brick thought, *he quits too easy*.

He settled into his rocking-chair squat while the infielders scurried back to position, and he kept his mouth shut. And in a second's time the air was filled with chatter, whistling, crackling chatter that poured out of third, short, second, first, even popping from the dugout well. Brick opened his mouth, and closed it. He could shut them up with one phrase, but he wouldn't. Let them rip, it's good for the team, and now he heard the fans talking it up, warming to the job of lifting Adcock from his mediocrity and from his 2-0 deficit.

And Adcock responded. He was in tight with his curve, flirting with the outside corner with the screwball, and the once-in-a-while fast one, coming right after the butterfly roundhouse, looked twice as swift. He got by the next two men, and after Osage had gone down one-two-three in their half of the inning, the left-hander picked right up and retired the side with not a ball hit out of the infield. And all the time Brick was silent, while Sweeney, the third baseman, yelped and yodeled; Rostelli, the shortstop, whistled and hollered; Furman, the second sacker, bellowed, clawed dirt, leaped and reared; and Muller, the blond first baseman, outdid them all with a double-talk gibberish that meant nothing but perked everybody up.

Brick Palmer, for all that came out of his throat, was not even at the park. But, in the dugout, Addison watched his $500 investment use his glove and his head in an exhibition of professional skill that made all the noise seem like a high school cheering section. His glove was always right, hugging the corners, taking his chances with Adcock's control, and always winning. A foul-tipped third strike he took in that glove, smothering its spin and fooling the crowd into thinking it had been a clean miss. And when Adcock fell behind three-and-nothing on one hitter, he examined the ball, turned it back to the ump, got it back again, returned it with a finger pointing to an invisible spot, got it back again, shrugged his shoulders, and fired it to third, where Sweeney sent it around the horn before it returned, the same ball, to Adcock. And the left-hander by this time had sucked in a couple of extra breaths, the tension draining away while the ball changed hands, and when he delivered again, the ball was where he wanted it. And so was the next one. And the next one.

Brick walked slowly to the dugout after that last pitch, to pull off his protector and guards. He batted fourth in the Osage order, and he wondered about the crowd as he stepped out to lead off the second inning for the Outlaws.

They saw him from the moment his head appeared outside the dugout, and they greeted him. The noise was a thunder, low and deep and menacing. It rolled out at him as he marched into it, and it grew with each step. No one voice could be heard, a joined mob they had become. He reached the batter's box, shaken by the sound, but more shaken by a feeling inside that he scarcely recalled ever having felt before. And he knew it was physical fear.

Slowly he put his bat down, slowly he straightened, each move twisted out of a body that strained to run. He wiped his hands slowly down his trouser legs, wiping off the sweat that clung to the wrinkles of his palm and invaded the hair at the back of his hands. He stopped there, his hands at his sides, and then he raised them, slowly, to his cap, while the crowd roared its wave of anger and hate. And he stiffly put his fingers to the peak of his cap, removed his hat, and bowed to the fans. First he bowed to the fans behind third base, reaching out to the left field fence; then he pivoted and swayed his body clumsily, stiffly from the waist, to the spectators behind the plate, and then to those behind first. And for a brief, startled moment, the wave broke, took on a sharper, shriller note, like the desperate cry of hyenas, and then resumed its even roll, deep and unending.

But he had reached them, Brick knew, and he felt elated as he stepped in to face the Victor pitcher. Maybe not today, or tomorrow, or the next day, but sometime before the season ran out its string he'd break that thunder in their throats, stifle it, and turn it to cheers. Not just cheers from a few, but from them all. He'd do it, he swore, if he had to beat in their heads with a baseball bat.

And then he was flat on his back, the dust all around him. The Victor pitcher's first delivery had smoked in, at his head, and Brick threw himself backward, the bat flying off. He just beat the ball, hearing it pop into the catcher's glove as he fell back, a pitch far more serious than any ordinary duster.

Brick had called for dusters throughout the years he had spent in baseball. When a man had dug in too close, too confident, the swift one came in at him, up close to his chin, driving him back and maybe loosening him so that he didn't get such a toehold the next pitch. But there's a difference between the duster that is aimed at the chin, or even at the temple, and the pitch that flies in at the batter, directed to hit him behind the ear, at the back of his head. When a man pulls back from such a pitch, he pulls his temple right into line with the ball for one frightening second. And then he's either away from it, sprawled on his back, or the pitch has crushed in his skull, and a career, a life perhaps, is ended.

Such was the pitch Brick barely avoided, a cannonball at the back of his head. And as he dug his way out of the dust and dirt, he once more heard the fans, pitched way up high, in that unearthly laugh of the bloodthirsty. He stepped out of the box again, and wiped his hands and saw that they were shaking. *Quit it,* he thought, *you knew it had to be this way.* He ran his hands up and down the bat, until the tremor left him, and then he started back, standing lightly in the box, his feet moving a bit, like a busher's. And as he started back he was thinking.

If he were behind the plate, calling for the next pitch, what would it be? The batter was nervous, jumpy, scared maybe, certainly not eager to dig in. He had just avoided an inside high fast ball. How about a fast hook on the outside corner, fast because the batter was fidgeting, hitching a bit, feet not steady. A curve away from the bat because the hitter wasn't going to step in, and the end of his bat will never reach the outside corner. Or perhaps just the fast one, on the outside edge? One or the other, nothing else. Fast it had to be, and on the outside, and as the pitcher wound up, Brick edged forward to the extreme front of the batter's box where he'd be able to beat the curve before it broke, and the feet that were moving now stopped, and as the right arm pinwheeled at him, his toes found dirt and dug in, and he was ready.

It was swift, all right, on the outside corner and probably it would have curved had it ever reached the catcher's glove, but Brick was stepping into it, his bat a savage club in savage hands. The whiplash was a blur of beauty, the crack a noise of triumph, and the ball a blinding streak into right-center field, on the line between the outfielders, striking grass about 380 feet away from the plate and leaping through the converging men who backtracked hastily and raced to the fence.

And Brick was on his way, a strange race against a ball bounding off a fence, while four thousand people sat still and prayed somehow the ball would win. He turned first and knew the coach was there someplace, his arm swinging a go-ahead, and he headed for second and could see the action in front of him, a bit to his right. The center fielder had the ball eight to ten feet from the fence, just short of the 420-foot sign, and his arm went back and rushed forward and the tiny whiteness left his hand and got bigger, and Brick turned second, his right foot kicking dust from the inside corner of the bag.

Now the real race was on, for it was apparent even to the praying fans that Brick had had two bases sewed up. It was the next ninety feet that counted, an aging truck horse of a man, his legs pumping up and down, pounding the hard earth underneath, and a flying ball that had to stop once more, in short right-center field where the second baseman stood. And a second later, less even, the ball had disappeared into his glove, had been plucked out again and was on its way to third, on a line, a magnificent throw that threatened to bite the dirt six inches in front of the sack.

Twelve feet from the bag Brick went into his slide, his body thrown forward and to the right, the whole right side of his body aimed for the foul line behind the base, while his left foot went pointing into the base, ready to twist and grab a corner of the bag and stop the rest of the body from ploughing on past. It was a long, low slide, no legs kicked high, no spikes showing, no knee ready to smash in the third sacker's mouth. And just as he dipped into the slide, his right thigh taking the first shock of the fall, he saw the baseman bend and come forward, his glove a bit to the inside of third, and Brick knew he had the base made. His foot clipped the bag violently, his body twisted away, outside the foul line, and then the tag was made, the glove rudely smashed into his left leg, and the man tripped over him and fell on top, his hands pushing Brick.

But the foot held, and he twisted his body, throwing off the weight of the third baseman and getting up, quickly, disdainfully, the foot still holding the bag. And then he looked at the umpire and saw him throw his hand into the air and saw the mouth make the word, "Out!" but didn't hear it, because the crowd was howling its glee.

Why, he thought, it wasn't even close! Not even the obvious ones would they give him, and he bent his knee and pushed his head forward, anger leaping to his lips, but the words stayed throttled there, behind his teeth, and he just took it, took the lousy decision that tickled the crowd, and maybe cost the Outlaws a run.

He walked away, the laughter following him all the way to the dugout, and he sat there and wondered what he was supposed to do. He heard a voice and looked up. It was Addison, calling him, and he walked over the lounging feet, sliding between Adcock and the manager. "Look," the old man said, his face weary, "don't you understand? You're out if the glove is anywhere near you. When you've got two bases, keep 'em, we need every runner. If there's a possibility of being thrown out, crawl back to the bag. They just won't give you anything."

"But I wasn't thrown out," Brick protested.

"No? Read the papers tomorrow. Some punk center fielder is going to have an assist, and some third baseman an out, and you'll have a double, not a triple. You were out. The ump said so. That's simple enough, isn't it?"

Brick shook his head. He knew Addison was right, but he found it impossible to believe an umpire not impartial. "Okay, okay," he said, "I'll catch on. Hit for three, take two."

The manager leaned back, satisfied. When he spoke again, his voice was softened. "That was nice, that hit. I didn't think you were ready."

Brick nodded. "These guys," he said, his hands sweeping to the Victors in the field, "they think out loud. The duster, then the outside pitch. The fast one, then the slow one. Like that," he said, pointing, as the next Osage batter went around on one leg, swinging too soon at the change of pace. Brick warmed to the subject, ignoring the men on the bench, riding their resentment and not caring, "It's like baseball from the book. A tall, skinny man can't hit a ball at his knees. A man who chokes his bat can't hit ditto. So on." He paused. "I guess it works, too, in this league." And he leaned back, and stared out at the field, and the hate came swarming off the bench to surround him. And inside, he laughed.

Addison nodded. "You're probably right." And then his voice regained its sharpness. "Except you're guessing too fast. Doesn't pay to case a league from two innings of play. Once a man asked me what kind of ball we play in this league, A or B or what. And I said I didn't know, but that an awful lot of people in Montreal come out here to watch us instead of the Royals. And that's Triple-A."

Brick stared at Addison. Triple-A ball was tops, outside of the majors. And then he remembered that throw, from short right-center field, by the Victor second baseman, the throw that bulleted in to third base, on the line all the way, and he remembered, too, how the second baseman had taken the throw from the center fielder and turned as he caught the ball, and released it as he turned, all in one fluid action. He stretched his memory back over the years, to Hughie Critz and Charlie Gehringer and Frisch and Gordon and Billy Herman, and he doubted that any of them had ever made a better throw.

The inning was over, and he was out into the squat again, and the game settled into a routine that football fans call monotonous, and baseball fans call baseball. It became precision baseball, the pitchers in command, the infield plays unspectacular and correct, the hits sharp but infrequent and never decisive. All there was to break the routine was the thunder that hovered over Brick Palmer's head, and even this seemed to lose its uniqueness merely by its unchanging quality.

The score remained 2-0 through the third and fourth, and Brick found himself picking up a bat to lead off the fifth, wondering whether he had not misjudged the league, or whether mediocrity versus mediocrity did not result in a contest so bitter that one forgot the ideal and settled for the relatively good. He was hitting—*had* hit—.336 for the Blues through the middle of August, and in his last year in the minors he batted .365, and he knew he was hitting better than ever. That meant he'd hit .365 or better, or else Addison was right about the calibre of play.

He had had time to study the Victor pitcher through four innings, and through two pitches, first hand. There was the big fast ball, smoky hot and with lots of lift, and there was a fair-to-middling curve, and a change-of-pace curve, and maybe that little slow wrinkle he threw sidearm was a slider. Two walks in four innings, five strikeouts, two hits.

There are high school pitchers with that sort of stuff, he thought, but back came the answer: *There also are major leaguers.* He shrugged his shoulders, postponing his decision, and he dug in, his mind on the pitcher, but his ears still hearing the steady wave beat down from the stands.

The first offering was in at the hands, and he took it, knowing it would be a called strike. Time he wanted, and a chance to see the rest of the stuff from the batter's box, the curve in both speeds, the slider, and whatever else lay in the sleeve. He crouched a bit, wigwagged once, twice, and held up, waiting, and the pitcher threw, sidearm, and Brick could see the whitened knuckle tips sticking out as the ball floated in, not a slider at all, but an ordinary knuckle ball, and Brick met it easily, stroking it, taking the power off his swing, for the big fly ball was not what he wanted, but the base hit. On a lazy line it went, over the shortstop's head, into short left-center field, and Brick steamed into first, rounded it wide and scurried back as the ball hurried into second. Two for two, he thought, 1.000. Bad, he thought, the law of averages would drop him .600 points in no time at all. And he grinned at the silent stands, the fans torn by the misery of rooting for Osage and hating the new Outlaw perched on first.

Rostelli, the shortstop, followed Brick, a rangy right-handed hitter who went for distance in batting practice, but who fouled out first time around. He swung late at the Victor's first pitch, the fast one, and Brick groaned inside. Another hitcher, a man who could overpower those fast ones, with wrists like that, but who never would until he smoothed the swing. But Brick could never say a word to help him, he knew, until the battle had ended, and they were playing on the same team.

He edged off first, not far, a snap throw might mean an out, or a spike might zip into his ankle or his hand. The pitch was the change-of-pace curve (*first the fast one, then the change-up*) and Brick wondered whether Rostelli had not heard his words in the dugout three innings back, for the batter stepped in and drilled it, and the score was tied the instant the ball landed on the other side of the left field fence, 340 feet away.

Brick trotted around, glad of the reprieve from running, the pain a silent companion of his legs. He stepped on home plate, and pointed down as he did so, catching the umpire's eye and ridiculing him with the gesture. Three strides from the plate Brick turned around, automatically, to extend his hand to Rostelli, and he fought back the rush of blood to his face as Rostelli ignored the hand and went prancing to the dugout. Never again, he thought, would he do them the honor. He slumped into the dugout, to hear the exultation of his teammates, and he felt like reaching over and grabbing Rostelli by the shirtfront and roaring into his impassive face, "Listen, you cheap bum, you owe me those two runs," and seeing how they'd react to the other Brick Palmer, the one who didn't sit and take it. But he didn't, and he couldn't.

And the game wore on, the afternoon sun turning useless once more, and the wind coming in to whip the dust in spirals at the plate where too many batters had ripped the ground through the long months behind. Brick breathed it in, the occupational disease of the catcher, and he thought that that wasn't so funny, look at poor Bill Delancey, the late Cardinal backstop.

Adcock was tiring, Brick knew, the screwball failing twice in the sixth, and again to the lead-off man in the seventh, and in the seventh the Victors took advantage of the lapse and broke the tie with a single run. And then filled the bases, with but one out. Brick called time and raced to the mound, before the infielders could beat him to it, and on the sideline he could hear the spat of a relief pitcher warming up. "How's it?" Brick asked mildly, wondering whether he'd get the turned back routine or just the guarded word. He got both. Adcock bent and picked up the rosin, and turned to face the outfield. "Okay," he said briefly, and stood there, staring into space. The interview was over.

But Brick opened it again. "I don't like you," he said, "any more than you like me. But I think you've pitched a nice game and I think you ought to take a nice shower before we're a dozen runs behind."

Adcock whirled, his mouth tight and his face gone white. "I didn't know your name was Addison," he said. "Since when do we take orders from you?"

Brick stood there patiently, for he knew no manager would stay in his dugout when the catcher was asking for a relief pitcher. And the shadow reached Brick first, then the sound of Addison's step, and then his cornbelt voice. "All right, Joe," he said, "you've done fine. I think you're tired." He put his arm around the hurler, and they walked off, and the crowd roared its appreciation for the six-plus inning stint. But before he reached the dugout, Adcock turned around and stared his hate at Brick, still at the mound, waiting for the reliefer.

That's two, he thought, Rostelli and Adcock. The rest would come later, but already there were two who detested him, and said so openly. He turned to the reliefer and wondered what this reaction would be. But the game had taken command, and the reliefer was all business. "I throw fast and low, not much of a curve, everything low, at the knees."

That's great, Brick thought. At the knees meant strikes in any other league, but with Brick Palmer catching, they were the same as wild pitches. "Hit my target," he said, "you must have control or they wouldn't be sending you out. Hit my glove, no matter how high I put it." He jogged back, and wondered what the blazes to do, and he wondered whether even Campanella could figure this one out. A walk meant a run and additional runs now probably would sew up the ball game. A pitcher who can hit the knees can make a man hit into the dirt, and with the bases filled that's what was called for. But they wouldn't be swinging, not with the umpire a tenth man on their side, calling every knee-high pitch a ball.

Well, he thought, they'd try the curve, the not-so-hot curve, because if it was not so hot maybe they wouldn't be expecting it; even in a Class D league word got around on which pitchers couldn't throw what. He faced the dugout, ready to walk over and tell Addison he wanted to try the curve, when he spotted the man at the end of the bench, hands on knees. The curve. Addison had figured it through right along with him, and he nodded his head at the bench, not in confirmation of the signal, but in admiration of the man's mind. A *major league mind*. This is the ball game, he knew, holding them off now so they could strike back, or losing them and never catching up. A 3-2 game could be salvaged, but the curve ball was the finger in the dike, and if it couldn't hold, what could?

The reliefer shook his head once, in doubt, but Brick flashed again, and the reliefer looked past him to the dugout and then imperceptibly shrugged, and nodded. Into the windup he went, and breaking free, the ball chest high on the inside, and the batter stepped in, swinging his chance for all the marbles. But the pitch broke, not suddenly, not much, just a quiver of a curve, enough to dip down and away, out of the home run slot and right into another. The slot that every pitcher wants, with the bases loaded and one man out, the slot that runs right back to the mound. The old come-back ball it was, a one-bounce smash to the box, and the reliefer speared it with his mitt at his shoulder, and then back to the plate it came, the throw to Brick for the force play, and Brick pivoted halfway and threw to first, past the straining runner, for the double play.

The inning was over, and with it, the game. Sometimes it happens that way, the critical play is made, and by its resolution every player, every fan in the park knows the game, too, has been decided. The score was 3-2 against the Outlaws, but in two turns at bat they were to go hit-crazy, going all the way around the order in the seventh for four runs, and piling two more on top in the eighth. Brick's contribution was small, an intentional pass, and a third hit, a single in the eighth after the rout had developed. The final score was 8-3, with Bobbett, the reliefer, opening up all the way, releasing his jagged fast ball past the beaten Victors, a steady stream of bullets into Brick Palmer's ever-loving glove.

Back in the steamy locker room they stepped, their enthusiasm for the job they had done a guarded thing, because among them was Brick Palmer. He found a corner, found it easily, for no one crowded in to swing an arm around his shoulder or to ask how the legs felt. Nor was there a trainer to set him up on the table for a quick rubdown, and Brick felt the knots forming more quickly than ever, first the cold air, then the steamy closed room and finally, the lukewarm shower. But as he dressed there was a man waiting for him, in the corridor. Addison, standing there, speaking a word to each man as he trooped out, but standing merely because he wanted to see Palmer.

Brick was out, last man to be dressed, and he was not surprised when Addison tapped his arm and drew him into his office. "It won't take more than a minute," he promised, as he swung behind his desk and pulled out a sheaf of papers. "Here's a batch of clippings on this league of ours, rosters of every team, the daily scores for the last month, and a book on the hitters. Not all of them, just those I could make book on." Brick knew what he meant. The rest of the batters, nobody knew. A fast ball struck one out today; yesterday the same pitch went over the fence. Another fanned twice in a row on the curve, and belted five straight hits next time around, same kind of pitch.

Brick took the papers and placed them in front of him, and looked at Addison to see if there was anything else. The old man tapped his finger on the desk and stared at Brick and tapped some more and finally spoke again. "One other thing, Palmer. I wanted to ask you what you'd've called for when they had the bases filled with one out in the seventh? You know, when we called in Bobbett." He waited for Brick to answer.

He's looking for the flaw, Brick thought. He wants to prove I'm a bum, that somewhere there's a streak in my ability, just as he thinks there's a streak in my person. Brick sucked in breath, and decided the hell with it. "The curve," he said simply.

Addison continued tapping his finger. "The curve?"

Brick nodded. *He doesn't believe me*, he thought. It was an old pattern now, not being believed. *None of it's true, Mr. Stutz, it's all a lie.* (Laughter) *I never got a blessed cent, Commissioner.* (Silence, scorn) *The curve.* (Finger tapping)

"All right, Palmer. See you tomorrow. We play Victoria again, same time." Addison leaned on his hands, preparing to get up. Brick turned and walked out, into the darkening twilight, and as the door closed behind him, Addison let his muscles relax and his weight was too much for his hands and he fell half forward, his head a foot from the desk top. He stayed in that position, shaking his head. "I dunno," he said, in a small whisper that died in the bare little office, "I dunno why he did it." He braced his arms once more and this time they held and he was up, for a last look at the locker room, and again his whisper crawled into an empty room, to fade away in a damp corner. "He plays like one of us, don't he, Joe?" And the answer, if indeed there was one, never got out of the damp darkness, nor did Addison wait for it. He closed the door swiftly, and was on his way back to the hotel to lie in bed and plot the next day's affairs, and to dream of pennant flags and World Series headlines, and always the headlines made him wake up....

CHAPTER VIII

Autumn came quickly, twenty days before its calendar promise, and Brick and Cathy, in their Chevvy, wondered what winter would be like, if an early September night was this cold. Two weeks had gone by since Brick Palmer joined the Outlaws, two weeks of pain and pressure.

They drove in from Malone, across the border, where another night game had gone into the dust of a scorer's notebook, and where Brick Palmer had finished his first series against the league-leading Maulers, two games up on the Outlaws, with two weeks to go. No rule on get-away contests, they'd be at night, maybe even a twi-night doubleheader, with a game scheduled fourteen hours after the last out, in some city forty rut-roaded miles away.

"Tired, hon?" Cathy asked, her head against his right shoulder, a touch of ghostly light in the eye-aching dark.

He nodded, his eyes glued on the road, trying to coax forty miles an hour from the Chevvy, so that the hotel would be less than an hour away, now.

Cathy shivered. For years she knew, Brick had carried the scars of baseball with seldom a word, the fractured skull, the broken fingers, the terrible aching thighs, the feet that collapsed and couldn't carry his weight, yet did. And now the scars were freshly cut open, and the blood was being laughed at.

Tonight, in Malone, for instance, she had seen him wince in the very first inning as he got into his squat. She saw him spilled by a runner in the fourth, and his face had twisted in pain.

Last week, at "home," he had staggered chasing a foul ball, and had gone to his knees. And for a second his body started to sink to the ground, and Cathy was half out of her seat, her fingers to her mouth to stifle the scream, but then he looked up and got to his feet, while the crowd laughed and pointed in derision.

On paper the two weeks had been a personal success. Brick was batting .389, twenty-three for fifty-nine at bats, five of them home runs, and he had driven in thirteen runs. Behind the plate they had charged him with two passed balls, once when Adcock crossed him up with a curve on the fast ball signal, and again when a pitch had hit the dirt to his left and bounced past on the hard surface, all the way to the screen, an obvious wild pitch, obvious to everybody but the scorer. But he had also thrown out three runners going down to second, while another had stolen successfully because a perfect throw had been jarred loose by a kicked spike.

During the two weeks, the Outlaws had closed the gap to one game, with thirteen to go. The team had united since Brick's arrival, united in a sullen, detesting club of eight, playing to win, yet hoping to do it without Brick's help.

But it wasn't all there on paper, those two weeks. In every game, at least once, he had been dusted, three times he had been hit, once a glancing pitch off the top of his head, and how the crowd had roared when Brick hadn't gone down, had merely stood there and rubbed the ache. A criss-cross of spike streaks went up and down his legs, testimony to the action at home plate, and his wrists and fingers were lanced bloody by zealous second basemen, playing the man instead of the bag.

And the fans, you couldn't put that down on paper. The size of the attendance, yes, that was there, the record stream of people who had jammed the parks of the Canadian-American Association, to see Brick Palmer step up and take his whipping. The words, a vocabulary of abuse and invective, a shrill chorus of indecency that came splitting out of the low rumbling thunder, never subsiding. In each new town it was the same, word had gone out that in Osage they had paper-cupped Brick, tossed pop bottles in Victoria, pulped fruit in Malone. His name was Goldbrick at "home," Trick in Malone, Money Bags in Absalom, and Itching in Waterbury. And all around the league the umps wouldn't give him the knees or the shoulders, just as Addison had predicted, the close plays at the plate always were safe, unless it was Brick who had come storming home.

But more than these, there was the knowledge that the two weeks had slowly cut down his huge strength, tore great holes out of his wind, branded him with pain that seldom budged even at night while he slept. His legs were trees, chipped and eaten by the worms of despair, and heavy as trees.

And the wind at night on the road, the cool, sunless days. They were breaking the man, Cathy knew, as she sat there in the car and counted the minutes until the hotel would come into sight and the old springs would creak as Brick lay there and, maybe, slept.

The lights of Osage hove into sight, dim and scattered over a tiny piece of land, an all-night saloon, a railroad crossing, a lumber mill, the hotel, a diner, and a few more saloons down at the other end of town. The Chevvy whined to a stop outside the hotel, and they got out and went upstairs, Cathy ahead, walking, for the elevator stopped running after 1:00 A.M., and even before unless you wanted to wake the underpaid operator.

Cathy pushed open the door, and they went in, stiff-legged and stumbling, fatigue crowding their eyeballs and shoving sand under the lids. They undressed in the dark, for light now, would hurt, and clothes were strewn over the nearest chair, on the doorknob of the closet, at the foot of the bed. And then followed the strangest ritual of all.

Brick lay face downward on the bed, bare from the waist up, his arms outstretched over and around his head, holding the rails of the head of the bed in a light grip. Cathy sat next to him, her fingers placed gently at the juncture of his head and neck, the fingers moving slowly, evenly, kneading the flesh, working it, trying to suck out the pain and return the elasticity of youth.

Her cool fingers on the brown muscles of his neck, at one-thirty in the morning, in a room that smelled of age and liniment.

"Cathy, Cathy," he murmured. "It isn't worth it."

Her fingers never ceased their rhythm. The neck, the shoulders, the great, wide, bent shoulders.

"It isn't worth it, hon. Not for this money or any. Where is it taking us?"

She went on, as though he had not spoken. Reaching in for the flesh, rubbing it with her fingers, hoping to transform it somehow to new flesh. She reached, she drew, she rubbed, she stretched, she released, and reached again, cool and gentle and kneading, and behind the fingers a face that showed up fading and yellow in the room of dust.

"Frozen bats," he said, "how do they expect a man to hit? Diamonds rocky here, mushy there. Pitchers who can't find the plate, or won't. They call it baseball."

On and on, reaching and working, and feeling finally the miracle of love and strain. The muscles started to warm, slowly, and in the night with her eyes closed Cathy could imagine the flesh starting to glow, like a baby's, and from her mind's eye she drew strength for her tired hands, the tiny muscles in her palms aching in a small ball.

"No rubdown before, no rub after, wind and dust. How can it be worth it?" His voice was small, like a child's, calling out in the dark for a helping hand to ward off the shadow patches of lions and tigers.

And the helping hand was there, at the shoulder, the right one, the bad one, giving it back something, something that might mean a thousand more throws to second. But while the flesh warmed up, Cathy felt no response from the heart within the flesh. "Any time at all," she said, "we can call it quits. I'm ready to go wherever you say."

The head went from side to side, slowly, but decisively. "No," he said, "we're here, we'll stick. If only—"

The fingers went on. "If only what, honey?"

The shoulders slumped, and Cathy was glad, for before they could not have done even this. "I don't know, don't mind me. I just have to gripe, I guess."

"Gripe," she said. "Go ahead, gripe."

He lay there silent, and the only sound was the touching of flesh against flesh. "It's more than that," he said finally. "It's more than just griping. It hurts so," he said, and his breath drew in sharply, to cut off the sob. "It just doesn't seem worth it."

"We can leave, Brick, we don't have to stay. We can go back, I can get a job in the store. There's no problem."

"The umps," he said, "chips on their shoulders, dirt in their eyes." And by his words, and more by his tone, Cathy knew he had not heard her. And she was glad. He was speaking aloud, yet to himself, castigating himself for coming up north, inflicting the pain on his already tortured body, and by that, releasing the chain around his guts. The slump to the shoulders, the long, deep breath that beat back the tears, all this was good, for the man was relaxing under his own punishment.

And she too went on speaking as though he were not there. "Or maybe it's time you get a job, like ordinary men, and I stay home, and have a baby." The fingers, pulling out the last length of elastic from the tired muscles, pulling slowly, gently, never losing the rhythm.

"It's not fair," he said. "How much are you supposed to bleed?"

"A child," she said. "That would be nice. A little girl."

His voice grew in volume and filled the shabby room. "What will I have when the month's over? Money to last another month, and a year's battering."

"A girl," she said, and now the direction to which she had forced her thoughts took over, and she spoke in a fantasy that was real behind her closed eyes. "Little fingers, pink and white, and a closet of dresses."

"Aches, and a check for half a grand, and no place to go. I come up a crook and I go back a crook. I wonder where my kid brother is?"

For a brief second the fingers stayed still, and then resumed. It was the first time Brick had mentioned Johnny, and not even this time by name. And his words tore her in two, up in the room where there was no light except the gold of her hair. It wasn't fair, she thought, and she wanted to smash something. But instead her fingers went on, with the patience of love. *He thought of Johnny when he said 'crook.'* But no, her heart murmured, it may have been when I said 'child.'

"Probably playing poker," she said, the last vestige of bitterness creeping into her words, and she was surprised.

"No," he said quietly, "he can't be. He's asleep or studying or on duty." Good lord, he thought, he mustn't let me down, how much can I stand.

She left one hand on Brick's back, fingers moving, and with her other hand she brushed hair from her eyes. Yes, she thought, he must be doing what Brick says. For only in Johnny was there reason for being up in the hotel room, at two o'clock in the morning.

He said it for her. "He's going to be all right, hon, he has to be. He'll grow up. He's—he's got to." He's got to, or else the world was chaos and there was no reason for Brick to be ducking the inside high one.

"Of course," she said softly, pressing her fingers a bit deeper in order that she might keep Brick from raising himself and turning before he was ready. "Of course," she said again, rotating her palms against the two heaps of muscle that lay at the side of his ribs. "Everything will be fine," she said. "Don't worry, he'll be fine."

He grunted into the pillow and nodded his head, his body sinking deeper into the mattress as he yielded to the constant pressure. "Sure he will."

"And so will we," she said, her hands careful and tender.

But the head went from side to side, in painful, slow dissent. "No," he said, "we won't. What'll we have, when it's over?"

She moved her own shoulders, to relieve the ache that was overtaking them. "What did you expect, hon? We came up to play ball and to see what would happen."

"And it happened, all right. The fans," he said, "what are they made of? Don't they know it's just a game?"

Very slowly she allowed herself to chuckle, the sound liquid and golden in the darkness. "No," she said, "to them it's not a game, it's a life. They live the games. Like you do. And you're no kid."

"No," he said, "I'm no kid. I'm hardly an anything any more. I must be a hundred years old."

Reach in, she thought, you've lost him, and it's two-thirty and there's a game in less than twelve hours, and he's slipping back, his body going stiff. She reached and pulled, and kept silent. Too much talk, she thought, he's thinking, and no man should think at two-thirty. Nor woman, she added, as her hand went automatically to her hair, and brushed it from her still closed eyes.

"I'm old," he said. "Old and washed up. Two weeks to go."

Two weeks, she thought, sitting here in the room at night and bringing him his strength, a few minutes at a time. The body gave again, and she reached in with more hope.

"One hundred and ninety pounds of ache. Every finger split. Every muscle crying. It's not worth it."

Just a play of a card, she thought, just a play of a card. The kid brother went yellow and signed Brick's name, and here they were on a hotel bed, half dead from fatigue and pain.

"Tomorrow I'll pull a muscle, it happens every other day and it didn't happen tonight. But tomorrow I don't get spiked. That happened today."

And every day you lie in the dust, she thought, and they laugh. All because the kid didn't have it, and he signed the name.

"Tonight," he said, "I thought Addison was going to smile at me, after the home run. He must have counted the house."

A wild pack they were, the fans. They jeered him after the home run, while he ran the bases and cut the lead to one game. And in return, Addison almost smiled. She shuddered, though the old window was closed fast and the steam pipe rattled and choked.

"How much longer?" he said. "You should be asleep."

She shook her head. "Just a bit more. You're coming along fine."

"What for?" he said. "They start to yowl, and I'm tight as a drum. They dust me off, once, and I'm tense the rest of the game."

"Yes," she said, "but what would happen if you weren't relaxed that first time?"

He nodded. "You're right. Only it seems so futile. Maybe it's the first pitch of the game, but sometimes not even that good. Maybe it's in batting practice."

She sucked in a breath. That she hadn't known. "They throw at you in batting practice? I hadn't noticed."

"Once in a while," he said. "Not at my head. Too obvious. A fast one at my feet, bouncing two feet in front of me and taking me in the shin or the knee. Just a slip, of course."

"Does Addison say anything?"

"Not a word." He spread his arms. "What does he care? He told me I play every game and so far I have. If I haven't quit by now, he figures I won't at all. What's a baseball rammed into your leg?"

"Even so," she said, "it's good you're ready for even that."

"Ah," he said, "but even being ready doesn't do any good. I stand outside the dugout before the game, and somebody's pepper game explodes, and a ball goes whizzing by my head. What good to be ready? My back is always turned."

"The men," she said, in a low voice, unbelieving, "they do that?"

"Who knows?" he said. "Somebody does it. Either it's batted or thrown, and there's always a pepper game going on when it happens. Somebody just lets go with a wild heave, or hits one too hard, and I happen to be in the way." He laughed, harsh, just once. "So what good is it? It's not worth it."

For a fleeting moment she almost believed he was right. It wasn't worth it, not when you play against your team, your manager, the fans, as well as the other club. But where her mind was formulating, her fingers decided. On they went, rotating and plucking, rubbing and stretching. "We've got to do it, though, and we'll do it as well prepared as we can."

"Yes," he said, but doubt carried his words, "as well as we can."

Five minutes more, she thought, her body on a pinnacle, swaying above the bed, ready to cave into the mattress. "It will be well enough," she said. It has to, she thought.

"Sure," he said, "just scrape the pieces together, get some scotch tape, and put a mask on it."

She opened her eyes and looked down at his body, the feeble light in the room seeming brighter than it really was, after her eyes had been closed tight so long. She ran her hands over his back, feeling the warmth and knowing she had won. "Send it up to the plate in a wheel chair?"

He laughed, and his body rose suddenly and then gave just as suddenly. He had yawned. "Well, you've done it again," he said. "My own little Lefty Fisher, except prettier." His body shifted deeper into the mattress.

"Was it worth it, then?" she asked, softly, watching his face, trying to find some light that would tell her his eyes were still open, but finding none.

"Was it?" he said, half to himself. "I don't know. Maybe it was, I just don't know. Tell you about it tomorrow, go to sleep, honey. Thank you, angel." He breathed deeply and slowly.

She stayed over him, her hands resting on his back, feeling it rise and fall, rise and fall, a half dozen times, a dozen, and then she lost count. But still she sat, until she knew, and then she bent her head to his back, and laid her cheek against him, feeling his heart pulse, steady and strong. She sat up, straight again, and her words could scarcely have been heard even by an awakened man. "Yes, darling, it's worth it. Every minute of it."

She rose from the bed and stood still, afraid to move lest the creaking floor rouse Brick. Finally she went, in her stocking feet, to the bathroom down the hall, and she stared at herself in the mirror, seeing the lines that he never saw, and she opened the medicine cabinet and took out the cold cream and peroxide. He must not know, she thought, he must never know—it would kill him.

Her fingers dipped into the cream and went to work against the tiny lines that crowded her eyes and nostrils. And then the tips of her hair regained their girl color as she touched the peroxide to her fingers and then to her head. She left the bathroom quickly, hating her presence there, and tiptoed back into their room. She crawled into bed, bone weary and pained, and she insisted on crowding another thought into her mind before sleep took over. "Worth it," she thought, "every minute."

Sometime in the early morning, he reached out and brought her close to him, and they slept that way until nine.

CHAPTER IX

The first news appeared in a UP dispatch, out of Montreal, and the first paper in the big city to grab it was the *Herald*. They buried it deep in the sports section, down where the trotting races get their play, just above the two-line fillers that tell you Babe Ruth hit 714 home runs in his big league career.

That afternoon the other sheets had it, a bit developed, still rather aimless as though the editors knew there was news in the item, but not knowing exactly what the news was.

And so the sports fans all over the country learned about Brick Palmer, ex-major league catcher, cashing in on his lousy press as he caught the dubious pitchers of an independent league on the Canadian border. His hitting exploits, the standing of the club, and the size of the crowds, that was all the UP man sent down, and that was all the newspapers had to go on.

That was more than enough for Randy York who wrote, on September 12, an extremely learned column on the foibles of human nature, how a man proved guilty of a treacherous crime (doing in his fellow teammates was, according to York, as serious an offense as swapping A-bomb secrets with the enemy), how a man presumed guilty until proved innocent had turned his folly into a money-making proposition. And wasn't this, went on York to his avid followers, typical of soft-hearted people all over (soft-headed, too, he implied), letting themselves be taken in by such a man. Wasn't Barnum right after all.

And a million heads nodded the correct answers at the correct times, and while their heads nodded, inside someplace there beat a full-blooded pulse, and the mob that is in each man reached out clutching fingers to grab this evil thing called Brick Palmer and throttle it. And a million as yet unspoken voices were added to the thunder of hate that swept across dingy ball fields up north.

Every day, now, there appeared a piece on the daily doings of the tarnished Goldbrick, his hits, runs, and errors, and the number of people who saw them. And as the league-leading Blues, Brick's former club, lost ground daily to the onrushing Tigers, comment was made in each day's story of the importance of Brick's crime, how badly the team had played since he had been barred, how young Fletcher behind the plate had failed to carry the big bat.

But every day, even with the rampaging Randy York lambasting Palmer, a small section of fans found themselves confused as to loyalty. For with each mention of Brick in the *Herald's* sports pages, there appeared a picture, from the newspaper's library. And somebody on the picture desk was passing on shots of Brick Palmer in his days of glory, the catcher crossing the plate after hitting a home run, his teammates shaking his hand, or Palmer braced at the plate, putting the ball on a sliding runner, defying spikes, knees, and the heel of a wandering hand. And while the fans, just a few of them, started wondering how come a guy with guts like that and who was liked by his own men like that could also be the same guy Randy York talked about; and while they were wondering, Timmons, the little photographer, innocently slipped in another picture, working nicely with his friends on the big desk, and more fans started wondering.

And in a short week, only the down-the-wire thrill of the major league pennant races, crucial series piling upon crucial series, had more appeal to the reader than the flag duel going on over the border. With their morning toast stiffening in their fingers, sports fans turned to their inside pages, sweeping past the news of the world, to see how the Blues had made out, and how Palmer's team was doing. And in the relentless way that chills a fan's spine, the Blues were fading, while the Outlaws kept coming, and the hate kept building as the league's darlings toppled from their perch, and the bully with the brass knucks slugged down the white-haired boys. It was not fair. Right was not winning.

The pool rooms heard the first real rustlings. It was the crinkling noise of green bills passing hands, the only real sound of the betting man, putting up. And in every gambling hall that masqueraded as a pool room a new white inning-by-inning scoreboard went up, listing the Outlaws and their daily opponents. The play was heavy, sentiment versus sense, the Outlaws running as high as 2-1 (9-11) against the second division clubs, 7-5 against the three- and four-spot teams, and even-six over the leading Maulers.

And when the Outlaws dropped one, the laughter in these halls was framed in cynicism, and the lips that issued the sound were white and thin, for the gamblers never knew whether Brick Palmer was maybe throwing a ball game for the do-re-mi.

Not all the gamblers, though. The big wheels who operated behind loan company offices and dead real estate fronts knew of the Palmer deal, and how he had been tapped for ten gees, and how he had kept his mouth shut to protect a kid brother. They knew that Palmer was broke, and playing for keeps, and their dough was compounding every day, and the odds on the Outlaws kept rising as the steady stream of smart money poured in.

But not even this was the real shrewd money. That was localized in one man, a skinny, gaunt-faced tool of a fat, florid-faced mob. He was the messenger boy punk who had met Brick Palmer in the lobby of the Statler and started the spitballs rolling. He was the same young man, seersuckered, cologned, flame-tied, and smelling faintly of rot as he breathed through his teeth. There was one difference. His nose had been sharply changed, the fine thin blade humping once at the bridge and twisting down at an angle. Around the nostrils there remained a tiny rawness, as though water had been assiduously applied over a period of weeks. As it had.

And inside there lived a bright, ugly light that burned all the time now, a light that poked and probed and found the dark hellholes of a twisted man's soul. Revenge was the light's name and it would burn until its beams fell upon Brick Palmer, and then it would flare once in bitter, terrifying brilliance before it expired.

The punk's name—not his real name, of course, that he had so long ago stopped using he seldom recalled it—was Pete Peterson, and the handful of smaller fry in the gang called him Petey. To the men, he was Boy.

And so it might seem surprising that the two men who hovered over Pete Peterson, men whose shoulders filled their wide jackets, whose bull heads towered six inches over the punk's—that these two men called him, respectfully, Petey. But where their muscle left off, nothing took over. This was the small fry of the mob, the clumsy, unthinking clubs that formed the first echelon of attack, the strange brute-men who pitched bricks through the windows of uncooperative shopkeepers, who patiently twisted arms behind backs until tendons stretched and snapped, who brought down the billies.

They stood in the shadows of the pool hall and spoke behind the click of balls and the rasp of tallies being racked up. "You understand," Pete said, "you might have nothing at all to do?"

The bull heads nodded. "But," said one, in a high-pitched voice, as though clutching hands had wound around his windpipe and left some irremediable lump in his throat, "but we get paid anyway?"

"Yes," Pete said, patiently, though this had been said many times before, "yes, you get your C-note, no matter what."

"Just for sitting there," insisted the other, "for doing nothing at all?"

"Look," Pete said sharply, "I'm buying insurance, that's all. Maybe he'll come across quick, with no persuasion." He looked from one to the other, and they hung on his words, like shaggy dogs waiting their bones. "Or maybe he won't. Then I need you. For that I'm willing to pay you each a hundred."

"And if he don't," high voice squealed, "we give him the works."

"Everything goes, you said," the other one spoke, "no rules or nothing."

Pete nodded, and the light inside grew in intensity as he fed on the fantasy of the two men beating Brick Palmer down into the ground while he stood and watched. "No rules. Just beat him down. And keep right on beating. I want him broken, so he can't bend or pick up a bat."

The two men stood silently, absorbing the words, their tongues moving once across their lips and their hands clenching in their pockets. It was beyond them, the motivation for such an action. Why anybody would give two hundred dollars for a couple of words or for a severe beating was not to be answered from the shallow convolutions of their dull minds. Their role they understood perfectly. Theirs was the glory, the power held in reserve until needed, and then exploding in savage fury.

"You'll take your knucks, your blackjacks," Pete reminded them.

They nodded, and felt instinctively for their back pockets where the knucks lay.

"Don't wait to use them. If you have to slug him, use them. Everything goes." He coughed suddenly into a handkerchief that appeared from nowhere. He spat into it and stared curiously at the lump of phlegm. "Slug him," he said ferociously, and the two men felt a strange warmness inside them, and they leaned a bit from their waists, their bodies swaying, their fists digging into their palms. "I don't care if you kill him."

Just as each hood ground his fist into the meat of his left hand, Brick Palmer tapped the pocket of his big glove. But his face was still, gray and drawn. His eyes flickered down the third base line where a rival runner strayed from the bag. The score was 1-0, Outlaws, and there was one away in the ninth. Pennington, the knuckle baller, studied Brick's glove, faced third, went into a stretch, and came down, breaking off a dinky curve on the inside corner. The batter swung and drove a ground ball towards the hole between short and third. Sweeney moved to his left and came up with the big bounce. The runner wheeled off third, racing a quick half-dozen steps toward the plate, and Sweeney pivoted to bluff him back to the bag, and then he turned and threw hurriedly, into the dirt at first. But Muller gloved it for the second out of the inning and then he was straightening to throw, for in from third streaked the runner. Muller's throw was high and on the third base side of the plate.

Brick went into the air and grabbed the toss, and let himself come down directly in the path of the runner. No attempt to make the delicate tag, but just plaster himself all over the man and keep him from reaching the plate. For he knew the ump would never see the tag. He landed on his knees first and then his upper body flattened down on the sliding runner and he felt spikes drive into his thighs, and his body trembled as it wanted to give ground, but it stayed. The whole play ended up twenty inches from home plate, with Brick jabbing the ball a dozen times into the runner's side, holding it so tight his knuckles were whiter than the ball. And the umpire finally jerked his thumb over his shoulder and walked away. The game was over.

Brick Palmer drew himself to his feet and let his gloved left hand hang over the ripped uniform trouser leg where the blood bubbled through the tear and started its descent to the ankle.

And as Brick walked off, by himself, the players stood in small clusters and stared at him, and Muller shook his head and said, "Damned if I can figure him," and Rostelli said sharply, "What's the matter, getting soft?" and immediately the shortstop wondered why he'd said that, for he, too, was unable to figure Brick Palmer.

Above the dugout a couple of fans stood and watched as Brick neared the well, and they could see the tear in Brick's trouser leg and they could see the blood, and they also wondered, for the first time, how come. Do crooks bleed, they asked themselves, and inside gave up a grudging answer, no, not usually. And respect, silent respect, started to build in two fans who had come to the stadium to shout insults at a crook.

The crook hobbled down the two steps and into the corridor. *One more,* he thought, *one more. Ten to go, and I quit....*

Back in the city, in a little hotel room that lit and darkened and lit again as a neon ad flashed and died and flashed, Pete Peterson lay on his back, a damp cigarette at his lips, and smoke curling to the ceiling. Next to him, on the bed was a slip of paper. It was an IOU, and the signatures on it were those of Brick and Johnny Palmer. The amount was for $10,000. It was a carbon copy of the original note Brick had seen once before, in the Statler lobby.

Once more, Pete thought, *once more, right from the beginning.* No slips were possible, he knew, but there was a joy akin to lust every time he thought it through. Ten games to go, up there in Canada, and the Outlaws were tied for first place. The Outlaws might win them all and the Maulers lose four, and the season was over. Or the Maulers might take seven and the Outlaws only three and that would end the race. But the kid knew the odds against either happening were good, and he was playing the good money.

More likely they'd hit those last three games with no more spread than two games between them, one was more probable, and none likeliest yet. And those three last games saw the Maulers move into Osage for the final series of the year.

If the Maulers held the edge going into the final three, Pete would keep his hand in check, placing modest hundred dollar bets on the Outlaws to win each next game, until they drew even, and then he'd move, putting the pressure on Brick Palmer, and betting five thousand on the result.

He stopped his thoughts, they were getting ahead of him. He picked up the slip of paper, the first convincer. Meet Palmer in the lobby, point to the two bully boys behind him, just to caution the big slob, and then show him the slip. Then they'd go upstairs, to Palmer's room, all four of them. They'd lock the door. He'd tell Palmer.

Look, he'd say, I tell everybody about the kid brother unless you play ball.

Palmer would want to know what he meant. And he'd explain, just like the last time, all he'd have to do was let a couple of pitches get away, and forget to hit. That's all.

And Palmer would see he had him. And that was all.

But if it wasn't, then the boys would put Palmer out of style for a bit, bust him up, and the Outlaws would play without him, and the bet would be just as solid, the five thousand riding on the Maulers at the early odds which would be plenty high, maybe even 2-1.

He started to grin at the thought, and then the grin broke into another sharp cough and a fleck of blood appeared at his shirt front, and he lay on his back, his hand clenching tight the little slip of paper. He lay with his eyes closed and quickly he let his thoughts go back to the beginning, and once more he acted out the play, except this time he didn't grin at the conclusion, but kept his teeth tight together and breathed deep to forestall the cough. And finally he relaxed and slept, fully dressed, as though he were afraid he'd have to go some place before morning....

While Pete Peterson slept, Johnny Palmer, the young interne came off duty at the hospital, stuffed clothes into his bedding to simulate a sleeping body, and changed to his civvies. The time was two in the morning, and his first hospital task would not occur for five hours. Which gave Johnny plenty of time for a couple of quick drinks, and a turn at the roulette wheel or maybe the poker deck. He had to, he thought, it was the only way he could pay back Brick. His luck would turn soon, it had to. And his right hand reached guiltily to his pocket where the sheaf of outstanding notes made a neat pile.

He took his hand from the pocket and brushed back his wavy hair. He'd have to hurry, less than an hour before they shut the doors of the night club. Fifty minutes for two drinks and eight, ten turns of the wheel. And back to the hospital bed, for three and a half hours' sleep.

He stopped running ten steps before he reached the club, and automatically his hand went to his hair. He went inside and straight to the bar.

"Rye," he said, "with a rye chaser." He slipped a five-dollar bill across the glossy wood and picked up the whiskey and smelled it deeply before placing it to his lips. Quickly he jerked his head back and downed the drink. He pocketed his change, waited five minutes while his fingers tapped the bar, waited for his head to cloud a trifle and then clear as he shook it once. Then down went the second, and again he waited five minutes, his eyes on the big clock above the door and his fingers tapping a horsebeat rhythm on the hardwood. He turned and walked upstairs and pushed open the door marked Private and walked in. Heads went up briefly and eyes met his fleetingly, and then dropped to the whirling table-center.

He stepped to the rim of the crowd and wormed inside the perimeter to the table. He made his bet and won, and bet and won, and won again. His fingers strayed to the pile of chips and he started to pocket half of them and then he shrugged and straightened his shoulders, like a little man, and bet the pile. And won again.

Now the noise rose and centered and drifted down on the blond youth who was hot. He was playing the red 7 and chips started to appear all over the outer rim, hoping to ride the streak.

The tall, bored, white-jacketed croupier spoke his monotonous spiel. "Place your bets; red 7 riding a string, bet a pile and start to sing. Place your bets."

And chips poured out of yielding pockets onto the red spot with the seven in the middle, and the blond boy with the man-	sized pile felt like God holding the puppet strings. He shoved out the bunch and forced his lips to smile, while inside of him he was thinking: "Win it and you're on your way. It's for Brick, remember, it's for Brick." But it wasn't, and he knew it, it was for himself, and while he thought his thoughts, a detached piece of mind went wandering over to the bar and bought the drinks he wanted and then picked up the car he wanted and maybe then the blonde. And the table started to spin while the center stood still, and then he realized it was the wheel that was moving, and a couple of thousand dollars was riding and so was his life, his miserable penny-ante life trying to grab the gold ring, real gold this time, and the wheel was a kaleidoscope of pretty colors and he was a child again, and his mother was there, pointing to the designs and every design was a win-ner, and then the kaleidoscope started to slow down, and he felt the fear climb his throat and he knew he had gone too far. The bored voice was there at the end of the ride, the conductor announcing it was his stop, the last stop. No, it wasn't the conductor, it was the real God; he, Johnny Palmer, wasn't God, the croupier with the mustache and the one-note voice was God, calling the turn of the wheel, and the stop wasn't a subway station, but a dead end, and it had a number and the number was 13, and it wasn't even red, but black.

Well, he thought, that's life, as he walked away, and the crowd's murmur followed him, "My, he takes it well, must have a sock to lose like that," and then he thought, No, it's not life, it's death, and he hurried out of the club and back to the hospital where he didn't sleep because a hump-backed man who looked strangely like his brother, Brick, kept invading his thoughts and when he did sleep, the hump-backed man was there again, wearing a mask and trying to play ball....

The days drifted by in a rigid pattern, and Brick Palmer wondered whether it wouldn't be better if the Outlaws would lose one, and then an-other, and then a third, and it would be all over, and he could relax. But every time that ball came ripping in and he swept his mask aside and made the play for the big out, and every time he wanted to let his body relax and ride with the runner out of the play, he stiffened his legs and dug with his toes and hung on, and the thrashing spikes beat holes in his guts, but he stayed there, no longer worrying about the amenities of the game but playing it to win, and he thought as he lay there on his belly and breathed in the dust, "This is the only way," although he never knew why.

There was just a week to go now, and the significance of the league had faded to one twin-fact. The Maulers were winning; the Outlaws were winning. And they were to meet those last few days, in the ghost moments of September, when the winds blew the last flecks of dust from the ball fields of Canada, and the hard-baked clay was a stone beneath your feet.

Out of Montreal they came, from Watertown, Malone, from the northern towns of P.Q., to see the Outlaws make their last drive for the flag, eight men and a crook, and they came to root for the Outlaws, and hate the crook. They flowed into the Brittany, and the elevator went on a double-shift, and bulbs appeared in lamps that were so coated with dust the manager couldn't remember when light had ever streamed from their sockets.

The county paper made it front-page news, and there was Max Addison's picture, with the caption, "We'll take it all," and next to it a picture of Bill Humphreys, the Malone shortstop and the league's leading home run hitter, with his own words (concocted by the paper's best sports reporter), "They'll have to beat us."

In the city, three men packed their bags for a trip to Canada, and took their hunting equipment with them—a piece of paper with two signatures on it, two pairs of brass knucks, two blackjacks, a short length of lead pipe, and a packet of bills. They rode a heavy sedan, swapping turns at the wheel, and the talk was meagre as their souls. They sucked cigarette smoke and drank from a bottle of bourbon and across their yellowing faces went the slender blade of emotion, naked and shining with savagery.

To two of them, this was a thrill to be seized and run dry. To meet the enemy, a few hundred miles away, to break him, and to leave—that was the mission, and their lips were moist with the joy of it. To the other, it was a flame, now, not just a light, but a bonfire inside, that sent roaring messages careening to his brain, and made him drunk with the content. Brick Palmer had pushed him around, and spun him, grabbed him, hit him. He squirmed with the thought of the fist that had come out of the night, while the other hand held his throat, and the dozen splitting sparks snaked through the back of his eyeballs and exploded in his brain. And how he woke that night, lying in his own blood, his nose smeared across his face. He, Pete Peterson, who hated big men because they could do just that, and who made big men do as he demanded, except when they wouldn't, and then he would lie on the pavement and the crimson would bubble from his lungs, and he knew he was a day closer to death.

But, so, he thought, was Brick Palmer. The man was soft, he knew, soft behind the bulk, the way women are soft. And he'd find that soft spot and press it and make pulp of the man, and then he'd do to him what he wanted. If it was money, then he'd get money from Palmer; if it was blood, why, then, the man would bleed. That's all. And he grinned in the darkness, a smile that lifted his lips from his upper teeth, while the rest of his face remained immobile, and the fire inside was something so fine he could hardly stand it.

Three men, they were, against one, and this, too, was good, for the result was foregone, two clubs and a brain against a hulk of a man, and they rode into the night of upper New York State, past the lights of people dancing, and they were strong with drink and cigarette smoke and death....

Timmons, the photographer, sat down at his typewriter and started another letter to Brick Palmer, up there in Osage. He'd received no answer from any previous one, and expected none from this. What Brick held inside him was Brick's business, not his. All he had to do was keep Brick alive to what was going on down here, the people who were talking about him now, out loud, people who no longer believed everything that had been said that first week Brick was ostracized. And when there wasn't anything to tell, why, then, Timmons made it up, filling his letter with the chatter of a friend who bucks up another one and doesn't let him know that's what he's doing.

"And, Brick," he wrote, "the *Herald* ran a little picture I took of you and Cathy at home after this year's All-Star game. You know, the one in the kitchen, trying to crack eggs with them big hands of yours. Can't figure out how come they let this stuff get in print (sez he) but they do. Somebody must know somebody on the *Herald*, and his name ain't Randy York. Well, I figure I'll be seeing you the end of the season when you come down to the city. Hit a couple of more for me—and for all us guys rooting for you."

The Outlaw locker room was snarling. Dust seeped up from the floor as the players clattered across to peel off their grime-coated uniforms and change into civvies. And before they were halfway to their lockers, cigarettes appeared and smoke filled the room.

"Good," Muller said, sinking into the relative luxury of the wooden bench. "I just want to sit here all night, I ain't never going to move." He straightened his shoulders as he pulled off the shirt, the blond hair on his chest hanging in limp wet strings. He spoke again, the words they were all thinking. "Three to go. Three blinking ball games and back to the farm."

Rostelli, the dark-browed shortstop with the nervous hands, sat heavily on the bench and stared down at his feet. "One good thing," he said, "no playoff."

The Outlaws had played out their string, all but the series with Malone, and the two teams were all even. Somebody had to take it, by one game or by three; there could be no other result once the three contests were over.

Sweeney lashed his towel at Adcock and stung the pitcher's back. "Oh, you bum," he said, "whoever said you could pitch!" And Adcock grinned through the sweat that notched his cracked lips. The memory was sweet, rival batters walking the silent walk back to the dugout, bats flung angrily away, curses spat into the dirt. And the long row of 0's, the futile nothingness of stilled bats, these things were sharp behind Adcock's eyes, his eighteenth win a big one, maybe the biggest he'd ever taken since pitching for the Outlaws.

And the song of victory, past and future, floated out of the shower room, launched by the bent shoulders of tired men who had come a long way and were almost there.

No one spoke of the pennant; the superstition of ball players crowded that out. But the thought was there. To have come this far, seven games behind in July, four in August, none today, to have climbed the backs of the league leaders was tantamount to complete victory. That would come in two days, they knew, and the song of today's win was but the dress rehearsal for tomorrow's and the next day's.

This they all knew, but Brick. The song he sang was a dirge, and it hung in his throat, unvoiced. He could not sink into the hardness of a bench, for no bone, no muscle would give. And while the noise was around him, he was outside it. The memory that invaded Adcock's mind was his, too, but the taste was bitter. He, too, saw the waving bats, and he still felt the crunch of Adcock's suddenly live fast one as it creased the pocket of his glove. Too old he was to want any of the credit, though his glove had never wavered as it sought out the blind spots and turned them into strikes. And too many shutouts had poured into his oily mitt. By now it was habit, carrying a second-rate pitcher on his broken back while the cheers centered on the mound and the catcher was just a despised automaton at the other end of a brilliantly unbroken streak of light.

But in his pain, he knew the truth. To this point in time he had come, his body that sloughed off pounds of weight, but no further. No longer could he walk from a ball field to claim precious hours of rest, for he had fought that battle for weeks, sleep versus pain, and pain had won. And now he didn't sleep, not until the morning light seeped into the dreary room and a giant hand clamped down on his gritty eyeballs and forced them shut.

Three games to go, and he couldn't make it. His arm was through, the 50,000 throws had been made to the bases, and the 200,000 more back to the pitcher's box. A quarter of a million times he had drawn back his arm, had aimed and thrown, until once more was impossible. His right arm hung at his side, dead and heavy as death, alive only to the pain that reached from his shoulder to the joints of his fingers. He raised his shoulder, and the whole arm lifted three inches, and then fell back again, and he wondered whether he'd even be able to lift a fork that night.

"Maybe left-handed," he thought, and he tried to raise his right arm once again. "No maybes about it," he thought sharply, as the pain went wickedly through his arm and left it shaking and useless.

But it wasn't just the arm, though that was enough. A bone at the bottom of his left foot crunched beneath him as he walked, and he knew he had a fracture. "Like a doughboy," he thought, "a march fracture," the unending hike in harness, from plate to dugout to plate, from plate to mound to plate, fifty feet backward, fifty feet forward, sixty feet six inches forward, sixty feet six inches back.

But it wasn't just the arm or the foot. Knots of muscle had bunched in his thighs and now they stayed bunched when he unbent and walked straight. Up and down he had come, down and up. Bend for the signal, straighten halfway for the pitch, come up the next two feet to return the ball, do it this way for years, until you learn how to do it all from the rocking chair, and then you give with the pitch and come bouncing back to give the elbow flick some momentum, and the ball is on its way to the pitcher, feather light and true. But still the knots form, rocking chair or no, and the pitchers in the bushes, like Osage, need more of a target than the squat, so it's up and down, down and up.

But it wasn't just the arm or the foot or the thighs. Brick's soul was dead. He walked from the locker room, his back damp with sweat, though the early evening was cold, and he wondered what Cathy would say when he told her he wouldn't play tomorrow, and quickly his mind snapped back. Not wouldn't, *couldn't.*

Chapter X

In a Montreal hotel room, Pete Peterson, lay on his back, his hands holding the yellow tape of the play-by-play account of the Osage victory. To him, the whole game was right there. *Muller out, 6-3. Palmer singles. Rostelli hits into DP, 6-4-3.*

He didn't know, and never would, that Palmer's single was a smash to deep short, knocked down by the fielder and beaten out by a lame-legged man who couldn't run. He didn't know, and wouldn't care, that the 6-4-3 DP saw Palmer sliding savagely into the bag, playing it hard and clean, and while he lay there, the shortstop nonchalantly walked over and stepped on his wrist.

All he knew were the cold figures; the game could have been played before an empty house, so devoid of thrill was the ticker tape account.

Pete Peterson seldom saw ball games. They made no sense, this insane roaring for a man to hit the ball, this craven pleading for a staggering pitcher to hold on for another inning. This was the game, this tape, one hundred and fifty inches of it, divorced of childish emotion, stripped down to the reality of the inexorable 6-4-3.

In the center of the room, heads bent in heavy concentration, the two muscle-men peered at their cards, and made their gin rummy plays with agonizing deliberation.

"We stay," Peterson said, finally, resting the paper on his chest. "One more day we stay here, before we move to Osage." The heads looked up and then bent to their cards. Where the table bit into their chests, there came a grunting sound of accord.

Peterson's voice was sharper this time. "We stay here, do you hear?"

This time the heads stayed up longer, puzzled by the edge that confronted them. "Yeah, sure, Petey, we stay here for another day. That's easy to understand."

"Sure," Pete said, bitterly. "Sure. Easy." He sat up and stared at them. "Do you know why we're staying another day?"

The one with the high-pitched voice looked at his friend, and then back at Pete. "Why," he said, "what difference does it make? You said stay, we stay." He went back to his cards. Pete groaned and sank to his bed. "Never mind," he said, his voice dull, "forget it." He lay there, thinking it through, and in a minute he had forgotten his displeasure at his companions, and felt glad he had not spoken more. They were staying another day because the league was all tied up, and the Maulers were visiting the Outlaws tomorrow. Let them play, bet the Outlaws on their home grounds. Bet them, because they had to win. In their win, the whole new picture lay. If the Outlaws won, the odds on them would be four, maybe five, to one. A game ahead with just two to play; that was duck soup. Don't make the move against Palmer tonight; let him sleep, let him play unburdened tomorrow, let the Outlaws win, and then get to Palmer, cinch the deal, and make the big bet, on the Maulers, at four, maybe five, to one....

"... don't cry, hon. There's nothing we can do, now." It was another hotel, another bed, another man.

"But," Cathy said, "what you've done to yourself, how could you stand it all these weeks? The pain." The tears stood in her eyes, old tears that had longed to have been shed days ago but somehow had stayed in damp hiding.

"It happened so gradually," he said, "I never knew it. The arm, it always hurt a bit, maybe I'd have a trembling after throwing too much. Nothing more. Then today, I could barely roll the ball back to the mound. Lucky," he laughed, "lucky that Adcock kept them off the bases, I'd never have thrown anybody out."

"But you didn't tell me," she said.

He shrugged. "What good would it have done? You couldn't have helped this."

"But," she said, helplessly, "I could have tried harder, at night, when I rubbed you down." And the tears rolled down her cheeks and stained the graying pillow case.

"Harder?" He stared at her, with wonderment. "Every night you gave me back my life, a day every night. What more could you have done?"

They sat there, silently, two aging people who had traveled so far to meet this destination, and when they got there, it was a dead end.

"Why did we do this?" Brick went on. "Why didn't they tell me it couldn't work? And even if it had, even if I went the whole way, what good would it have done?"

Cathy shook her head, her eyes closed, and she thought he probably was right. But still, she wondered, where had it gone wrong, not counting the leg, the arm, the back. They had figured on the fans' hatred, on the teammates', even on the manager's, and on all three they had been right.

Where, then, had it made so much difference? They had come up aglow, though they knew Brick would be face down in the dirt as dusters blew by, that runners would criss-cross his body with spike scars. Was it just the injuries, or something deeper? And her mind shrank from the answer that lay in her husband's whitened face and bewildered, pained eyes.

She stood up, abruptly, and brushed her hands together, as though wiping clean a slate. "Well," she said brightly, "we're five hundred dollars richer. That's why we came up, isn't it, to get a sock?"

He shook his head. "I'm giving it back," he said. "Addison said five hundred for a month's ball. I didn't give him the whole month. I didn't earn the money." He pressed his hands to his thighs and got up, using his arms for leverage. He walked to the other end of the room, to the window, and looked out. "I'll go up to see him. Maybe he'll let me keep carfare back. I'll ask him."

No, she thought, *keep it all or give it back, whatever you think you should. But don't beg for peanuts.* "Go on up soon, honey, you should get lots of sleep."

"What for?" he said, bitterly. "There's no game tomorrow."

"Maybe," she started to say, "maybe you'll feel—" and she stopped. For she knew he wouldn't feel better the next day.

"Maybe," he said, and he walked to the door. "It won't be long. I'll be up—" and he, too, stopped what he was saying. "Yes, it will," he said. "Don't wait up, I'll be there a while, I think. At least I'll tell him the whole story before I leave."

"The whole story?" she said, her eyes widening. "You mean the bribe and everything?"

"Oh, no," he said, amazed. How could she think he'd tell Addison that? "I mean I'll tell him what I think of him, of his team, the fans, everything. I couldn't tell him about Johnny, about the gambling debt. You know that."

"Yes," she said, dully, "I know that. I don't know what I was thinking."

He turned and softly shut the door, and walked heavily down the stairs to Addison's room.

He knocked on the door, and he remembered the first time he and Cathy had stood there, in the musty corridor, and they thought an adventure was starting. Now it had ended. All that remained was closing the book.

The door swung open, and Brick sucked in his breath. *Why*, he thought, *the man is old.*

"Come in, Palmer," Addison said, his face tight as a drum, emotionless.

Old, and unmovable, Brick thought. He stepped in and sat down; no formality could keep him standing with all that pain.

"I'm leaving," Brick said swiftly, and suddenly he felt confused. "I can't play tomorrow, nor any more." He looked up at Addison and waited for his response.

There was none. Or maybe that soft creaking little sound was a man sighing and not the floor giving. Addison walked slowly across the room to the door, his fingers tented before him, and he stopped there, his back to Brick. Finally he spoke, his voice gentled with age.

"Is it your arm, Brick? Or your back?"

"Both, I guess," Brick said. *How the devil does he know*, he thought.

"You were back in the rocking chair today. I thought it must have been the arm." He turned and Brick found himself drawing in his breath once more. *I've hurt him*, Brick thought. *What the hell.*

"Well," Addison went on, "I guess it was to be expected. Too many night games, weather too cold."

Brick nodded, self-pity feeding him for a minute. "Yes," he said with a rush, "and getting dusted and hit and spiked."

Addison bent suddenly and he barked out, "And getting booed?"

Brick colored before the thrust. "Yes," he snapped back, "and getting booed. And being snubbed by your own men. Ignored by your manager. Yes, that too. That's why."

Addison straightened, and then he slumped a trifle. "I'm sorry, Brick," he said, the voice soft again, even softer maybe than before. "That was uncalled for. I know what you went through." He stared out into the night, and again Brick felt the man held memories too tight to his chest and someday he'd burst.

But still the self-pity was there, and he resented Addison's words. "No," he said, "you don't know what I've gone through. Nobody knows."

Addison walked to the edge of the bed and he sat, and stared straight into Brick's eyes. "Listen," he said, "I'm going to tell you something, something maybe I shouldn't because I still don't know you. But you've got the right to know, now you're leaving, you deserve to know."

Brick fought off the feeling to shiver as he watched the dancing pinpoints of Addison's eyes. What was this going to be, he thought. Will he gloat over me?

"This team," Addison said, "what do you really think of it, now? Not the men, but the team."

Brick frowned. It had been so long since he had seen major league baseball. How could he tell? "Pretty good," he said, "better than I thought a month ago."

"How good?" Addison insisted. "B, A, Double-A or what?"

"I don't know," Brick said, "sometimes I guess it's Double-A. Somewhere around there."

"Good," Addison breathed, "I thought you wouldn't be unfair. Yes, it's good ball, maybe Double-A. Like I said, they come from Montreal to see us play. Even before you came," he added, hastily.

What has this got to do with it, Brick thought, is this what he wants to tell me?

"And the men now," Addison went on, "what do you really think of them?"

Brick breathed in slowly, deeply. Now. "I hate their guts," he said. "I've never met such men in my life."

Addison sat still, his eyes losing their light for a second. "Yes, I guess you hate them. But you shouldn't, you really shouldn't. There's nothing to hate in them. It's all in you."

Brick waved aside the insult. "Nothing to hate? If they were silent only, nothing else, I'd hate them. But they're more than that." He balled up his fist and waved it under Addison's eyes. "Look at those knuckles. Pennington took the middle one, with a knuckler." He waited.

"So?" Addison said.

"So nothing. Only I called for a fast ball. And he threw the knuckler."

"Pitchers miss signals, Brick," Addison spoke, his words just a breath in the room.

Brick shook his head. "No. You give a man on the bench the sign. That's one. He gives it to me. That's two. I give it to Pennington. That's three. You can't miss a signal given three times. Why, half the time I think the other team's on to it."

"Maybe he didn't miss my signal. Maybe you forgot, and called for the knuckler."

Brick was silent. What was he doing, fighting for a lump of bone, now that the whole arm was gone? "Forget it," he said wearily, "t'hell with my hands. I still hate the men."

"Don't, Brick," Addison said, and he laid his hand on Brick's left shoulder. "Listen to me, and don't hate them. You don't know what they've gone through. Yes, you *do* know. And that's why you mustn't hate them." He paused and looked out into the blackness of Osage's main street, still but for the moaning wind.

"Muller, at first," Addison went on, "he played in the American Association, nine years ago. He had some trouble at home, with his wife, I guess. I don't remember, it's been so long. He was playing Milwaukee in August, hotter'n hell, the league all tied up in knots. Maybe the ump missed one, maybe not. All I know is that Muller went nuts for a second.

"And when it was over there was the ump stretched out, knocked cold by Muller. He didn't come to for two days, brain concussion, minor hemorrhage. They barred Muller for life."

Brick's body tensed for a second, his shoulder coming up hard against the hand that lay on it. *Barred for life.* Like himself. No, not like himself. Different. No years in the big time. No name in the record book that counts. No World Series money. No big crowds, roaring their admiration. Different. *Worse.*

The manager waited, skillfully, using the man's intelligence against himself, knowing that Brick was thinking thoughts that were new and that had to be thought slowly. He waited, and closed his eyes, and thought of old days, his mind paralleling Brick's, hearing the noise of the crowds.

"That's Muller," he said. "Rostelli, he's another." Again the pause, again the stiffening body as another blow ripped Brick. "He threw his bat at a fan who'd been needling him every afternoon, from the same box seat, for three seasons, down in the Texas League."

Three seasons, Brick thought. Three years at home, over two hundred, two twenty-five, games. "Every afternoon," he said, his voice a shocked whisper. "Why?"

Addison barely lifted his shoulder in a shrug. "Who knows? He paid his money and he booed his man. Fan's privilege."

"Three years," Brick whispered again.

"Three years," Addison replied.

"And I—" Brick started and stopped, amazement filling him.

"And you, you've been up here a month, less," Addison finished for him.

"He threw his bat, and they barred him?"

"For life," Addison said. "You see, he hit the man and there was a law suit, for a hundred grand. They settled out of court. The guy got twenty thousand and they railroaded Rostelli out of baseball."

Brick shivered. The whole pattern of the team came swarming over him, and before Addison opened his mouth, he knew what was coming.

"Joe Adcock. The bench wolves got on him early, just a kid lefty, wet behind the ears. They rode him into three fist fights in one month, in Baltimore, Rochester, Jersey City."

"The International League?" Brick asked, incredulous.

"Sure," Addison said. "Just two years ago. The Giants wanted him, they say."

"The Giants? Why?"

"I know," Addison said, "he's not much of a pitcher, now. But he had it then. He could throw that fast ball, still can, once in a while. But his arm, he hurt it, a ligament, that last fight."

Brick narrowed his eyes, looking back into the dust of the afternoon. Adcock, throwing the fast one the last two innings, as though he had two dozen fast balls left in his arm, and he didn't want them to go rotten. And throwing them past the empty bats.

And on the voice droned, and Brick suddenly knew what the word meant, *Outlaws.*

"Sweeney, at third, fighting. He once even slugged his manager." Sweeney, who never looked at Brick, who sat off by himself, fighting. Fighting his old teammates, his own manager.

"Riley, jumped his team, went home to a sick wife, and stayed. That's all I know, of Riley."

Riley, the slender center fielder who moved so swiftly, who couldn't hit because he fidgeted too much and never got set. But who threw blind from the base of the fence today, on a line to third base to cut down a runner, and maybe a run. *He quit his team, once.* For his wife.

"Ostowski, he also hit an ump. Rizzo, drink."

Down the roster he went, every man an outlaw. A list of thugs, alcoholics, assaulters. And on every uniform shirt the word *Outlaws.*

"My number," Brick said, "33. That's why you gave it to me." Addison nodded. "They wear their guilt, on their chests. And they play to win, as Outlaws."

Brick thought of his number. Worn through the years, behind the great dented plates of the major leagues, huddling with the great pitchers of his team. And then, burned, the number. "You gave it back to me, to let me know I could wear it, here."

"Yes," Addison said. "I didn't think you'd understand, but I couldn't tell you."

"But why not?" Brick asked, bewildered, leaning forward. So much to learn, he thought, and somewhere in his right arm a muscle leaped.

"Because you were different, somehow, and I didn't know you."

"Different?"

"Yes," Addison said, "you were something new to the men. You had sold out your own team. Took a bribe. Or didn't take it; just forgot to report it. They don't understand that. That's dirty, to them."

Brick was silent, and for the first time the unresolved guilt that had lain at the base of his soul came smoking up, and he understood why he had never felt right, since he pinned a check in a punk racketeer's pocket.

"So I couldn't tell you, about the number, or anything else, until now. I'm not doing it for you, you see, I'm doing it for the men. They don't deserve to be hated the way you hate."

Brick reached into his brain, to stop the throbbing. "But why did you give me the number, if you thought I was so dirty. Why did you bring me up in the first place? For the money you'd make?"

And Addison sagged, his body sinking three inches into the mattress, a shriveled old man. "No," he said weakly. "I did it for me."

"For you?" Brick said.

The manager turned watery eyes to Brick. "You're not the first major leaguer on this team to do what you did."

"But you said—"

Addison shook his head. "No, none of the players. Me. I did it, thirty years ago. Took a bribe, like you."

Brick ignored the accusation. "Thirty years ago?"

"Yes," Addison said. "The Chicago White Sox. 1919."

"Oh," Brick said, and then he fell silent. Thirty years guilty, he thought, and he wanted to share it with somebody, finally. With me.

"The name, *Addison*, it's phony, of course. I changed it. I wore my number up here, but that wasn't enough. I was hiding from me, for thirty years. And then you came along, just as guilty. And you hadn't changed your name. So the fans could give it to you, your own men, the other team, the umps. And I couldn't hide any more. Every time they dusted you, I felt the pitch. They abused you, and I heard them and they were abusing me." He stopped suddenly, and Brick knew the man had talked it out, and would say no more.

Brick got up, and he wondered, foolishly, whether there was blood un-

der the man's socks, and he knew how Addison had learned of his sore arm,
his back. Addison and he, he and Addison, they had been the same person
this past month. He walked to the door and he said good night and he went
out swiftly, waiting for no answer. For no answer could come. The room was
filled with the horrible retching sound of an old man crying.

He stumbled through the corridor and up the stairs, and inside of him
there was a wild thing tearing him up. The glory of them, he thought, the
pride of such men. Playing out their lives in a graveyard of dreams, a boneyard
heap of unwanted ball players. And that man in the room, the room that
smelled only of old memories, how had Addison stood it, these thirty years?
Ordering his men to wear the word *Outlaws* on their shirts, so that he could
feel his guilt, so that he'd never forget what he had done.

Brick burst into the room, and stopped short. The light was on, and Cathy
sat at the edge of the bed, and the bags were packed, and then he remembered.

"No," he said, the blood singing in his ears, "we're not going."

Her eyes widened and she stared at her husband curiously. "What do you
mean?" she whispered.

"Three days more don't mean that much," he said, trying to explain, and
failing, and starting in again. "It doesn't hurt, that's what it is, it doesn't really hurt. Not where it counts."

And she understood, this. "Are you sure?" she said, knowing he was, and
knowing he had come alive again.

"Even if it did hurt," he went on, "I'd play. These men, you don't know
them, but they're magnificent. Why, do you know why they hate me?" he
said, leaning forward, his eyes young and urgent.

She shook her head. "Why?" she repeated obediently.

"Because I'm dirty," he said, triumphantly. "Because I'm not a team man,
and they are."

"Oh," she said, "how wrong they are."

"No," he said, "they're right. I didn't understand, until now. I sold out
the important teams, me and you, me and baseball, just for the kid brother.
I took you up here, I put you through hell. I quit the big leagues, I let baseball take the rap. The only two teams that count, and I sold them out. And
now I can't sell out the third team."

"The Outlaws?" she said.

"Yes, the Outlaws."

"But you never would have sold them out," she said.

"You're wrong," he said, "I already had. But that's over. I'd been playing for me, for Brick Palmer and five hundred dollars and a toehold on the future. No more now. It's inside of me, you can practically hear it, like a college kid playing for his letter. A new feeling. No, an old one. Oh," he said, "I
can't wait."

His voice was a roar now and Cathy started to laugh, rolling to her side.

"You big fool," she said, "you've got school spirit, that's what's inside of you."

"Yes," he said, "that's what it is. After fifteen years I've learned to play again, like I did as a kid. You'll see, tomorrow. Come out tomorrow, you'll see."

"Are you sure?" she said, her eyes grave again. "Your arm, your foot, that bone sticking out?"

"Yes," he said, "I'm sure. Why, Gehrig," he said, "he couldn't stand up, he fell down trying to tie his laces and couldn't get up, and he was still playing every day. All I've got are bruises, like you get in the subway rush. Come out, you'll see." And for the moment he believed it, believed that the pain had gone, and for believing it, it had. He flexed his right arm and the life in it was a torrent. He stood on his toes, spreading them and sinking all his weight into his arches, and he believed nothing happened, and nothing did.

"Oh," he said, "these three days. There'll never be anything like them."

"No," she said, "I'll stay here, in this room. I'm not going to jinx you, these three days." But he wasn't listening. The fantasy grew in his mind, and he saw the stands jammed, and the sudden roar as the runner broke for second, and he saw the catcher straighten and throw, and the beauty of it, the fluid grace of it brought tears to his eyes, for the catcher was himself and the day was tomorrow.

The glory, he thought, wasn't in the fame, but in the doing of it. It never mattered when a man did what his ability said he could do. That was expected. It was only when a man did what he couldn't do, that was where the glory lay. And tomorrow, he knew, he would do things his arms and legs and back couldn't do, and he thought of DiMaggio crawling off the bench up in Boston and hitting the ball further than even DiMaggio could.

Suddenly he was tired, the good tiredness that poleaxes a man, and even the wild-hoofed horse that raged inside him was still, and soon all that was left was a hum in his heart and this, too, soon changed to the drone of sleep.

Chapter XI

And the sun came back to Canada, September's dying sun, full and rich for a moment, warding off the winter. It poured down on Osage, and with the suction strength of spring, it drew the moisture up and turned the baked clay to sponge.

With it came the people. From Malone they came, across the border in buses and cars, from Montreal, and from the logging camps of Osage, ten thousand of them, filling the stands early, filling them and spilling out of them so that ropes were thrown up to hold back the overflow.

On the field were the Maulers, the league champions, silent men in gray, clustering unintentionally around their broad-backed shortstop, Bill Humphreys. As he moved, the team seemed to follow. He moved, now, for the one-bounce shot into the hole and came up with it, and he threw nonchalantly to first and then he drifted over to second base to take the catcher's peg. And the eyes were on him, players' and fans'. He was tiger grace and power, a twenty-year-old magician who would soon go south to claim his piece of glory, and every man in the park knew he was an artist, playing his last series.

The rest of the club was solid, the pitching deep and keen, and the power was left-handed, which meant trouble for the Outlaws, with Adcock unavailable, and every other Osage thrower a righty.

But in the Osage locker room, where just two men remained, there was the certainty of victory. Brick Palmer lay face down on the rubbing table, and over him Max Addison worked his own magic. The arm that had been dead yesterday leaped to Addison's touch. The purple lump at the bottom of his foot was still there, but ice packs had cut its size and the soft sock padding, reinforced with a layer of sponge, took away the dull pain.

And while Addison worked the back and shoulders, Brick slowly raised his feet, alternately, bending his knees, and the pull was on his thighs, easing out the knots.

In his imagination, cruel and sharp, Brick thought he had been battling four elements, the fans, his opponents, his own teammates, and, lastly, his own manager, Addison. One of these foes was now on his side, or, rather, Brick had joined his manager.

One down, he thought, and three to go. And he remembered that first day when a play at the third base foul railing had shaken sparse cheers from the crowd. The fans, he thought, he'd get to them, he had to. For the glory of it. And even now, these last few days, he thought he could feel a difference. The sound they made was automatic, he thought, without any feeling behind it. They seemed to boo him because they had formed a habit, and even so, he

could sense something building in them, a silent, maybe even resentful, respect, but a respect none the less. Brick grinned to himself. Who was he kidding. Respect! What a laugh. But, still, he felt it might be so.

His own men, that hardly mattered now, for he knew why they were as
they were. And the Maulers, his bat would smash them and his arm hold them
in check.

A whistle blew and the dull tone of the crowd outside changed, and Brick
knew the Maulers were leaving the field, the Outlaws replacing them for their
infield drill, and he swung off the table.

"No," Addison said, "you don't have to catch warm-up. Lukas can do it."
He pressed his hand into Brick's upper right arm, his fingers still rotating.

Brick shook him off. "I'd rather. Anyway, I want to talk to Pennington.
I want him to hold off on the knuckler, as long as he can."

Addison stared at Brick. "You anticipate me," he said, finally, "that's what
I wanted to talk to you about." He mused for a moment, his head down, his
mouth making sounds against his own lips. "Once I said you were the best
since Cochrane. I didn't mean it then. I was just trying to warm you up, trying to let you know I was on your side. But now I mean it. You're the best I
ever saw, and I've seen them all."

They walked out of the room. "Not Campanella, you haven't," Brick said,
but now he didn't know, himself, how good he was, for today he felt better
than he had ever felt in his life, and suddenly he wanted to be the best, better than Campy and Dickey and Black Mike and Bresnahan and Muddy Ruel.

He stepped onto the field, and though he wasn't prepared the noise that
hit him was not so terrible as it had once sounded. Ten thousand strong, they
laced out at him and the sound bounced off and inside of him there remained
a rock, a stillness that would not be moved today, not by ten thousand jeering voices or one hundred thousand.

And then Brick realized, with a shock, no, it's not just me. They're not
making as much noise as they used to. The biggest crowd we've drawn, and
they sound like half that size. There was something building in them, he knew.

There would be no bow today, no mocking gesture. Too long, Brick knew,
he had been all gesture and no body. The bow that first day, the strong man
act in the locker room when he had chinned by one arm, the words he threw
into his teammates' faces when they had tested him with the epithet on his
locker door, all these were for the show, and the show was over. There were
ten thousand fans in the stands, but he wasn't playing for fans today. He was
playing for nobody, one man alone against the absolute standards of honor and
truth, and only he would know whether Brick Palmer had played well or not.

Good, he thought, the sun feels good, and his feet crunched against the
warm dirt and a drop of sweat tickled his shoulder blades as it went by. For
a moment he felt frightened, so fine did he feel, wondering whether any man
could hold this point for long, and then he was right again, the fear gone, be-

cause he knew he had it, and nothing would change it today.

He warmed up Pennington, doing nothing more than just that, keeping the pitcher busy throwing, but not throwing hard. He had the right-hander pull the string on the fast ball, merely lobbing it up, trying to hit the target, and putting no twist on the knuckler. Strength he'd need, Pennington, for he was going to throw his speed at the Maulers, with the knuckler kept in mothballs until the swiftness waned. Two games he'd pitch, Pennington, one with one speed, the second with another. Swift for as long as he could go, bruising Brick's glove with the speed, brushing back the Maulers and then blistering the fast one across the outside, at the knees.

And then, when they stopped waving at the ball and started leveling, in the fourth, or fifth, or, please God, the sixth or seventh, then Pennington would pitch his second game, the one with the knuckler every other delivery.

"That's it," he said when he saw the pitcher wipe his forehead. "Let's go in," and he turned and walked to the dugout, not caring that Pennington deliberately waited until Brick had reached his seat before he entered the low enclosure and looked for a spot of his own, at the other end of the bench.

Two minutes later the whistle blew again, and Brick was on his feet and out on the field, first man, and the crowd was confused, wanting to blast the man, but behind him was the team, fighting from the bottom of the heap to today's tie, and so they were quiet, and it sounded not like a crucial ball game but instead like an ordinary Tuesday contest in May, between two second division clubs.

The Mauler lead-off man stepped in, and Pennington, all business, went right to work, throwing sidearm, almost crossfire, splitting the plate with a fast ball for a called strike. And in eleven pitches, Pen had turned them back, two on strikes, the third man on a weak roller down the first base line where Muller took it, his foot on the bag.

They were chopping at the Osage right-hander, hitting foul balls to the wrong field or else punching out too late, while the sizzling hot pitch rested in Brick's glove. And Brick grinned broadly as he went to the dugout and Addison caught the grin, and returned it.

Sweeney gave the crowd what it wanted, hitting the big Mauler ace's first pitch down the third base line and bounding into the overflow, for a ground rule double. Riley bunted deftly, moving Sweeney to third, and Muller ran the count the whole way, fouled off a half-dozen pitches, and finally got his walk, on an inside half-speed ball that sent him staggering from the plate. The crowd jeered the Mauler right-hander, Littauer, for the near-duster, and then they spotted Brick as he walked up, and the jeers continued.

Brick knocked dirt from his cleats and studied the coach's box for a sign and found none. He stepped in, and the waves of hate washed against him and moved him not and washed away, and then he was alone, the sound of the thud beneath his ribs the only noise he could hear, and his body stretched and tensed and then settled into the immovable poise of the hitter, and Littauer threw.

Brick strode smoothly, long and silken, getting out ahead of the inside fast ball at his chest and his breath oof-ed out of him as he turned his bat on the ball, his wrists unlocking as he connected, and then he was running, his palms stinging and his eyes taking one swift glance at the rising line drive that siz-zled into left-center field, between the fielders and through. Sweeney lum-bered in, and the crowd roared, and Muller sped around second and into third, and around as the coach waved him on.

Against the fence, 380 feet away, a frantic Mauler fielder clutched the bounding ball, his back to the diamond, and then he spun and threw, and Brick rounded second as the shortstop took the throw in short left field and pivoted, his eyes traveling first to the plate where Muller was thundering across, and then to the base paths where the big Osage catcher, on his toes and flying, raced towards third base, and then he whipped his arm around and made the toss to third, a flat line shot that bounced once and sped into the baseman's glove, waiting at the sack.

Brick held his slide until he knew where the peg would be taken and un-til he was sure he could jostle the Mauler third baseman. Now, he thought, eight feet from the bag, and he threw himself forward, awkwardly, his body twisted and high, and like a blocking back he hit the Mauler and caved him in and somewhere he heard the cry of the crowd, high pitched and sudden, and he knew the ball was loose and he was up, kicking free of the grunting fielder, and running again. On his toes he went, and this time it was the pitcher he had to beat, covering third base and retrieving the ball and straightening for the throw to the plate.

But the Mauler catcher had learned something in the last fifteen seconds, and he stayed back of the plate, straddling it instead of coming out and block-ing it off to eat spike and runner. And Brick was underneath him, his spikes cutting cruelly into the catcher's shoes and lifting the man up and then down on him, but without the ball that was scurrying to the railing behind the plate. Brick's palm fished for the plate, so high was the dust, and he pounded it and got up and dug his cleats into it, and then he turned and trotted off, and the Outlaws led 3-0.

Addison's face was white, but behind the drawn skin and thin aging mouth was a grin and his head nodded once, slightly, as Brick swept into the dugout, and he thought, please Lord, hold him together, just a little while longer.

They stood shaken at the mound, the Maulers' pitcher and the shortstop Humphreys, and for longer than the rule book permits, they stood and talked and a relief pitcher took off his jacket and started to throw, hurriedly. But in Humphreys was the quicksilver, and the tremor passed, and he dug into his genius and found the leak and plugged it. No one man, Palmer or anybody, would beat him to death, and his voice found itself, and the twenty-year-old body leaned over the pitcher and coddled him and soothed him, and the rally that promised to be a rout was snuffed out, and the first inning was history.

It was Humphreys who led off the second frame for the Maulers, and Brick knew this was the man they had to keep saddled all day. He saw the sloping shoulders and the thick brown wrists, and he saw the power there and in the locked hips. And, despite the knowledge that his own voice would auto-matically turn off the infield tap of chatter, Brick called out to Pennington.

"Come on, Penny boy, pitch to me, boy, nobody hits, nobody hits." And the right-hander came by way of third base with his long, swinging sidearm delivery and bulleted a fast one past the lunging bat.

One, he thought, *one strike. Does he have two more in him*, and he thought not, and he put the glove on the outside corner, hoping Pennington kept in the groove, and then the pitch was on its way, and Brick felt his glove inch over towards the center of the plate and he shuddered even before Humphreys swung, and then as the bat lashed around, there was time for one more thought, and this was a prayer, *let it get by, let it fool him*, but he knew it was a prayer. Brick winced and he felt sick inside, because it was so easy to wipe out a three-run lead with a man like Humphreys waiting for the mistake and the mistake was just two inches long, and that was too much.

He straightened to watch the ball as it flew out into left field, climbing until he thought it had to start to come down and then climbing some more and finally describing its arc and disappearing over the fence. The crowd was shocked into silence for a second, Mauler and Outlaw fans alike, so stagger-ing was the size of the blow, and then they roared, astonished and thrilled, and the young giant trotted around the bases, the battle still on his face, and as he crossed home plate he stared at Brick and Brick felt the cold power of the man, and again he shuddered.

But then he was by, wheeling into the shadows of the visitors' dugout, and Brick knew he was just another hitter who had landed one, and he was human and could be stopped. He walked out to the mound, his step slow and sure, and his voice mild.

"All right," he said, "that's one, it's down the drain, let's forget it." But he wasn't ready for the snarl that came from the pitcher.

"Forget it?" Pennington said, his face twisted and his eyes on fire. "Why, you cheap bonehead. What do you think this is, sandlot ball? Where do you get off calling two fast ones in a row, on Humphreys? I must be crazy, pitch-ing what you call for."

Brick frowned and started to answer, and then he stopped, and turned and waved his hand to the dugout and Addison appeared at the entrance and stared out at the diamond. Brick waved once more, and as Addison slowly stepped out and across to the box, the crowd's noise grew restive and dis-agreeable.

"What is it, Palmer?" Addison asked, carefully avoiding Pennington.

"I want you to call them from now on, just as you did the first couple of weeks. Penny doesn't like my calls." He waited, hoping Addison would not carry this further, for Pennington must not get cold.

Addison stared at the catcher, and for a fearful second, Brick thought he'd ask why, and then the manager nodded once. He looked at Pennington, and he was troubled, and Brick wanted to put his arm around the old man's shoulder and tell him it was all right, he'd carry him through, he'd done it before, but he couldn't and he wondered whether there were enough runs in his bat.

Addison nodded again. "Fast balls," he said to the pitcher, "nothing but fast balls, until I say no."

"To everybody?" Pennington asked. "To Humphreys?"

"To everybody," the old man said. "Just hit Palmer's glove, that's all."

And the three men turned to their places, Addison to the lonely dugout where he had to play his game, all nine positions and the blood and tears of a tenth; Pennington to the mound, where the sun beat down and where the fans were staring and he felt cheated somehow, let down by his manager, and in his disappointment rose a new fury and his fingers clenched the ball; and Brick to the dirt and dust of the plate.

He crouched there and held his glove for Pennington, and then the big right-hander was bending back and leaning forward, and the ball was a blur, eating its way into Brick's pocket, and behind Brick came the call, "*Stuh-rike.*"

And Pennington went red hot, whiplashing the ball past the Maulers and sending them back to their bench, popeyed and talking to themselves, and the game settled into the routine, the Outlaws clutching their 3-1 lead, the Maulers clawing away, but always with empty hands.

They whisked through the second inning, and Brick got his licks in the third, and again he met the first pitch, a blistering line belt past the startled Mauler hurler, through the middle of the diamond, but it was Humphreys who turned the noise, three giant steps to his left and then the catapult dive, glove extended waist high, and the spat of the white smoke against the pocket of his mitt turned him around in the air and he fell on his back, but always the glove was visible, held aloft, never touching dirt, and the afternoon air was split open by the ten thousand voices.

And Brick, ten strides to first base, stopped and then continued another step, not believing what he had seen, and again he stopped, and he thought, *the way Marion did it, in '42,* and for the first time that day he felt some pain, in his back, and he wondered whether it could ever happen that way, that the glory was split in two parts, and they'd come together on the same ball field and slug it out.

But, no, he thought, the man is human, and he grinned, for what he meant was, he's got to be human, and the third inning sped by, and in the fourth it was Humphreys again, coming to the plate, and this time there was a Mauler on base, and only one out. The crowd roared at the sight of the big shortstop, and then realizing they had roared all day, they got up, in the fourth inning, and their hands beat together and their feet stomped against the wooden planks and the noise was rolling thunder.

The sweat had popped out of Pennington, trickling down the seams of his face, and his jaw had gone lean and firm an inning ago, sticking out as he punished himself. Fast balls they called for, faster than he'd ever thrown them, and faster yet he'd give them. It was Humphreys now, who ate fast balls, and Pennington went sweeping into his pitch, his eyes cutting a track to Palmer's glove and his arm following through and the ball then whistling in, swift as light, and in close to the letters, bending the batter away, and Humphreys was down in the dirt. The duster it was, as Brick called for it, and the hate that was in the pitcher, hate for his catcher, hate for his manager, came down in the pitch, the fastest ball Brick had caught in Canada, and he knew now that Humphreys had to come out of the dirt and face a man who was not afraid of knocking him down every time he got up.

And Brick wondered how Humphreys would take it, and then the shortstop was up, dusting himself off and snarling abuse at Pennington and Pennington raised himself up on his toes and shouted back, all his hate on this batter now, on this batter who, more than any, represented all batters, and the ugly duel between pitcher and hitter went on, and Brick was glad.

"Pitch to me, boy," he said, "pitch to me. Nobody hits, he'll never dig in," while his eyes watched Humphreys take his foothold, deeper than ever, and then he thought, now, now we throw our first knuckle ball, and he flashed the signal, and he saw Pennington's face light up and then go stolid again and nod, and he wound and threw.

Humphreys stepped forward, eager and blazing mad, and Brick nearly laughed as the ball floated in, spinning so slowly it seemed not to spin at all, and then Brick sucked in his breath for Humphreys fooled once, and fooled badly, stepped back and then stepped in for a second time, and Brick knew the man was great, he had never seen a greater at his age. But the damage had been done, the bat was wobbling in its chopping swing and it was the comeback ball, hit on one hop to the mound where Pennington gobbled it and whirled and threw to second, and Furman, the second sacker, was high off the ground, avoiding the onrushing spikes and throwing, and the umpire made the call, his thumb tossed high, a bang-bang play at first, the flying Humphreys a half-step late, and the inning was over.

Rostelli tripled to the center field wall in the fifth, and three outs later he still stamped around third base, and the Maulers came up and went down, Pennington blowing the fast one by, and in the stands they chanted each strikeout and the total was nine. It was big Pen in the sixth, stroking the first pitch into left field for a base hit, his bat flying from sweat-slick hands, but Sweeney hit down to Humphreys and it was 6-4-3, so swift and smooth you couldn't believe it.

And in the Maulers' seventh Brick knew it had happened. Pennington had gone as far as the fast ball could take him, the first pitch leveling off and drooping, the hop gone and the ball fat. He went out to the mound after the dust had cleared at second base and the Mauler had beaten the throw in for a double, and Brick called time.

"You all right?" he said, knowing he wasn't and hoping the right-hander had his guts in his hands, because he'd need them now.

"Sure," he snapped, "it just got away, that last one."

"I know," Brick said, "he was lucky." Lucky. Lucky the ball didn't rise, it've cleared the left field wall, instead of hugging the line, six feet high all the way. "I think we fool them again," he said.

"Knuckle balls?" Pennington said, the willing pupil, and not even knowing it.

Brick nodded. "Knuckle balls, every possible motion. Overhand when I touch dirt, sidearm when I don't, alternate it every inning beginning now. If I don't talk, throw the slider."

Pennington frowned. "Max, he don't like the slider."

"Neither do I, but it breaks different from the sidearm knuckler, and everything goes now. Nine outs, that's all we need."

And he felt Humphreys standing behind him, the shadow of the man reaching out to the mound.

The pitcher shrugged, and Brick saw the slow rise of the shoulders and he wondered whether there were nine outs or nine pitches left. "All right," Pennington said, "only—"

Brick looked at him sharply. "Only what?"

"Nothing," the pitcher said, and he turned away, and Brick knew he was frightened.

Good, he thought, no time for thinking how he hates me, no double-cross when I call for the knuckler and he wants to break my hand. Stay frightened, boy, and we'll get by.

He was behind the plate, staring into the dirt, and Humphreys stepped in, and Brick started to talk, his hand out-stretched, clear of the dirt, calling for the sidearm knuckler that bent away from a right-handed hitter. "Come to me, boy, no hitter here, boy, no hitter," and Pennington wound and gave it plenty of schmaltz and then he threw, the motion a replica of the fast ball, but instead out of his right hand came the floating, tantalizing knuckler shooting for the outside corner, and Humphreys was stepping in and swinging for all the marbles.

And then Brick was up, the pitch in his glove for the strike and then his bare hand had grabbed it and he threw down to second to Rostelli who had sneaked behind the runner and the peg was on the bag, in the shortstop's glove and the Mauler was climbing Rostelli's thigh, trying to get back in, but failing, and the umpire's hand swept up and up, and his voice was sharper than the crowd's roar, "Yer out!"

And Pennington turned to Brick and made a half-step from the mound and his mouth started to move, but Brick couldn't, not yet, and he spun away to toss a jeering word at the retreating Mauler runner. *No*, Brick thought, *don't thank me, I'm not ready yet.*

It was still Humphreys, though, and the game was not over, eight outs not over, and Brick was down in his crouch, thinking it through, and signaling for the overhand knuckler, the one that looped fifteen feet in the air and sank like a rock, Rip Sewell's pitch, the kind you could stroke, maybe, into left field for a lazy single, or else hit high to the fences but not over, and Brick wondered whether Humphreys did not have the power to beat them after all. Pennington threw, and the ball started to come down, shoulder high three feet in front of the batter, chest high, maybe, when it would have reached the plate, and waist high had Brick ever caught it.

But instead the gamble lost, and the teams were just one run apart, Humphreys leveling with all his mighty strength, turning his cold fury on the ball, accepting the dare like Ted Williams, and hitting to the wall, all right, but over, 440 feet on the fly, on a pitch that walked up to the plate. And the crowd ooh-ed at the sight of it, and Brick hated Humphreys and wanted to kiss him, all at the same time, for here was the game laid naked and true, and Brick knew how much he had to beat to win it. He had to beat Humphreys, and that was impossible yet he had to do it, and there was the beauty of it all, the glory and the truth.

Out at the mound was Pennington, bewildered and frightened, for he had nothing in his arm left to offer and still he had to go on. He threw wild, past Brick, and then laid a sidearm one in there, but Riley flew into the left-center field slot and climbed the sky, and brought it in, and then Sweeney went behind third for the one-bounce shot, gloving it backhand, his body turned away from the diamond, and then he straightened and threw and Muller went into the dirt and swept it up, to retire the side.

In the dugout they were desperate, even Addison, all but Brick. And he never thought of the throw to second that nipped the Mauler and saved the tying run, for he knew it didn't matter, they could have tied it and gone ahead, he still had to beat Humphreys and he was going to do it.

He felt a hand on his knee, and he turned and saw Addison, and he was again surprised at the age of the man. "Palmer," the manager said, "how is your arm?"

Brick flexed his right arm and raised it, and smiled. "Fine," he said, "couldn't be better," and so was his back and his legs and the chunk of bone on the bottom of his foot. And even the pain that haunted him, that couldn't have been better, and he felt the thud in his chest, and then it was his turn to hit, and he faced Humphreys before he stepped in and their eyes met. *For* you, bunko, he thought, *this one is for you, with loving hate.*

He dug in, his left hand held out imperiously, dictating to the pitcher that he was not ready, and then he squared away, and his eyes traveled in, from the fence in dead center field, to the chalked bag at second, to the slowly swinging right arm, and he knew what he must do, and then the ball was on him and thought was impossible now for the body took over as he strode in to meet the pitch. He did not get the rise Humphreys had, and for a second he felt the bitterness in his mouth, but then his hands told him that his eyes were lying, and then his eyes told him that his hands were right, for the ball went on a line into center field, fifteen feet off the ground, and halfway to the fence it started to rise, and Brick was slowing down to watch it as he turned first base. It rose another dozen feet and seemed to hang for a second and then, like a golf drive, rose again and swiftly dropped, and disappeared from sight, and Brick was trotting the whole way around, in the silence of the afternoon, and past second base he looked at Humphreys and saw the coldness of the man and he felt like laughing.

Hate me, boy, he thought, *that's good, hate me.* They could have laid a tape measure out, he knew, to the spot where the ball hit dirt, and they would have found a mark next to it where Humphrey's ball had landed, so alike in distance had they been. Hate me today, boy, because you'll never touch me today, no matter how many you hit. Two you've got, and I've got four runs, so hate me, boy, I love it.

And in the dugout, once more, there was Addison, his pale blue eyes speaking silent thanks and still Brick couldn't look for Pennington, because still he wasn't ready. It's still me, Brick thought, me against the Maulers, and that's the way it will be today. But tomorrow, I'll be an Outlaw, and then maybe I'll look for their thanks.

That was all for the Outlaws, in the seventh, and Brick was out on the diamond again for the Mauler eighth. The two-run bulge was sliced to one as the Maulers got to Pennington, scoring and then filling the bases on a couple of line shots and a walk. But finally the slider worked, and around the horn shot the ball, for a double play, and the score was 4-3. The crowd had stopped counting the strikeouts now, and instead they winced every time Pen threw, so fat the pitch looked.

Addison was on his feet in the dugout as the Outlaws came in to take their eighth inning licks. "All right," he said, "take your time. Creep up to the plate, stall around. I want Pennington to get a breather. Take the first pitch, take the 2-0, take the 3-1. If you think there's a question, call the ump on his decision. If you get on, tie your laces. Tie 'em even if you don't. We want time. Time."

And for twenty minutes the Outlaws made the clock crawl. Not a man got on base, Riley, Lukas and Pennington going down in order, but Riley knocked three pounds of dirt out of his cleats, Lukas removed foreign matter from his eye, and Pennington switched bats twice, tied his laces once, ran the count to three-and-two, fouled off five pitches, and finally struck out.

Brick started out for the plate, but Addison stopped him. "How is Pennington?" he asked the catcher.

Brick shrugged. "All right. Tired, but all right. The knuckler's starting to straighten out."

Addison nodded. "I know. And the slider is nothing. What do you think? Does he have any speed left?"

Brick squinted, looking into the past of five hundred pitchers who had wobbled and staggered, and then threw a half-dozen big ones in the last inning. Larry Jansen, he thought of, rocked in the opening frames and airtight from the sixth on. And Joe Page, falling behind 3-0, getting his early lumps and then going four, five, maybe six hitless innings. But Pennington? Frightened and tired. He didn't know.

"Yes," he said, "a little speed, maybe." He waited.

Addison turned away and spoke over his shoulder. "All right," and his voice was tired and thin, "if he can throw fast, let him."

It was the top of the order, in the ninth, and Pennington was white-faced as he went into his swinging delivery. And the Mauler lashed out at the wrinkling knuckler on the outside corner, drilling the ball down the first base line past the sprawling Muller and into the corner, and the throw into second base was too late.

Brick straightened, and he felt the muscles in his back give but grudgingly, and he called time and made the walk to the mound.

"Look," he said, "they're not going to score. You're not going to let them. Just pitch where I call for them, and don't worry, they're not going to score."

The big pitcher looked down at the dirt at his feet, and slowly he scraped the side of his shoe against it, flattening it. "Will they bunt?" he asked.

Will they? Brick thought. He didn't know. They might, they probably would, but he didn't know. How many times didn't Durocher bunt when everyone knew he would. And didn't Mack bunt when the rule said swing away? But Pennington didn't care about the others; he wanted to know. He had to know.

"Yes," Brick said, "they'll bunt. And we'll let them. Pitch to my glove, and start moving in, to your right. Sweeney will anchor at third, Muller will come in and cover everything between the first base line and the box. I'll take the bunt if it's hit slow. The play is third."

All this Pennington knew, but Brick also knew he wanted to hear it again, the way the Giants under Terry perfected the defensive maneuvers against a bunt with a man on second. The pitcher nodded and licked his lips and bent to the rosin.

Brick squatted behind the plate and flashed the signal, alerting Muller and Sweeney, and he held his glove at the waist, a bit below, where the Mauler could get his light wood on it and send the ball bouncing into the dirt. And, Brick thought, if I'm wrong, he won't be able to level off and get too much rise.

The pitch was in, then, and Brick was right, and half the battle was over, the runner coming thirty feet down, waiting to see whether the ball was bunted, and whether it was on the ground or in the air. And the hands shifted, the body squared away, and the ball was tapped, straight out towards the mound, a poor bunt, hit too hard, on one big bounce at the charging Pennington. And then the pitcher froze, the ball bounding off his glove and falling at his feet, and he grabbed at it, and missed, and grabbed again, whirled to face third, saw he had no play, and then threw to first, to the second baseman covering, barely in time. The sacrifice had worked, and the Mauler perched on third, with one away.

And Brick felt the chill hit him, the afternoon sun dying and the evening coming in fast. But it wasn't so much the breeze Brick felt, but the knowledge that Humphreys would soon bat again.

He saw the misery on Pennington's face and he knew he could not walk out to the mound again, so alone was the pitcher and so alone must he stay until he had beaten this thing, or else gone down in the dirt. Throw the ball, Brick thought, that's all you have to do. And Pennington threw, breaking his knuckler into the dirt and Brick was on it, smothering the ball and then cocking his arm, chasing the Mauler back to third. Big Pen threw again and the batter swung and connected, and Brick braced himself at the plate, but the ball was foul, kicking up dust outside third, and streaking into the crowd.

All even, he thought, one-and-one, and don't fall behind. He called for the slider, on the outside, but the pitch didn't break and the Mauler hit sharply again, and again there was dust, five feet outside the right field line for another foul, another strike. Again, he thought, the slider again, and he'll make it break, he'll have to. Pennington lifted his chest and released the breath, and nodded, and pitched and the batter went after it, swinging and missing, and there were two out, the runner still on third, and the thunder of noise from the stands was two-edged as Humphreys stepped in.

Now, Brick thought, now I can talk to him again. He's got it back, his nerve. He trotted out to the mound, and Pennington was breathing full and easy. Brick took the ball from the pitcher and put his hand on Pennington's right arm. "Can you throw fast, once, twice maybe?"

The pitcher nodded. "Sure," he said, "I'm still strong."

"We curve him," Brick said, "on the corners. If he swings, fine, we've got strikes. No matter what, he gets nothing good. I don't care if you walk him, he'll never score. The man on third, he's the one that counts. Curve balls, fast balls. Whatever I call." He stared at Pennington, and the pitcher nodded, and kept on nodding while Brick looked, trying to see inside the man, where his heart was.

He turned at last, hoping he'd walked sixty-and-six the last time that day, and then he saw Humphreys. He nodded his head at the big shortstop, and there was an answering light in Humphreys' eyes, and then they moved away, Brick behind the plate, and the batter to his rectangle of chalk.

"Son," Brick said, his voice carrying just to Humphreys, and no further, "you're good, and you're going to go good. But not now. Now you're dead."

The man's back stiffened and the bat stopped swishing air, and then it continued.

"No more batting practice, no more bush league stuff," Brick went on, his glove shielding his sign, "now it's for keeps, and you're through."

The bat kept slicing air, smooth and softly menacing, and out on the mound Pennington froze at the top of his pitching motion, and then threw to Brick's big mitt. It was the sidearm knuckler, twisted out of pained fingers, and the ball broke sharply at the hands, and Humphreys started to swing too late, checked it, and looked foolish as the pitch wafted over for a called strike.

"That's one," Brick spoke, and Humphreys was out of the box, kicking dirt and rubbing a hand down the length of bat. "One down, and two to go, Billy boy."

Pennington tried to do his part in the little drama at the plate, but the first fast ball he'd thrown in three innings missed the target and zoomed outside, taking Brick out of his crouch for a backhand grab, and the crowd sucked noisy breath at the near wild pitch.

"We give you one, Billy," Brick said, "and now we take it away. On the hands again, the knuckle ball on the inside corner, and you won't even be swinging."

And Pennington threw, as Brick called it, the sidearm sweeping knuckle ball, scarcely spinning and then stabbing across the plate, and Humphreys pulled away, and then chopped at the pitch, and Brick laughed aloud. "One more to go, Billy," he said, "and we all go home." And then Humphreys stepped out of the box and spun around and looked down at Brick, and the wild light of hate was in his eyes, not cold now, but hot and furious, and Brick felt sorry for the boy who was fighting two battles, the pitcher's skill and the catcher's words.

Brick held his glove on the outside corner and called for the fast one, and his heart prayed it would be the fastest one Pennington had in his arm, for it might be the last, and then the pitch was on its way, a flashing streak of white in the late graying day, and Humphreys' bat was frozen on his shoulder as the ball veered for the glove, a perfect pitch, clipping a half-inch from the outside corner of the plate, and smoking into Brick's glove.

And behind him, the umpire called out, "Ball two," and Brick swung around, the ball in his hand, his mouth open and the surprise and hate popping out of his eyes. Oh, no, he thought, how could he do that to Pen. And then he knew. He had forgotten, in the battle with Humphreys, he had forgotten that the corners weren't his, ever, up here, and that he had no right to call for a pitch so close to the edge of the plate, for the umps would never give him the corner, not with the game hanging on the call.

He turned away from the umpire, not saying a word, and he could scarcely look out at Pennington, who had just won a ball game, except for one little thing. The last big out was getting four strikes, instead of three.

He worked his shoulders, easing the chest protector from under his chin, and then he made his sign to Pennington, and looked up at the pitcher, and Pennington didn't shake it off, but nodded. It was another fast one, and Brick held his glove in the middle of the plate, hoping Humphreys would be expecting anything but a pitch right through the middle, belt high and straight.

Pennington wound slowly, and from third base skittered the Mauler runner, coming down a half-dozen steps, and then the crowd went silent, and from behind the plate Brick could see nobody but Pennington, and only his swinging right arm, over his head and around and a white speck coming up to him, getting bigger and bigger, aimed to hit his glove where it hung, and into the corner of Brick's eye came a new figure, Humphreys striding forward, and swinging, and then everything changed and the whole picture was shattered.

The ball, that was the thing, Brick thought, the ball. And as soon as he heard the too-loud sound of bat against ball he knew Humphreys had hit under the hopping fast ball, and somewhere overhead and behind him was the ball, popped foul. His mask was off as he turned and then he saw it, forty feet high, at the peak of its rise, and near the Outlaw dugout, and then it started to come down. He moved for it, ten feet, twenty, thirty, and the ball was rushing towards him, and he towards the gaping mouth of the dugout, and he heard a voice, Addison's maybe, *and then a volley of voices, warning him shrilly,* and he was on top of the dugout now, he and the ball, and then his glove reached for it, and his left foot came down, but the ground wasn't there any more, just air, and then not air but the impact of wooden planks, and his glove was stabbing and his right hand closing over the pocket, and he crashed face down into the benches, taking the full shock of it on his head and chest, his arms twisting away from his body, the glove held out, stiffly, away from him and pointed towards the playing field, for anybody to see. And the ball was in it, the ball was in it, and nobody could take it away, not even when the knowledge came to Brick that somewhere in his body pain had returned, and the somewhere was everywhere.

And then, like a god clapping his hands, came the sound of thunder, more loud than ever, the crowd's noise, roaring for the catch, for the Outlaws, for the win that put them in first place, a game ahead, with two to go....

Chapter XII

Sleep, he thought, sleep might do it. He walked stiffly, a tired man in pain, and he fastened his eyes on the hotel lights ahead, knowing the bed was there, and sleep. Cathy had failed to meet him at the park with the car, and he frowned. It was not like her. Something must have come up, or maybe he had sounded too confident before the game, and she had been afraid to find out. Or else she had napped, and overslept. It didn't matter, he thought, the walk may ease the pain.

Brick had waited for her, the other ball players piling into their rattletraps, looking once at the big catcher and then chugging away. Not one of them had offered him a lift, nor had he expected it.

But still, he thought, they must have known how much it hurt. His hand went to his face, touching the bruises on his cheekbones, patting down the bandaid under his eye.

The night had swung in, cold and clear, and he stretched out, to keep warm. The town was on him now, first the saloon at the far end, and inside he could see the crowd, a noisy, celebrating crowd, drinking their beers to Pennington's win, and to tomorrow's. And then the small shops, closed for the day, a tight-aisled diner, open all night, and crowded, and finally the hotel. And one step inside, he saw him.

He saw the punk, sitting deep in a lobby chair, his hands hidden in his gray topcoat pockets, and as Brick walked to him he could see the punk's eyes, narrowed and deep, and he sensed a change more basic than the new nose the kid wore. And then he saw the other two, standing behind the chair, near the elevator, lounging, their hands hidden in perfect imitation, but he could see the pockets working, as though fists were being clenched.

"Hello," Brick said. "I should have guessed."

The punk said nothing, but stood up, and Brick was shocked by the man's eyes, by the holes in his face where the flesh seemed drained off. Why, he thought, the kid is dying, and he felt nothing.

"You've brought a couple of your chums, I see," Brick said, and he wondered how the words came out. "They're even prettier than you."

The eyes flashed for a second, and died, and Brick saw the kid was composed and sure, and he wondered why he didn't understand what was going on. It should have been simple, he knew.

The punk spoke at last, his voice even and soft. "Shall we go upstairs, and talk?"

"Shall we?" Brick said. "You tell me."

The kid looked over his shoulder and nodded to the men, and they moved from the wall, and Brick saw their size and the fatty tissue under their eyes. The punk walked out ahead, to the elevator, and the three others followed, in silence.

"You know," Brick said, "I don't even know your name, and I should, by now."

"Shut up!" the kid said fiercely, and Brick blinked in surprise. Why, they're touchy, Brick thought, like movie stars. His name's been in the papers, and I don't even know it.

And, as they stepped out and walked down the dim corridor, Brick kept the needle firm, knowing he had reached the punk. "I might even say the face is familiar, but I can't. Somebody's had a plastic done on his nose, I think, or else somebody bent it out of shape since I last saw it."

The kid whirled, and again there was flame in the eyes, and this time it stayed. "Look," he said, and the voice had lost its evenness, "look, it can happen now, right here. All I got to do is say so, and that's all. Stop it, you hear, stop it."

Brick shrugged, and then they were at the door, and suddenly he remembered Cathy. Well, he thought, she'll have a surprise. Company. And he pushed the door open, and felt for the light and the room was empty.

And now he whirled, and his hand came up in a fist, but the pain stopped him, and the fingers flexed in agony, and only his voice carried his violence. "Cathy!" he said. "What did you do to her?"

The punk paled and his foot started to move back and then he remembered the presence behind him, and he stopped. "Nothing," he said, "I didn't think you'd want her to hear this. She's gone off to Montreal for a couple of hours."

"Montreal?" Brick said, his head thick and heavy. "Why Montreal?"

"She thinks you've been hurt," the punk said, and inside of him the light flashed again, "and maybe she's right, maybe you will be if you play it dumb. I sent her a telegram, that you hurt your leg, a possible fracture, and were in a hospital in Montreal, and wanted to see her."

The beauty of it, Brick thought, and maybe it's just as good. They can't hurt her this way. Whatever they want, they'll have by the time she gets back, and they'll be gone.

"What do you want?" he said, lifelessly.

"Just a word from you, that's all," the punk said, and behind him the two men quickly slipped out of their coats, their hands in trouser pockets now. And they stepped apart, each to a corner of the room, and Brick thought, how silly, I can't even raise my right arm.

"What word?" Brick asked. "Money?"

The punk laughed, hollow and unmirthful, and then he cut it short and put his hand to his mouth, as if to clamp down on the one barking cough that came out of his throat.

"No, not money," he said through tight lips. "Just a word like yes. Yes, you'll drop a couple of throws tomorrow, call a few wrong, whiff in the pinch.

That's all. Just the word yes."

"And if I don't?" Brick asked.

Now the kid laughed again, and there was joy in it, and he didn't care that the cough came barking out, once, twice. "That's what's so nice, it don't matter. Don't say yes, and we'll turn a carbon of the IOU, with your brother's name on it, over to the baseball commish. And you won't let that happen, will you?"

Brick was silent, and a new pain started, between his eyes, beating slowly, and he thought, all over again, it's starting all over again. "That's it?" he said, finally.

The kid nodded. "Half of it, anyway," and he waited, his face aglow, his lips moist.

"All right," Brick said, "stop playing. What's the other half?" Christ, he thought, I'm tired.

The punk jerked his thumb over his shoulder to the men behind him. "The boys, they're the other half. We beat you, like you never got beat before, so you don't play tomorrow. So our bet is just as good, on the Maulers."

And then the picture was clear, and Brick sat down on the edge of his bed, and put his head between his hands. He knew immediately that this was what he had been running from; a little seed of his conscience knew that the hounds had never finished, that they had not run him into the ground for good, and that they would not rest until they had.

He shut out the room with his hands, and his eyes closed, but the throb-throb between his eyes reminded him of the alien presence in the room, his and Cathy's room. Cathy. What would she want? His blood on the floor, or his soul rotting away? What would she say?

Addison. He had bought a ball player, given him a piddling half a grand, made him leak blood through the worst month a man ever spent, what would he say? And Brick remembered... *boneyard heap of ball players, graveyard of dreams*. No, he could not ask Addison.

The men. They hated him, abused him, shunned him. He could sell them out now, in return for the pain they had inflicted. Muller, *barred for life*. Rostelli, *barred for life*. Every man an Outlaw, and proud as Yankees. No, he could not.

Who then? Who could he ask? And the answer was as bleak as the room. No one.

"Well, what is it?" came the crackling voice of the kid and Brick looked up in surprise.

What if I say yes, and double-cross them? he thought. And he looked at the two sappers covering the door, and he shuddered. They'd chase him some more, and they'd have the paper again, and they'd beat him. Maybe they'd kill him, what use would they have of him afterwards. And how could the Outlaws win, if he played a game carrying the load of a future beating, maybe his death?

And then he laughed. How well could he play tomorrow, anyway? The pain gripped his shoulders and held them tight. Who was he kidding?

And again he laughed. These three men, that's who he was kidding. They didn't know he was maybe through for the year, that he'd never be at his best against the Maulers tomorrow, or the next day. And they were waiting for his answer, hoping they could send a healthy Brick Palmer into action, so that he would be clear-headed about throwing the ball into center field and vicious in his swing when he struck out.

"All right," the kid said, but Brick could see it wasn't all right, worry lines dented his forehead, "all right, cut the comedy and give us the word. Yes or no."

On the line. No more stalling. He tried anyway. "I thought you fellows were washed up. That Brooklyn D.A. and Murphy, the new police commissioner. I thought they had you guys on the run."

Now the kid snorted, and even the two muscular morons smiled. "Don't be a chump," the kid said. "Did you see anybody crying because they couldn't get bets down on Louis-Charles?" Brick shook his head, but the wonderment still remained. This was a world he knew nothing about, except for a word in the columns of the big newspapers.

"Sure," the kid went on, "the little guys, they're on the run, and some dumb cops who couldn't stand the heat, but not us. Not the Capone boys. We got class. Nobody touches us."

Why, the poor fool, Brick thought. He's proud of it. Proud of the billies his boys are carrying, of the brass knucks and guns and shivs. The elite.

And Brick suddenly turned cold with rage. What right did these men have to do this? To take advantage of a kid's weakness, like Johnny Palmer's, and how many million Johnny Palmers were there? To chase him around, him and Cathy, like frightened hares, from one job to another, from one nation to another? And always on their heels.

Didn't they know it was *wrong?* And in the fine depths of Brick's soul, he could find no reason for men acting this way, and somehow he felt he must know.

"Why are you doing this?" he asked, sharply, and he saw the glint in the kid's eyes change as the eyes opened wide for the first time.

"Why?" the punk answered. "For money, of course. Why else? I got money on the Maulers, at six-to-one, and I don't want to lose it. That's why."

And Brick thought: why had he and Cathy run up here, for this terrible month? For money. For Johnny Palmer, too? he questioned himself. Once he had thought yes, but now, he didn't know. How could he protect Johnny, every minute of the time? And how could Johnny feel protected, knowing he was losing his heart and soul every time Brick stood up and took his lumps for him? That's not protection, he thought, that's coddling. The boy must grow up, and he'll need room to do that, more room than there is under the shadow of a wing.

And so what was the difference then, between him and the punk? He had come up here for money, despite the scars he had left on baseball, and there *was* no difference between himself and the punk.

But now there would be. There were standards more dear than money. He'd found them for sure on the diamond today, the shining lines of honor and truth and courage; he'd found them in beaten men like Addison and Pennington, in the giant Humphreys, and, yes, in himself.

He looked up at the kid, and he saw the lines deepen on the forehead, and he pressed home his glance until it seemed his eyes were streaking the kid's brow and eating in.

"Well, what is it?" the kid asked. "Yes or no?"

He'd never be able to let them know, the Outlaws. But he'd know. And Cathy. And that was all that mattered, just so long as you stood by the standards. He got to his feet, wearily, and he faced the two men at the door.

"No," he said, and his voice was strange in his ears, and he heard the kid squeal. Then they were on him....

He did not know how long he lay there, but it could not have been long. He pressed his hands into the damp carpet and pushed up, the tufts of wool pulling the caked blood from his cheek. He raised himself and then pulled his knees up under his body and squatted, breathing lightly because it hurt too much to breathe full.

He sat, his head lolling against the arm of a chair, and he held his sides, trying to contain the pain with each breath. He knew there was something he had to do, but he could not remember what it was. His head hurt, in layers of pain, and his nose and mouth felt strange. Thick and numb. He gently rubbed his lower teeth against his upper lip and felt the puffiness and tasted the blood. And then he had to take his teeth away from his lip, because it closed his mouth and with his mouth closed he couldn't breathe.

That was his first awareness that his nose was broken and useless. He raised his right hand to his face and touched his bruises and felt cautiously the spreading flesh of his nose, and withdrew his hand to stare at it. There were small dark stains of blood, and one knuckle was skinned raw and the whole hand was puffy and blue, as though it had been stepped on, hard.

He brought his left hand, slowly, before him, and it was the same blue, and the first joint of his middle finger was more crooked and humped than usual, and he knew it had been broken.

And then he remembered what had been bothering him. Cathy wasn't home. She was out, worrying about him, on the road from Montreal and he had to be all right when she got back to the hotel room. He dropped his hands to the carpet and once again pushed down, raising his body. He got his feet under him and strained upward, and the pain lanced his side, but he was standing. He walked over to the mirror, across the room, and he wondered why his legs didn't hurt him. And then he saw his face.

His stomach rolled once, and he thought he was going to faint, and then he thought he'd be sick, but nothing happened, and he   l o o k e d again. It was not his face, he thought, not with the left cheekbone caved in, the nose spread across his face and twisted to the left, his mouth caked with blood and thick as sausage. He swallowed, and tasted more blood, and then he was all right again.

Brick turned to the bed and sat, and his right hand lifted the phone, and he wondered what he was doing.

The sleepy voice downstairs answered, as though nothing had happened, and Brick found his mouth working, though his mind seemed blank.

"Hello," he said, "I want to call Presbyterian Hospital, John Palmer, person to person, emergency." He stopped and frowned, and then he spoke again. "Please."

The other voice, barely more alert now, said, "Okay, call you when call's in. Ought to be just a couple of minutes." And Brick held a dead phone.

He started to lie down, but he couldn't breathe that way, and he sat up quickly and began to unbutton his shirt. And then he couldn't get it off, because he couldn't raise his arms to pull the sleeves, and he turned the shirt away from his flesh, instead, and stared down at his sides. There was nothing to see, the faintest discoloration possibly, but no more, and that was strange, for he remembered the soft thud of feet against his sides, as he lay on the carpet and the two men grunted over him. They had kicked him, he was sure, until he had passed out, and then probably for a bit longer.

He dropped his face into his hands, and his eyes closed, and instantly he felt sleep wash over him. He shook his head and sat up stiff. "I mustn't," he thought, "the call will come through soon, and I'll never hear it. And Cathy, what will she think if she sees me lying here?" He stretched his eyes wide open. "She'll think I'm dead, that's what," he thought, and then the phone rang.

He picked it up, and he still didn't know why he had called Johnny, and then the operator said something and another voice, a man's he thought, tried to say something, and he said, "Yes," and then Johnny said, "Brick, what the hell?"

And then he knew why he had called his brother. There were two things. "Johnny," he said, and he had to talk very slowly because it didn't sound like "Johnny" to him, his lips were so thick and numb and his nose was clogged up with something, bone ends and blood or something, and he had to make this very clear. "Johnny," he tried again, and he stopped. He had to be sure.

"Yes, yes, I hear you, what's wrong, Brick?"

"Johnny," he said, for the third time, and then the words were coming out, one at a time, "I've been beaten up by some gangsters," and then he stopped.

There was a shocked silence, and Brick wondered whether the words made sense. "Are you hurt?" Johnny said.

"No," he said, "yes. My nose is broken, I think, and a finger, maybe two. My ribs hurt. I can't breathe good."

"Oh, my God," the boy at the other end whispered, and it was a boy, Brick knew, you could tell by the way he said it. "Are you in a hospital?"

"No," Brick said, "it just happened, twenty, thirty minutes ago. I can't go to the hospital." And that was the one thing he had to tell him. He couldn't go to the hospital. Why? he thought. Because I have to play ball tomorrow, he answered, and he shivered at the insane thought. "I can't go to the hospital," he said, "I have to play ball tomorrow. I want you to come up and see what you can do."

There was silence at the other end.

"Johnny," Brick said, and he remembered, be patient, speak clearly, he *has* to understand. "Do you hear me?"

"Oh, yes, Brick, yes," the boy whispered again, and Brick wondered whether the kid was sick. "I'll come right up. I'll take a plane, first plane out."

"Good," Brick said, and he thought, he sounds like a boy, but he used to sound like a man when he was a boy. And then Brick remembered the second thing, and for a second he froze, the words a fright. "One other thing kid," he said, *one at a time*, "I wouldn't do something they wanted, so maybe they'll hurt you. No, not hurt you this way, I mean maybe they'll talk about the IOU." He waited. "Do you understand?"

"Oh, yes, Brick," and the voice was sharper, impatient now, as though this part ought to end soon, the voice was in a hurry. "Don't worry about that, Brick. It's about time."

"Yes," Brick said, "that's what I thought." He started to hang up and then he spoke again into the phone. "You have my address, don't you, Johnny?"

"The Brittany, Osage, yes, I have it, Brick."

"Kid?" Brick said, and this he had to ask, to make sure. "Is it all right?"

"Oh, Brick, shut up," the boy said, and there were tears there, and the phone clicked in Brick's ears, and he put it down.

And then the whole conversation came swarming over like eager base runners going wild, and he lurched to his feet and stumbled over to the mirror.

Why, you crazy fool, he thought, you can't play ball tomorrow. He looked at the man's face he saw in the mirror, and somehow he thought nobody would really know how bad he was hurt, even with that face. They'd think the fall against the bench on the last play, on Humphreys' foul pop, they'd think he landed harder than anybody had realized, that the bruises were slow in showing, like bruises are, like the bruise on his ribs was, slow in showing, but turning a dirty brown now, and purple underneath.

They'd wonder about his nose and cheekbone, but didn't Williams break his elbow in the All-Star game, and play eight more innings? And Slaughter, a few years before, daring Red Sox runners to move, *with a broken arm*, risking his career right at its pinnacle on a couple of throws, just so they'd never know he was bluffing? And DiMaggio, skillfully shielding *his* pained, useless throwing arm from American League base runners, *all year?* More, more, oh, there were so many more, staining the whole glorious history of baseball with their blood. Bill Terry, crawling off the bench out west, in Chicago, or Pittsburgh, he couldn't remember now, and showing his Giants how to do it, running out two triples on crippled legs, driving his team home when he could hardly stand. Burgess Whitehead, his cheek laid open by errant spikes, sent in as a pinch runner the next day, and sliding home, on his face, the frail Burgess Whitehead. Seminick in '50, on one leg; Lou Brissie, his game leg smashed by a line drive off the bat of Williams, on opening day, getting up and finishing the job he started, beating the Red Sox.

Oh, yes, he could play. Or maybe he couldn't, but he would. And the kid brother, he'd fix him up, he'd have to. They owed each other that. Patch him up and get him in harness, worthless bruised flesh, but who'd know, who'd know? And he straightened up, exulting, and he raised his arms from his side, and a scream tore from his mouth. Nobody would know, he thought, except himself. The ribs. How could he hide that? The scream, he hadn't been able to stop that, and he hadn't even done anything, like block the plate or come out of the squat and throw.

And then he turned, slowly, for he could hear her heels coming, and he held the grin so that she could see, and the door burst open, and for the second time in less than a minute the room heard a scream.

"Brick," she said, "what happened?" She started forward, and then stopped, not touching him, for she could see the pain in his twisted mouth where he was trying to laugh.

"It's nothing," he said, quickly, "don't worry. I'm not really hurt."

"But," she said, her eyes searching him, "the wire—"

He explained it to her, standing there for he was afraid to sit down and show her the pain, but she knew.

"When do you expect Johnny?" she said, when he had finished.

He shrugged. "I don't know."

She picked up the phone and called the desk. He waited, where he stood, until she hung up. She turned to him, at last, her face dull with fear. "The next plane reaches Montreal at midnight, a few minutes past."

He looked down at the bed and wondered how long he could stand this way, knowing he'd have to sit sooner or later, and then she gave him his chance. "Wait," she said, "I'll get some ice and some towels," and she started out of the room. At the door she wheeled around and walked to him and stood close, her face strained up to his. She looked at him, at each bruise, and then she lifted her lips to his broken mouth, and tenderly she kissed him. Then she was gone.

With a groan he sank to the bed and his hands found their places at his sides, holding his ribs and coaxing each breath. He lay there, on his back, sucking air out of the room of dust and musk. The ribs, he thought, are gone. The nose, the cheek, broken. One finger for sure, maybe two. His hands were active over his body. That was all, he thought. The rest didn't count. And somehow they hadn't reached deep inside him where the pain lay in his spine and in his thighs and in his shoulder. That was the same as ever, bad enough, but he had played with that pain today—*was it still the same day?*—and he could play with that tomorrow.

But why? he thought. If the punk talked, he was clear. If he didn't, what difference would it make to anyone? He couldn't give the Outlaws the game he wanted to give them, not half-broken and useless. So why play?

There was a knock at the door, and he thought, *so quickly?* He said, "Come in," but it wasn't Cathy; it was Addison.

He walked over and stood above Brick, looking down at the wreckage of his half a grand. "Your wife told me; I thought maybe I could help before your brother arrived."

Brick didn't ask how much she had told him; it couldn't have been everything, there hadn't been that much time. And Cathy wouldn't implicate Johnny, not unless he had said she could talk.

He waved his hand to a chair. "Sit down. Not much you can do, I guess." He spoke quickly, shielding the pain.

Addison sat but his eyes stayed on Brick. "No," he said, "you can't play tomorrow, you know."

"Can," Brick said. Oh, no, he thought, let's not argue, I don't have the breath.

"But you can't," Addison said, leaning forward.

Brick raised himself, an inch at a time, and then twisted over so that he was on his left side. "I will, though, I have to. Why," he said, and he leaned forward despite the pain, "I have a history of quitting. Do you know what they'll think of me if I don't show up tomorrow? Do you know what they'll call me?" Brick pressed home his words, knowing that Addison would understand this, if nothing else. He, too, had lived through the next day after quitting. "Once they thought I sold out my team, that I quit on them, took a bribe, like an ordinary crook. Me, a ball player! Just today, on that last out, I heard them yell. That was the first time they cheered me, a bunch of them. I liked it, and I can't let them do the other thing again. I've *got* to play, that's all there is to it. I've *got* to."

"But, man, you'll kill yourself," Addison said.

Brick laughed, hollowly. "No," he said, "nor will anybody else. Not any more. I'm immortal."

Addison sat back. He knew he was beaten, and he was glad. "I'll tell the men you hurt yourself in the fall, on the last out. Your nose, your cheek, your mouth. I'll tell them I patched you up last night. Come to the park early, if you can, and you can dress in my room. So they can't see your body, your sides, I mean."

Brick nodded. The man knew so much, so quickly. "Thank you," he said. "You see, I have to play."

Addison nodded. "Maybe it will rain tomorrow. Another day's rest. I can call the game for almost any reason."

"No," Brick said. "There are things I have to prove." He stopped there, afraid to talk too much. *For the boy's sake.*

"Does it hurt?" Addison said, suddenly.

"Yes," Brick said. "Mostly the ribs, when I breathe. The rest, I'll get by."

Cathy came in then, with a basin of ice cubes and a handful of towels, and a damp, warm washcloth. She sat at the edge of the bed, without a word, and started to dab at Brick's face. Tentatively she washed around the stained flesh, staying away from the nose and mouth, wiping off the black flecks of caked blood and carpet wool, and Brick said nothing, moving his head only when the cloth covered his mouth, and he couldn't breathe.

In five minutes she was through, and they could see the full extent of his facial hurts, Cathy and Addison, and they looked at each other, wondering what next to do.

Brick laughed at their faces. "It's not that bad," he said, "it couldn't be."

Cathy shuddered, and tears sprang to her eyes. "It's even worse, honey," she said. "You're insane."

I guess I am, he thought. For he knew the punk wouldn't talk, there was nothing to gain. He had had his revenge, and for all the kid knew, Brick was out of the game, tomorrow and the next day, and the bet had its insurance riding. Why talk, and implicate himself, the whole Capone gang, right along with Johnny Palmer?

They packed half a dozen cubes into a towel and placed them at the bridge of his nose, and another handful on the swollen upper lip. Brick raised his hands to his face and kept the towel moving on his lip, giving himself space, to suck breath, and at the same time letting the ice work on his mangled hands. The ribs, he thought, there was nothing they could do there. Not until Johnny came. Midnight. No, midnight in Montreal. One o'clock in the morning, tomorrow morning, the morning of the game.

"Can you sleep, honey?" Cathy asked.

"Sleep?" he said. "I don't know. I can't breathe too good."

"Try," she said, "you're going to need it. I'll keep the towel away from your mouth."

He nodded his head and closed his eyes, and he felt Cathy untying his shoe laces and he tried to relax so she could pull them off easily, but his legs were tight, and she jerked, and the pain rocketed to his brain, and back.

He opened his eyes and saw the tears in Cathy's, and he grinned down at her, open-mouthed and terrible, and she smiled back. She went to the other shoe, and it came off, without the great jolt, and then his socks. Her hands loosened his belt and his trousers were off, and then she pulled the spread from the foot of the bed and placed it around him, loosely, and again he nodded.

They worked silently, the frightened blonde girl and the tired old man, the ice towels moving and stopping, and patches of white showed for a second when the towel moved away, and then the blood rushed in. Cathy turned on a table lamp, across the room, and snapped off the overhead light, and Brick felt the sleep come over him again, and he wondered when Johnny would come.

For three hours they worked, the first half-hour in silence until the ugly rasp of Brick's breathing started to steady itself and they knew he was asleep. And then they spoke single words, in tiny whispers until they had grown used to each other, and again it was silent.

At midnight, ten minutes before, Brick stirred, his hand going to his side, and he was awake. He looked to the far wall, to the dresser beyond them, and at the clock, and he grinned.

"Good," he said.

"Hush," Cathy said, "go back to sleep."

He shook his head. "Johnny'll be here soon. Let me wake up."

He looked at the basin of water, and at a second basin, filled with cubes. "How many did you use?" he asked.

"Three, four basins," Addison said. "How do you feel?"

"I don't know," Brick said. "Whenever you wake up, you feel good. I'm relaxed. Wait till I tighten up, then I'll know."

"Sleep," Cathy said, "and you won't tighten up. You don't know when Johnny will get here. Maybe another hour, maybe more."

Brick shook his head. It had to be sooner. That's all. It had to.

He lay there, helping them move the towels, ice cold and clean the feeling, and then he knew why the pain hadn't returned. His face was frozen numb. He wondered idly whether people got frostbite from this sort of anesthetic. "Look," he said to Addison, "there's no reason for you to stay up. Go to bed."

"Don't be silly," the old man snapped.

"Well, then," Brick said, "let's make some use of this time. I'm not in much shape to catch, but I got an idea."

"Bobbett?" Addison asked, softly.

How does he know? Brick wondered. Bobbett, the reliefer, who worked fast and low, not much of a curve, good control, always working low, around the knees. "Yes," he said, "Bobbett. I can catch him in the rocking chair. Maybe I'll never even have to stretch. Target at the knees."

Addison shook his head. "No, not at the knees. Higher. Between the knees and the waist. Otherwise," he shrugged, and spread his hands. Otherwise the umps wouldn't see them, as strikes.

"Yes," Brick said, "knees and waist. That's it." He felt a sudden warmness. Maybe they could get away with it. Keep the men off the base. If they get on, have Bobbett keep 'em so close they'll never break. Cock the arm a couple of times. They don't run much, anyway, he thought. Nor do they lead off too far, certainly not after he had picked that Mauler off second right before Humphreys hit his second home run, this afternoon. No, he thought, not this afternoon any more, yesterday afternoon. The time was 12:15, and Johnny was coming, Johnny was coming.

And then he thought, *Bobbett.* What about him, could he pitch to the target, inning after inning? He hadn't started a game all year, hadn't gone over six innings all year. Could he do it? For after Bobbett, there was nobody. Maybe Adcock for an inning or two, but his stuff was so slow and tricky, and his control had been off the last couple of times out. Pennington could go an inning, maybe, but not a man further. And that was that. The rest of the staff, its rotation ripped, was tired, overworked. It had to be Bobbett.

"Don't frown so," Cathy said, "you're getting all tight again."

"No," he said, "I'm not." Not tight, still relaxed. But he was concentrating on this terrible gamble he and Addison were taking, and he realized therein lay another way of beating the pain. Talk. Think. "About Humphreys. Maybe we can throw him that dinky little curve that worked so well that first game I caught."

Addison nodded quickly. "Anything you say. You know these hitters better than I do. Better than anybody, as a matter of fact."

Brick liked that. There was a new pattern starting, he felt, a new-old pattern of applause, adulation, praise. He had missed it, though he would have sworn he had never noticed it when it was always present, back in the old days when he was a Blue. He needed it, up here, where his name was an anathema, and where he carried hate on his shoulders. Again the warmth was flooding through him, and he closed his eyes to bask in it, only for a second, he thought, only for a second. And he slept.

But still, coming out of this second sleep, he was the first to hear Johnny. He jerked his head up, his eyes wide open, and then they, too, heard the footsteps, and three heads faced the door, and somewhere a half-mile away a lonely church clock softly struck two, and there was a knock on the door.

"Come in, Johnny," Cathy called, and the door flew open and out of the dimness he came with his black bag in his hand, wearing no topcoat, but an old suit jacket, wrinkled, pockets bulging.

There was a briskness about him, in his step, in the curt nod he gave Addison, the way he sat at the edge of the bed, but withal, a certain reluctance, and Brick felt sorry for the kid.

The dirty scarf over the table at the side of the bed was whisked off, and a clean towel replaced it, and on it appeared the weapons of the trade, and Brick felt as though it were old times, and he was about to be rubbed down. The kid nodded at the ice cubes and the damp towels, and then he bent and looked at Brick's sides, his fingers exploring from chest cavity to back, running the length of each rib, pressing, looking up at Brick's face for the inevitable reaction, and nodding imperceptibly, once, twice, three times, and Brick knew. Three of them. Cracked.

Suddenly the kid sat up and snapped his fingers. "Turn the lights on, I can't see a blasted thing." And Cathy switched on the overhead light, but she knew he was covering up; he had seen more than he had wanted to see.

The examination was brief, and only the digging at the ribs hurt and the time the kid put his index finger of his left hand into Brick's mouth, high behind the upper teeth, feeling for the lowest point of the cheekbone, while his right hand probed on the outside, and then the bone wobbled between the two hands, and Johnny looked at Brick fiercely, and whispered a sound that wasn't a word, and the fingers seemed to meet and the pain went whipping through Brick's head.

That was the only part that hurt; the novocain injections were mere pricks and the pressure of the entering liquid was controlled by the kid's thumb, and all it felt like was a severe sinus ache. Once the novocain took effect, Johnny went to work on the nose, cleaning it out and taping the inside of the nostrils, high up until it seemed to Brick that the kid was poking his eyeballs. Johnny drew a splint around the one broken finger on the left hand, and kept the other hand in ice, to reduce the swelling around the dislocation. "No break," he said, and Brick breathed more easily, for it was his throwing hand, and in the ice he started to flex and relax, flex and relax, working the hand even before the ice had started to bring down the size.

"All right," Johnny said, and the time was three-thirty, "sit up. Now we go to work." Brick sat and swung his legs over the side of the bed, his feet touching the chilly floor. Johnny drew out the four-inch tape and started to unroll it. "You're sure?" he said to Brick. "Sure you're going to play tomorrow?"

Brick nodded. "Sure," he said, his jaw tight.

The kid sucked his lower lip. "Look," he said, "I don't know whether I should say this, with Cathy here, but you've got three bad ribs. Not busted clean through, nothing chipped off, but plenty cracked. You could get hurt tomorrow." He stopped and resumed his sucking. "Not hurt, I don't mean. You could get killed, I mean." There was a choked sob across the room, and then Brick laughed.

"Nonsense," he said. "You've been reading too many medical books.

Why, I might step off a curb tomorrow, and get killed by a car."

"Okay," Johnny said, "that's what I wanted to know. You don't care, so play. But it's no nonsense. You could get killed. Those ribs, they might break clean through the first time somebody takes you out at the plate. And who's going to guarantee which way they'd break, whether the ends'll go in and clip the lungs."

Brick laughed again. "You," he said, "that's why you're here. You're to guarantee that. That's why you're taping me. You know whether they'll break in or out. You know whether the ends will puncture the lungs. Don't you?"

The kid stared at Brick. Without an X-ray he couldn't tell, and even then not for sure. Brick must know that, he thought. And then he understood. For Cathy's sake. "Yes," he said, "I was just trying to scare you. I don't think you ought to play, and I was trying to make it sound worse than it really is. No, you're safe. They probably won't even break any worse than they are, now. You might as well know, if you're going to go through with this."

And Brick held the kid's eyes with his, and the boy didn't waver, and they each smiled. He's grown, Brick thought, he's grown.

"All right, Brick," Johnny said, softly, "take a deep breath, let some out, and hold it." Brick slowly sucked in air, despite the pain, released a bit and then held it while Johnny turned the tape around and around him, closeting the breath with it, and Cathy and Addison leaned over and watched until the line of white grew to the armpits, and worked down again to the waist, and then back on up. "There," the kid said, "it'll work like a cushion, thick like that." Brick punched his chest lightly and smiled at the insulation and then he tapped his side with it, and held the smile. But inside he turned sick once more. For the little tap, with the tips of his fingers, had jolted him and the pain flared inside, wild and red.

Nobody saw it, though, not even Cathy, and it was four o'clock, and the night was over, and they were exhausted, all four of them. Addison got up, as though it had been a social evening, and shook hands with Johnny and bowed slightly to Cathy and said good night, and closed the door behind him, glad to be out of the room where they had all been so naked and vulnerable.

Johnny curled up in the big chair, in his clothes, and Cathy went down the hall to bring Brick a glass of cold water so that he could wash down his sleeping pills, and Brick lay on his back, and started thinking how they could stop Humphreys.

Chapter XIII

It rained all right, a slow miserable drizzle that first tamped down the dust and then went through and made a coat of slick over the thick sod and finally bit holes into the ground and left half-inch puddles. But the crowd had started to pile up outside the stadium at 10 A.M. and when the gates opened at eleven-thirty, there were three thousand people outside, patient and sodden.

And at noon, it stopped, and when Max Addison looked out of his hotel room window, he knew he had no choice, nor did he want one, just so long as it was all right with Palmer.

It was all right with Brick. He lay on his back, forcing himself to relax, the codeine long since worn off, and the pain and stiffness a blanket over him. Cathy, like Addison, stood at the window, and she felt relief when the yellow sun broke hazily through and filtered to the damp sidewalk below. The waiting and the hoping had ended, and soon it would all be over. Even Johnny, busy alternately with hot water bags and ice packs, trying to loosen the muscles and reduce the swellings, was glad to see the sun.

"Game's on," Brick said, his eyes steady on the window pane, where the drops of rain turned silvery bright. "I'll have to get up." And without a word he sat up. They could not see how he had done it, his hands pressing the mattress, hidden by the blanket, and pushing down to raise his body from the waist. And they couldn't feel the palms go slippery with sweat and the wrists liquid-weak with pain.

"Are my slippers there?" he asked, his feet dangling above the floor. He knew they were, but time, time he needed.

"Yes," Cathy said, "how do you feel, honey?"

"Not so good," he grinned. "Like I didn't have enough sleep."

"Not half enough," Cathy said, her face white. "You should have slept through today's game. Then it wouldn't matter any more."

He looked at her, trying to tell her. "Yes it would, honey," he said gently. "It's the whole thing, my playing."

She sighed and got up from the window sill where she had been half-sitting, half-resting, and walked across the room, her back to him.

Brick looked at her, and then to Johnny. "Well, kid, I guess you better take off. Nothing more you can do. They'll miss you at the hospital."

Johnny looked at him sharply. "Don't be silly," he said. "I'm not going back to the hospital. I couldn't, now."

"Why not, kid?" Brick asked.

"For one thing, you're not allowed to leave without permission, and you're not allowed to treat people outside of the hospital—oh, that's not what I wanted to say. You see, I'm not blaming you—damn," he said, and he, too, got up and started to walk away, to the window, where he stood and looked far down the street. Then he turned, as though he had to make it clear. "This whole thing, it begins with me. We both know that. Maybe I've done some good, last night, this morning. I didn't think it could be done, putting you back together, but I think we've licked it. I've heard about things like this, read about them in medical case histories. Guys beat up like you, and then patched up, practically as good as new. I never believed it before. Now I don't know. I still don't think you should play, and if I had my way you wouldn't." He stopped again. When he went on, a half-minute later, his voice had changed, almost dull in its quality, and the words came out without effort. "Yes, you would. I want you to play, Brick. I'm selfish that way. I want you to play for me."

"For you, kid?" Brick said.

"Yes. So I can feel I've done some good. So I can feel good, that's what I mean. I haven't felt good since, since—the whole business began a month ago. Clean, that's how I want to feel. You know what I mean?"

Brick nodded. "Sure," he said, "I know what you mean." He wanted the kid to talk, to get it all out in one flood of self-abuse and pity.

Johnny started the walk again, back across the room, to the door, and back to the window, and half back again, where he stopped. "I'm not going back to the hospital. I'll go some place, out West some place, maybe even fake some references, change my name. If that doesn't work, I'll go back to school, and learn something else."

Like Addison, Brick thought. New name, new job. New life. With the old one, in the shadows, dim, dark, but always there. And he wondered whether the kid could do it. And then he didn't wonder any more, for the kid *had* to do it, no matter what the penalty. "Yes," he said, "that sounds good. Doesn't it, Cathy?"

Cathy looked down at him, and she nodded, and Brick knew she hadn't heard a word of it. "Well," he said, "game time in an hour," and he dropped his feet into the slippers and stood up, and started talking, too rapidly, "Guess I'll wash up, come along, Johnny, I may need some help, see you in a few minutes, hon." And he took his first step, behind the cover of words, and then the foot was down and his weight shifted to it, and passed on to the other, and he was walking, slowly, stiffly, and though the pain tried to fill him, it didn't quite, and a little corner inside remained untouched and that corner lit up a smile, a wild grin that swept Johnny and Cathy, and they smiled back, and then they started to laugh, and with every sound pain slid along his ribs, and yet every sound was louder, and the room was laughing and swaying and he was out of the room, going down the corridor to the bathroom, Johnny behind him, watching, watching, and both of them laughing....

He got to the ball park twenty minutes later, forty minutes before game time. He walked through the soft dirt tunnel to the little office, and hesitated, and then stepped across the narrow underway to the other room, to the locker room, and he pushed open the door and went in. There was a whoosh of breath, and somebody whispered a single word and in the corner of the room he thought he heard the word, "What—" and it sounded like Muller's voice. He walked across the room, to his locker, and flung it open, and then turned around. He didn't know what Addison had told them, if anything. "It was a hard bench," he said, and then he gathered up his uniform and walked out, to Addison's office.

The old man was sitting at his desk when Brick threw open the door. He smiled at Brick, but the smile didn't hold, and then he was away from the desk, his right hand gripping Brick's shoulder. "How is it?" he asked, his eyes fearful.

"Not bad," Brick said. He emptied his pockets on Addison's desk. "Here," he said, "the novocain. Where Johnny showed you." He started to undress, slowly, the pain urgent now, with every move.

In twenty minutes it was over. The shot in the hand, into the hunched muscles of the palm and a second one between the first two fingers. Then across the chest, in three places, and already the numbness took over his left hand. "No rubdown," Brick said, "it hurts too much to touch." He stood in his uniform, a strange sight, his nose spread wide and ugly red, tape ends showing at his nostrils; his cheek purple and black and puffy now; his mouth mashed and fat. He looked down at his feet, and then he lowered his knees, an inch, two, three, waiting for the pain in his thighs to return, but it didn't, and then he tapped his sides, the thick cushion of tape, and that, too, was painless, but that he knew would return when the novocain wore off, in a couple of innings.

He walked out onto the diamond, and he turned his face away from the stands and looked out at the far-off center field fence. From the stands, he knew, he looked like just another beat-up ball player, and that was what he wanted. No sympathy. No pity. He watched Bobbett lob in his last few pitches to the relief catcher, and he waited for the crowd to spot him and shout down their abuse, but no sound came, and he knew they were waiting, on the borderline, waiting to be taken, one way or the other. And he wondered whether there was strength enough in him to win this battle, with the fans, to capture their loyalty 100 per cent when he made the throw or caught hold of one or put the ball on a runner for the big out. There they sat, ten thousand or more, remembering that last play yesterday when Brick took the foul pop in the dugout, and they also remembered ugly black headlines which called Brick Palmer a crook. And so they waited, in silence.

In the dugout he let Addison clamp on the knee guards, and he wondered whether he'd be able to take them off himself, and then he heard someone down the line mutter, "Mama's boy," and somebody else answer, harshly, "Shut up." He kept his head down, watching Addison, ready to anticipate any wrong move, so that he could mask his face when pain struck. But Addison was gentle and slow, and suddenly there was a giant roar from the crowd as the Outlaws left the bench and went trotting onto the wet diamond.

They were alone, for a brief half-minute, he and Addison. "Thank you," the old man said, and Brick nodded his head. "Don't be a fool, boy," Addison went on, and again Brick nodded. He waited for the manager to say something else, but he was looking out at the men on the diamond, at the relief catcher warming up Bobbett, his fast ball smoking through the sunlight, and Brick got up, and walked slowly out.

Brick moved behind the plate, stiff-legged and tentative, his mitt held by a hand without feeling, his chest rising and falling in rhythmic numbness. He faced the flags, while they played the anthems, his cap in his hand and he squared his shoulders and felt a twinge at his ribs, and he thought, "So soon."

Then the crowd roared again, and this time the roar didn't die, for it was going to be a roaring crowd, every pitch, every foul ball, every pop fly. And behind the shield of the roar, Brick lowered his knees, his glove on the ground supporting him, and he squatted, deep into the rocking chair. He stayed that way, his weight on his glove, and then he raised the mitt, and his thighs cried out and trembled and then they held firm, and Bobbett was going into his first motion, the Mauler lead-off man crowding up close and waving his bat, and Brick felt himself draw away, sway back two inches, his whole body flinching as the ball streaked in.

And then the batter was whirling away from the plate, twisting his body frantically, his bat flying out of his hands, and the third base coach yelled, "Watch out!" and Brick's left hand went up and to the left and speared the duster.

He was out of the rocking chair on the first pitch and his ribs were on fire. He had not held firm, he knew, his glove a wobbling, indistinct target, and Bobbett, of the impeccable control, missed badly. He started to throw the ball back to the pitcher, and then he realized he couldn't, and he walked out to the mound instead, and the crowd's roar turned into a mumble of discontent.

"I'm sorry," he said to Bobbett, and the pitcher nodded, his lips tight. Brick handed him the ball, and turned and walked back to the plate and he could see Addison's white face at the edge of the dugout, and he smiled at the old man.

Back into the chair he went, and though the shadow of the Mauler's waving bat was a constant menace, and though pain was his twin, he stuck his glove up for all the world and Bobbett to see, and he held it, even while the bat hitched back and then lashed forward, and the tiny white pill grew and grew and exploded, in his waiting pocket. And at the last second, the last hundredth of a second actually, he let his body relax, and with the explosion, that hundredth of a second before, he rocked back, and then he rocked forward, the ball in his right hand and with a gentle jerk of the elbow, a flick of the wrist, the clean white baseball returned to the size of a pill, and then disappeared in Bobbett's down-snapping glove. And behind Brick, the umpire whirled counterclockwise, his right hand rising slowly, and the word came out, "Stuh-rike."

And there, in that last corner of his body not plugged with pain he felt the heat of exultation rise and for the first time that day his voice barked out. The game, already two pitches and three minutes old, was just beginning for Brick Palmer.

"Attaboy, Bobby boy," he said, "come to me, boy, nobody hits, nobody hits." And with his words, a veil of silence drifted over the rest of the infield, Sweeney, Rostelli, Furman, Muller, all of them quiet now, and Brick didn't care. It was his voice, alone, that swept through the grass, and though Bobbett lost the rest of his infield, he felt the strength of the man behind the plate, and reluctantly perhaps, he drew from it, as a thousand pitchers of the past had drawn from it, and his next delivery was a pellet of dynamite, the ball just a slender cream of white.

The rest of the Mauler half-inning was a breeze, stirred up by a crackling fast ball and pushed along by futilely waving bats. And Humphreys, in his clean-up position, never entered the batter's box, even as Brick never again left his rocking chair.

In the dugout Brick found his place next to Addison, and each understood the other's veiled words. "How is it going?" the manager asked, and Brick answered, "Fine." And then they turned and watched Sweeney take a third strike, and Riley pop one up behind the plate, and Muller hit one on the line, but right at Humphreys, for the third out.

And Brick saw that he couldn't win, no matter what. He was glad he hadn't been forced to take off his shin guards and protector, yet that meant he hadn't batted, that the Outlaws had gone down one-two-three, and you don't win games sending twenty-seven men to the plate, and back again. And he'd have to lead off the second, get the guards off fast, and the strange paradox confused him as he started to hope the Maulers were at bat a long time, so that he'd have time to prepare his body for the next problem.

But while he gave in thus to pain, his glove betrayed his self-catering, a glove held by a deadened hand that even now was puffing and squishing water below the purple skin. For the glove was alive, coaxing the ball from Bobbett, waiting hungrily for its next mouthful. And all the time, behind the glove, words came twisting out of a wrecked mouth, "Nobody hits, Bobby boy, you're the boss, boy, you're the boss." And nobody hit, not even Humphreys, lofting to Riley in dead center, 400 futile feet away, and the second inning was gone, and Brick was in the dugout, his hands at the straps, and the shin guards lay at his feet, before he could think.

He had not taken batting practice, and he did not know whether he could swing at the ball, the pain already starting to grow in his chest. He planted himself in the box, not even digging his tiny toe holes, but standing flat-footed and heavy, the bat on his shoulder, and then the Mauler pitcher, another big right-hander with lots of speed and a good change-up, sent in his first pitch, at the shoulders, on the inside corner.

Brick took it, and the crowd roared, even before the umpire went into his swinging strike sign, pointing his right hand at the watching heavens. And again, a second time he took, for a second strike, the nothing ball, at half speed, splitting the plate.

The crowd howled, and Brick could hear a single voice, "Hey, what's a matter, Goldbrick, tired?" And, "You ain't getting paid to stand there, Palmer—or are you?"

No, Brick thought, nobody's paying me. I'm doing the paying. He could feel the sweat forming at his eyebrows, poised at the bridge of his nose, and then he shook his head, and tiny beads of water went flying off, and he started to dig his toes in. Take your cut, he told himself, and the Mauler pitcher was in his graceful motion, his right arm appearing suddenly out of the sky in far-off left-center field, and the pitch came pouring in. It was the fast one, on the outside, maybe an inch or two off the corner, but Brick knew the rules—an inch or two off was as good as a couple of inches in, and he swung, laboriously, fearfully, a lagging, sweeping swing, with wrists locked, and the bat went poking at the ball, and he hit it.

He dropped his bat and dug his right foot hard into the ground, his eyes watching the blooping fly ball rise above the infield and then come swiftly down, and he saw, too, the second baseman turn tail desperately and sprint out, his back to the diamond, and Brick knew it would drop in, and he held up what little speed he might have mustered, and trotted to first.

And the stands were silent, except for one snorting fan, behind the first base boxes. "Oh you lucky burn, you! Where do you buy your hits?"

It was only at first, standing on the bag, that Brick remembered how badly hurt he was, and he knew that the game itself would save him—for another few innings—for in the action, in the swing, in the running, there was no brain at work, only the controlled reflexes of a hundred thousand swings, a hundred hundred thousand steps.

He stepped off first, down the line with the next pitch, and then he was digging for second, as Rostelli stepped into the delivery and hit it, sharply, to the shortstop side of second, and Brick could see Humphreys now, in all his grace and beauty, running, bending, scooping, stepping on second a dozen strides before Brick, and firing the ball right at Brick's cap, on the line to the first baseman, as Brick ducked, for the double play.

And a minute later Brick was letting Addison strap on the guards, and out he went, for the third. Slow he was, and leaden, and the crowd laughed and roared when he let a foul pop land a dozen feet behind him, and then somebody shouted down, as they had all month, "Hey, Tricky, how much they paying you?" but this time it hurt, and Brick stopped dead and removed his mask and searched the crowd, trying to spot the offending voice. But all he saw was the wall of white faces, splotched by black pits, round and moving, from which the voices came.

But the inning was over, though the Maulers put two men on base, one with a hit and a second with a base on balls, when the umpire failed to give Bobbett a corner he owned. It was Rostelli who stopped them, going into short left field for a fading fly ball that threatened to drop in, snaring it over his shoulder as his cap flew off, for the last out.

The Malone right-hander continued to pitch what Brick once called, a long month ago, high school ball. The fast one, the change-up, the fast one, the change-up. And nobody hit.

The number three man for the Maulers led off the fourth inning, and Bobbett made his first mistake. Though the glove was steady, at the knees, four inches above, on the inside corner, the pitch missed, coming in at the belt, right through the middle slot, and the Mauler strode and swung, and the ball went streaking into left-center field, Riley racing over and back, making the greatest play of his life, going high into the air and stopping the bounding ball with his bare hand, and whirling and throwing to second base, a half-second late.

And Humphreys stepped in, and Brick was silent now, saving his breath that came and went out of his open mouth. Would they bunt, he thought, with none out? The play was bunt, he knew, except Humphreys was up, and he had never seen the big shortstop bunt. It still was bunt, he thought, except, except.... He didn't know why his reason said bunt and everything else said no. Maybe it was because he put himself in the Maulers' spot, and they figured Bobbett would pitch up high, at the chest, to get Humphreys to bunt the ball in the air, and instead they'd have Humphreys swing away, level off on the high fast one.

Brick stopped thinking, and gave Bobbett the signal, and he thought he saw the pitcher's mouth twitch a bit, in what might have been fear, or a smile. It was the curve, if you could call that thing Bobbett threw a curve, a little wrinkler that broke maybe an inch and a half, if that.

Bobbett dropped his arms to his belt and held them there, looking over his right shoulder at the prancing Mauler, off second base, and he hunched his shoulder once, driving the runner back, and then he turned, and threw. Humphreys stepped in on the waist-high pitch, at the outer third of the plate, and he started to swing, and then, halfway around, his wrists still in a vise, he checked himself, and Brick gathered in the pitch for a called strike, and he knew that Humphreys had beaten them, this time up.

He called for the fast one, at the knees, and Bobbett came through, but so did Humphreys' bat, fairly swishing as it lashed out, and Rostelli's dive into the hole between short and third was futile, the ball past him before he hit the ground, and the runner was around third and storming in while Riley made his play to second, to keep Humphreys from stretching. It was 1-0, Maulers.

And though the stands rocked with noise, and Humphreys kept Bobbett busy, the Outlaw hurler dug in and blew the fast ball by, and the inning was over, with Humphreys no nearer the plate.

It was one-two-three, again, for the Outlaws in the fourth, Brick waiting on deck for his turn, but not getting it, his shin guards still on, and he realized with a shock that the Mauler pitcher had a one-hitter going, and that only twelve men had gone to bat against him.

In the fifth, though he could barely bend, Brick had to come out of his rocking chair, a swinging bunt dribbling eight feet in front of him down the third base line, and he made the play, in time by a half-step. The crowd was silent, and Brick wondered whether there was a baseball brain in the whole lot, for he had played the ball badly, slow to start, slow to bend, grappling for the ball, and barely winning with his throw that lobbed its way to first. It was the wet grass that saved him, he knew, slowing down the ball, slowing down the runner, and establishing the obvious excuse for his weak throw—the ball must have slipped.

And that was the Mauler fifth, with Bobbett just as strong as he had been in the first, nobody sending the ball to the outfield, and the Outlaws were in for their bats, still trailing, and time was building as the empty space on the scoreboard dwindled away to half its size.

There was no luck in Brick's bat this time, taking again the first pitch, waving weakly at the second while the crowd jeered, and then, paralyzed by the pain that had set in, taking again, as the ball missed the inside corner, and hearing the umpire roar out the third strike. He turned, without a word, for he knew the ball was close enough, even if the umps weren't stealing inches from his bat. Yesterday, any day, even in the big league, he would have swung. Today was today, and he couldn't, and back to the dugout he could hear the crowd, and now it was no longer taunting him out of habit. There was a new note, sullen and deep-throated, and Brick knew what was happening.

They thought they were being taken. They thought Brick Palmer, crook, was quitting on them, for a price. And he could feel their eyes, their hate-filled eyes, as he walked out to take his position for the sixth, and suddenly he wondered what he could do, for his strength was gone, his arm was gone, his hand was a throb of meat, and his ribs, his whole chest and sides, ah, he had never known such pain.

For one brief play, yesterday, he had held them in the palm of his hand, but now they were lost. On the borderline they had been sitting, waiting, and now they made their decision. Crook, he was, a man to be hated. And Brick felt he could do nothing about it.

What had happened to the yesterday Brick Palmer, the Brick Palmer who had felt once more the full power of his body, the great strength hidden in his arms and legs? In one day, that man had been wiped out, reduced to the alien flesh of baseball's old age. He knew, now, more than he had ever known before, how Marty Marion must feel when he bends for the grass cutter in the hole, how DiMag must feel now that his great legs are dying and his arm is an empty shell. Through the years he had seen them come, out of the bushes, fresh from college, green and strong, oh so strong, their bodies supple and swift and never, never betraying them. And he had seen them go, a step at a time, sometimes beginning in the back, sometimes the legs, too many charley horses, too many bone bruises, too many days and nights.

He knelt, now, Brick Palmer, old and beaten, and there paraded before his eyes the old-timers he had seen in their glory. And where were they, Gehringer, Mize, and Paul Waner, where were they, Frisch, Terry Moore and Marion? Ah, no, they were not still around, not even Mize and Marion, they had gone, long ago, over the hill and into the shadows, though men who resembled them still played, and sometimes out of the shadows they'd come, ghosts of their old glory, great ghosts, perhaps, but ghosts.

And as he flinched at the sight in his mind, even as he flinched from the sound of the stands, heaping down its abuse, and from the pain that wrapped around him, tight and unyielding now, he thought one more dreadful thought. And that was: the fans, they cheered the stars in their glory, and when they went down, the fans cheered them again, or at least they watched in silence, in respect. Whereas he, Brick Palmer, he still remembered the shouts of praise, the years of glory, but now that he had been wrecked, the noise was louder, the shouts more audible, but they were not of praise.

And as the Mauler batter stepped in and lifted a dinky foul fly, behind the plate, on Bobbett's first delivery, to open the sixth inning, what could Brick Palmer do? He stayed there, deep in his crouch, his ears telling him that the ball was landing twenty-five feet behind him, ten feet from the railing. There was nothing he could do, and he felt the new mob feeling in the crowd, *like a lynch mob*, he thought, angry and restless, and a tremble swept through Brick, as the grandstands seemed to push down closer, and he shut his eyes for a moment, and then opened them, and saw Bobbett.

Here, here was the game, he thought. Bobbett. Pitching in the sixth inning, as far as he could go, and showing no quit, showing nothing but strength and courage. Bobbett. An Outlaw. A man he had hated, until a few days ago. Bobbett had suffered as he had. Barred for life. And now he was suffering in the other way, like Brick. Physically. Pitching beyond his ability, beyond his strength, beyond his body's deficiencies. With his heart.

And Brick came out of the rocking chair. No more of this, he thought. Live, he thought, you're not dead. *Play*, he thought, *not half play*. What had been the meaning of that pretty little speech to Addison, last night in the hotel room, how he *had* to play because otherwise the fans would call him a quitter? What was he now, sitting here, letting foul pops land behind him? And the answer was a brand on his flesh. Quitter. He stood there, braced and ready, and a red smear ran across his eyes, shutting out his sight for a moment, and the band of pain tightened, but his glove was still, and his voice was working.

"C'mon, you Outlaw," he said, though the words were coming out of a mouth too sore to speak, "look alive in there, nobody hits." And he shouted a word to Sweeney, down there at third, ninety feet and four hundred miles away, a blocky white body swimming in the haze of third base, "Talk it up, Sweeney, boy, let's hear the chatter, boy," and, unwillingly perhaps, Sweeney found himself talking, and then Rostelli, and Furman and Muller. Talking, dispiritedly, but making noise, and Bobbett responded to it, going through the sixth inning on six pitches, the lead-off man fanning on four, and the next two men popping up Bobbett's first delivery.

But it was no use, Brick thought, this pitching beyond yourself, for the Outlaws weren't hitting, and the Mauler right-hander was getting hotter every inning, the sixth going down the drain, and both sides, up and down in the seventh, and the eighth, with Maulers on base, three of them, but nobody scoring, and the Outlaws, breaking out of their hitless skein, but getting no man past third. And it was 1-0 into the ninth, and Bobbett was slump-shouldered and drawn, going out to the hill.

For Brick, the pain was habit, kin to him now, and out of the slits of his eyes, closing every inning as the sun puffed up the raw flesh of his cheekbones, he squinted to see Bobbett and his pitch. There was a Mauler stepping in, no name to him, just a dim familiar sight, *the man who whiffed on the outside pitch last time, some time, ten years ago.* And so they pitched him outside, the tired arm that went back and then forward, aimed at the heavy wet glove.

And then there was another one, another Mauler, dim and familiar, and this time it was inside and then change-up, and the ball was popped up, and now Brick's ear failed him, he couldn't tell whether the ball was too far away for him to play it, so he spun out of his half-crouch, and went digging back, head up, looking for it, and finding it, and clamping his heavy mitt around it, and then feeling his body hit the railing, and bounce gently off.

And a third Mauler, bigger than the others, not so dim now, and even more familiar, Humphreys his name was, and out of the thinning sight, Brick could see Bobbett square his shoulders and he could see Bobbett move his lips, in a curse or a prayer, and then the arm, back and forth, once, twice, three times. And Humphreys, tired now himself, strained and desperate, swinging, once, twice, three times, and walking out to his position at shortstop.

The shadows had swept the field, and the chill had fallen, and some strange gust of wind had found a tree of golden leaves, and sent them flying over the fence in center field, whirling over the Mauler center fielder's head, and then falling to the grass over 400 feet from the plate. And the fans stood, in the bottom half of the ninth, roaring and moving, and stamping their feet, to keep the chill out perhaps, or to fire up the Outlaws, for this last time.

And while Brick sat next to Addison and felt the man's gentle hand on his knee, and while he heard the crowd's roar change tone, grow shrill and then tense and then ear-splitting, and while he again felt the hand, not so gentle now, but gripping tight and then leaving his knee as the man, Addison, jumped to his feet, and his voice joined the ear-splitters—all the while, Brick sat there, not knowing what was happening, until somebody yelled, "Palmer," and he walked out to the diamond, and squatted in the "on deck" circle, and then he was moving again, closer to the plate, and into the batter's box, and his eyes cleared for a second, and he brushed the pain from his forehead, and there were Outlaws on base, and the scoreboard said one out, and the score was 1-0, still.

And then he knew what it was. It was the last of the ninth, not only of the game, but of his baseball career, his last licks, with men on first and third, and one out, and the bat was in his hands, too heavy to swing, too heavy to hold, even. Yet he was holding it, he knew, and therefore he could swing it.

Could, he thought, and would. And the painful simplicity of it terrified him, for it went against all the rules. His body *couldn't* stand up, yet did. His arms *couldn't* swing the bat, yet would.

And the first pitch was by him, the speed of it a shock, and he hadn't swung, and the crowd drifted down that sullen noise. Why, he thought, there is but one thing to do, and he would do it, and he looked past the pitcher, as he had done yesterday, and he looked at Humphreys, and saw in him all that had once been himself, and he wondered whether Humphreys knew that it wasn't all in the body, in the strength, but some of it, the most some of it was in the heart, in the soul, or whatever you want to call it.

And the second pitch was coming in, and he thought, this is what you can be some day, Humphreys, and he swung, a ruined body propelling a too heavy bat, and the ball had been hit, solidly, he thought, but he couldn't tell, there was no sting in his palms, and the crowd's noise seemed no different, but he was running, that he knew.

And as he reached first, he turned and saw the action in one blindingly clear instant, no man on third now, but a runner, an Outlaw runner, Riley it was, racing, racing like a long, slender greyhound, shoulders high, head forward, running from second to third, and beyond him, in deep left center field, a man, a Mauler, drawing his arm back, and throwing, and in closer, Humphreys, no mistake about him, motionless, glove in front of him, back to the diamond, waiting for the ball, and Brick pounded to second, no longer watching the action, for there were things to do.

He hit the base, and he saw the ball fly past him, towards the plate, but he dared not look to his left, to see Riley thunder homeward, for he was on his way to third base. If they got Riley at the plate, Brick thought, he'd have to make third. Why, he didn't know, for a man on second, with two out, is practically as good as a man on third, and why risk that third out, a tired broken man running to a base too far away, so easy a target. He didn't know why. He just felt it. It was another thing he had to do, for who knows, a wild pitch, and the man on third may score, even with two out; the infield hit, the swinging bunt, the error, all these may score the man from third, even with two out. And so he ran, on feet of blood and crushed bone, and then he was near to the bag, and he did what runners do, what else would he do? He threw himself into the air, broken-boned and splintered, and slid into third, his eyes on that outside corner of the sack, his toe reaching for what his eyes saw. And then he hit the ground, and the red smear rose up and enveloped him, and he never even felt his foot touch the base, nor could he have heard the umpire, ninety feet away, at home plate, yell "Safe!" as Riley beat the throw from Humphreys, nor did he see the crowd spill over the stands, a howling maniacal mob, roaring in the lust of victory. Nor did he know, Brick Palmer, lying there in the mud and dirt of third base, where no play had to be made, that the score was 2-1, Outlaws, and that the game was over.

This he didn't know until the crowd suddenly stopped roaring, in pieces, as they started to notice the figure lying there, motionless at third base, ignored by the players, Osage and Malone alike. And then, though Brick never heard them or saw them, they held their noise, and edged toward the still ball player, held their noise in respect, stepping aside as first Addison reached Brick, and then the rest of the Outlaws.

This he didn't know, until he had been told about it, and he never heard the gasp when Addison reached down and ripped open Brick's shirt, and stripped it off, and there was the tape, inch after inch of it, letting them all see what held the man together and letting them see the ugly purple swelling of flesh around the edges of the tape, where streaks of angry blood showed beneath, like blackened claws. And then they whispered, in appreciation, and this, too, he never heard, except in the retelling, and then there was water on his face, and Brick felt hands all over him, and he thought he had to escape the groping hands, for the hands could tag him, and this must not happen, and he struggled, and then lay still, as the hands were too many, and faces started to appear above the hands, and he knew that these were not third basemen, not all of them.

He sat up, numb to the agony of himself, and he saw Addison, and there was a smile on the old man's face, but behind it were tears, and he wondered if they had lost, the Outlaws. And then he saw where he was, and then he thought he had been called out, and he got to his feet, ready to play the next inning. And then he heard them, frighteningly close, the crowd, roaring, and he looked into the white wall of faces around him, and he saw just the faces of people, and they were cheering. *Cheering.*

Cathy was there, in the locker room, the men standing in towels, embarrassed and silent and watching. Johnny was there, too, his fingers easing the tape off the stained flesh, while ice, blessed ice appeared, and his hand rested in it, and more for his face.

The novocain had dulled him, again, and he didn't care, somehow, what Johnny did, or what he said. Whether they had broken through, whether his hand was gone for good, never to clasp another baseball, whether his foot would need an extra arch support all the rest of its limping life. He was happy, for he had heard the noise, and he had seen the faces of his men, his own Outlaws, and, more than that, they, *we* had won.

Ah, he thought, and maybe he thought aloud, for everybody stared at him, this is good. And his broken hand came out of the ice and reached for Cathy's and he squeezed hers, and the men watched and then turned away, talking to themselves, too loud and too quickly.

And then Brick realized something. These men, they still didn't know about the bribe, a month ago, nor did the crowd. Yet they respected him, though they believed he was a man who had sold out his team, once. And, he thought, it doesn't matter now, whether they ever know. They've bought me, on their terms, which were false ones, but so much tougher than the true ones. And he was glad they had thought he was an outlaw. An *Outlaw.*

He turned to Johnny, so busy, so efficient, so quick and mature. "Don't tell them," he said, "it doesn't matter any more."

And Johnny looked up, once, from the tape and medicine, and said quickly, "Don't be a fool. I already have. The papers. The hospital. The Commissioner. Maybe it doesn't matter to you, any more. But it does to me."

Brick looked at him, and saw the truth in the boy, and he knew that Johnny had done what he had to do. Live with yourself, that was the important thing.

Johnny went on, not looking up now, still working, patching, putting together a man who needed no putting together, except of flesh. "Also, I told that school, out in Wisconsin. Where they promised you that job."

And Cathy leaned forward, and kissed the boy, the *man* on the cheek, and Brick closed his eyes and smiled.

And then he was up again, his eyes bright, and he turned to Addison, and he asked, "How did the Blues make out today?" and Addison smiled and said, "That's how I feel about the White Sox. Even now. I'll put on the radio. We'll find out." He turned to his office.

THE END

A Conversation with Arnold Hano

• •

At a recent gathering of writers whose novels hit the shelves in the 1950s and 1960s, Arnold Hano held court. With him were Matthew Gant, Gil Dodge, Ad Gordon and Mike Heller. Not surprisingly, Arnold did all the talking. His companions were, in fact, his pseudonyms under which Hano published the lion's share of his novels.

Arnold Hano turned 90 in the spring of 2012, and at a heavily-attended gathering in celebration of that milestone, he, not surprisingly, got the biggest laughs and proved that he's still as sharp as ever, critiquing the accuracy and presentation of his many tributes with his ear for detail that served him so well as managing editor of the now legendary paperback publishing operation, Lion Books, from its inception in 1949 until his departure in 1954. Hano is justifiably proud of his editorship of Lion both for his courage to publish classics other houses had either overlooked or shied away from, and for his ability to work with and help launch or enhance the careers of a stable of writers including David Goodis, Richard Matheson and, of course, Jim Thompson. Hano's lifelong friendship and editorial stewardship of Thompson's career began with Lion's *The Killer Inside Me* in 1952. With the rediscovery of Thompson, the legacy of the Thompson-Hano-Lion collaboration became the stuff of hardboiled publishing history.

But what remains largely under-reported is Arnold Hano's own writing career. With the exception of his baseball classic, *A Day in the Bleachers* (1955), the first novel written from the perspective of a true fan, and now regarded as one of the great sports novels of all time – the remainder of Hano's 26 books are no longer in print. With the publication of this trio of his early works – one of them under his own name for the first time – it is hoped that all of Hano's works will ultimately find their way back into print, allowing new readers to discover one of the surest and most original voices in fiction. It was this desire that compelled this writer to team with contemporary crime writer/editor Gary Phillips and begin the search for a new publisher. Happily, that search eventually led to Stark House, and the publication of the book you're now holding.

A brief bio: Arnold Hano was born in 1922, and moved with his family to the Bronx in 1926. After attending DeWitt Clinton High School, he went to Long Island University, playing varsity baseball his senior year. In 1941, he joined the *New York Daily News* as a copy boy before entering the Army in 1942. He saw combat in WWII in the Pacific at Attu and Kwajalein. Arnold also married in 1942, and his son Stephen was born in 1944, his daughter Susan in 1946.

After the war, he was a high school English teacher and editor of a Dept. of Labor newsletter before joining Bantam Books as an editor of western novels in 1947. Later, he became managing editor, finding the company's first million-seller, *The Chinese Room* by V.S. Connell. He also began reading manuscripts for the Scott Meredith, sold his short story *Hand in Glove*, and began selling to pulp magazines during that period.

In 1949, he was fired from Bantam for trying to unionize their shop. That same year, he was hired by Magazine Management to start Lion Books, which he edited and ran from 1949-1954. At the same time, he was selling his own writing both to Lion and other publishers. In 1951, he sold his first novel, *The Big Out*, to Barnes.

Following divorce from his first wife, he married Bonnie Abraham – to whom he is still happily married – on June 30, 1951. During the rest of that decade, Arnold continued to write and sell novels in various genres and under assorted pseudonyms to an array of publishers (see his bibliography), with the most significant of these being his personal memoir of attending the first game of the 1954 World Series, *A Day in the Bleachers*.

In 1955, Arnold, Bonnie and their daughter Laurel moved west to Laguna Beach, California. Continuing to write novels, columns, hundreds of articles for *TV Guide* and *Sport* magazine, Arnold also became very active in local and national politics. From 1964-1976, he also taught writing classes at the University of California, Irvine. In 1963, he received the Sidney Hillman Award for magazine writing and was also named Magazine Sportswriter of the Year. In 1977, he received a Master's degree from California State Fullerton. From 1983-1987, he was a professor of writing at the USC School of Journalism; in 1990, he was a visiting professor at Pitzer College. And from 1991-93, he and Bonnie served in the Peace Corps in Costa Rica, where he began work on his autobiography, entitled *Hack*.

As of 2012, Arnold and Bonnie are still living in Laguna Beach and very active in their community. Arnold is busily editing *Hack* and continuing to write as the Hanos anticipate their 61st anniversary.

In the following interview, Arnold's voice is as strong, fresh and insightful as ever, leavened by his love of puns, jokes and his self-deprecating sense of humor. As we talked about the three books included here and highlights from his career, it became abundantly clear that not only is Arnold Hano a writer's writer, he's a socially-conscious advocate for important causes, an encyclopedic sports authority... and a hell of a great guy. And we'll all credit Bonnie's unwavering support for his amazing longevity.

The interview began with a general question about the writing of Arnold's first novel, *The Big Out*. With that, he was off and running.

Arnold Hano: While working at Lion Books in the early 1950s, I decided to try my hand at a baseball novel. I had become intrigued with the Shoeless Joe Jackson story—the throwing of the 1919 World Series by the Chicago White Sox. What interested me was not the 1919 Series but what had happened to those eight White Sox players who had taken money and then been banned from organized ball. Had they just drifted out of baseball and into tending bar? Or had some continued to play ball, at a different level? Sandlot ball? Semi-pro ball?

I invented a baseball league in my novel, outside the aegis of organized baseball. My role as an outsider, I suppose. A league where such players could still play ball professionally, still display their fine art to a smaller, less discerning audience, but at least to a crowd of some sort. Their need to be memorialized as other than crooks. I took one of those old White Sox players banned from baseball and made him the manager of my team of outlaws. Whom I called the "Outlaws."

The manager was not my protagonist, but he gave the novel the bad-good quality I look for in my characters. Villain-hero. Not one or the other but both, and often both at the same time.

My protagonist was more straightforward. He was a big-league catcher accused of taking a bribe to throw a game, and ultimately banned from organized ball for life. The catcher joins an outlaw league. Now, I don't believe any such league ever existed. But just as there had never been a black cowboy, so I was told, and had to invent one [in *The Last Notch* (1958)], I decided I would pass off this outlaw league as though it did exist.

On May 3, 1950, I wrote a proposal to John Lowell Pratt, president and publisher of A. S. Barnes, a hundred-year-old house that was the major publisher of sports books at the time. I suggested my novel to him. Back came a reply dated the next day, May 4, 1950, wherein Pratt gave me a go-ahead. "You are correct in saying the subject of unorganized or independent baseball has not been covered, and I think you could write a grand story." It would appear from his words I had pulled off a hoax—he had bought my idea of a league that never was.

Because I had a regular job at the time, as editor of Lion Books, and was taking home books and manuscripts nightly to read for possible publication, I had to fight to find time to write this, my first novel. I did it by getting up an hour early every day and working for that hour. The phone would not ring;

there were no interruptions. I sat down and the words appeared magically on the paper as the typewriter keys chattered on, seemingly unstruck.

In a month of these one-hour stints I had three finished chapters and an outline which I sent to Barnes. The rest of the novel went about as smoothly as the early chapters and I was paid about as poorly as one would expect, and the book came out with a nice cover, the catcher, looking eerily like my brother, on a green ball field.

I waited for my fame. Weeks went by. No reviews. I walked by a clutch of bookstores in midtown Manhattan one day and stopped at Scribner's, my favorite then, to ask a woman clerk, "Do you have copies of *The Big Out?*" She looked me over and said quickly, "Oh, you must be the author." Just by looking at me. Yes, she had a few copies of the book and asked me to sign them, so I did, perhaps four or five copies. Although the book had come out in an invisible state, she had made me feel important.

Six months later, after the book had totally disappeared both from any bookshelf and my immediate concern, I was leafing through a Sunday *New York Times* book review section, and there was a review of *The Big Out*. And it was a splendid review. I do remember the reviewer, Ralph Adams Brown, said the book was one of the most thrilling sports novels he had ever read.

Today I see the message. I had moved ahead of my time—books about Joe Jackson and the Black Sox scandal have since come thick and fast. But mine was first. Story of my life—a book too soon and a review too late.

Q: That was your first experience in writing a novel. Was there a feeling of this being a major accomplishment?

AH: I was writing for my brother when I was eight years old in the avenue newsletter, things like that. And at college in the late 1930s, I was the sports editor of the weekly paper the school put out and the next year the editor in chief. So, I was always being published. So, I did not go through a process where it was "Wow."

Q: You were already in the publishing business.

AH: I wrote again and something was published, and the fact that it was a novel or a short story or a poem or anything, it didn't impress me that much. I enjoy very much when somebody likes something I've written, writes how much they like it. But, I don't even remember that much about it once it's gone.

Q: By the time you wrote Flint *in 1957, you'd been a western editor and already written two westerns of your own,* Valley of Angry Men *(1953) - written in eight days by "Matthew Gant," and* Slade *(1956) - writing as "Ad Gordon." How did* Flint *evolve?*

AH: Jim Thompson's close-in writing—where the reader and the protago-nist seem to be inches apart, smelling each other's breath—influenced my own writing. After his novel *Savage Night* (1953) came out as a Lion original—to my mind, the best crime syndicate novel ever—I saw that the story could be translated into a western, changing time and place, but little else.

I asked Jim's permission to use his plot in a western setting and he gra-ciously gave it to me. I wrote a psychological suspense western—once again, a unicorn—titled *Flint*. I also included a dedication to Jim that said something like, "To Jim Thompson, who wrote this story first and wrote it best, and then gave me permission to try my own version." New American Library did not run the dedication. When I saw that the galley proofs lacked the ac-knowledgment, editor Marc Jaffe said it was just a slip, that it would appear in the finished book. It didn't, and I wondered whether New American Li-brary saw my acknowledgment as a confession of plagiarism. It doesn't come close. Read the two books and decide. My book appeared under a pseudonym they chose for me, a dreadful choice for an offbeat western.

The idea of my plagiarizing Jim would have amused him. In a sense we had swapped roles. Jim had written a novel based on a synopsis Lion had handed him; now I was writing a western on a plot Jim had given me. It would have brought on one of Jim's soft easy chuckles. He did say to me later, but he was drunk when he said it, "Yours is better than mine," which was generous and untrue and we both knew it. Jim was a kind man who had kind words for peo-ple he liked.

Jim's style of in-your-face writing became my own. It was mine before I'd met Thompson, but Jim's success with it cemented it for me. If Jim could write that way, so chillingly close to the reader, I could too, and would, and did.

Q: Flint *is written almost entirely in first person, just as* Savage Night *is.*

AH: Flint was written when I was still back east. And then when I came back here [to the West Coast], I had to solve the problem of the shift from first-person to third-person, and it occurred to me how to make that work. I penciled in the schizophrenic clues so people would understand that this breakdown would occur. And when I did that, New American Library im-mediately bought it.

By the way, the western editor there was Ed [E.L.] Doctorow. And he actually literally removed the climactic next-to-last chapter from the manu-script. And when I read the galleys and saw it was gone, I had to call and make sure they put it back in, because it made no sense. Doctorow had done that.

I like *Flint*, and people who don't know westerns, when I mention it, they say, "*Flint*, I read that once, that was wonderful."

Also, in the very first beginnings when "Flint" is approached to take on this extra job of killing somebody, and the snakes in his stomach kind of roil, when I'm writing sometimes and I suddenly stop writing from my head and my fingers, something else takes over. I don't know what that is. I think it happens to a lot of writers, and most writers at a certain point.

Robert Kirsch said, "The writing writes the writer," and I believe that's true at times. And when that happens I would feel it in my belly that this thing had occurred. And that let me know that I was on the right track. So, I guess I'm a hired killer also, among other things.

Q: What do you remember about the reception to Flint?

AH: I recall a torn copy of it that was mailed back to me by some irate father who wrote, "You ought to be ashamed of yourself. I bought this for my child," or something like that. And, to a degree, having sex in a novel, in a western novel, is very unusual. And there's some sex in this one. This is a more internal novel. And I like to try to do new things. And with *Flint* and *The Last Notch**we broke down some rules there.

(*The Last Notch (1958), written as "Matthew Gant," was the first western to feature a black protagonist. Hano had to fight to convince his editors there were, in fact, black cowboys. Philip Durham's book on African American cowboys appeared a short time later, making Arnold's case after the fact. We sincerely hope to see *The Last Notch* back in print again soon.)

Q: Were you aware of how your books were doing in terms of sales?

AH: There was a time when I had nine books in print, paying royalties beyond the advance. Nine books. So, I'm getting 18 checks a year. I never made a lot of money from any one thing, but there they all were. I didn't know, for instance, that my first biography of Willie Mays sold 480,000 copies. I didn't know that until recently. And that is more than all the other Mays books put together. And I did know about the Sandy Koufax book because they kept saying they put it on the stands, and that book disappeared every time they put it on the stands. They sold as many copies as they printed.

Q: In 1957, you're living in Laguna Beach and you write So I'm a Heel, *published by Gold Medal. Its setting is a thinly-disguised Laguna Beach, and it has a very different feel from your other books.*

AH: Well, the editor at Gold Medal didn't like it because he didn't like novels about heels.

Q: Did you send it to Gold Medal with that title?

AH: I don't think so. I'm not sure. I think they titled it. What I do remember was that Anthony Boucher reviewed it in the *New York Times*. And he said very kind things about the first half of the novel. I like the fact that this was a paperback novel and Boucher reviewed it. And that was partly because of what we had done with Jim Thompson earlier. And Boucher became the first person to recognize that. He started to review paperback novels. So, I feel that I was part of that process.

Q: Did people around Laguna Beach know you were "Mike Heller"?

AH: I gave a friend of mine a copy and she kind of scolded me for being nasty and not proper. And she recognized all the characters. There was a local business executive who was a very strange man. He was a very strange man, a terrible right-winger. He would rant against gays and child molesters. And then each time he left town, he had to check in with the police department to tell them where he was going because he was a registered child molester. So, people who knew, they could tell.

Q: Your protagonist in So I'm a Heel *has an artificial jaw. Where did you get the idea for that?*

AH: In World War II, when I was on a combat ship in the Pacific on the way to Kwajalein, there was a journalist named Keith Wheeler interviewing these guys who are going into combat. I told him that my first wife was pregnant and any time now she's going to have a baby. He was terrific. He came back two or three days later and said, "Nothing's happened. It's going to be maybe another week or two, so I'll keep you in touch if I know." So we land on this island just off Kwajalein to set up our artillery, and we get off and we're pulling our guns. And Keith Wheeler gets off, and the next thing I see, he's down, he's been shot in the jaw. They had to take him to the battleship or the infirmary and patch him back up. Keith Wheeler.

Q: Can you talk about your choice of pseudonyms?

AH: "Matthew Gant" began with Bonnie and me sitting around saying, gee, what name could we use as a pseudonym. But, "Matthew Gant" was probably based on some short stories, but it came first. And I think "Eugene Gant" in Thomas Wolfe's first two novels...I thought "Gant" had grit to it. I liked that. And "Matthew" was a good name. And that seemed to work. We did that together. I don't know which one of us did what, but we did it together. And I should have thrown out all the other pseudonyms. That would have worked for westerns, for hardboiled, for pretty good stuff.

"Ad Gordon" was for my friend Adina Gordon, who's an art historian, when I wrote *The Flesh Painter* [about French artist Paul Gauguin]. Adina wasn't actually involved in the book or research at all.

Q: You didn't say, "Now I'm 'Ad Gordon,' so now I'm going to approach this western differently than I did as Matthew Gant"?

AH: No. And the one I find the most trouble with is "Gil Dodge" for *Flint*, because "Gil Dodge" sounds like a typical kind of shoot-em-up western writer. And I remember Marc Jaffe [editor, New American Library] saying, "We have a great name for your pseudonym this time, 'Gil Dodge.'" And I thought, "Oh, my God." But that was that. They imposed that one on me. And I should have done something about it beforehand.

Q: And "Mike Heller" for So I'm a Heel?

AH: "Mike Heller" fits that novel. That name worked pretty well. I think either Bonnie and I came up with that one. Or I did.

Q: But why use pseudonyms in the first place?

AH: The major reason why I used pseudonyms at all was because I was an editor at Lion Books, and if I were to do a western novel—and we were publishing westerns—and I used my own name, people could say, "Gee, of course, it's a cinch for him to do that." Or, if I used my own name and it landed at Gold Medal, they could say, "It wasn't even good enough to do at his own house." So, it was one of those 'you can't win for losing' sort of situations.

Q: You've written 26 books. So far. Is there something you can pinpoint, some unifying impulse that sets a novel by Arnold Hano apart from other writers?

AH: Other than the fact that they're better? [he laughs, we all do] I think what impresses me about me is the variety of things that I do. I write short stories, I write long short stories, I write novels, I write westerns, I write suspense, I write historical, I write biography, autobiography. I once won a small prize in a national lyric writing contest. I wrote libretto notes for two years of opera. There is almost nothing that I have not written. The variety of stuff is what impresses me about me.

We're impressed. We believe you will be, too.

Dan Duling, Fall 2012.

1-933586-26-5 **Benjamin Appel** Sweet Money Girl / Life and Death of a Tough Guy $21.95
1-933586-03-6 **Malcolm Braly** Shake Him Till He Rattles / It's Cold Out There $19.95
1-933586-10-9 **Gil Brewer** Wild to Possess / A Taste for Sin $19.95
1-933586-20-6 **Gil Brewer** A Devil for O'Shaugnessy / The Three-Way Split $14.95
1-933586-24-9 **W. R. Burnett** It's Always Four O'Clock / Iron Man $19.95
1-933586-31-1 **Catherine Butzen** Thief of Midnight $15.95
1-933586-38-9 **James Hadley Chase** Come Easy--Go Easy / In a Vain Shadow $19.95
0-9667848-0-4 **Storm Constantine** Oracle Lips (limited hb) $45.00
1-933586-30-3 **Jada M. Davis** One for Hell $19.95
1-933586-43-5 **Bruce Elliot** One is a Lonely Number /
                Elliott Chaze Black Wings Has My Angel $19.95
1-933586-34-6 **Don Elliott** Gang Girl / Sex Bum $19.95
1-933586-12-5 **A. S. Fleischman** Look Behind You Lady / The Venetian Blonde $19.95
1-933568-28-1 **A. S. Fleischman** Danger in Paradise / Malay Woman $19.95
1-933586-35-4 **Orrie Hitt** The Cheaters / Dial "M" for Man $19.95
0-9667848-7-1 **Elisabeth Sanxay Holding** Lady Killer / Miasma $19.95
0-9667848-9-8 **Elisabeth Sanxay Holding** The Death Wish / Net of Cobwebs $19.95
0-9749438-5-1 **Elisabeth Sanxay Holding** Strange Crime in Bermuda / Too Many Bottles $19.95
1-933586-16-8 **Elisabeth Sanxay Holding** The Old Battle Ax / Dark Power $19.95
1-933586-17-6 **Russell James** Underground / Collected Stories $14.95
0-9749438-8-6 **Day Keene** Framed in Guilt / My Flesh is Sweet $19.95
1-933586-33-8 **Day Keene** Dead Dolls Don't Talk / Hunt the Killer / Too Hot to Hold $23.95
1-933586-21-4 **Mercedes Lambert** Dogtown / Soultown $14.95
1-933586-14-1 **Dan Marlowe/Fletcher Flora/Charles Runyon** Trio of Gold Medals $15.95
1-933586-07-9 **Ed by McCarthy & Gorman** Invasion of the Body Snatchers: A Tribute $19.95
1-933586-09-5 **Margaret Millar** An Air That Kills / Do Evil in Return $19.95
1-933586-23-0 **Wade Miller** The Killer / Devil on Two Sticks $17.95
1-933586-27-3 **E. Phillips Oppenheim** The Amazing Judgment / Mr. Laxworthy's Adventures $19.95
0-9749438-3-5 **Vin Packer** Something in the Shadows / Intimate Victims $19.95
1-933586-05-2 **Vin Packer** Whisper His Sin / The Evil Friendship $19.95
1-933586-18-4 **Richard Powell** A Shot in the Dark / Shell Game $14.95
1-933586-19-2 **Bill Pronzini** Snowbound / Games $14.95
0-9667848-8-x **Peter Rabe** The Box / Journey Into Terror $21.95
0-9749438-4-3 **Peter Rabe** Murder Me for Nickels / Benny Muscles In $19.95
1-933586-00-1 **Peter Rabe** Blood on the Desert / A House in Naples $21.95
1-933586-11-7 **Peter Rabe** My Lovely Executioner / Agreement to Kill $19.95
1-933586-22-2 **Peter Rabe** Anatomy of a Killer / A Shroud for Jesso $14.95
1-933586-32-x **Peter Rabe** The Silent Wall / The Return of Marvin Palaver $19.95
0-9749438-2-7 **Douglas Sanderson** Pure Sweet Hell / Catch a Fallen Starlet $19.95
1-933586-06-0 **Douglas Sanderson** The Deadly Dames / A Dum-Dum for the President $19.95
1-933586-29-X **Charlie Stella** Johnny Porno $15.95
1-933586-39-7 **Charlie Stella** Rough Riders $15.95
1-933586-08-7 **Harry Whittington** A Night for Screaming / Any Woman He Wanted $19.95
1-933586-25-7 **Harry Whittington** To Find Cora / Like Mink Like Murder / Body and Passion $23.95
1-933586-36-2 **Harry Whittington** Rapture Alley / Winter Girl / Strictly for the Boys $23.95

STARK HOUSE PRESS
www.StarkHousePress.com